Love in Excess

Or the fatal enquiry, a novel.

In three parts

Mrs. Haywood

Alpha Editions

This edition published in 2020

ISBN : 9789354025167

Design and Setting By
Alpha Editions
email - alphaedis@gmail.com

LOVE in Excess;

OR THE

FATAL ENQUIRY,

A

NOVEL.

In THREE PARTS.

By Mrs. HAYWOOD.

----- In vain from Fate we fly,
For first or last, as all must die,
So 'tis as much decreed above,
That first or last, we all must Love.

LANSDOWN.

The Fourth EDITION Corrected.

LONDON:

Printed for D. BROWNE *jun.* at the *Black Swan* without *Temple Bar.* MDCCXXII.

TO
Mrs. ELIZ. HAYWOOD,
ON HER
NOVEL
CALL'D
Love in *Excess*, &c.

FAIN wou'd I here my vast Ideas raise,
To paint the Wonders of Eliza's *praise;*
But like young Artists where their Stroaks decay,
I shade those Glories which I can't display.
Thy Prose in sweeter Harmony refines,
Than Numbers flowing thro' the Muse's Lines;
What Beauty ne'er cou'd melt, thy Touches fire,
And raise a Musick that can Love inspire;
Soul-thrilling Accents all our Senses wound,
And Strike with softness, whilst they Charm with sound!
When thy COUNT *pleads, what Fair his Suit can flye?*
Or when thy Nymph laments, what Eyes are dry?

Ev'n

Verses to Mrs. HAYWOOD.

Ev'n Nature's self in Sympathy appears,
Yeilds Sigh for Sigh, and melts in equal Tears;
For such Descriptions thus at once can prove
The Force of Language, and the Sweets of Love.

The Myrtle's Leaves with those of Fame entwine,
And all the Glories of that Wreath are thine?
As Eagles can undazzl'd view the Force
Of scorching Phæbus *in his Noon-day Course;*
Thy Genius to the God its Luster plays,
Meets his fierce Beams, and darts him Rays for Rays!
Oh Glorious Strength! Let each succeeding Page
Still boast those Charms and luminate the Age;
So shall thy beamful Fires with Light divine
Rise to the Sphere, and there triumphant Shine.

RICHARD SAVAGE.

By

By an unknown Hand.

To the most Ingenious Mrs HAYWOOD, on her NOVEL Entitled,

Love in Excess:

A Stranger Muse, an Unbeliever too,
That Womens Souls such Strength of Vigour knew!
Nor less an Atheist to Love's Power declar'd,
Till YOU *a Champion for the Sex appear'd!*
A Convert now, to both, I feel that Fire
YOUR *Words alone can paint!* YOUR *Looks inspire!*
Resistless now, Love's shafts new pointed fly,
Wing'd with YOUR *Flame, and blazing in* YOUR *Eye.*
With sweet, but pow'rful Force, the Charm-shot Heart
Receives th' Impression of the Conqu'ring Dart,
And ev'ry Art'ry huggs the Joy-tipt Smart!

No more of Phœbus, *rising vainly boast,*
Ye tawny Sons of a luxuriant Coast!
While our blest Isle is with such Rays replete,
Britain *shall glow with more than Eastern Heat!*

VERSES

VERSES

Wrote in the Blank Leaf of

Mrs. *Haywood's* NOVEL.

OF all the Passions given us from above,
The Noblest, Truest, and the Best, is Love;
'Tis Love awakes the Soul, informs the Mind,
And bends the stubborn Temper to be kind,
Abates the Edge of ev'ry poi'nant Care
Succeeds the Wishes of the trembling Fair,
And ravishes the Lover from Despair.
'Tis Love Eliza's *soft Affections fires,*
Eliza *writes, but Love alone inspires;*
'Tis Love, that gives D'Elmont *his manly Charms,*
And tears Amena *from her Father's Arms;*
Relieves the Fair one from her Maiden Fear,
And gives Melliora *all her Soul holds dear,*
A generous Lover, and a Bliss sincere.

Receive, my Fair, the Story, and approve,
The Cause of Honour, *and the Cause of* Love;
With kind Concern, the tender Page peruse,
And aid the Infant Labours of the Muse.
So never may those Eyes forget to shine,
And bright Melliora's *Fortune be as Thine;*
On thy best Looks, an happy D'Elmont *feed,*
And all the Wishes of thy Soul succeed.

LOVE

LOVE in EXCESS:

OR, THE

FATAL ENQUIRY.

PART the FIRST.

N the late War between the *French* and the *Confederate* Armies, there were two BROTHERS, who had acquir'd a more than ordinary Reputation, under the Command of the great and intrepid LUXEMBOURGH. But the Concluſion of the Peace taking away any further Occaſiſions of ſhewing their Valour, the Eldeſt of 'em, whoſe Name was COUNT D'ELMONT, return'd to PARIS, from whence he had been abſent two Years, leaving his Brother at St. OMER's, 'till the Cure of ſome ſlight Wounds were perfected.

THE Fame of the *Count's* brave Actions arriv'd before him, and he had the Satisfaction of being receiv'd by the KING and COURT, after a Manner that might gratify the Ambition of the proudest. The Beauty of his Person, the Gayity of his Air, and the unequal'd Charms of his Conversation, made him the Admiration of both Sexes; and whilst those of his *own* strove which should gain the largest share in his Friendship; the *other* vented fruitless Wishes, and in secret, curs'd that Custom which forbids Women to make a Declaration of their Thoughts. Amongst the Number of these, was ALOVISA, a Lady descended (by the Father's Side) from the Noble Family of the D' LA TOURS formerly Lord of BEUJEY, and (by her Mothers) from the equally Illustrious House of MONTMORENCY. The late Death of her Parents had left her Coheiress (with her Sister,) of a vast Estate.

ALOVISA, if her Passion was not greater than the rest, her Pride, and the good Opinion she had of her self, made her the less able to support it; she sigh'd, she burn'd, she rag'd, when she perceiv'd the Charming D'ELMONT behav'd himself toward her with no Mark of a distinguishing Affection. What (said she) have I beheld without Concern a Thousand Lovers at my Feet, and shall the only Man I ever endeavour'd, or wish'd to Charm, regard me with Indifference? Wherefore has the agreeing World join'd with my deceitful Glass to flatter me into a vain Belief I had invincible Atractions? D'ELMONT sees 'em not! D'ELMONT is insensible. Then would she fall into Ravings, sometimes cursing her own want of Power, sometimes the Coldness of D'ELMONT. Many Days she pass'd in these Inquietudes, and every time she saw him (which was very frequently) either at Court, at Church, or publick Meetings, she found fresh Matter for her troubled Thoughts to work upon: When on any Occasion he happen'd to speak to her, it was with that Softness in his Eyes, and that engaging tenderness in his Voice, as would half perswade her, that, that God had touch'd his Heart,

whic'n

which ſo powerfully had Influenc'd hers; but if a glimmering of ſuch a Hope gave her a Pleaſure inconceiveable, how great were the enſuing Torments, when ſhe obſerv'd thoſe Looks and Accents were but the Effects of his natural Complaiſance, and that to whomſoever he Addreſs'd, he carried an equality in his Behaviour, which ſufficiently evinc'd, his Hour was not yet come to feel thoſe Pains he gave; and if the afflicted fair Ones found any Conſolation, it was in the Reflection, that no Triumphant Rival could boaſt a Conqueſt, each now deſpair'd of gaining. But the impatient ALOVISA diſdaining to be rank'd with thoſe, whom her Vanity made her conſider as infinitely her Inferiors, ſuffer'd her ſelf to be agitated almoſt to Madneſs, between the two Extreams of Love and Indignation; a thouſand *Chimeras* came into her Head, and ſometimes prompted her to diſcover the Sentiments ſhe had in his Favour: But theſe Reſolutions were rejected, almoſt as ſoon as form'd, and ſhe could not fix on any for a long time; 'till at laſt, Love (ingenious in Invention,) inſpir'd her with one, which probably might let her into the Secrets of his Heart, without the Shame of revealing her own.

THE Celebration of Madam the Dutcheſs of BURGUNDY's Birth-day being Solemniz'd with great Magnificence, ſhe writ this *Billet* to him on the Night before.

To Count D'ELMONT.

RESISTLESS as you are in War, you are much more ſo in Love: Here you conquer without making an Attack, and we Surrender before you Summons; the Law of Arms obliges you to ſhow Mercy to an yielding Enemy, and sure the Court cannot inspire less generous Sentiments than the Field. The little God lays down his Arrows at your Feet, confesses your superior Power, and begs a Friendly Treatment; he will appear to you to morrow Night at the Ball, in the Eyes of the most passionate of all his Votresses; search therefore for him in Her, in whom (amongst that bright Assembly) you would most desire to find Him; I am confident you have too much Penetration to miss of him, if not byass'd by a former Inclination, and in that Hope, I shall (as patiently as my Expectations will let me) support, 'till then, the tedious Hours.

Farewell.

THIS she sent by a trusty Servant, and so disguis'd, that it was impossible for him to be known, with a strict Charge to deliver it to the *Count*'s own Hands, and come away before he had read it; the Fellow perform'd her Orders exactly, and when the *Count*, who was not a little surpriz'd at the first opening it, ask'd for the Messenger, and commanded he should be stay'd; his Gentleman (who then was waiting in his Chamber,) told him he ran down Stairs with all the speed imaginable, immediately on his Lordship's receiving it. D'ELMONT having never experienc'd the Force of Love, could not presently comprehend the Truth of this Adventure; at first he imagin'd some of his Companions had caus'd this Letter to be wrote, either to sound his Inclinations, or upbraid his little Disposition to Gallantry; but these Cogitations soon gave Place to others; and tho' he was not very vain, yet he found it no difficulty to perswade himself to an Opinion, that it was possible for a Lady to distinguish him from other Men. Nor did he find any thing so unpleasing in that Thought as might make him endeavour to repell it; the more he consider'd his own Perfections, the more he was confirm'd in his Belief, but who to fix it on, he was at a Loss as much as ever;

ever; then he began to reflect on all the Discourse, and little Railleries that had pass'd between him and the Ladies whom he had convers'd with since his Arrival, but cou'd find nothing in any of 'em of Consequence enough to make him guess at the Person: He spent great part of the Night in Thoughts very different from those he was accustom'd to, the Joy which naturally rises from the Knowledge 'tis in one's Power to give it, gave him Notions which till then he was a Stranger to; he began to consider a Mistress as an agreeable, as well as fashionable Amusement, and resolv'd not to be Cruel.

IN the mean time poor ALOVISA was in all the Anxiety imaginable, she counted every Hour, and thought 'em Ages, and at the first dawn of Day she rose, and calling up her Women, who were amaz'd to find her so uneasy, she employ'd 'em in placing her Jewels on her Cloaths to the best Advantage, while she consulted her Glass after what Manner she should Dress, her Eyes, the gay, the languishing, the sedate, the commanding, the beseeching Air, were put on a thousand times, and as often rejected; and she had scarce determin'd which to make use of, when her Page brought her Word, some Ladies who were going to Court desir'd her to accompany them; she was too impatient not to be willing to be one of the first, so went with them immediately, arm'd with all her Lightnings, but full of unsettled Reflections. She had not been long in the Drawing Room, before it grew very full of Company, but D'ELMONT not being amongst 'em, she had her Eyes fix'd towards the Door, expecting every Moment to see him enter; but how impossible is it to represent her Confusion, when he appear'd, leading the young AMENA, Daughter to Monsieur *Sanseverin*, a Gentleman, who tho' he had a very small Estate, and many Children, had by a partial Indulgence, too common among Parents, neglecting the rest, maintain'd this Darling of his Heart in all the Pomp of Quality. The Beauty and Sweetness of this Lady was present-

Death to ALOVISA's Hope's; ſhe ſaw, or fancy'd ſhe ſaw an uſual Joy in her Eyes, and dying Love in his; Diſdain, Deſpair, and Jealouſie at once crowded into her Heart, and ſwell'd her almoſt to burſting; and 'twas no wonder that the violence of ſuch terrible Emotions kept her from regarding the Diſcourſes of thoſe who ſtood by her, or the Devoirs that D'ELMONT made as he paſs'd by, and at length threw her into a Swoon; the Ladies ran to her aſſiſtance, and her charming Rival, being one of her particular Acquaintance, ſhew'd an extraordinary aſſiduity in applying Means for her Relief, they made what haſt they cou'd to get her into another Room, and unfaſten herRobe, but were a great while before they could bring her to herſelf; and when they did, the Shame of having been ſo diſorder'd in ſuch an Aſſembly,and the Fears of their ſuſpecting the Occaſion, added to her former Agonies, had rack'd her with moſt terrible Revulſions, every one now deſparing of her being able to aſſiſt at that Night's Entertainment, ſhe was put into her Chair, in order to be carry'd Home; AMENA who little thought how unwelcome ſhe was grown, would needs have one call'd, and accompany'd her thither, in ſpight of the Intreaties of D'ELMONT, who had before engag'd her for his Partner in Dancing; not that he was in Love with her, or at that time believ'd he cou'd be touch'd with a Paſſion which he eſteem'd a Trifle in it ſelf, and below the Dignity of a Man of Senſe; but Fortune (to whom this Lady no leſs enamour'd than ALOVISA) had made a thouſand Invocations, ſeem'd to have allotted her the glory of his firſt Addreſſes; ſhe was getting out of her Chariot juſt as he alighted from his, and offering her his Hand, he perceiv'd hers trembled, which engaging him to look upon her more earneſtly than he was wont, he immediately fancy'd he ſaw ſomething of that languiſhment in her Eyes, which the obliging Mandate had deſcrib'd. AMENA was too lovely to make that Belief diſagreeable, and he reſolv'd on the Beginnings of an Amour, without giving himſelf the trouble of conſidering the Conſequences;

the

the Evening being extreamly pleasant, he ask'd if she wou'd not favour him so far as to take a turn or two within the Palace-Garden; She who desir'd nothing more than such a particular Conversation, was not at all backward of complying; he talk'd to her there for some time, in a manner as could leave her no room to doubt he was entirely Charm'd, and 'twas the Air such an Entertainment had left on both their Faces, as produc'd those sad Effects in the jealous ALOVISA. She was no sooner led to her Apartment, but she desir'd to be put to Bed, and the good natur'd AMENA, who really had a very great kindness for her, offer'd to quit the Diversions of the Ball, and stay with her all Night; but the unfortunate ALOVISA was not in a Condition to endure the Presence of any, especially her, so put her off as civilly as her Anxiety wou'd give her leave, chusing rather to suffer her to return to the Ball, than retain so hateful an Object (as she was now become) in her sight; and 'tis likely the other was not much troubled at her Refusal. But how, (when left alone, and abandon'd to the whirlwinds of her Passion,) the desperate ALOVISA behav'd, none but those, who like her, have burn'd in hopless Fires can guess, the most lively Description wou'd come far short of what she felt; she rav'd, she tore her Hair and Face, and in the extremity of her Anguish was ready to lay violent Hands on her own Life. In this Tempest of Mind, she continu'd for some time, till at length rage beginning to dissipate it self in Tears, made way for cooler Considerations; and her natural Vanity resuming its Empire in her Soul, was of no little Service to her on this Occasion. Why am I thus disturb'd? Mean Spirited as I am! Said she, D'ELMONT is ignorant of the Sentiments I am possess'd with in his favour; and perhaps 'tis only want of Incouragement that has so long depriv'd me of my Lover; my Letter bore no certain Mark by which he might distinguish me, and who knows what Arts that Creature might make use of to allure him. I will therefore (persu'd she, with a more cheerful Countenance) direct his erring Search.

As she was in this Thought (happily for her, who else might have relaps'd) her Women who were waiting in the next Room, came in to know if she wanted any thing; yes, answer'd she, with a Voice and Eyes wholly chang'd, I'll rise, one of you help me on with my Cloaths, and let the other send CHARLO to me, I have instant Business with him. 'twas in vain for 'em to represent to her the Prejudice it might be to her Health to get out of her Bed at so unseasonable an Hour, it being then just Midnight: They knew her too absolute a Mistress not to be obey'd, and executed her Commands, without disputing the Reason. She was no sooner ready, then CHARLO was introduc'd who being the same Person that carry'd the Letter to D'ELMONT, guess'd what Affair he was to be concern'd in, and shut the Door after him. I commend your Caution, said his Lady, for what I am now going to trust you with, is of more concernment than my Life. The Fellow bow'd, and made a thousand Protestations of an eternal Fidelity. I doubt it not, resum'd she, go then immediately to the *Court*, 'tis not impossible but in this hurry you may get into the Drawing Room; but if not, make some pretence to stay as near as you can 'till the Ball be over; listen carefully to all Discourses where you hear COUNT D'ELMONT mention'd, enquire who he Dances with, and above all, watch what Company he comes out with, and bring me an exact Account. Go, continu'd she hastily, these are all the Orders I have for you to Night, but to Morrow I shall employ you farther. Then turning to her *Escritore*, she sat down, and began to prepare a second Letter, which she hop'd wou'd be more lucky than the former. She was not long writing, Love and Wit, suggested a World of passionate and agreeable Expressions to her in a Moment: But when she had finish'd this so full a Discovery of her Heart, and was about to sign her Name to it; not all that Passion which had inspir'd her with a Resolution to scruple nothing that might advance the compassing her Wishes, nor the vanity which assur'd her of Success, were forcible enough

enough to withſtand the ſhock it gave her Pride; No, let me rather die! Said ſhe, (ſtarting up and frighted at her own Deſigns) than be guilty of a Meanneſs which wou'd render me unworthy of Life, Oh Heavens! To offer Love, and poorly ſue for Pity! 'tis inſupportable! What bewitch'd me to harbour ſuch a Thought as even the vileſt of my Sex wou'd bluſh at? To pieces then (added ſhe, tearing the Paper) with this ſhameful Witneſs of my Folly, my furious Deſires may be the deſtruction of my Peace, but never of my Honour, that ſhall ſtill attend my Name when Love and Life are fled. She continu'd in this Temper (without being able to compoſe herſelf to reſt) till Day began to appear, and CHARLO returned with News which confirmed her moſt dreaded Suſpicions. He told her that he had gain'd admittance to the Drawing Room ſeveral Times, under pretence of delivering Meſſages to ſome of the Ladies; that the whole Talk among 'em was, that D'ELMONT, was no longer inſenſible of Beauty; that he obſerv'd that Gentleman in very particular Conference with AMENA, and that he waited on her Home in his Chariot, her own not being in the way, I know it, ſaid ALOVISA (walking about in a diſorder'd Motion) I did not doubt but that I was undone, and to my other Miſeries, have that of being aiding to my Rival's Happineſs: Whatever his Deſires were, he carefully conceal'd 'em, till my curſed Letter prompted a Diſcovery; tenacious as I was, and too, too confident of this little Beauty! Here ſhe ſtop'd, and wiping away ſome Tears which in ſpight of her ran down her Cheeks, gave CHARLO leave to ask if ſhe had any more Commands for him. Yes (anſwer'd ſhe) I will write once more to this undeſcerning Man, and let him know, 'tis not AMENA that is worthy of him; that I may do without prejudicing my Fame, and 'twill be at leaſt ſome Eaſement to my Mind, to undeceive the Opinion he may have conceiv'd of her Wit, for I am almoſt confident ſhe paſſes for the Authoreſs of thoſe Lines which have been ſo fatal to me; in ſpeaking this, without any further Thought, she once more took her Pen, and wrote these Words.

To Count D'ELMONT.

IF Ambition be a Fault, 'tis only in those who have not a sufficient stock of Merit to support it; too much Humility is a greater in you, whose Person and Qualities are too admirable, not to render any Attempt you shall make justifiable, as well as successful. Heaven when it distinguish'd you in so particular a Manner from the rest of Mankind, design'd you not for vulgar Conquests, and you cannot without a manifest Contradiction to its Will, and an irreparable Injury to your self, make a present of that Heart to AMENA, *when one, of at least an equal Beauty, and far superior in every other Consideration, would Sacrifice all to purchase the glorious Trophy; continue then no longer in a wilful Ignorance, aim at a more exalted flight, and you will find it no difficulty to discover who she is that languishes, and almost dies for an Opportunity of confessing (without too great a breach of Modesty) that her Soul, and all the Faculties of it, are, and must be,*

Eternally Yours.

THIS she gave to CHARLO, to deliver with the same Caution as the former; but he was scarce got out of the House before a new Fear assaulted her, and she repented her uncircumspection. What have I done, cry'd she! Who knows but D'ELMONT may shew these Letters to AMENA, she is perfectly acquainted with my Hand, and I shall be the most expos'd and wretched Woman in the World. Thus Industrious was she in forming Notions to Torment herself;

herſelf; nor indeed was there any thing of Improbability in this Conjecture. There are too many ungenerous enough to boaſt ſuch an Adventure; but D'ELMONT tho' he would have given good Part of his Eſtate to ſatisfy his Curioſity, yet choſe rather to remain in a perpetual Ignorance, than make uſe of any Means that might be diſadvantagious to the Lady's Reputation. He now perceiv'd his Miſtake, and that it was not AMENA who had taken that Method to engage him, and poſſibly was not diſguſted to find ſhe had a Rival of ſuch Merit, as the Letter intimated. However, he had ſaid too many fine Things to her to be loſt, and thought it as inconſiſtent with his Honour as his Inclination to deſiſt a Purſuit in which he had all the Reaſon in the World to aſſure himſelf of Victory; for the young AMENA (little vers'd in the Art of Diſſimulation, ſo neceſſary to her Sex) cou'd not conceal the Pleaſure ſhe took in his Addreſſes, and without even a ſeeming reluctancy, had given him a Promiſe of meeting him the next Day in the *Tuilleries*; nor could all his unknown Miſtreſs had writ, perſwade him to miſs this Aſſignation, nor let that be ſucceeded with another, and that by a third, and ſo on, 'till by making a ſhew of Tenderneſs; he began to fancy himſelf really touch'd with a Paſſion he only deſign'd to repreſent. 'Tis certain this way of Fooling rais'd Deſires in him little different from what is commonly call'd Love; and made him redouble his Attacks in ſuch a Manner, as AMENA ſtood in need of all her Vertue to reſiſt; but as much as ſhe thought her ſelf oblig'd to reſent ſuch Attempts, yet he knew ſo well how to excuſe himſelf, and lay the Blame on the Violence of his Paſſion, that he was ſtill too Charming, and too Dear to her not to be forgiven. Thus was AMENA (by her too generous and open Temper) brought to the very brink of Ruin, and D'ELMONT was poſſibly contriving Means to compleat it, when her Page brought him this Letter.

To

To Count D'ELMONT.

SOME Malicious Persons have endeavour'd to make the little Conversation I have had with you, appear as Criminal; therefore to put a stop to all such Aspersions, I must for the future deny my self the Honour of your Visits, unless Commanded to receive 'em by my Father, who only has the Power of disposing of

AMENA.

THE Consternation he was in at the reading these Lines, so very different from her former Behaviour, is more easily imagin'd than express'd, 'till casting his Eyes on the Ground, he saw a small Note, which in the opening of this, had fallen out of it, which he hastily took up, and found it contain'd these Words.

I guess the Surprize my lovely Friend is in, but have not time now to unriddle the Mystery: I beg you will be at your Lodgings towards the Evening, and I will invent a Way to send to you.

'TWAS now that D'ELMONT began to find there were *Embarassments* in an Intrigue of this Nature, which he had not foreseen, and stay'd at Home all Day, impatiently expecting the clearing of an Affair, which at present seem'd so ambiguous. When it grew a little Duskish, his Gentleman brought in a Young Woman, whom he immediately knew to be ANARET, an Attendant on AMENA; and when he had made her sit down, told her he hop'd she was come to make an *Eclaircisment*, which would be very obliging to him, and therefore desir'd she wou'd not defer it.

MY

MY Lord, said she, 'tis with an unspeakable Trouble I discharge that Trust my Lady has repos'd in me, in giving you a Relation of her Misfortunes; but not to keep you longer in suspence, which I perceive is uneasy to you; I shall acquaint you, that soon after you were gone, my Lady came up into her Chamber, where, as I was preparing to undress her, we heard Monsieur SANSEVERIN in an angry Tone ask where his Daughter was, and being told she was above, we immediately saw him enter, with a Countenance so inflam'd, as put us both in a mortal Apprehension. An ill use (said he to her) have you made of my Indulgence, and the Liberty I have allow'd you! Could neither the Considerations of the Honour of your Family, your own Reputation, nor my eternal Repose, deter you from such imprudent Actions, as you cannot be ignorant must be the inevitable Ruin of 'em all. My poor Lady was too much surpriz'd at these cruel Words, to be able to make any Answer to 'em, and stood trembling, and almost fainting, while he went on with his Discourse. Was it consistent with the Niceties of your Sex, said he, or with the Duty you owe me, to receive the Addresses of a Person whose Pretensions I was a Stranger to? If the Count D'ELMONT has any that are Honourable, wherefore are they conceal'd? The Count D'ELMONT! (cry'd my Lady more frighted than before) never made any Declarations to me worthy of your Knowledge, nor did I ever entertain him otherwise, than might become your Daughter. 'Tis false (interupted he furiously) I am but too well inform'd of the contrary; nor has the most private of your shameful Meetings escap'd my Ears! Judge, Sir, in what a Confusion my Lady was in at this Discourse; 'twas in vain, she muster'd all her Courage to perswade him from giving Credit to an Intelligence so injurious to her; he grew the more enrag'd, and after a thousand Reproaches, flung out of the Room with all the Marks of a most violent Indignation, But tho' your Lordship is too well acquainted

quainted with the mildness of AMENA's Disposition, not to believe she could bear the Displeasure of a Father (who had always most tenderly lov'd her) with indifference; yet 'tis impossible for you to imagine in what an excess of Sorrow she was plung'd, she found every Passage of her ill Conduct (as she was pleas'd to call it) was betray'd, and did not doubt but whoever had done her that ill Office to her Father, wou'd take care the Discovery should not be confin'd to him alone. Grief, Fear, Remorse, and Shame by turns assaulted her, and made her incapable of Consolation; even the soft Pleas of Love were silenc'd by their Tumultuous Clamours, and for a Time she consider'd your Lordship in no other view than that of her Undoer. How! cry'd D'ELMONT (interrupting her) cou'd my AMENA, who I thought all sweetness, judge so harshly of me. Oh! my Lord, resum'd ANARET, you must forgive those first Emotions, which as violent as they were wanted but your Presence to dissipate in a Moment; and if your Idea had not presently that Power, it lost no Honour by having Foes to struggle with, since at last it put 'em all to flight, and gain'd so entire a Victory, that before Morning, of all her Troubles, scarce any but the Fears of losing you remain'd. And I must take the Liberty to assure your Lordship, my Endeavours were not wanting to establish a Resolution in her to despise every thing for Love and you. But to be as brief as I can in my Relation; the Night was no sooner gone, than Monsieur her Father came into the Chamber, with a Countenance, tho' more compos[illegible] than that with which he left us, yet with such an Air of Austerity, as made my timerous Lady lose most of the Spirit she had assum'd for this Encounter. I come not now AMENA, said he, to upbraid or punish your Disobedience, if you are not wholly [illegible]ndon'd by your Reason, your own Reflections will [illegible]ficiently your Tormentors. But to put you in a [illegible]y, (if no[illegible] your Fame, yet to take away a[illegible]cation of future Calumny,) you must write to Count D'ELMONT.

I will have no denials continu'd he, (ſeeing her about to ſpeak) and leading her to her Eſcritore, conſtrain'd her to write what he dictated, and you receiv'd; juſt as ſhe was going to Seal it, a Servant brought word that a Gentleman deſir'd to ſpeak with Monſieur SANSEVERIN, he was oblig'd to ſtep into another Room, and that abſence gave her an Opportunity of writing a Note, which ſhe dextrouſly ſlip'd into the Letter, unperceiv'd by her Father at his return, who little ſuſpecting what ſhe had done, ſent it away immediately. Now, ſaid he, we ſhall be able to judge of the ſincerity of the Count's Affections, but till then I ſhall take care to prove my ſelf a Perſon not diſintereſted in the Honour of my Family. As he ſpoke theſe Words, he took her by the Hand, and conducting her, thro' his own, into a little Chamber (which he had order'd to be made ready for that purpoſe) ſhut her into it; I follow'd to the Door, and ſeconded my Lady in her Deſires, that I might be permitted to attend her there; but all in vain, he told me, he doubted not but that I had been her Confident in this Affair, and ordered me to quit his Houſe in a few Days. As ſoon as he was gone out, I went into the Garden, and ſaunter'd up and down a good while, hoping to get an Opportunity of ſpeaking to my Lady through the Window, for I knew there was one that look'd into it; but not ſeeing her, I bethought me of getting a little Stick, with which I knock'd gently againſt the Glaſs, and engag'd her to open it. As ſoon as ſhe perceiv'd me, a Beam of Joy brighten'd in her Eyes, and gliſten'd tho' her Tears. Dear MARGARET, ſaid ſhe, how kindly do I take this proof of thy Affection, 'tis only in thy Power to alleviate my Misfortunes, and thou I know art come to offer thy Aſſiſtance. Then after I had aſſur'd her of my willingneſs to ſerve her in any command, ſhe deſir'd me to wait on you with an Account of all that had happen'd and to give you her Vows of an eternal Love. My Eyes, ſaid ſhe weeping, perhaps may ne'er behold him more, but Imagi-

Imagination ſhall ſupply that want, and from my Heart he never ſhall be Abſent. Oh! do not talk thus, cry'd the Count, extreamly touch'd at this Diſcourſe. I muſt, I will ſee her, nothing ſhall hold her from me. You may, anſwer'd ANARET, but then it muſt be with the Approbation of Monſieur SANSEVERIN, he will be proud to receive you in Quality of a Suitor to his Daughter, and 'tis only to oblige you to a publick Declaration that he takes theſe Meaſures. D'ELMONT was not perfectly pleas'd with theſe Words: he was too quick ſighted not to perceive immediately what Monſieur SANSEVERIN drove at, but as well as he lik'd AMENA, found no inclination in himſelf to Marry her; and therefore was not deſirous of an Explanation of what he reſolv'd not to ſeem to underſtand. He walk'd two or three turns about the Room, endeavouring to conceal his Diſguſt, and when he had ſo well overcome the ſhock, as to baniſh all viſible Tokens of it, I would willingly ſaid he coldly, come in to any proper Method for the obtaining the Perſon of AMENA, as well as her Heart; but there are certain Reaſons for which I cannot make a Diſcovery of my Deſigns to her Father, 'till I have firſt ſpoken with her. My Lord, reply'd the ſubtle ANARET (eaſily gueſſing at his Meaning) I wiſh to Heaven there were a poſſibility of your Meeting; there is nothing I would not riſque to forward it, and if your Lordſhip can think of any way in which I may be ſerviceable to you, in this ſhort Time I am allow'd to ſtay in the Family, I beg you would command me. She ſpoke this with an Air which made the Count believe ſhe really had it in her Power to ſerve him in this Occaſion, and preſently hit on the ſureſt Means to bind her to his Intereſt. You are very obliging, ſaid he, and I doubt not but your Ingenuity is equal to your good Nature, therefore will leave the Contrivance of my happineſs entirely to you, and that you may not think your Care beſtow'd on an ungrateful Perſon, be pleas'd (continu'd he, giving her a Purſe of *Lewis-Dor's*) to accept this ſmall Earneſt

neſt of my future Friendſhip, ANARET, like moſt of her Function, was too mercinary to reſiſt ſuch a Temptation, tho' it had been given her to betray the Honour of her whole Sex; and after a little pauſe, reply'd, Your Lordſhip is too generous to be refus'd, tho' in a Matter of the greateſt Difficulty, as indeed this is; for in the ſtrict Confinement my Lady is, I know no way but one, and that extreamly hazardous to her; however, I do not fear but my Perſwaſions, joyn'd with her own Deſires, will influence her to attempt it. Your Lordſhip knows we have a little Door at the farther End of the Garden, that opens into the *Tuillerys*. I do, cry'd D'ELMONT interrupting her. I have ſeveral times parted from my Charmer there, when my Entreaties have prevail'd with her to ſtay longer with me than ſhe wou'd have the Family to take notice of. I hope to order the Matter ſo, reſum'd ANARET, that it ſhall be the Scene this Night of a moſt happy Meeting. My Lady unknown to her Father, has the Key of it, ſhe can throw it to me from her Window, and I can open it to you, who muſt be walking near it, about Twelve or One a Clock, for by that time every body will be in Bed. But what will that avail, cry'd D'ELMONT haſtily; ſince ſhe lies in her Father's Chamber, where 'tis impoſſible to paſs Without alarming him. You Lovers are ſo impatient re-joyn'd ANARET ſmiling, I never deſign'd you ſhould have Entrance there, tho' the Window is ſo low, that a Perſon of your Lordſhip's Stature and Agility might mount it with a Galliard ſtep, but I ſuppoſe it will turn to as good an Account, if your Miſtreſs by my Aſſiſtance ſtets out of it. But can ſhe, interrupted he; will ſhe, doſt thou think? Fear not, my Lord, reply'd ſhe, be but punctual to the Hour, AMENA, ſhall be yours, if Love, Wit and Opportunity have power to make her ſo. D'ELMONT was tranſported with this Promiſe, and the Thoughts of what he expected to poſſeſs by her Means, rais'd his Imagination to ſo high a pitch, as he cou'd not forbear kiſſing and embracing

her

her with such Raptures, as might not have been very pleasing to AMENA, had she been witness of 'em. But ANARET who had other things in her Head than Gallantry, disengag'd her self from him as soon she cou'd, taking more Satisfaction in forwarding an Affair in which she propos'd so much Advantage, than in the Caresses of the most accomplish'd Gentleman in the World.

WHEN she came Home, she found every thing as she cou'd wish, MONSIEUR Abroad, and his Daughter at the Window, impatiently watching her return she told her as much of the Discourse she had with the COUNT as she thought proper, extolling his Love and Constancy, and carefully concealing all she thought might give an umbrage to her Vertue. But in spight of all the Artifice she made use of, she found it no easie Matter to perswade her to get out of the Window; the fears she had of being discover'd, and more expos'd to her Father's Indignation, and the Censure of the World, damp'd her Inclinations, and made her deaf to the eager Sollicitations of this unfaithful Woman. As they were Disputing, some of the Servants happ'ning to come into the Garden, oblig'd 'em to break off; and ANARET retir'd, not totally dispairing of compassing her Designs, when the appointed Hour should arrive, and AMENA should know the darling Object of her Wishes was so near. Nor did her Hopes deceive her, the Resolutions of a Lover, when made against the Interest of the Person belov'd, are but of a short duration; and this unhappy Fair was no sooner left alone, and had leisure to Contemplate on the Graces of the Charming D'ELMONT, but Love plaid his part with such Success, as made her repent she had chid ANARET for her Proposal, and wish'd for nothing more than an Opportunity to tell her so. She pass'd several Hours in Disquietudes she had never known before, till at last she heard her Father come into the next Room to go to Bed, and soon after some Body knock'd softly

ſoftly at the Window, ſhe immediately open'd it, and perceiv'd by the Light of the Moon which then ſhone very bright, that it was ANARET, ſhe had not Patience to liſten to the long Speech the other had prepar'd to perſwade her, but putting her Head as far as ſhe could, to prevent being heard by her Father. Well ANARET, ſaid ſhe, where is this Adventrous Lover, what is it he requires of me? Oh! Madam, reply'd ſhe, overjoy'd at the compliable Humour ſhe found her in, he is now at the Garden Door, there's nothing wanting but your Key to give him Entrance; what farther he requeſts, himſelf ſhall tell you. Oh Heavens! cry'd AMENA, ſearching her Pockets, and finding ſhe had it not; I am undone, I have left it in my Cabinet in the Chamber where I us'd to lie. Theſe Words made ANARET at her Wits end, ſhe knew there was no poſſibility of fetching it, there being ſo many Rooms to go thro', ſhe ran to the Door, and endeavour'd to puſh back the Lock, but had not Strength; ſhe then knew not what to do, ſhe was ſure D'ELMONT was on the other ſide, and fear'd he would reſent this uſage to the diſappointment of all her mercenary Hopes, and durſt not call to acquaint him with his Misfortune for fear of being heard. As for AMENA, ſhe was now more ſenſible than ever of the violence of her Inclinations, by the extream vexation this Diſappointment gave her: Never did People paſs a Night in greater uneaſineſs, than theſe three; the *Count* who was naturally impatient, could not bear a balk of this nature without the utmoſt chagrin. AMENA languiſh'd, and ANARET fretted to Death, tho' ſhe reſolv'd to leave no Stone unturn'd to ſet all right again. Early in the Morning ſhe went to his Lodgings, and found him in a very ill Humour, but ſhe eaſily pacify'd him, by repreſenting with a great deal of real Grief, the Accident that retarded his Happineſs, and aſſuring him there was nothing cou'd hinder the fulfilling it the next Night. When ſhe had gain'd this Point, ſhe came Home and got the Key into her poſſeſſion, but could not find an opportunity all Day of ſpeaking to her La-

dy

dy, Monsieur SANSEVERIN did not stir out of Doors, and spent most of it with his Daughter; in his Discourse to her, he set the Passion the COUNT had for her in so true a light, that it made a very great alteration in her Sentiments; and she began to reflect on the Condescensions she had given a Man, who had never so much as mention'd Marriage to her, with so much shame, as almost overwhelm'd her Love, and she was now determin'd never to see him, till he should declare himself to her Father in such a manner as would be for her Honour.

IN the mean time ANARET waited with a great deal of Impatience for the Family going to Bed; and as soon as all was hush, ran to give the COUNT Admitance; and leaving him in an ALLEY on the farther side of the Garden, made the accustom'd Sign at the Window. AMENA presently open'd it, but instead of staying to hear what she would say, threw a Letter out, Carry that, said she, to COUNT D'ELMONT, let him know the Contents of it are wholly the result of my own Reason. And as for your part, I charge you trouble me no farther on this Subject; then shutting the Casement hastily, left ANARET in a strange Consternation at this suddain Change of her Humour; however she made no delay, but running to the Place where the COUNT waited her return, deliver'd him the Letter, but advis'd him (who was ready enough of himself) not to obey any Commands might be given him to the hindrance of his Designs. The Moon was then at the full, and gave so clear a Light, that he easily found it contain'd these Words.

To-

To Count D'ELMONT.

TOO many Proofs have I given you of my weakness not to make you think me incapable of forming or keeping any Resolution to the Prejudice of that Passion you have inspir'd me with: But know, thou undoer of my Quiet, tho' I have Lov'd and still do Love you with a Tenderness, which I fear will be Unvanquishable; yet I will rather suffer my Life, than my Virtue to become its Prey. Press me then no more I conjure you, to such dangerous Interviews, in which I dare neither Trust my Self, nor You, if you believe me worthy your real Regard, the way thro' Honour is open to receive You; Religion, Reason, Modesty, and Obedience forbid the rest.

Farewel.

D'ELMONT knew the Power he had over her too well, to be much discourag'd at what he read, and after a little consultation with ANARET, they concluded he should go to speak to her, as being the best Sollicitor in his own Cause. As he came down the Walk, AMENA saw him thro' the Glass, and the sight of that beloved Object, bringing a thousand past Endearments to her Memory, made her incapable of retiring from the Window, and she remain'd in a languishing and immoveable Posture, leaning her Head against the Shutter, 'till he drew near enough to discern she saw him. He took this for no ill Omen, and instead of falling on his Knees at an humble Distance, as some Romantick Lovers would have done, redoubled his Pace, and Love and Fortune which on this Occasion were resolv'd to befriend him, presented to his View a large Rolling-Stone which the Gardiner had accidentally

tally left there; the Iron-work that held it was very high, and strong enough to bear a much greater weight than his, so he made no more to do, but getting on the top of it, was almost to the Waste above the bottom of the Casement. This was a strange Trial, for had she been less in Love, good Manners would have oblig'd her to open it; however she retain'd so much of her former Resolution, as to conjure him to be gone, and not expose her to such Hazards; that if her Father should come to know she held any clandestine Correspondence with him, after the Commands he had given her, she were utterly undone, and that he never must expect any Condescensions from her, without being first allow'd by him. D'ELMONT, tho' he was a little startled to find her so much more Mistress of her Temper than he believ'd she could be, yet resolv'd to make all possible use of this Opportunity, which probably might be the last he shou'd ever have, look'd on her as she spoke, with Eyes so piercing, so sparkling with Desire, accompany'd with so bewitching softness, as might have thaw'd the most frozen reservedness, and on the melting Soul stamp'd Love's Impression. 'Tis certain they were too irresistable to be long withstood, and putting an end to AMENA's grave Remonstrances, gave him leave to reply to 'em in this manner. Why my Life, my Angel, said he, my everlasting Treasure of my Soul, shou'd these Objections now be rais'd? How can you say you have given me your Heart? Nay, own you think me worthy that inestimable Jewel, yet dare not trust your Person with me a few Hours: What have you to fear from your adoring Slave? I want but to convince you how much I am so, by a thousand yet uninvented Vows. They may be spar'd, cry'd AMENA, hastily interrupting him, one Declaration to my Father, is all the Proof that he or I demands of your Sincerity. Oh! Thou Inhuman and Tyrannick Charmer, answer'd he, seizing her Hand, and eagerly kissing it) I doubt not but your faithful ANARET has told you, that I could not without the highest Imprudence, presently discover the Passion I have for you to the World.

I have, my Lord, said that cunning Wench who stood near him, and that 'twas only to acquaint her with the Reasons why, for some Time, you would have it a Secret, that you much desir'd to speak with her. Besides (rejoyn'd the COUNT) consider my Angel how much more hazardous it is for you to hold Discourse with me here, than at a farther distance from your Father; your denying to go with me is the only way to make your Fears prove true; his jealousie of you may possibly make him more watchful than ordinary, and we are not sure but that this Minute he may tear you from my Arms, whereas if you suffer me to bear you hence, if he should happen to come even to your Door, and hear no noise, he will believe you sleeping, and return to his Bed well satisfy'd. With these and the like Arguments she was at last overcome, and with the assistance of ANARET, he easily lifted her down. But this rash Action, so contrary to the Resolution she thought herself a few moments before so fix'd in, made such a confusion in her Mind, as render'd her insensible for some Time of all he said to her. They made what haste they could into the *Tuilleries*, and D'ELMONT having plac'd her on one of the most pleasant Seats, was resolv'd to loose no time; and having given her some Reasons for his not addressing to her Father, which tho' weak in themselves, were easily believ'd by a Heart so willing to be deceiv'd as hers, he began to press for a greater confirmation of her Affection than Words; and 'twas now this inconsiderate Lady found herself in the greatest Strait she had ever yet been in; all Nature seem'd to favour his Design, the pleasantness of the Place, the silence of the Night, the sweetness of the Air, perfum'd with a thousand various Odours, wafted by gentle Breezes from adjacent Gardens, compleated the most delightful Scene that ever was, to offer up a Sacrifice to Love; not a breath but flew wing'd with desire, and sent soft thrilling Wishes to the Soul; CYNTHIA herself, cold as she is reported, assisted in the Inspiration, and sometimes shone with all her brightness, as it were to feast their

their raviſh'd Eyes with gazing on each others Beauty; then veil'd her Beams in Clouds, to give the Lover boldneſs, and hide the Virgins bluſhes. What now could poor AMENA do, ſurrounded with ſo many Powers, attack'd by ſuch a charming Force without, betray'd by tenderneſs within: Virtue and Pride, the Guardians of her Honour, fled from her Breaſt, and left her to her Foe, only a modeſt Baſhfulneſs remain'd, which for a time made ſome Defence, but with ſuch weakneſs as a Lover leſs impatient than D'ELMONT, would have little regarded. The heat of the Weather, and her Confinement having hindred her from dreſſing that Day; ſhe had only a thin ſilk Night Gown on, which flying open as he caught her in his Arms, he found her panting-Heart beat meaſures of Conſent, her heaving Breaſt ſwell to be preſs'd by his, and every Pulſe confeſs a wiſh to yeild; her Spirits all diſſolv'd, ſunk in a Lethargy of Love; her ſnowy Arms, unknowing, graſp'd his Neck, her Lips met his half way, and trembled at the touch; in fine, there was but a Moment betwixt her and Ruin; when the tread of ſome Body coming haſtily down the Walk, oblig'd the half-bleſs'd Pair to put a ſtop to farther Endearments. It was ANARET, who having been left Centinel in the Garden, in order to open the Door when her Lady ſhould return, had ſeen Lights in every Room in the Houſe. and heard great Confuſion, ſo ran immediately to give 'em notice of this Misfortune. Theſe dreadful Tidings ſoon rous'd AMENA from her Dream of Happineſs, ſhe accus'd the influence of her Amorous Stars, upbraided ANARET, and blam'd the Count in Terms little differing from diſtraction, and 'twas as much as both of 'em could do to perſwade her to be calm. However, 'twas concluded that ANARET ſhould go back to the Houſe. and return to 'em again, as ſoon as ſhe had learn'd what accident had occaſion'd this Diſturbance. The Lovers had now a ſecond Opportunity, if either of'em had been inclin'd to make uſe of it, but their Sentiments were entirely chang'd with this Alarm;

A-

AMENA's Thoughts were wholly taken up with her approaching Shame, and vow'd she wou'd rather die than ever come in to her Father's Presence, if it were true that she was miss'd; the Count, who wanted not good Nature, seriously reflecting on the Misfortunes he was likely to bring on a young Lady, who tenderly lov'd him, gave him a great deal of real Remorse, and the Consideration that he should be necessitated, either to own an injurious Design, or come into Measures for the clearing of it, which would in no way agree with his Ambition, made him extreamly pensive, and wish AMENA again in her Chamber, more earnestly than ever he had done, to get her out of it; they both remain'd in a profound Silence, impatiently waiting the approach of ANARET; but she not coming as they expected, and the Night wearing away apace, very much encreas'd the Trouble they were in; at length the Count, after revolving a thousand Inventions in his Mind, advis'd to walk toward the Garden, and see whether the Door was yet open. 'Tis better for you, Madam, said he, whatsoever has happen'd, to be found in your own Garden, than in any Place with me. AMENA comply'd, and suffer'd herself to be led thither, trembling, and ready to sink with Fear and Grief at every Step; but when they found all fast, and that there was no hopes of getting Entrance, she fell quite senseless, and without any signs of Life, at her Lover's Feet, he was strangely at a loss what to do with her, and made a thousand Vows if he got clear of this Adventure, never to embark in another of this Nature; he was little skill'd in proper Means to recover her, and 'twas more to her Youth and the goodness of her Constitution that she ow'd the Return of her Senses, than his awkard Endeavours; when she reviv'd, the piteous Lamentations she made, and the perplexity he was in how to dispose of her, was very near reducing him to as bad a Condition as she had been in; he never till now having had occasion for a Confident, render'd him so unhappy as not to know any one Perſon at whoſe Houſe he cou'd, with any Convenience, truſt her, and to carry her to that where he had Lodgings, was the way to be made the talk of all *Paris*. He ask'd her ſeveral times if ſhe would not command him to wait on her to ſome Place where ſhe might remain free from Cenſure, tell ſhe heard from her Father, but cou'd get no Anſwer but upbraidings from her. So making a Virtue of Neceſſity, he was oblig'd to take her in his Arms, with a deſign to bring her (tho' much againſt his Inclinations) to his own Apartment: As he was going thro' a very fair Street which led to that in which he liv'd, AMENA cry'd out with a ſort of Joy, looſe me, my Lord, I ſee a Light in yonder Houſe, the Lady of it is my deareſt Friend, ſhe has power with my Father, and if I beg her Protection, I doubt not but ſhe will afford it me, and perhaps find ſome way to mitigate my Misfortunes; the *Count* was overjoy'd to be eas'd of his fair Burthen, and ſetting her down at the Gate, was preparing to take his leave with an indifference, which was but too viſible to the afflicted Lady. I ſee, my Lord, ſaid ſhe, the pleaſure you take in getting rid of me, exceeds the trouble for the Ruin you have brought upon me; but go, I hope I ſhall reſent this Uſage as I ought, and that I may be the better enabled to do ſo, I deſire you to return the Letter I writ this fatal Night, the Reſolution it contain'd will ſerve to remind me of my ſhameful Breach of it.

MADAM (anſwer'd he coldly, but with great Complaiſance) you have ſaid enough to make a Lover leſs obedient, refuſe; but becauſe I am ſenſible of the Accidents that happen to Letters, and to ſhew that I can never be repugnant even to the moſt rigorous of your Commands, I ſhall make no ſcruple in fulfilling this, and truſt to your Goodneſs for the re-ſettling me in your Eſteem, when next you make me ſo happy as to ſee you. The formality of this Compliment touch'd her to the Quick, and the thought of what ſhe was

like

like to suffer on his account, fill'd her with so just an Anger, that as soon as she got the Letter, she knock'd hastily at the Gate, which being immediately open'd, broke off any further Discourse, she went in, and he departed to his Lodging, ruminating on every Circumstance of this Affair, and consulting with himself how he shou'd proceed. ALOVISA (for it was her House which AMENA by a whimsical effect of Chance had made choice of for her Sanctuary) was no sooner told her Rival was come to speak with her, but she fell into all the Raptures that successful Malice could inspire, she was already inform'd of part of this Night's Adventure; for the cunning CHARLO who by her Orders had been a diligent Spy on Count D'ELMONT's Actions, and as constant an Attendant on him as his shadow, had watch'd him to Monsieur SANSEVERIN's Garden, seen him enter, and afterwards come with AMENA into the *Tuilleries*; where perceiving 'em Seated, ran Home, and brought his Lady an Account; Rage, Jealousie and Envy working their usual Effects in her, at this News, made her promise the Fellow infinite Rewards if he would invent some Stratagem to separate 'em, which he undertaking to do, occasion'd her being up so late, impatiently waiting his return; she went down to receive her with great Civility, mix'd with a feign'd surprize to see her at such an Hour, and in such a Dishabilee; which the other answering ingeniously, and freely letting her into the whole Secret, not only of her Amour, but the coldness she observ'd in D'ELMONT's Behaviour at parting, fill'd this cruel Woman with so exquisite a Joy, as she was hardly capable of dissembling; therefore to get liberty to indulge it, and to learn the rest of the particulars of CHARLO, who she heard was come in, she told AMENA she would have her go to Bed, and endeavour to compose her self, and that she would send for Monsieur SANSEVERIN in the Morning, and endeavour to reconcile him to her. I will also added she, with a deceitful smile, see the Count D'ELMONT, and talk to him in a manner as shall make him truly ſenſible of his Happineſs; nay, ſo far my Friendſhip ſhall extend, that if there be any real Cauſe for making your Amour a Secret, he ſhall ſee you at my Houſe, and paſs for a Viſitor of mine; I have no body to whom I need be accountable for my Actions and am above the Cenſures of the World. AMENA, thank'd her in Terms full of gratitude, and went with the Maid, whom ALOVISA had order'd to conduct her to a Chamber prepar'd for her; as ſoon as ſhe had got rid of her, ſhe call'd for CHARLO, impatient to hear by what contrivance this lucky Chance had befallen her. Madam, ſaid, he, tho' I form'd a thouſand Inventions, I found not any ſo plauſible, as to alarm Monſieur SANSEVERIN'S Family, with an out-cry of Fire. Therefore I rang the Bell at the fore-gate of the Houſe, and bellow'd in the moſt terrible accent I could poſſible turn my Voice to, Fire, Fire, riſe, or you will all be burnt in your Beds. I had not repeated this many times, before I found the Effect I wiſh'd; the Noiſes I heard, and the Lights I ſaw in the Rooms, aſſur'd me there were no Sleepers left; then I ran to the *Tuilleries*, deſigning to obſerve the Lover's proceedings, but I found they were appriz'd of the Danger they were in, of being diſcover'd, and were coming to endeavour an entrance into the Garden. I know the reſt, interrupted ALOVISA, the Event has anſwer'd even beyond my Wiſhes, and thy Reward for this good Service ſhall be greater than thy Expectations. As ſhe ſaid theſe Words ſhe retir'd to her Chamber, more ſatisfy'd than ſhe had been for many Months. Quite different did poor AMENA paſs the Night, for beſides the grief of having diſoblig'd her Father, baniſh'd her ſelf his Houſe, and expos'd her Reputation to the unavoidable Cenſures of the unpitying World; for an ungrateful, or at beſt an indifferent Lover. She receiv'd a vaſt addition of Afflictions, when taking out the Letter which D'ELMONT had given her at parting, poſſible to weep over it; and accuſe her ſelf for ſo inconſiderately breaking the noble Reſolution ſhe had form'd, when it was writ, She found it was ALOVISA's Hand

Hand, for the *Count* by mistake had given her the second he receiv'd from that Lady, instead of that she desir'd him to return. Never was Surprize, Confusion, and Dispair at such a height, as in AMENA's Soul at this Discovery; she was now assur'd by what she read, that she had fled for Protection to the very Person she ought most to have avoided; that she had made a Confident of her greatest Enemy, a Rival dangerous to her Hopes in every Circumstance. She consider'd the High Birth and vast Possessions that ALOVISA was Mistress of in opposition to her Father's scanted Power of making her a Fortune. Her Wit and Subtilty against her Innocence and Simplicity: her Pride, and the respect her grandeur commanded from the World, against her own deplor'd and wretch'd State, and look'd upon her self as wholly lost. The violence of her Sorrow is more easily imagin'd than express'd; but of all her melancholy Reflections, none rack'd her equal to the belief she had that D'ELMONT was not unsensible by this time whom the Letter came from, and had only made a Court to her to amuse himself a while, and then suffer her to fall a Sacrifice to his Ambition, and feed the Vanity of her Rival; a just Indignation now open'd the Eyes of her Understanding, and considering all the Passages of the *Count's* Behaviour, she saw a thousand Things which told her, his Designs on her were far unworthy of the Name of Love. None that were ever touch'd with the least of those Passions which agitated the Soul of AMENA, can believe they would permit Sleep to enter her Eyes: But if Grief and Distraction kept her from repose; ALOVISA had too much Business on her Hands to enjoy much more; She had promis'd AMENA to send for her Father, and the *Count*, and found there were not too many Moments before Morning, to contrive so many different forms of Behaviour, as should deceive 'em all three, compleat the Ruin of her Rival, and engage the Addresses of her Lover; as soon as she thought it a proper Hour, she dispatch'd a Messenger to Count D'ELMONT, and another to Monsieur SANSEVERIN, who full of Sorrow as he was, immediately obey'd her Summons. She receiv'd him in her Dressing-room, and with a great deal of feign'd Trouble in her Countenance, accosted him in this manner. How hard is it, said she, to dissemble Grief, and in spite of all the Care, which I doubt not you have taken to conceal it, in consideration of your own, and Daughter's Honour, I too plainly perceive it in your Face to imagine that my own is hid: How, Madam, cry'd the impatient Father, (then giving a loose to his Tears) are you acquainted then with my Misfortune? Alas, answer'd she, I fear by the Consequences you have been the last to whom it has been reveal'd. I hop'd that my Advice, and the daily Proofs the *Count* gave your Daughter of the little regard he had for her, might have fir'd her to a generous Disdain, and have a thousand Pardons to ask of you for Breach of Friendship, in concealing an Affair so requisite you should have known: Oh! Madam, resum'd he, interrupting her, I conjure you make no Apologies for what is past, I know too well the greatness of your goodness, and the favour you have always been pleas'd to Honour her with; not to be assur'd she was happy in your Esteem, and only beg I may no longer be kept in Ignorance of the fatal Secret. You shall be inform'd of all, said she, but then you must promise me to Act by my Advice; which he having promis'd, she told him after what manner AMENA came to her House, the coldness the *Count* express'd to her, and the violence of her Passion for him. Now, said she, if you should suffer your rage to break out in any publick Manner against the *Count*, it will only serve to make your Daughter's Dishonour the Table-Talk of all *Paris*. He is too great at Court, and has too many Friends to be compell'd to any Terms for your Satisfaction; besides, the least noise might make him discover by what means he first became acquainted with her, and her excessive, I will not say troublesome fondness of him, since; which should he do, the shame wou'd be wholly her's, for few wou'd condemn him for accepting the offer'd Caresses of a

Lady

Lady ſo young and beautiful as AMENA. But is it poſſible, cry'd he (quite confounded at theſe Words) that ſhe ſhould ſtoop ſo low to offer Love. Oh Heavens! Is this the Effect of all my Prayers, my Care, and my Indulgence. Doubt not, reſum'd ALOVISA, of the Truth of what I ſay, I have it from herſelf, and to convince you it is ſo, I ſhall inform you of ſomething I had forgot before. Then ſhe told him of the Note ſhe had ſlip'd into the Letter he had forc'd her to write, and of ſending ANERET to his Lodgings, which ſhe heightned with all the aggravating Circumſtances her Wit and Malice cou'd ſuggeſt; till the old Man believing all ſhe ſaid as an Oracle, was almoſt ſenſeleſs between Grief and Anger; but the latter growing rather the moſt predominant, he vow'd to puniſh her in ſuch a manner as ſhould deter all Children from Diſobedience. Now, ſaid ALOVISA, it is, that I expect the performance of your Promiſe; theſe threats avail but little to the retrieving your Daughter's Reputation, or your quiet; be therefore perſwaded to make no Words of it, compoſe your Countenance as much as poſſible to ſerenity, and think if you have no Friend in any Monaſtry where you could ſend her till this Diſcourſe, and her own fooliſh Folly be blown over. If you have not, I can recommend you to one at *St.* DENNIS where the Abbeſs is my near Relation, and on my Letter will uſe her with all imaginable Tenderneſs. Monſieur was extreamly pleas'd at this Propoſal, and gave her thoſe thanks the ſeeming kindneſs of her offer deſerv'd. I would not, reſum'd ſhe, have you take her Home, or ſee her before ſhe goes; or if you do, not till all things are ready for her Departure, for I know ſhe will be prodigal of her *Promiſes* of Amendment, 'till ſhe has prevail'd with your Fatherly Indulgence to permit her ſtay at *Paris*, and know as well ſhe will not have the Power to *keep* 'em in the ſame Town with the *Count*. She ſhall, if you pleaſe, remain conceal'd in my Houſe, 'till you have provided for her Journey, and it will be a great Means to put a ſtop to any farther Reflections the malicious may make on her; if you give out ſhe is already gone to ſome Relations in the Country. As ſhe was ſpeaking, CHARLO came to acquaint her, one was come to viſit her. She made no doubt but 'twas D'ELMONT, therefore haſten'd away Monſieur SANSEVERIN, after having fix'd him in a Reſolution to do every thing as ſhe adviſ'd. It was indeed Count D'ELMONT that was come, which as ſoon as ſhe was aſſur'd of, ſhew threw off her dejected and mournful Air, and aſſum'd one all Gaiety and good Humour, dimpl'd her Mouth with Smiles, and call'd the laughing Cupids to her Eyes.

MY Lord, ſaid ſhe, you do well by this early viſit to retrieve your Sexes drooping fame of Conſtancy, and prove the nicety of AMENA's diſcernment, in conferring favours on a Perſon, who to his excellent Qualifications, has that of aſſiduity to deſerve them; as he was about to reply, the ruſh of ſomebody coming haſtily down the Stairs which faced the Room they were in, oblig'd 'em to turn that way. It was the unfortunate AMENA, who not being able to endure the Thoughts of ſtaying in her Rivals Houſe, diſtracted with her Griefs, and not regarding what ſhou'd become of her, as ſoon as ſhe heard the Doors were open, was preparing to fly from that deteſted Place. ALOVISA was vex'd to the Heart at the ſight of her, hoping to have had ſome Diſcourſe with the *Count* before they met; but ſhe diſſembled it, and catching ho'd of her as ſhe was endeavouring to paſs, ask'd where ſhe was going, and what occaſion'd the Diſorder ſhe obſerv'd in her. I go, (anſwer'd AMENA) from a falſe Lover, and a falſer Friend, but why ſhou'd I upbraid you (continu'd ſhe looking wildly ſometimes on the *Count*, and ſometimes on ALOVISA) Treacherous Pair, you know too well each others Baſeneſs, and my Wrongs; no longer then, detain a Wretch whoſe Preſence, had you the leaſt Senſe of Honour, Gratitude, or even common Humanity, wou'd fill your Conſciences with Remorſe

and

and Shame; and who has now no other wish, than that of shunning you for ever. As she spoke this, she struggled to get loose from ALOVISA's Arms, who, in spite of the Amazement she was in, still held her. D'ELMONT was no less confounded, and intirely ignorant of the Meaning of what he heard, was at a loss how to reply, 'till she resum'd her reproaches in this manner: Why, ye Monsters of barbarity, said she, do you delight in beholding the Ruins you have made? Is not the knowledge of my Miseries, my everlasting Miseries, sufficient to content you? And must I be debarr'd that only Remedy for Woes like mine? Death! Oh cruel Return for all my Love, my Friendship! and the confidence I repos'd in you. Oh! to what am I reduc'd by my too soft and easie Nature, hard fate of tenderness, which healing others, only wounds it's self.----- Just Heavens!------ here she stopp'd, the violence of her Resentment, endeavouring to vent it self in sighs, rose in her Breast with such an impetuosity as choak'd the Passage of her Words, and she fell in a Swoon. Tho, the *Count*, and ALOVISA were both in the greatest Consternation imaginable, yet neither of 'em were negligent in trying to Recover her; as they were busi'd about her, that fatal Letter which had been the Cause of this Disturbance, fell out of her Bosom, and both being eager to take it up (believing it might make some discovery) had their Hands on it at the same time; it was but slightly folded, and immediately shew'd 'em from what source AMENA's despair proceeded: Her upbraidings of ALOVISA, and the Blushes and Confusion which he observed in that Ladies Face, as soon as ever she saw it open'd, put an end to the Mistery, and one less quick of Apprehension than D'ELMONT, wou'd have made no difficulty in finding his unknown Admirer in the Person of ALOVISA: She, to conceal the Disorder she was in at this Adventure as much as possible, call'd her Women, and order'd 'em to Convey AMENA into another Chamber where there was more Air; as she was preparing to follow, turning a little

little towards the *Count*. but ſtill extreamly confus'd, you'll Pardon me, my Lord, ſaid ſhe, if my concern for my Friend obliges me to leave you. Ah Madam, reply'd he, forbear to make any Apologies to me, rather Summon all your goodneſs to forgive a Wretch ſo blind to happineſs as I have been: She either cou'd not, or wou'd not make any anſwer to theſe Words, but ſeeming as tho' ſhe heard 'em not, went haſtily into the Room where AMENA was, leaving the *Count* full of various and confus'd Reflections; the ſweetneſs of his Diſpoſition made him regret his being the Author of AMENA's Misfortunes, but how miſerable is that Woman's Condition, who by her Miſmanagement is reduc'd to ſo poor a Comfort as the pity of her Lover; that Sex is generally too Gay to continue long uneaſy, and there was little likelihood he cou'd be capable of lamenting Ills, which his ſmall Acquaintance with the Paſſion from which they ſprung, made him not comprehend. The pleaſure the Diſcovery gave him of a Secret he had ſo long deſir'd to find out, kept him from being too much concern'd at the Adventure that occaſion'd it; but he could not forbear accuſing himſelf of intollerable Stupidity, when he conſider'd the Paſſages of ALOVISA's Behaviour, her ſwooning at the Ball, her conſtant Glances, her frequent Bluſhes when he talk'd to her, and all his Cogitations whether on ALOVISA, or AMENA, were mingled with a wonder that Love ſhould have ſuch Power. The diverſity of his Thoughts wou'd have entertain'd him much longer, if they had not been interrupted by his Page, who came in a great hurry, to acquaint him, that his Brother, the young Chevalier BRILLIAN was juſt come to Town, and waited with Impatience for his coming Home: As much a Stranger as D'ELMONT was to the Affairs of Love, he was none to thoſe of Friendſhip, and making no doubt but that the former ought to yield to the latter in every reſpect; contented himſelf with telling one of ALOVISA's Servants, as he went out, that he wou'd wait on

her

her in the Evening, and made what hast he cou'd to give his beloved Brother the welcome he expected after so long an absence; and indeed the manner of their Meeting, express'd a most intire and sincere Affection on both sides. The *Chevalier* was but a Year younger than the *Count*, they had been bred together from their Infancy, and there was such a sympathy in their Souls, and so great a Resemblance in their Persons, as very much contributed to endear 'em to each other with a Tenderness far beyond that which is ordinarily found among Relations, After the first Testimonies of it were over, D'ELMONT began to Question him how he had pass'd his Time since their Separation, and to give him some little Reproaches for not writing so often as he might have Expected. Alas! my dearest Brother, reply'd the *Chevalier*, such various Adventures have hap'ned to me since we parted, as when I relate 'em, will I hope excuse my seeming Negligence; these Words were accompany'd with Sighs, and a Melancholly Air immediately overspreading his Face, and taking away great part of the Vivacity, which lately sparkled in his Eyes, rais'd an impatient Desire in the *Count* to know the Reason of it, which when he had express'd, the other (after having engag'd him, that whatever Causes he might find to ridicule his Folly, he wou'd suspend all appearance of it till the end of his Narration) began to satisfy in this Manner.

THE

THE STORY OF THE Chevalier BRILLIAN.

AT St. *Omers*, where you left me, I happen'd to make an Acquaintance with one Monsieur BELPINE, a Gentleman who was there on some Business; we being both pretty much Strangers in the Place, occasion'd an Intimacy between us, which the disparity of our Tempers, wou'd have prevented our Commencing at *Paris*; but you know I was never a lover of Solitude, and for want of Company more agreeable, was willing to encourage his. He was indeed so obliging as to stay longer at St. *Omers* then his Affairs required, purposely to engage me to make *Amiens* in my way to *Paris*. He was very Vain, and fancying himself happy in the esteem of the fair Sex, was desirous I should be witness of the Favours they bestow'd on him. Among the Number of those he used to talk of, was Madamoiselle ANSELLINA de la TOUR, a *Parisian* Lady, and Heiress of a great Estate, but had been

some

ſome time at *Amiens* with Madam the Baroneſs *de* BERONVILLE her God-Mother. The Wonders he told me of this young Lady's Wit, and Beauty, inclin'd me to a deſire of ſeeing her; and as ſoon as I was in a Condition to Travel, we took our Way towards *Amiens*, he us'd me with all the Friendſhip he was capable of expreſſing; and ſoon after we arriv'd, carry'd me to the *Baroneſſes*: But oh Heavens! How great was my Aſtoniſhment when I found ANSELLINA as far beyond his faint Deſcription, as the Sun Beams the Imitation of Art; beſides the regularity of her Features, the delicacy of her Complexion, and the juſt Simmetry of her whole Compoſition, ſhe has an undeſcribable Sweetneſs that plays about her Eyes and Mouth, and ſoftens all her Air: But all her Charms, dazling as they are, would have loſt their captivating Force on me, if I had believ'd her capable of that weakneſs for BELPINE, that his Vanity would have me think. She is very Young and Gay, and I eaſily perceiv'd ſhe ſuffer'd his Addreſſes more out of Diverſion then any real Regard ſhe had for him; he held a conſtant Correſpondence at *Paris*, and was continually furniſh'd with every thing that was *Novel*, and by that means introduc'd himſelf into many Companies, who elſe wou'd not have endured him; but when at any time I was ſo happy as to entertain the lovely ANSELLINA alone, and we had Opportunity for ſerious Diſcourſe, (which was impoſſible in his Company) I found that ſhe was Miſtreſs of a Wit, Poynant enough to be Satyrical, yet it was accompanied with a Diſcretion as very much heighten'd her Charms, and compleated the Conqueſt that her Eyes begun. I will confeſs to you, Brother, that I became ſo devoted to my Paſſion, that I had no leiſure for any other Sentiments. Fears, Hopes, Anxities, jealous Pains, uneaſie Pleaſures, all the Artillery of Love, were garriſon'd in my Heart, and a thouſand various half form'd Reſolutions fill'd my Head. ANSELLINA's inſenſibility among a Crow'd of Admirers, and the diſparity of our Fortunes,

tunes, wou'd have given me juſt Cauſes of Deſpair, if the Generoſity of her Temper had not diſſipated the one, and her Youth, and the hope her Hour was not yet come, the other. I was often about letting her know the Power ſhe had over me, but ſomething of an awe which none but thoſe who truly Love can gueſs at, ſtill prevented my being able to utter it, and I believ'd ſhould have languiſh'd 'till this Moment in an unavailing ſilence, if an accident had not hapen'd to embolden me: I went one Day to viſit my Adorable, and being told ſhe was in the Garden, went thither in hopes to ſee her, but being deceiv'd in my Expectation, believ'd the Servant who gave me that Information was miſtaken, and fancying ſhe might be retir'd to her Cloſet, as ſhe very often did in an Afternoon, and the pleaſantneſs of the Place inducing me to ſtay there till ſhe was willing to admit me. I ſat down at the Foot of a DIANA, curiouſly carv'd in Marble, and full of melancholy Reflections without knowing what I did, took a black lead Pen out of my Pocket, and writ on the Pedeſtal theſe two Lines.

Hopeleſs, and Silent, I muſt ſtill adore,
Her Heart's more hard than Stone whom I'd implore.

I had ſcarce finiſh'd 'em, when I perceiv'd ANSELLINA at a good diſtance from me, coming out of a little Arbour; the reſpect I had for her, made me fear ſhe ſhould know I was the Author of 'em, and gueſs, what I found, I had not gain'd Courage enough to tell her. I went out of the Alley, as I imagin'd, unſeen, and deſign'd to come up another, and meet her, before ſhe cou'd get into the Houſe. But tho' I walk'd pretty faſt, ſhe had left the Place before I cou'd attain it; and in her ſtead (caſting my Eyes toward the Statue with an Intention to rub out what I had writ) I found this Addition to it.

You wrong your Love, while you conceal your Pain,
Flints will diſſolve with conſtant drops of Rain.

But

BUT, my dear Brother, if you are yet insensible of the wonderful Effects of Love, you will not be able to imagine what I felt at this View; I was satisfy'd it could be writ by no Body but ANSELLINA, there being no other Person in the Garden, and knew as well she could not design that Encouragement for any other Man, because on many Occasions she had seen my Hand; and the Day before had written a Song for her, which she desir'd to learn, with that very Pen I now had made use of; and going hastily away at the sight of her, had forgot to take with me. I gaz'd upon the dear obliging Characters, and kiss'd the Marble which contain'd 'em, a thousand times before I cou'd find in my Heart to efface 'em; as I was in this agreeable Amazement, I heard BELPINE's Voice calling to me as he came up the walk, which oblig'd me to put an end to it, and the Object which occasion'd it. He had been told as well as I, that ANSELLINA was in the Garden, and expressing some wonder to see me alone, ask'd where she was, I answer'd him with a great deal of real Truth, that I knew not, and that I had been there some Time, but had not been so happy as to Entertain her. He seem'd not to give Credit to what I said, and began to use me after a Fashion as would have much more astonish'd me from any other Person. I would not have you, said he, be concern'd at what I am about to say, because you are one of those for whom I am willing to preserve a Friendship; and to convince you of my Sincerity, give you leave to address after what manner you please to any of the Ladies with whom I have brought you acquainted, excepting ANSELLINA. But I take this Opportunity to let you know, I have already made choice of her, with a design of Marriage, and from this time forward, shall look on any Visits you shall make to her, as injurious to my Pretensions. Tho' I was no Stranger to the Vanity and Insolence of BELPINE's Humour, yet not being accustomed to such arbitrary Kind of Treatment, had certainly

certainly resented it (if we had been in any other Place) in a very different Manner than I did, but the consideration that to make a Noise there, would be a Reflection, rather than a Vindication on ANSELLINA's Fame; I contented myself with telling him he might be perfectly easie, that whatever Qualifications the Lady might have that should encourage his Addresses, I should never give her any Reason to boast a Conquest over me. These Words might have born two Interpretations, if the disdainful Air with which I spoke 'em, and which I could not dissemble, and going immediately away had not made him take 'em, as they were really design'd, to affront him; He was full of Indignation and Jealousy (if it is possible for a Person to be touch'd with that Passion, who is not capable of the other, which generally occasions it) but however, having taken it into his Head to imagine I was better receiv'd by ANSELLINA than he desired; Envy, and a sort of a Womanish Spleen transported him so far as to go to ANSELLINA's Apartment, and rail at me most profusely (as I have since been tod) and threaten how much he'd be reveng'd, if he heard I ever should have the assurance to Visit there again. ANSELLINA at first laugh'd at his Folly, but finding he persisted, and began to assume more Liberty than she ever meant to afford him; instead of list'ning to his Entreaties, to forbid me the Privilege I had enjoy'd of her Conversation; she pass'd that very Sentence on him, and when next I waited of her, receiv'd me with more Respect than ever; and when at last I took the boldness to acquaint her with my Passion; I had the Satisfaction to observe from the frankness of her Disposition, that I was not indifferent to her; nor indeed did she, even in Publick, affect any reservedness more than the decencies of her Sex and Quality requir'd; for after my Pretensions to her were commonly talk'd of, and those who were intimate with her, wou'd rally her about me; she pass'd it off with a Spirit of Gaity and good Humour peculiar to her self, and bated nothing of her usual freedom to me; she permitted me to Read to her;

her, to Walk and Dance with her, and I had all the Opportunities of endeavouring an encreaſe of her Eſteem that I cou'd wiſh, which ſo incens'd BELPINE, that he made no ſcruple of reviling both her and me in all Companies wherever he came; ſaying, I was a little worthleſs Fellow, who had nothing but my Sword to depend upon; and that ANSELLINA having no hopes of Marrying him, was glad to take up with the firſt that ask'd her. Theſe ſcandalous Reports on my firſt hearing of 'em had aſſuredly been fatal to one of us, if ANSELLINA had not commanded me by all the Paſſion I profeſs'd, and by the Friendſhip ſhe freely acknowledged to have for me, not to take any Notice of 'em. I ſet too high a Value on the favours ſhe allow'd me, to be capable of Diſobedience; and ſhe was too nice a Judge of the Punctillio's of our Sexes Honour, not to take this Sacrifice of ſo juſt a Reſentment, as a very great proof how much I ſubmitted to her will, and ſuffer'd not a Day to paſs without giving me ſome new mark how nearly ſhe was touch'd with it. I was the moſt contented and happy Perſon in the World, ſtill hoping that in a little time, ſhe having no Relations that had Power to contradict her Inclinations) I ſhould be able to obtain every thing from her that an honourable Paſſion could require; 'till one Evening coming Home pretty late from her, my Servant gave me a Letter, which he told me was left for me, by one of BELPINE's Servants; I preſently ſuſpected the Contents, and found I was not miſtaken; it was really a Challenge to meet him the next Morning, and muſt confeſs, tho' I long'd for an Opportunity to Chaſtiſe his Inſolence, was a little troubled how to excuſe my ſelf to ANSELLINA but there was no poſſibility of evading it, without rendering my ſelf unworthy of her, and hop'd that Circumſtance wou'd be ſufficient to clear me to her. I will not trouble you, Brother, with the particulars of our Duel, ſince there was nothing material, but that at the third paſs (I know not whether I may call it the effect of my good or evil Fortune) he receiv'd my Sword a good depth in in his Body, and fell with all the Symptoms of a Dying-Man. I made all possible hast to send a Surgeon to him. In my way I met two Gentlemen, who it seems he had made acquainted with his Design (probably with an intention to be prevented). They ask'd me what Success, and when I had inform'd 'em, advis'd me to be gone from *Amiens* before the News should reach the Ears of BELEPINE's Relations, who were not inconsiderable in that Place. I made 'em those Retributions their Civilities deserv'd; but how eminent soever the Danger appear'd that threatned me, cou'd not think of leaving *Amiens*, without having first seen ANSELLINA. I went to the *Baronesses*, and found my Charmer at her Toylet, and either it was my Fancy, or else she really did look more amiable in that Undress, than ever I had seen her, tho' adorn'd with the utmost Illustrations. She seem'd surpriz'd at seeing me so early, and with her wonted good Humour, asking me the reason of it, put me into a mortal Agony how to answer her, for I must assure you, Brother, that the fears of her Displeasure were a thousand times more dreadful to me, than any other apprehensions; she repeated the Question three or four times before I had Courage to Reply, and I believe she was pretty near guessing the Truth by my Silence, and the disorder in my Countenance before I spoke; and when I did, she receiv'd the account of the whole Adventure with a vast deal of trouble, but no anger; she knew too well what I ow'd to my Reputation, and the Post his Majesty had honour'd me with, to believe, I cou'd, or ought to dispence with submitting to the Reflections which must have fallen on me, had I acted otherwise than I did. Her Concern and Tears, which she had not Power to contain at the thoughts of my Departure, joyn'd with her earnest Conjurations to me to be gone, let me more than ever into the Secrets of her Heart, and gave me a Pleasure as inconceivable as the necessity of parting did the contrary. Nothing cou'd be more moving than our taking leave, and when she tore her self half willing, and half unwilling, from my my Arms, had ſent me away inconſolable, if her Promiſes of coming to *Paris*, as ſoon as ſhe could, without being taken notice of, and frequently writing to me in the mean time, had not given me a Hope, tho' a diſtant one, of Happineſs. Thus Brother, have I given you, in as few Words as I cou'd, a Recital of every thing that has happen'd to me of Conſequence ſince our Separation, in which I dare believe you will find more to Pity than Condemn. The afflicted Chevalier cou'd not conclude without letting fall ſome Tears; which the *Count* perceiving, ran to him, and tenderly embracing him, ſaid all that cou'd be expected from a moſt affectionate Friend to mitigate his Sorrows, nor ſuffered him to remove from his Arms 'till he had acompliſh'd his Deſign; and then believing the hearing of the Adventures of another, (eſpecially one he was ſo deeply intereſted in) would be the ſureſt Means to give a Truce to the more melancholy Reflections on his own; related every thing that had befallen him ſince his coming to *Paris*. The Letters he receiv'd from a Lady *Incognito*, his little Gallantries with AMENA, and the accident that preſented to his View, the unknown Lady in the Perſon of one of the greateſt Fortunes in all *France*. Nothing cou'd be a greater Cordial to the Chevalier, than to find his Brother was belov'd by the Siſter of ANSELLINA; he did not doubt but that by this there might be a poſſibility of ſeeing her ſooner than elſe he cou'd have hop'd, and the two Brothers began to enter into a ſerious conſultation of this Affair, which ended with a Reſolution to fix their Fortunes there. The *Count* had never yet ſeen a Beauty formidable enough to give him an Hours uneaſineſs (purely for the ſake of Love) and would often ſay, *Cupid*'s Quiver never held an Arrow of force to reach his Heart; thoſe little Delicacies, thoſe trembling aking Tranſports, which every ſight of the belov'd Object occaſions, and ſo viſibly diſtinguiſhes a real Paſſion from a Counterfeit, he look'd on as the Chimera's of an idle Brain, form'd to inſpire Notions of an imaginary Bliſs, and make Fools

loſe

lose themselves in seeking; or if they had a Being; it was only in weak Souls, a kind of a Disease with which he assur'd himself he should never be infected. Ambition was certainly the reigning Passion in his Soul, and ALOVISA's Quality and vast Possessions, promising a full Gratification of that, he ne'er so much as wish'd to know a farther Happiness in Marriage.

BUT while the *Count* and *Chevalier* were thus Employ'd, the Rival Ladies past their Hours in a very different Entertainment, the despair and bitter Lamentations that the unfortunate AMENA made, when she came out of her swooning, were such as mov'd even ALOVISA to Compassion, and if any thing but resigning D'ELMONT cou'd have given her Consolation, she wou'd willing have apply'd it. There was now no need of further Dissimulation, and she confessed to AMENA, that she had Lov'd the Charming *Count* with a kind of Madness from the first Moment she beheld him: That to favour her Designs on him, she had made use of every Stratagem she cou'd invent, that by her means, the Amour was first discover'd to *Monsieur* SANSEVERIN, and his Family Alarm'd the Night before; and Lastly, that by her Persuasions, he had resolv'd to send her to a Monastry, to which she must prepare her self to go in a few Days without taking any leave even of her Father; have you (cry'd AMENA hastily interrupting her) have you prevail'd with my Father to send me from this hated Place without the Punishment of hearing his upbraidings? Which the other answering in the Affirmative, I thank you, resum'd AMENA, that Favour has cancell'd all your Score of Cruelty, for after the Follies I have been guilty of, nothing is so dreadful as the Sight of him. And, who wou'd, oh Heavens! (continued she bursting into a Flood of Tears) wish to stay in a World so full of Falshood. She was able to utter no more for some Moments, but at last, raising herself on the Bed where she was laid, and endeavouring to seem a little more compos'd: I have two Favours, Madam, yet to ask of you (rejoin'd she) neither of 'em 'em will, I believe, ſeem difficult to you to grant, that you will make uſe of the Power you have with my Father, to let my Departure be as ſudden as poſſible, and that while I am here, I may never ſee Count D'ELMONT. It was not likely that ALOVISA ſhou'd deny Requeſts ſo ſuitable to her own Inclinations, and believing, with a great deal of Reaſon, that her Preſence was not very grateful, left her to the Care of her Women, whom ſhe order'd to attend her with the ſame Diligence as herſelf. It was Evening before the Count came, and ALOVISA ſpent the remainder of the Day in very unneaſie Reflections; ſhe knew not, as yet, whether ſhe had Cauſe to rejoyce in, or blame her Fortune in ſo unexpectedly diſcovering her Paſſion, and an inceſſant viciſſitude of Hope and Fears, rack'd her with moſt intollerable Inquietude, till the darling Object of her Wiſhes appear'd; and tho' the firſt ſight of him, added to her other Paſſions, that of Shame, yet he manag'd his Addreſs ſo well, and ſo modeſtly and artfully hinted the Knowledge of his Happineſs, that every Sentiment gave place to a new Admiration of the Wonders of his Wit; and if before ſhe lov'd, ſhe now ador'd, and began to think it a kind of Merit in herſelf, to be ſenſible of his. He ſoon put it in her Power to oblige him, by giving her the Hiſtory of his Brother's Paſſion for her Siſter, and ſhe was not at all backward in aſſuring him how much ſhe approv'd of it, and that ſhe wou'd write to ANSELLINA by the firſt Poſt, to engage her coming to *Paris* with all imaginable Speed. In fine, there was nothing He cou'd ask, refus'd, and indeed it would have been ridiculous for her to have affected Coyneſs, after the Teſtimonies ſhe had long ſince given him of one of the moſt violent Paſſions that ever was; this fore-Knowledge ſav'd abundance of Diſſimulation on both Sides, and ſhe took care that if he ſhould be wanting in his kind Expreſſions after Marriage, he ſhould not have it in his Power to pretend (as ſome Husbands have done) that his Stock was exhauſted in a tedious Courtſhip. Every thing was preſently

ſently agreed upon, and the Wedding Day appointed, which was to be as ſoon as every thing cou'd be got ready to make it Magnificent; tho' the *Count's* good Nature made him deſirous to learn ſomething of AMENA, yet he durſt not enquire, for fear of giving an Umbrage to his intended Bride; but ſhe, imagining the Reaſon of his Silence, very frankly told him, how ſhe was to be diſpos'd of, this Knowledge made no ſmall Addition to his Contentment, for had ſhe ſtay'd in *Paris*, he could expect nothing but continual Jealouſies from ALOVISA; beſides, as he really wiſh'd her happy, tho' he could not make her ſo, he thought Abſence might baniſh a hopeleſs Paſſion from her Heart, and Time and other Objects efface an Idea, which could not but be deſtructive to her Peace. He ſtay'd at ALOVISA's Houſe 'till it was pretty late, and perhaps they had not parted in ſome Hours longer, if his impatience to inform his Brother his Succeſs, had not carried him away. The young *Chevalier* was infinitely more tranſported at the bare Hopes of being ſomething nearer the Aim of all his Hopes, than D'ELMONT was at the Aſſurance of loſing his in Poſſeſſion, and could not forbear rallying him for placing the ultimate of his Wiſhes on ſuch a Toy, as he argu'd Woman was, which the *Chevalier* endeavouring to confute, there began a very warm Diſpute, in which, neither of 'em being able to convince the other, Sleep at laſt interpos'd as Moderator. The next Day they went together to viſit ALOVISA, and from that time were ſeldom aſunder: But in Compaſſion to AMENA, they took what Care they could to conceal the Deſign they had in Hand, and that unhappy Lady was in a few Days, according to her Rival's Contrivance, hurried away, without ſeeing any of her Friends. When ſhe was gone, and there was no farther need of keeping it a Secret, the News of this great Wedding was immediately ſpread over the whole Town, and every one talk'd of it as their particular Intereſts or Affections dictated. All D'ELMONT's Friends were full of Joy, and he met no inconsiderable Augmentation of it himself, when his Brother receiv'd a Letter from ANSELLINA, with an Account, that BELPINE's Wound was found not Dangerous, and that he was in a very fair way of Recovery. And it was concluded, that as soon as the Wedding was over, the *Chevalier* should go in Person to AMIENS, and fetch his belov'd ANSELLINA, in order for a Second, and as much desir'd Nuptial. There was no Gloom now left to Cloud the Gaiety of the happy Day, nothing could be more Grand than the Celebration of it, and ALOVISA now thought her self at the end of all her Cares; but the Sequel of this glorious Beginning, and what Effect the Despair and Imprecations of AMENA (when she heard of it) produc'd, shall, with the continuance of the *Chevalier* BRILLIAN's Adventures, be faithfully related in the next Part.

End of the FIRST PART.

LOVE

LOVE in Excess:

OR, THE

FATAL INQUIRY,

A

NOVEL.

PART the SECOND.

By *Mrs.* HAYWOOD.

Each Day we break the bond of Humane Laws
For Love, and vindicate the common Cause.
Laws for Defence of civil Rights are plac'd; (*waste*
Love throws the Fences down, and makes a gen'ral
Maids, Widows, Wives, without distinction fall,
The sweeping deluge Love, comes on and covers all.

DRYDEN.

LONDON:
Printed for W. CHETWOOD, J. WOODMAN, D. BROWN, and S. CHAPMAN.

LOVE in EXCESS: OR, THE FATAL ENQUIRY.

PART the SECOND.

THE Contentment that appear'd in the Faces of the new Married Pair, added so much to the Impatience of the *Chevalier* BRILLIAN to see his belov'd ANSELLINA, that in a few Days after the Wedding, he took leave of them, and departed for *Amiens*: But as human Happiness is seldom of long continuance, and ALOVISA placing the Ultimate of *her's* in the Possession of her Charming Husband, secure of that, despis'd all future Events, 'twas time for *Fortune*, who long enough had smil'd, now to turn her Wheel, and punish the presumption that defy'd her Power.

As they were one Day at Dinner, a Messenger came to Acquaint *Count* D'ELMONT that *Monsieur* FRANKVILLE was taken, suddenly, so violently Ill, that his Physicians despair'd of his Life; and that he beg'd to speak with him immediately: This Gentleman had been Guardian to the COUNT during his Minority, and the Care and Faithfulness with which that Trust had been Discharg'd, made him, with Reason, to regret the danger of losing so good a Friend: He delay'd the Visit not a Moment, and found him as the Servant had told him, in a Condition which cou'd cherish no hopes of Recovery, as soon as he perceiv'd the COUNT come into the Chamber, he desir'd to be left alone with him, which Order being presently obey'd, My dear Charge, (said he taking him by the Hand, and pressing to his trembling Bosom) you see me at the point of Death, but the knowledge of your many Virtues, and the Confidence I have that you will not deny me the request I am about to ask, makes me support the Thoughts of it with Moderation. The other assuring him of his readiness to serve him in any Command, encourag'd the old Gentleman to prosecute his Discourse in this manner: You are not Ignorant, my Lord (Rejoin'd He) that my Son (the only one I have) is on his Travels, gone by my Approbation, and his own Desires to make the Tour of *Europe*; but I have a Daughter, whose Protection I wou'd entreat you to undertake; her Education in a Monastery has hitherto kept her intirely unacquainted with the Gayeties of a Court, or the Conversation of the *Beau Monde*, and I have sent for her to *Paris* purposely to Introduce her into Company, proper for a young Lady, who I never design'd for a Recluse; I know not whether she will be here time enough to close my Eyes, but if you will promise to receive her into your House, and not suffer her artless and unexperienc'd Youth to fall into those Snares which are daily laid for Innocence, and take so far a Care, that neither she, nor the Fortune I leave her, be thrown away upon a Man unworthy of her, I shall dye well satisfy'd. D'ELMONT answer'd this

Request

Request, with repeated assurances of fulfilling it, and frankly offer'd, if he had no other Person in whom he rather wou'd confide, to take the management of the whole Estate he left behind him, till young FRANKVILLE should return ----- The anxious Father was transported at this Favour, and thank'd him in Terms full of Gratitude and Affection; they spent some Hours in settling this Affair, and perhaps had not ended it so soon, if Word had not been brought that the young Lady his Daughter was alighted at the Gate; 'tis impossible to express the Joy which fill'd the old Gentleman's Heart at this News, and he began afresh to put the COUNT in mind of what he had promis'd concerning her: As they were in this endearing, tho' mournful Entertainment, the matchless MELLIORA enter'd, the Surprize and Grief for her Father's Indisposition (having heard of it but since she came into the House) hindered her from regarding any thing but him, and throwing herself on her Knees by the Bedside, wash'd the Hand which he stretch'd out to raise her with, in a flood of Tears, accompany'd with Expressions, which, unstudy'd and incoherent as they were, had a delicacy in 'em, that show'd her Wit not inferiour to her Tenderness, and that no Circumstance cou'd render her otherwise than the most lovely Person in the World; when the first transports of her Sorrow were over, and that with much ado she was persuaded to rise from the Posture she was in: The Affliction I see thee in my Dear Child, (said her Father) wou'd be a vast addition to the Agonies I feel, were I not so happy as to be provided with Means for a mitigation of it, think not in losing me thou wilt be left wholly an Orphan, this worthy Lord will dry thy Tears. Therefore, my last Commands to thee shall be to oblige thee to endeavour to deserve the Favours he, is pleas'd to do us in accepting thee for --- He wou'd have proceeded, but his Physicians (who had been in Consultation in the next Room) coming in prevented him, and *Count* D'ELMONT taking the charming MELLIORA by the Hand, led her to the Window, and beginning to ſpeak ſome Words of Conſolation to her, the ſoftneſs of his Voice, and graceful Manner with which he deliver'd himſelf (always the inſeparable Companions of his Diſcourſe, but now more particularly ſo) made her caſt her Eyes upon him; but alas, he was not an Object to be ſafely gaz'd at, and in ſpight of the Grief ſhe was in, ſhe found ſomething in his Form which diſſipated it; a kind of painful Pleaſure, a mixture of Surprize, and Joy, and doubt, ran thro' her in an inſtant; her Fathers Words ſuggeſted to her Imagination, that ſhe was in a poſſibility of calling the charming Perſon that ſtood before her, by a Name more tender than that of Guardian, and all the Actions, Looks, and Addreſs of D'ELMONT ſerv'd but to confirm her in that Belief. For now it was, that this inſenſible began to feel the Power of Beauty, and that Heart which had ſo long been Impregnable, ſurrender'd in a Moment; the firſt ſight of MELLIORA gave him a Diſcompoſure he had never felt before, he Sympathiz'd in all her Sorrows, and was ready to joyn his Tears with hers, but when her Eyes met his, the God of Love ſeem'd there to have united all his Lightnings for one effectual Blaze, their Admiration of each others Perfections was mutual, and tho' he had got the ſtart in Love, as being touch'd with that Almighty Dart, before her Affliction had given her leave to regard him, yet the ſoftneſs of her Soul made up for that little loſs of time, and it was hard to ſay whoſe Paſſion was the Strongeſt; ſhe liſtned to his Condolements, and aſſurances of everlaſting Friendſhip, with a pleaſure which was but too viſible in her Countenance, and more enflam'd the COUNT. As they were exchanging Glances, as if each vyed with the other who ſhould dart the fierceſt Rays, they heard a ſort of ominous Whiſpering about the Bed, and preſently one of thoſe who ſtood near it, beckon'd them to come thither; the Phyſicians had found *Monſieur* FRANKVILLE in a much worſe Condition than they left him in, and ſoon after perceiv'd evident Symptoms in him of approaching Death, and indeed there were but a very few Moments

ments between him and that other unfathomable World; the uſe of Speech had left him, and he cou'd take no other leave of his dear Daughter than with his Eyes; which ſometimes were caſt tenderly on her, ſometimes on the COUNT, with a beſeeching Look, as it were, to Conjure him to be careful of his Charge; then up to Heaven, as witneſs of the Truſt he repos'd in him. There cou'd not be a Scene more Melancholly than this dumb Farewell, and MELLIORA, whoſe ſoft Diſpoſition had never before been ſhock'd, had not Courage to ſupport ſo dreadful a one as this, but fell upon the Bed juſt as her Father Breath'd his laſt, as motionleſs as he. It is impoſſible to repreſent the Agony's which fill'd the Heart of D'ELMONT at this View, he took her in his Arms, and aſſiſted thoſe who were endeavouring to recover her, with a wildneſs in his Countenance, a trembling Horror ſhaking all his Fabrick in ſuch a manner, as might have eaſily diſcover'd to the Spectators (if they had not been too buſily employ'd to take notice of it) that he was Actuated by a Motive far more powerful than that of Compaſſion. As ſoon as ſhe came to herſelf, they forc'd her from the Dead Body of her Father (to which ſhe Clung) and carried her into another Room, and it being judg'd convenient that ſhe ſhould be remov'd from that Houſe, where every thing wou'd ſerve but to remind her of her Loſs, the COUNT deſir'd the Servants of *Monſieur* FRANKVILLE ſhou'd be call'd, and then in the preſence of 'em all, [illegible]'d their Maſter's laſt Requeſt, and order'd an Account of all Affairs ſhou'd be brought to his Houſe, where he wou'd immediately Conduct their young Lady, as he had promis'd to her Father. If MELLIORA had been without any other cauſe of Grief, this Eclairciſſment had been ſufficient to have made her Miſerable: She had already entertained a moſt tender Affection for the COUNT, and had not ſo little diſcernment as not to be ſenſible ſhe had made the like Impreſſion on him; but now ſhe wak'd as from a Dream of promis'd Joys, to certain Woes, and the ſame Hour which gave Birth to her Passion, commenc'd an adequate Despair, and kill'd her Hopes just budding.

INDEED there never was any Condition so truly deplorable as that of this unfortunate Lady; she had just lost a dear and tender Father, whose Care was ever watchful for her, her Brother was far off, and she had no other Relation in the World to apply her self to for Comfort, or Advice; not even an Acquaintance at *Paris*, or Friend, but him who but newly was become so, and whom she found it dangerous to make use of, whom she knew it was a Crime to Love, yet cou'd not help Loving; the more she thought, the more she grew Distracted, and the less able to resolve on any Thing; a thousand Times she call'd on Death to give her ease, but that pale Tyrant flies from the Pursuer, she had not been yet long enough acquainted with the ills of Life, and must endure (how unwilling soever) her part of Sufferings in common with the rest of human kind.

As soon as D'ELMONT had given some necessary Directions to the Servants, he came to the Couch, where she was sitting in a fix'd and silent Sorrow (tho' inwardly toss'd with various and violent Agitations) and offering her his Hand, entreated her to permit him to wait on her from that House of Woe. Alas! Said she, to what purpose shou'd I remove, who bear my Miseries about me? Wretch that I am! --- a flood of Tears, here interpos'd, and hindred her from proceeding, which falling from such lovely Eyes, had a Magnetick Influence to draw the same from every beholder; but D'ELMONT who knew that was not the way to Comfort her, dry'd his as soon as possible, and once more beg'd she wou'd depart; suffer my return then (answer'd she) to the Monastery, for what have I to do in *Paris* since I have lost my Father? By no means, Madam (resum'd the *Count* hastily) that were to disappoint your Fathers Designs, and contradict his last Desires; believe most lovely MELLIORA (continu'd he taking her by the Hand and letting fall some Tears which he cou'd not restrain, upon it) that I bear at least an equal Share in your Affliction, and lament for you, and for my self: Such a regard my grateful Soul paid *Monsieur* FRANKVILLE for all his wondrous Care and Goodness to me, that in his Death methinks I am twice an Orphan. But Tears are fruitless to reinspire his now cold Clay, therefore must transmit the Love and Duty I owed him living, to his Memory Dead, and an exact performance of his Will; and since he thought me worthy of so vast a Trust as MELLIORA, I hope she will be guided by her Fathers Sentiments, and believe that D'ELMONT (tho' a Stranger to her) has a Soul not uncapable of Friendship. Friendship! Did I say? (rejoyn'd he softning his Voice) that term is too mean to express a Zeal like mine, the Care, the Tenderness, the Faith, the fond Affection of Parents, --- Brothers, --- Husbands, --- Lovers, all Compriz'd in one! One great Unutterable! Comprehensive Meaning, is mine! for MELLIORA! She return'd no Answer but Sighs, to all he said to her; but he renewing his Entreaties, and urging her Father's Commands, she was at last prevail'd upon to go into his Chariot, which had waited at the Door all the Time of his being there.

As they went, he left nothing unsaid that he believ'd might tend to her Consolation, but she had Griefs which at present he was a Stranger to, and his Conversation, in which she found a thousand Charms, rather Encreas'd, than Diminish'd the trouble she was in: Every Word, every Look of his, was a fresh Dagger to her Heart, and in spight of the Love she bore her Father, and the unfeign'd Concern his sudden Death had given her, she was now convinc'd that COUNT D'ELMONT's Perfections were her severest Wounds.

WHEN they came to his House, He presented her to ALOVISA, and giving her a brief Account of what had happened, engag'd that Lady to receive her

 with

with all imaginable Demonſtrations of Civility and Kindneſs.

HE ſoon left the two Ladies together, pretending Buſineſs, but indeed to ſatisfie his Impatience, which long'd for an opportunity to meditate on this Adventure. But his Reflections were now grown far leſs pleaſing than they uſed to be; real Sighs flew from his Breaſt uncall'd: And MELLIORA's Image in dazling Brightneſs! In terrible Array of killing Charms! Fir'd Him with (impoſſible to be attain'd) Deſires: he found by ſad Experience what it was to Love, and to Deſpair. He Admir'd! Ador'd! And wiſh'd, even to Madneſs! Yet had too much Honour, too much Gratitude for the Memory of Monſieur FRANCKVILLE; and too ſincere an Awe for the lovely Cauſe of his Uneaſineſs, to form a Thought that cou'd encourage his new Paſſion. What wou'd he not have given to have been Unmarried? How often did he Curſe the Hour in which ALOVISA's fondneſs was diſcover'd? And how much more his own Ambition, which prompted him to take Advantage of it, and hurry'd him Precipitately to a Hymen, where Love, (the nobleſt Gueſt) was wanting? It was in theſe racks of Thought, that the unfortunate AMENA was remembr'd, and he cou'd not forbear acknowledging the Juſtice of that Doom, which inflicted on him, theſe very Torments he had given her. A ſevere Repentance ſeiz'd on his Soul, and ALOVYSA for whom he never had any thing more than an Indifferency; now began to ſeem Diſtaſteful to his Fancy, he look'd on her, as indeed ſhe was, the chief Author of AMENA's Misfortunes, and abhorr'd her for that Infidelity, But when he conſider'd her, as the Bar 'twixt Him and MELLIORA ſhe appear'd like his ill Genius to him, and he cou'd not ſupport the Thoughts of being oblig'd to love her (or at leaſt to ſeem as if he did) with Moderation. In the midſt of theſe Reflections, his Servant came in and deliver'd a Letter to him which had been juſt left by the Poſt. The COUNT immediately knew the Hand to be AMENA's, and was cover'd with the utmost Confusion and Remorse when he read these Lines.

To the too Charming and Perfidious D'ELMONT.

NOW Hopes, and Fears, and Jealousies are over! Doubt is no more! You are for ever lost! And my unfaithful, happy Rival! Triumphs in your Arms, and my Undoing! ---- I need not wish you Joy, the haste you made to enter into Hymen's Bonds, and the more than ordinary Pomp with which that Ceremony was Celebrated, assures me you are highly satisfied with your Condition; and that any future Testimonies of the Friendship of so wretched a Creature as AMENA, *wou'd be receiv'd by you, with the same Disregard, as those she has given you of a more tender Passion. ---- Shameful Remembrance! Oh that I cou'd Blot it out! ---- Erace from the Book of Time those fond deluded Hours! Forget I ever saw the Lovely false* D'ELMONT! *Ever listned to his soft persuasive Accents! And thought his love a mighty Price for Ruin ------ My Father writes that you are Married, Commands my Return to* Paris, *and assume an Air as Gay, and Chearful as that with which I us'd to appear. ---- Alas! How little does he know his Daughters Heart? And how impossible is it, for me to Obey him, can I look on you as the Husband of* ALOVYSA, *without remembring you were once the Lover of* AMENA? *Can Love like mine, so fierce, so passionately, tender, e're sink to a calm, cold Indifference? Can I behold the fond Endearments of your bridal Joys (which you'd not be able to Restrain, even before me) and not burst with Envy? No, the Sight wou'd turn me quite Distracted, and I shou'd commit some Desperate Violence that wou'd Undoe us all. --- Therefore, I hide my self for ever from it, bid an everlasting*

Adieu

Adieu to all the gay Delights and Pleasures of my Youth.----- To all the Pomp and Splendor of the Court. ----- To all that the mistaken World calls Happiness.--- To Father, Friends, Relations, all that's Dear---- But your Idea, and that, not even these consecrated Walls, nor Iron Gates keep out; Sleeping or Waking you are ever with me, you mingle with my most solemn Devotions; and while I Pray to Heaven that I may think on you no more, a guilty Pleasure rises in my Soul, and contradicts my Vows! All my Confessions are so many Sins, and the same Breath which tells my Ghostly Father I abjure your Memory, speaks your dear Name with Transport. Yes----Cruel! Ungrateful!---Faithless as you are, I still do Love you---- Love you to that infinite degree, that now, methinks fir'd with thy Charms (repenting all I've said) I cou'd wish even to renew those Moments of my Ruin! ---- Pity me D'ELMONT, *if thou hast Humanity.----- Judge what the rackings of my Soul must be, when I resolve, with all this Love, this Languishment about me; never to see you more.*

Every thing is preparing for my Reception into holy Orders, (how unfit I am Heaven knows) and in a few Days I shall put on the Vail which excludes me from the World for ever; therefore, if these distracted Lines are worth an Answer, it must be speedy, or it will not come to my Hands. Perhaps not find me Living.----- I can no more ----- Farewel (thou dear Destroyer of my Soul)

Eternally Farewel, AMENA.

P. S. I do not urge you to write, *Alovisa* (I wish I cou'd not say your Wife) will perhaps think it too great a Condescention, and not suffer you so long from her Embraces. ---- Yet if you can get loose.---- But you know best what's proper to be done ---- Forgive the restlesness of a dispairing Wretch, who cannot cease to Love, tho' from this Moment she must cease to tell you so--- Once more, and for Ever,

Adieu.

HAD-

HAD this Letter came a Day sooner, 'tis probable it wou'd have had but little Effect on the Soul of D'ELMONT, but his Sentiments of Love were now so wholly chang'd, that what before he wou'd but have laugh'd at, and perhaps despis'd, now fill'd him with Remorse and serious Anguish. He read it over several Times, and found so many Proofs in it of a sincere and constant Affection, that he began to pity Her, with a Tenderness like that of a Relation, but no more: The charming MELLIORA had Engross'd all his fonder Wishes; else it is not impossible but that ALOVISA might have had more Reason to fear her Rivalship after Marriage, than before. That Lady having been without the presence of her dear Husband some Hours, had not patience to remain any longer without seeing Him, and making an excuse to MELLIORA for leaving her alone, came running to the Closet where he was; how unwelcome she was grown, the Reader may imagine, he receiv'd her, not as he was wont; the Gaity which used to sparkle in his Eyes, (at once declaring, and creating Amorous desires) now gave Place to a sullen Gloominess, he look'd not on her, or if by chance he did; 'twas more with Anger than with Love, in spite of his endeavours to conceal it, she was too quick sighted (as all are that truly Love) not to be sensible of this Alteration. However she took no notice of it, but Kissing and Embracing him (according to her Custom whenever they were alone) beg'd him to leave his solitary Amusement, and help her to Comfort the afflicted Lady he brought there. Her Endearments serv'd but to encrease his Peevishness, and heighten her Surprize at his Behaviour; and indeed, the Moment that she enter'd the Closet was the last of her Tranquility.

WHEN with much perswasions she had prevail'd with him to go with her into the Room where MELLIORA was, he appeared so disorder'd at the second Sight of that Charmer, as wou'd certainly have let

AL-

ALOVYSA into the ſecret of his Paſſion, had ſhe not been retir'd to a Window to recover herſelf from the Confuſion her Husbands coldneſs had thrown her in, and by that fortunate diſregard of his Looks at that critical Inſtant, given him (who never wanted preſence of Mind) leave to form both his Countenance and manner of Addreſs, ſo as to give no ſuſpicion of the Truth.

THIS little Company was very far from being Entertaining to one another; every one had their particular Cogitations, and were not diſpleas'd not to be Interrupted in them. It growing late, ALOVYSA conducted MELLIORA to a Chamber which ſhe had order'd to be prepar'd for her, and then retir'd to her own, hoping that when the COUNT ſhou'd come to Bed, ſhe might be able to make ſome Diſcovery of the Cauſe of his Uneaſineſs. But ſhe was deceiv'd, he ſpoke not to her, and when by a thouſand little Inventions ſhe urg'd him to reply to what ſhe ſaid, it was in ſuch a faſhion as only let her ſee, that he was extreamly troubled at ſomething, but cou'd not gueſs at what. As ſoon as Day broke, he roſe, and ſhutting himſelf into his Cloſet, left her in the greateſt Conſternation imaginable; ſhe cou'd not think it poſſible that the Death of *Monſieur* FRANKVILLE ſhou'd work this Transformation, and knew of no other Misfortune that had happened. At laſt ſhe remembred ſhe had heard one of the Servants ſay, a Letter was brought to their Maſter by the Poſt, and began to reflect on every Thing (in the power of *Fortune* to determine) that cou'd threaten a Diſturbance, yet was ſtill as ignorant as ever. She lay not long in Bed, but putting on her Cloaths with more Expedition than uſual went to the Cloſet, reſolving to ſpeak to him in a manner as ſhou'd oblige him to put an end to the uncertainty ſhe was in, but finding the Door lock'd, her Curioſity made her look thro' the Keyhole, and ſhe ſaw him ſometimes very intirely reading a Letter, and ſometimes writing, as tho' it were an Anſwer to it. A ſudden Thought came into her Head, and ſhe

ſhe immediately went ſoftly from the place where ſhe was, without knocking at the Door, and ſtay'd in a little Chamber adjacent to it, where none could paſs to, or from the Cloſet without being perceiv'd by her; ſhe had not waited long, before ſhe heard the *Count* Ring, and preſently ſaw a Servant enter, and ſoon after return with a Letter in his Hand; ſhe wou'd not ſpeak to him then, for fear of being over heard by her Husband, but follow-ed him down Stairs, and when he came towards the bottom, call'd to him in a low Voice to tarry 'till ſhe came to him; the Fellow durſt not but Obey, and there being no body near 'em, commanded him to de-liver her the Letter; But he either afraid or unwilling to betray his Truſt, excus'd himſelf from it as well as he cou'd, but ſhe was reſolv'd to have it; and when Threats wou'd not avail, condeſcended to Entreaties, to which ſhe added Bribes, which laſt Article join'd to the promiſe ſhe made of never revealing it, won him to her Purpoſe. She had ſcarce patience to forbear opening it before ſhe got to her Chamber: The Su-perſcription (which ſhe ſaw was for AMENA) fir'd her with Diſdain and Jealouſie, and it is hardly poſſi-ble to imagine, much leſs to deſcribe the Torrent of her Indignation, when ſhe found that it contain'd theſe Words.

To the Lovely AMENA.

Y*OU accuſe me of Cruelty, when at the ſame Time you kill me with yours: How Vile! How deſpicable, muſt I be grown in your Opinion, when you believe I can be Happy, when you are Miſerable? --- Can I enjoy the Pleaſures of a Court, while you are ſhut within a Cloy-ſter? ---- Shall I ſuffer the World to be depriv'd of ſuch a Treaſure as* AMENA? *For the Crime of worthleſs* D'ELMONT *---- No, no Fair, injur'd Softneſs, Re-turn, and bleſs the Eyes of every Beholder! Shine out again*

again in your native Lustre, uneclips'd by Grief, the Star of Beauty and the guide of Love. --- And, if my unlucky Presence will be a Damp to the Brightness of your Fires, I will for ever quit the Place. ---- Tho' I cou'd wish, you'd give me leave sometimes to gaze upon you, and draw some hop'd Presages of future Fortune from the Benignity of your Influence, --- Yes, AMENA, *I wou'd sigh out my Repentance at your Feet, and try at least to obtain a Pardon for my Infidelity. ---- For, 'tis true, what you have heard, ---- I am Marry'd --- But oh* AMENA! *Happiness is not always an Attendant on* Hymen. -- *However, I yet may call you Friend -- I yet may Love you, tho' in a different way from what I once pretended to; and believe me, that the Love of Souls, as it is the most uncommon, especially in our Sex, so 'tis the most refin'd and noble of all Passions, and such a Love shall be for ever yours. Even* ALOVISA *(who has robb'd you of the rest) cannot justly resent my giving you that part, ---- You'll wonder at this Alteration in my Temper, but 'tis sincere, I am no more the Gay, the Roving* D'ELMONT, *and when you come to* Paris, *perhaps you will find me in a Condition more liable to your Pity than Indignation. What shall I say* AMENA? *My Crime is my Punishment, I have offended against Love, and against you, and am, if possible, as Miserable, as Guilty: Torn with Remorse, and Tortur'd with ---- I cannot ---- must not Name it ---- but 'tis something which can be term'd no other than the utmost severity of my Fate. --- Haste then to Pity me, to comfort, to advise me, if (as you say) you yet retain any remains of your former Tenderness for this Ungrateful Man,*

D'ELMONT.

UNGRATEFUL indeed! Cry'd ALOVISA (Transported with Excess of Rage and Jealousie) Oh the Villain! --- What Miseries! What Misfortunes are these thou talk'st of? What Unhappiness has waited on thy *Himen*? 'Tis I alone am wretched! base Deceiver!

THEN,

THEN, as if ſhe wanted to diſcover ſomething farther to heighten the Indignation ſhe was in, ſhe began to read it over again, and indeed the more ſhe conſider'd the meaning of what ſhe read, the more her Paſſions ſwell'd, 'till they got at laſt the entire Dominion of her Reaſon: She tore the Letter in a thouſand pieces, and was not much leſs unmerciful to her Hair and Garments 'Tis poſſible, that in the Violence of her Fury, ſhe might have forgot her promiſe to the Servant, to vent ſome part of it on her Husband, if her Woman coming into the Room to know if ſhe was ready to dreſs, had not prevented her, by telling her the *Count* was gone abroad, and had left Word, that he ſhou'd not return 'till the Evening. ALOVISA had thrown herſelf on the Bed, and the Curtains being drawn diſcover'd not the diſorder ſhe was in, and which her Pride made her willing ſhou'd be ſtill a Secret, therefore diſmiſt her with ſaying, ſhe wou'd call her when ſhe wanted any thing. Tho' ALOVISA was too apt to give a looſe to her Paſſions on every occaſion, to the Deſtruction of her own Peace, yet ſhe knew well enough how to diſguiſe 'em, when ever ſhe found the Concealing of them wou'd be an Advantage to her Deſigns: And when the Tranſports of her Rage was ſo far over, as to give her Liberty of Reflection, and ſhe began to Examine the State of her Affection to the *Count*, ſhe ſoon perceiv'd it had ſo much the better of all other Conſiderations, that in ſpite of the injuſtice ſhe thought him guilty of to her, ſhe cou'd not perſwade her ſelf to do any thing that might give him a pretence to Quarrel with her. She thought ſhe had done enough in Intercepting this Letter, and did not doubt but that AMENA wou'd take his not writing to her ſo much to Heart, as to prevent her ever returning to *Paris*, and reſolv'd to omit nothing of her former Endearments, or make a ſhew of being in the leaſt diſoblig'd; this ſort of Carriage ſhe imagin'd wou'd not only lay him more open and unguarded to the diligent watch ſhe deſign'd to make on all his

his Words and Actions, but likewiſe awaken him to a juſt Senſe of her Goodneſs, and his own Ingratitude. ----- She rightly judg'd that when Poeple are Marry'd, Jealouſie was not the proper Method to revive a decay'd Paſſion, and that after Poſſeſſion it muſt be only Tenderneſs, and conſtant Aſſiduity to pleaſe, that can keep up deſire, freſh and gay: Man is too Arbitrary a Creature to bear the leaſt Contradiction, where he pretends an abſolute Authority, and that Wife who thinks by ill humour and perpetual Taunts, to make him weary of what ſhe wou'd reclaim him from, only renders her ſelf more hateful, and makes that juſtifiable which before was blameable in him. Theſe, and the like Conſiderations made ALOVYSA put on a Countenance of Serenity, and ſhe ſo well acted the part of an Unſupecting Wife, that D'ELMONT was far from imagining what ſhe had done: However he ſtill behav'd with the ſame Caution as before, to MELLIORA; and certainly never did People diſguiſe the Sentiments of their Souls more artfully than did theſe three --- MELLIORA vail'd her ſecret Languiſhments, under the Covert of her grief for her Father, the COUNT his Burning anguiſh, in a gloomy Melancholy for the Loſs of his Friend; but ALOVYSA's Task was much the hardeſt, who had no pretence for grief (raging, and bleeding with neglected Love, and ſtifled Pride) to frame her Temper to a ſeeming Tranquility ---- All made it their whole ſtudy to deceive each other, yet none but ALOVYSA was intirely in the dark; for the *Count* and MELLIORA had but too true a gueſs at one another's meaning, every look of his, for he had Eyes that needed no Interpreter, gave her Intelligence of his Heart, and the Confuſion which the underſtanding thoſe looks gave her, ſufficiently told him how ſenſible ſhe was of 'em. ---- Several Days they liv'd in this Manner, in which time *Monſieur* FRANKVILLE was Interr'd. Which Solemnity, the *Count* took care ſhou'd be perform'd with a Magnificence ſuitable to the Friendſhip he publickly profeſt

to

to have born him, and the ſecret Adoration his Soul paid to his Remains.

NOTHING happned of Moment,'till a Day or two after the Funeral, a Gentleman newly arriv'd at *Paris*, came to viſit the *Count*, and gave him an Account of AMENA's having taken the Habit; how, (ſaid D'ELMONT Interrupting him) is it poſſible? ---- Has ſhe then profeſt? Yes, anſwer'd the Gentleman, having a Siſter whom I always tenderly lov'd at the Monaſtery at St. *Dennis*, my affection oblig'd me to make it in my way to viſit her. AMENA was with her at the Grate, when ſhe receiv'd me; I know not how, among other Diſcourſes, we hapned to talk of the fine Gentlemen of *Paris*, which it was Impoſſible to do, without mentioning *Count* D'ELMONT, the COUNT anſwer'd not this Complement as he wou'd have done at another time, but only bowing with an humble Air, gave him Liberty to proſecute his Diſcourſe; the moment (reſum'd he) that AMENA heard your Name, the Tears run from her fair Eyes; in ſuch abundance, and ſhe ſeem'd oppreſt with ſo violent a Grief, that ſhe was not able to ſtay any longer with us. When ſhe was gone, my Siſter whom ſhe had made her Confidant, gave me the Hiſtory of her Misfortunes, and withal, told me, that the next Day ſhe was to be Initiated into Holy Orders: My Curioſity engag'd me to ſtay at St. *Dennis*, to ſee the Ceremony perform'd, which was Solemn; but not with that Magnificence which I expected; it ſeems it was AMENA's deſire that it ſhould be as private as poſſible, and for that Reaſon, none of her Relations were there, and ſeveral of the Formalities of Entrance omitted: After it was over, my Siſter beckon'd me to come to the Grate, where I ſaw her before, and Conjur'd me in the Name of her new Siſter, to give this to your Hands; in ſpeaking theſe Words, he took a Letter out of his Pocket, which the COUNT immediately opening, to his great ſurprize, found it contain'd, as follows,

To the Inhuman D'ELMONT.

TO be pity'd by you, and that you shou'd tell me so, was all the recompence I ask'd for Loss of Father, Friends, Reputation, and Eternal Peace; but now, too late, I find that the fond Maid who scorns the World for Love, is sure to meet for her reward the scorn of him she Loves ---- Ungrateful Man! Cou'd you not spare one Moment from that long Date of Happiness, to give a last farewel to her you have undone? What wou'd not this Barbarous Contempt have drawn upon you, were I of ALOVISA'*s Temper? Sure I am, all that disdain and rage, cou'd Inspire Malice with, had been Inflicted on you, but you well know my Soul is of a another Stamp.---- Fool that I was, and little vers'd in the base Arts of Man, believ'd I might by tenderness, and faithful Friendship, gain esteem; tho' Wit and Beauty the two great Provocatives to create Love were wanting. But do not think that I am yet so mean as to desire to hear from you; no, I have put all future Correspondence with you out of my Power, and hope to drive it even from my wish: Whether your disdain, or the Holy Banner I am listed under, has wrought this Effect, I know not, but methinks I breath another Air, think on you with more Tranquility, and bid you without dying,*

Eternally Adieu, AMENA.

P.S. LET ALOVISA know I am no more her Rival, Heaven has my Soul, and I forgive you both.

D'ELMONT was strangely fir'd at the reading these Lines, which left him no Room to doubt that his Letter had miscarried, he could not presently imagine by what means, but was resolv'd if possible, to find it out. However, he dissembled his Thoughts 'till the Gentleman had taken his leave; then calling for the Servant,

Servant, whom he had entrusted with the carrying it, he took him by the Throat, and holding his drawn Sword directly to his Breast, swore that Moment should be his last, if he did not immediately confess the Truth; the poor Fellow, frighted almost to Death, trembling, and falling on his Knees, implor'd Forgiveness, and discover'd all. ALOVISA who was in the next Chamber, hearing her Husband call for that Servant, with a Tone somewhat more imperious than what he was accustom'd to, and a great Noise soon after, imagin'd some Accident had happen'd to betray her, and ran in to know the Certainty, just as the *Count* had discharg'd the Servant, at once from his Service and his Presence. You have done well Madam (said D'ELMONT, looking on her with Eyes sparkling with Indignation) you have done well, by your impertinent Curiosity and Imprudence, to rouze me from my Dream of Happiness, and remind me, that I am that wretched Thing a Husband! 'Tis well indeed (answer'd ALOVISA, who saw now that there was no need of farther Dissimulation) that any thing can make you remember, both what you are, and what I am. You, (resum'd he, hastily interrupting her) have taken an effectual Method to prove your self a Wife! ---- a very Wife! ---- Insolent --- Jealous --- and Censorious! --- But Madam (continued he frowning) since you are pleas'd to assert your Priveledge, be assur'd, I too shall take my turn, and will exert the --- Husband! In saying this, he flung out of the Room in spite of her Endeavours to hinder him, and going hastily through a Gallery which had a large Window that looked into the Garden, he perceived MELLIORA lying on a green Bank, in a melancholy, but a charming Posture, directly opposite to the Place where he was; her Beauties appear'd, if possible, more to Advantage than ever he had seen them, or at least, he had more Opportunity thus unseen by her, to gaze upon 'em; he in a Moment lost all the Rage of Temper he had been in, and his whole Soul was taken up with softness; he stood for some Moments fix'd in silent

ſilent Admiration, but Love has ſmall Dominion in a Heart, that can content it ſelf with a diſtant Proſpect, and there being a Pair of back-Stairs at the farther end of the Gallery, which led to the Garden. He either forgot, or not regarded what Conſtruction ALOVISA might make on this private Interview, if by Chance, from any of the Windows ſhe ſhould be Witneſs of it.

MELLIORA was ſo intent on a Book ſhe had in her Hand, that ſhe ſaw not the *Count* 'till he was cloſe enough to her to diſcern what was the Subject of her Entertainment, and finding it the Works of *Monſieur* L'FONTENELLE; Philoſophy, Madam, at your Age (ſaid he to her with an Air, which expreſt ſurprize) is as wond'rous as your other Excellencies; but I am confident, had this Author ever ſeen MELLIORA, his Sentiments had been otherwiſe than now they ſeem to be, and he would have been able to write of nothing elſe but Love and her. MELLIORA bluſh'd Extremely at his unexpected Preſence, and the Complement he made Her; but recollecting her ſelf as ſoon as ſhe cou'd; I have a better Opinion of *Monſieur* L'FONTENELLE, (anſwer'd ſhe) but if I were really Miſtreſs of as many Charms as you wou'd make me believe, I ſhould think my ſelf little beholding to Nature, for beſtowing them on me, if by their means I were depriv'd of ſo choice an Improvement as this Book has given me. Thank Heaven, then Madam, (reſum'd he) that you were born in an Age ſucceſſive to that which has produc'd ſo many fine Treatiſes of this kind for your Entertainment; ſince (I am very Confident) this, and a long ſpace of future Time will have no other Theme, but that which at preſent you ſeem ſo much averſe to. MELLIORA found ſo much difficulty in endeavouring to Conceal the diſorder ſhe was in at this Diſcourſe, that it rendered her unable to reply; and He, who poſſibly gueſt the occaſion of her ſilence) taking one of her Hands and tenderly preſſing it between his, look'd ſo full in her

her Eyes, as heighten'd her Confusion, and discover'd to his ravish'd View, what most he wish'd to find: Ambition, Envy, Hate, Fear, or Anger, every other Passion that finds Entrance in the Soul; Art, and Discretion, may Disguise, but Love, tho' it may be feign'd, can never be Conceal'd, not only the Eyes (those true and most Perfect Intelligencers of the Heart) but every Feature, every Faculty betrays it! It fills the whole Air of the Person possest with it; it wanders round the Mouth! Plays in the Voice! trembles in the Accent! And shows it self a thousand different, nameless ways! Even MELLIORA's Care to hide it, made it more apparent, and the Transported D'ELMONT not considering where he was, or who might be a witness of his Rapture, cou'd not forbear catching her in his Arms, and grasping her with an Extasie, which plainly told her what his thoughts were, tho' at that time he had not Power to put 'em into Words; and indeed there is no greater proof of a vast and elegant Passion, than the being uncapable of Expressing it: ---- He had perhaps held her in this strict embrace, 'till some Accident had discover'd and separated him from her; if the Alarm this manner of Proceeding gave her Modesty, had not made her force her self from him. - -- They both stood in a silent Consternation, nor was he much less disorder'd at the Temerity, the violence of his ungovernable Passion had made him guilty of, than she was at the Liberty he had taken; he knew not how to Excuse, nor she, to Reproach; Respect (the constant Attendant on a sincere Affection) had tyed his Tongue, and shame mixed with the uncertainty after what manner she shou'd resent it, Hers. At last, the Natural Confidence of his Sex Encourag'd him to break this mute Entertainment.--- There are Times Madam (said he) in which the wisest have not Power over their own Actions--- If therefore I have offended, impute not the Crime to me, but that unavoidable impulse which for a Moment hurry'd me from my self; for be assured while D'ELMONT can Command his Thoughts, they shall be most

most obedient to your Wishes —— As MELLIORA was about to reply, she saw a Servant coming hastily to speak to the COUNT, and was not a little glad of so favourable an opportunity to retire without being oblig'd to continue a Discourse in which she must either lay a severe Punishment on her Inclinations by making a quarrel with him, or by forgiving him too easily, Trespass against the strict Precepts of Virtue she had always profess'd: She made what haste she cou'd into her chamber, and carry'd with her a World of troubled Meditations, she now no longer doubted of the COUNT's Passion, and trembled with the Apprehension of what he might in time be prompted to; but when she Reflected how dear that Person she had so much cause to fear, was to her, she thought her self, at once the most unfortunate and most Guilty of her Sex.

THE Servant who gave 'em this seasonable Interruption delivered a Letter to his Master, which he opening hastily, knowing that it came from his Brother by the Seal, found the Contents as follows.

I Hop'd (my Dearest Friend, and Brother) by this day to have Embrac'd you, but Fortune takes delight to disappoint our wishes, when highest rais'd, and nearest to their Aim.---- The Letter I carry'd from her, whom I think it my Happiness to call Sister, joyn'd with my own Faith, Love, and Assiduity; at length Triumph'd over all the little niceties and objections my Charmer made against our Journey, and she Condescended to order every thing requisite for our departure from Amiens *shou'd be got ready.--- But how shall I Express the Grief, the Horrour, the Distraction of my Soul, when the very Evening before the Day we shou'd have set out, as I was sitting with her, a sudden, but terrible Illness, like the Hand of Death seiz'd on her, she fell (oh! my Brother) Cold, and Speechless in my Arms ------ Guess, what I endur'd at that Afflicting Moment, all that I had of Man, or Reason left me; and sure had not*

not the Care of the Baronness and some other Ladies (whom my Cries drew in to her Assistance) in a little time recover'd her, I had not now surviv'd to give you this Account: Again, I saw the Beauties of her Eyes! again, I heard her Voice, but her Disorder was yet so great, that it was thought convenient she should be put to Bed; the Barroness seeing my Despair, desired me not to quit her House, and by that Means I had News every Hour, how her Fever encreas'd, or abated. for the Physicians being desir'd to deal freely, assur'd us, that was her Distemper: For severa Days she continued in a Condition that could give us no Hopes of her Recovery; in which Time, as you may imagine, I was little capable of Writing. ----- The wildness of my unruly Grief, made me not be permitted to come into her Chamber; but they cou'd not, without they had made use of Force, hinder me from lying at her Door: I counted all her Groans, heard every Sigh the Violence of her Pain drew from her, and watch'd the Countenance of every Person who came out of her Chamber, as Men who wou'd form a Judgment of future Consequences, do the Signs in Heaven. ---- But I trouble you with this tedious recital, she is now, if there is any Dependance on the Doctors Skill, past Danger, tho' not fit to Travel, at least this Month, which gives no small Alienation to the greatness of my Joys (which otherwise wou'd be unbounded) for her Recovery, since it occasions so long a Separation from the best of Brothers, and of Friends: Farewell, may all your Wishes meet Success, and an Eternal round of Happiness attend you; to add to mine, I beg you'll write by the first Post, which, next to seeing you, is the greatest I can Taste. I am, my Lord, with all imaginable Tenderness and Respect, your most Affectionate Brother and Humble Servant,

BRILLIANT.

THE *Count* judg'd it proper that ALOVISA shou'd see this Letter, because it so much concern'd her

 Sister,

Sister, and was ordering the Servant to carry it to her, (not being himself willing to speak to her) just as she was coming towards him: She had receiv'd a Letter from the *Baroness* DE BERONVILL, at the same time that the *Chevalier* BRILLIAN's was brought, and was glad to take the Opportunity of Communicating the Contents of it, in hopes by this Conversation, to be reconcil'd to her Husband: But the gloomy Sullenness of the Humour he had left her with, return'd at Sight of her, and after some little Discourse of Family Affairs, which he could not avoid answering, walk'd carelesly away: She follow'd him at a distance, 'till he was got up to the Gallery, and perceiving he went toward his Closet, mended her Pace, and was close to him when he was going in. My Lord, (said she) with a Voice but half assur'd, and which would not have given her leave to utter more, if he had not interrupted her, by telling her he would be alone, and shutting the Door hastily upon her, but she prevented his Locking of it, by pushing against it with all her Force, and he, not exerting his, for fear of hurting her, suffer'd her Entrance: But look'd on her with a Countenance so forbidding, as in spite of the natural Haughtiness of her Temper, and the Resolution she had made to speak to him, render'd her unable for some Moments to bring forth a Word; but the silent Grief, which appear'd in her Face, pleaded more with the good Nature of the *Count*, than any thing she could have said: He began to pity the unhappiness of her too violent Affection, and to wish himself in a Capacity of returning it, however, he (like other Husbands) thought it best to keep up his Resentments, and take this Opportunity of Quelling all the *Woman* in her Soul, and humbling all the little Remains of Pride that Love had left her. Madam, (resum'd he) with an Accent, which tho' something more softned, was still imperious enough, if you have any Thing of Consequence to impart to me, I desire you will be as brief as you can, for I would be left to the Freedom

dom of my Thoughts --- ALOVISA cou'd not yet anſwer, but letting fall a Shower of Tears, and throwing her ſelf on the Ground, Embrac'd his Knees with ſo Paſſionate a Tenderneſs, as ſufficiently expreſt her Repentance for having been guilty of any thing to diſoblige him: D'ELMONT was moſt ſenſibly touch'd at this Behaviour, ſo vaſtly different from what he cou'd have expected from the greatneſs of her Spirit, and raiſing her with an obliging Air. I am ſorry (ſaid he) that any thing ſhould happen to occaſion this Submiſſion, but ſince what's paſt, is out of either of our Powers to recall: I ſhall endeavour to think of it no more, provided you'll promiſe me, never for the future to be guilty of any thing which may give me an uneaſineſs by the ſight of yours---- 'Tis impoſſible to repreſent the Tranſport of ALOVISA at this kind Expreſſion, ſhe hung upon his Neck, kiſſed the dear Mouth which had pronounc'd her Pardon, with Raptures of unſpeakable Delight, ſhe ſigh'd with Pleaſure, as before ſhe had done with Pain, ſhe wept, ſhe even dy'd with Joy! ---- No, no, my Lord, my Life, my Angel, (cry'd ſhe, as ſoon as ſhe had Power to ſpeak) I never will Offend you more, no more be Jealous, no more be doubtful of my Happineſs! You are! -- you will be only mine, I know you will---- Your kind Forgiveneſs of my Folly, aſſures me that you are mine, not more by Duty than by Love! A Tye far more valuable than that of Marriage. The *Count* conſcious of her Miſtake, had much ado to conceal his Diſorder at theſe Words, and being unwilling ſhe ſhould proceed; as ſoon as he could (without ſeeming unkind or rude) diſingag'd himſelf from her Arms, and took a Pen in his Hand, which he told her he was about to employ in anſwering the *Chevalier* BRILLIAN's Letter; ALOVISA who now reſolv'd an entire Obedience to his Will, and remembring he had deſired to be alone, withdrew, full of the Idea of an imagin'd Felicity ---- Her Heart was now at eaſe, ſhe believ'd, that if her Husband had any Remains of Paſſion for AMENA, the impoſſibility of ever ſeeing her again, would ſoon extinguiſh them, and ſince ſhe was ſo happily reconcil'd, was far from repenting her intercepting of his Letter: But poor Lady, ſhe did not long enjoy this Peace of Mind, and this Interval of Tranquility ſerv'd but to heighten her enſuing Miſeries,

THE *Count*'s ſecret Paſſion for MELLIORA grew ſtronger by his endeavouring to ſuppreſs it, and perceiving that ſhe carefully avoided all Opportunities of being alone with him one Moment, ſince his Behaviour to her in the Garden, he grew almoſt Diſtracted with the continual Reſtraint he was forc'd to put on all his Words and Actions: He durſt not Sigh nor ſend an amorous Glance, for fear of offending her, and alarming his Wive's Jealouſy, ſo lately lull'd to Sleep: He had no Perſon in whom he had Confidence enough to truſt with his Misfortune, and had certainly ſunk under the Preſſure of it, if ALOVISA, who obſerving an Alteration in his Countenance and Humour, fearing he was really indiſpos'd (which was the excuſe he made for his Melancholly) had not perſwaded him to go into the Country, hoping that change of Air might do him good: He had a very fine Seat near *Anjerville* in the Province of *Le Beauſſe*, which he had not been at for ſome Years, and he was very willing to comply with ALOVISA's Deſires of paſſing the remainder of the Summer in a Solitude, which was now become agreeable to him; the greateſt Difficulty was, in perſwading MELLIORA to accompany them thither; he gueſs'd by her reſerv'd Behaviour, that ſhe only waited an Opportunity to leave the Place where he was, and was not miſtaken in his Conjecture: One Day as they were talking of it, ſhe told them ſhe was reſolv'd to return to the Monaſtery where ſhe had been Educated, that the World was too noiſy a Place for one of her Taſte, who had no reliſh for any of the Diverſions of it: Every Word ſhe ſpoke, was like a Dagger to D'ELMONT's Heart; yet, he ſo artfully manag'd his Endeavours, between the Authority

thority of a Guardian, and the Entreaties of a Friend, that ſhe was at laſt overcome. 'Tis hard for the ſevereſt Virtue to deny themſelves the Sight of the Perſon belov'd, and whatever Reſolutions we make, there are but few, who like MELLIORA might not by ſuch a Lover be prevail'd upon to break them.

As ſoon as their coming into the Country was ſpread abroad, they were viſited by all the Neighbouring People of Quality, but there was none ſo welcome to D'ELMONT as the *Baron* D'ESPERNAY; they had before the COUNT's going into the Army been very intimate Acquaintance, and were equally glad of this opportunity to renew a Friendſhip, which Time and Abſence had not entirely erac'd. The *Baron* had a Siſter young, and very agreeable, but gay even to Coquetry; they liv'd together, being both ſingle, and he brought her with him, hearing the *Count* was Married, to viſit his Lady: There were ſeveral other young Noble Men and Ladies there, at the ſame time, and the Converſation grew ſo delightfully Entertaining, that it was impoſſible for Perſons leſs prepoſſeſt than the COUNT and MELLIORA, to retain their *Chagrin*; but, tho' there were ſcarce any in the Company that might not have liſt'ned with a pleas'd Attention, to what thoſe two admirable Perſons were capable of ſaying, yet their ſecret Sorrows kept them both in ſilence, 'till MELANTHA, for that was the Name of the *Barons* Siſter, took upon her to divert the Company with ſome Verſes on Love; which ſhe took out of her Pocket-Book and read to 'em: Every Body extoll'd the ſoftneſs of the Stile, and the Subject they were upon. But MELLIORA who was willing to take all opportunities of Condemning that Paſſion, as well to conceal it in her ſelf as to check what ever hopes the *Count* might have, now diſcovered the force of her Reaſon, the Delicacy of her Wit, and the Penetration of her Judgment, in a manner ſo ſweetly ſurprizing to all that were Strangers to her, that they preſently found, that it was not want of Noble, and truly agreeable Thoughts or Words

E 3 to

to expreſs 'em, that had ſo long depriv'd them of the Pleaſure of hearing her; ſhe urg'd the Arguments ſhe brought againſt the giving way to Love, and the Danger of all ſoftning Amuſements, with ſuch a becoming fierceneſs, as made every Body of the Opinion that ſhe was born only to create Deſire, not be ſuſceptible of it her ſelf. The *Count* as he was moſt Concern'd, took the moſt particular Notice of all ſhe ſaid, and was not a little alarm'd to ſee her appear ſo much in earneſt, but durſt not anſwer, or Endeavour to confute her, becauſe of ALOVYSA's preſence: But it was not long before he had an opportunity, a few Days after he met with one, as full as he cou'd wiſh. Returning one Evening from the *Baron* D'ESPERNAY's, whom he had now made the Confident of his Paſſion, and who had Encourag'd him in it, he was told that ALOVYSA was gone out to take the Air, and hearing no mention of MELLIORA's being with her, he ſtay'd not to enquire, but running directly to her Chamber, made his Eyes his beſt Informers: He found her lying on a Couch in a moſt charming Diſſabillee, ſhe had but newly come from Bathing, and her Hair unbraided, hung down upon her Shoulders with a negligence more Beautiful than all the Aids of Art cou'd form in the moſt exact *Decorum* of Dreſs; part of it fell upon her Neck and Breaſt, and with it's Lovely Shadineſs, being of a Delicate dark Brown, ſet off to vaſt Advantage, the matchleſs whiteneſs of her Skin: Her Gown and the reſt of her Garments were white, and all ungirt, and looſely flowing, diſcover'd a Thouſand Beauties, which Modiſh Formalities conceal. A Book lay open by her, on which ſhe had reclin'd her Head, as if been tir'd with Reading, ſhe Bluſh'd at ſight of the *Count*, and roſe from off the Couch with a Confuſion which gave new Luſtre to her Charms, but he not permitting her to ſtir from the place ſhe was in, ſat down by Her, and caſting his Eyes on the Book which lay there, found it to be *Ovid's-Epiſtles*, How Madam (cry'd he, not a little pleas'd with the Diſcovery) dare you, who the other Day ſo warmly

inveigh'd

inveigh'd against Writings of this Nature, trust your self with so Dangerous an Amusement? How happens it, that you are so suddenly come over to our Party? Indeed my Lord (answer'd she, growing more disorder'd) it was Chance rather than Choice, that directed this Book to my Hands, I am yet far from approving Subjects of this Kind, and believe I shall be ever so: Not that I can perceive any Danger in it, as to my self, the Retirement I have always liv'd in, and the little Propensity I find to entertain a Thought of that uneasie Passion, has hitherto secur'd me from any Prepossession, without which, *Ovid's* Art is Vain. Nay, Madam, reply'd the *Count*, now you Contradict your former Argument, which was, that these sort of Books were, as it were, Preparatives to Love, and by their softning Influence, melted the Soul, and made it fit for amorous Impressions, and so far, you certainly were in the right, for when once the Fancy is fixed on a real Object, there will be no need of Auxillary Forces, the Dear Idea will spread it self thro' every Faculty of the Soul, and in a Moment inform us better, than all the Writings of the most Experienc'd Poets, cou'd do in an Age. Well, my Lord, (said she endeavouring to Compose her self) I am utterly unambitious of any Learning this way, and shall endeavour to retain in Memory, more of the Misfortunes that attended the Passion of *Sappho*, than the Tender, tho' never so Elegant Expressions it produc'd: And if all Readers of Romances took this Method, the Votaries of *Cupid* wou'd be fewer, and the Dominion of Reason more Extensive. You speak (Answer'd D'ELMONT) as tho' Love and Reason were Incompatible, there is no Rule said (she) my Lord, without Exception, they are indeed sometimes united, but how often they are at Variance, where may we not find Proofs, History is full of them, and daily Examples of the many Hair-brain'd Matches, and slips, much less excusable, sufficiently evince how little Reason has to do in the Affairs of Love, I mean (continu'd she, with a very serious Air) that sort of Love, for there are two, which hurries People on to an immediate Gratification of their Desires, tho' never so prejudicial to themselves, or the Person they pretend to Love. Pray Madam (said the *Count* a little nettled at this Discourse) what Love is that which seems at least to Merit the Approbation of a Lady so extreamly nice? It has many Branches (reply'd she) in the first Place that which we owe to Heaven, in the next to our King, our Country, Parents, Kindred, Friends, and Lastly, that which Fancy inclines, and Reason guides us to, in a Partner for Life, but here every Circumstance must agree, Parity of Age, of Quality, of Fortune, and of Humour, Consent of Friends, and Equal Affection in each other, for if any one of these particulars fail, it renders all the rest of no Effect. Ah, Madam (cry'd the *Count* not able to suffer her to proceed. What share of Pity then can you afford to a Man who, loves where almost all these Circumstances are wanting, and what Advice wou'd you give a wretch so Curst? I wou'd have him *think*, (said she more Gravely than before) (How Madam, resum'd he) think did you say? Alas! 'Tis Thought that has undone him, that's very possible (answer'd she) but yet 'tis want of thinking justly, for in a Lovers Mind Illusions seem Realities, and what at an other time wou'd be look'd on as Impossible, appears easie then: They indulge, and feed their new-born Folly with a prospect of a Hope, tho' ne're so distant a one, and in the vain pursuit of it, fly Consideration, 'till dispair starts up in the midway, and bar's their promis'd View; whereas if they gave way to due Reflection, the Vanity of the Attempt wou'd presently be shown, and the same cause that bid 'em cease to hope, wou'd bid 'em cease to wish: Ah Madam (said he) how little do you know of that Passion, and how easily cou'd I disprove you by the Example of my Friend; despair and Love are of an equal Age in him, and from the first Moment he beheld his Adorable Charmer, he has Languished without the least mixture of a flattering Hope. I Grant the Flames with which our Modern Gallants are ordinarily animated, cannot long subsist ɔfift without Fewel, but where Love is kindled in a :nerous Heart by a juft Admiration of the real Me- s of the Object belov'd, Reafon goes Hand in Hand th it, and makes it lafting as our Life. In my Mind ıfwer'd MELLIORA Coldly) an Efteem fo Ground- may more properly be afcribed to Friendfhip, then it fo Madam, (rejoyn'd the *Count* briskly) Friend- p and Love, where either are fincere, vary but little their meaning, there may indeed be fome Diftincti- s in their Ceremonies, but their Effentials are ftill fame: And if the Gentleman I fpeak of were fo ppy as to hope his Friendfhip wou'd be acceptable, are promife that he never wou'd complain his Love re not fo. You have a ftrange way (faid fhe) to ıfound Idea's, which in my Opinion are fo vaftly erent, that I fhou'd make no Difficulty in grant- my Friendfhip to as many of my Acquaintance, ad Merit to deferve it; but if I were to Love in general Manner, 'twould be a Crime wou'd juft- ender me Contemptible to Mankind: Madam (re- d the *Count*) when I fpoke of the Congruity of e and Friendfhip, I did not mean that fort, which ne, feems unworthy of the Name of either, but Exalted one, which made *Oreftes* and *Pilades*, *Thee-* and *Perithous* fo Famous. That, which has no erve, no feparate Intereft, or divided Thoughts, it which fills all, --- gives all the Soul, and efteems ı Life a Trifle, to prove it felf fincere ----- What Love do more than yield every thing to the object v'd? And Friendfhip muft do fo too, or it is not ndfhip! Therefore take heed fair Angel (conti- he, taking her Hand, and kiffing it) how you nife Friendfhip, where you ne're mean to Love: obferving fhe was Silent, your Hand, (faid he) Lip, your Neck, your Breaft, your All.----- All whole Heaven of Beauty muft be no longer in own Difpofal ---- All is the Prize of Friendfhip! nuch Confus'd as MELLIORA was, at thefe ds, which gave her fufficient, Reafon to fear he 'd now declare himfelf more fully than fhe defir'd, ſhe had Spirit and Reſolution enough to withdraw her Hand from his, and with a look, that ſpoke her Meaning but too plainly for the repoſe of the Enamour'd D'ELMONT: I ſhall take care my Lord (ſaid ſhe) how I Commence a Friendſhip with any Perſon who ſhall make uſe of it to my Prejudice.

THE *Count* was now ſenſible of his Error in going ſo far, and fearing he had undone himſelf in her Eſteem by his raſh Proceeding, thought it was beſt at once to throw off a Diſguiſe which, in ſpight of his Endeavours wou'd fall off, of it ſelf, and by making a bold and free Confeſſion of his real Sentiments, oblige her to a Diſcovery of hers.---- I do not doubt your Caution, Madam, (anſwer'd he) in this point: Your Reſerved Behaviour, even to me, convinces me, but too fully, how little you are diſpoſed to give, or receive any Proofs of Friendſhip: But perhaps (continu'd he, with a deep ſigh) my too preſuming Eyes have rendred me a ſuſpected Perſon, and while you find in me the Wretch I have diſcrib'd, you find nothing in me worthy of a happier Fortune; you are worthy every thing my Lord, (ſaid MEELLIOR, quite beſide her ſelf at theſe Words) nor are you leſ happy than you deſerve to be, and I wou'd rathe that theſe Eyes ſhou'd looſe their ſight than view yo otherwiſe than now I ſee you, bleſt in every Circum ſtance, the Darling of the World, the Idol of th Court, and Favourite of Heaven! Oh ſtop! (Cry' D'ELMONT haſtily Interrupting her) forbear to Cur me farther, rather Command my Death, than wi the Continuance of my preſent Miſeries. Cruel ME LIORA, too well, alas, you know what I have e dur'd from the firſt fatal Moment I beheld you, a only feign an Ignorance to diſtract me more: A Tho ſand times you have read my Riſing wiſhes, ſparkli in my Eyes, and glowing on my Cheeks, as often ſe my Virtue ſtruggling in ſilent Tremblings, and Li waſting Anguiſh to ſuppreſs deſire. Nay, Mada (ſaid he Catching faſt hold of both her Hands, ſeei her about to riſe) by all my ſleepleſs Nights, and reſtl

Da

Days, by all my countless burning Agonies; by all the Torments of my gall'd, bleeding Heart, I swear, that you shall hear me: I have heard too much (cry'd MELLIORA not able to contain her self) and tho' I am unwilling to believe you have any farther aim in this Discourse than your Diversion, yet I must tell your Lordship, that there are Themes more proper for it, than the Daughter of your Friend, who was entrusted to your Care with a far different Opinion of your Behaviour to her. What have I done (resum'd the almost the Distracted *Count*, falling at her Feet, and grasping her Knees) what have I done, Inhuman MELLIORA! To deserve this Rigour? My Honour has hitherto prevail'd above desire, fierce, and raging as it is, nor had I any other hopes by making this Declaration, than to meet that pity my Misfortunes merit; and you cannot without Ingratitude deny: Pity, even to Criminals is allow'd, and sure, where the offence is unvoluntary, like mine, 'tis due: 'Tis impossible to guess the Conflict in MELLIORA's Breast at this Instant, she had heard a most Passionate Declaration of Love from a married Man, and by Consequence, whatever his Pretences were, cou'd look on his Designs no otherwise than aim'd at the Destruction of her Honour, and was fir'd with a virtuous Indignation. But then she saw in this married Man, the only Person in the World, who was capable of Inspiring her with a tender Thought, she saw him reduc'd to the last Extremity of Despair for her sake: She heard his sighs, she felt his Tremblings as he held her, and cou'd not refrain shedding some Tears, both for him, and for her self, who indeed suffer'd little less; but the *Count* was not so happy as to be Witness of this Testimony of her Compassion: He had reclin'd his Head on her Lap, possibly to hide those that forc'd their way thro' his Eyes, at the same time; and ALOVISA's Voice which they heard below, giving them both an Alarm; they had no further opportunity for Speech, and the *Count* was but just gone out of the Room, and MEL-

LIORA

LIORA laid on the Couch in the ſame careleſs Poſſture which he had found her in; when ALOVISA enter'd the Chamber, and after having a little pleaſantly Reproach'd her, for being ſo lazy as not to accompany her in the Walk ſhe had been taking, ask'd her if ſhe had not ſeen the *Count*, who ſhe had been told was come home: Poor MELLIORA had much ado to conceal the Diſorder ſhe was in at this Queſtion, but recovering her ſelf as well as ſhe could, anſwer'd in the Affirmative; but that he had not ſtaid there longer than to enquire where ſhe was gone, and that ſhe knew not but he might be gone in ſearch of her: This was enough to make ALOVISA take her leave, impatient for the Sight of her dear Lord, a Happineſs ſhe had not enjoy'd ſince Morning, but ſhe was diſappointed of her Hope. The *Count*, as late as it was in the Evening, went into his Chaiſe, which had not been ſet up ſince he came from the *Baron* D'ESPERNAY's, and drove thither again with all the Speed he could.

THE *Baron* was extreamly ſurpriz'd at his ſudden Return, and with ſo much Confuſion and Melancholy in his Countenance. But much more ſo, when he had given him an Account of what had paſs'd between him and MELLIORA, and cou'd not forbear rallying him exceſſively on the Occaſion. What, ſaid he, a Man of Wit, and Pleaſure like *Count* D'ELMONT, a Man, who knows the Sex ſo well, could he let ſlip ſo favourable an Opportunity with the fineſt Woman in the World; One, for whoſe Enjoyment he wou'd Die. ---- Cou'd a Frown, or a little angry Coyneſs, (which ten to one was but affected) have Power to freeze ſuch fierce Deſires. The *Count* was not at preſent in a Humour to reliſh this Merriment, he was too ſeriouſly in Love to bear that any thing relating to it, ſhould be turn'd into Ridicule, and was far from repenting he had done no more, ſince what he had done, had occaſion'd her Diſpleaſure: But the *Baron*, who had Deſigns in his Head, which he knew cou'd not

not by any means be brought to succeed, but by keeping the *Count's* Passion warm, made Use of all the Artifice he was Master of, to embolden this respective Lover, to the Gratification of his Wishes: And growing more grave than he had been, My Lord, said he, you do not only injure the Dignity of our Sex in general, but your own Merits in particular, and perhaps even MELLIORA's secret Inclinations, by this unavailing distant Carriage, and causeless Despair. ---- Have you not confess'd that she has look'd on you with a Tenderness, like that of Love, that she has blush'd at your Sight, and trembled at your Touch? ---- What would you more that she should do, or what indeed, can she do more, in Modesty, to prove her Heart is yours? A little Resolution on your side would make her all yours ---- Women are taught by Custom to deny what most they covet, and to seem Angry, when they are best Pleas'd; believe me, D'ELMONT, that the most rigid Virtue of 'em all, never yet hated a Man for those Faults, which Love occasions: All this answer'd the *Count*, is what I readily agree to: --- But O her Father's Memory! My Obligation to him! Her Youth and Innocence are Daggers to my cool Reflections --- Wou'd it not be Pity (*D'espernay!* continued he with a deep Sigh) even if she shou'd consent, to ruin so much Sweetness? The *Baron* could not forbear laughing at these Words, and the *Count* who had started these Objections, only with the Hope of having them remov'd, easily suffer'd himself to be perswaded to follow his Inclinations; and it was soon concluded betwixt them, that on the first Opportunity, MELLIORA should fall a Sacrifice to Love.

THE *Count* came not Home 'till the next Morning, and brought the *Baron* with him, for they were now become inseparable Friends: At his return, he found ALOVISA in a very ill Humour for his being abroad all Night, and in spite of the Resolution she had made of shewing a perfect Resignation to her Husband's Will,

Will, could not forbear giving him ſome Hints, how unkindly ſhe took it, which he but little regarded, all his Thoughts were now bent on the gaining MELLIORA. But that Lady alarm'd at his late Behaviour, and with Reaſon, doubting her own Power of reſenting it as ſhe ought, or indeed reſiſting any future Attempts he might make, feign'd the neceſſity of performing ſome private Rules of Devotion, enjoyn'd her as a Pennance, and kept her Chamber that ſhe might not ſee him.

THE Diſquietudes of D'ELMONT for being forc'd to live, but for three or four Days without the happineſs of beholding her, convinc'd him how impoſſible it was for him to overcome his Paſſion, tho' he ſhould never ſo vigorouſly endeavour it, and that whatever Method he ſhou'd make uſe of to ſatisfy it, might be excus'd by the Neceſſity.

WHAT is it that a Lover cannot accompliſh when Reſolution is on his Side? D'ELMONT after having formed a Thouſand fruitleſs Inventions, at laſt pitch'd on One, which promis'd him an aſſurance of Succeſs: In MELLIORA's Chamber there was a little Door that open'd to a Pair of Back Stairs, for the Convenience of the Servants coming to clean the Room, and at the Bottom of that Deſcent, a Gate into the Garden. The *Count* ſet his Wits to work, to get the Keys of thoſe two Doors; that of the Garden ſtood always in it, nor cou'd he keep it without its being miſs'd at Night, when they ſhou'd come to faſten the Gate, therefore he carefully took the Impreſſion in Wax, and had one made exactly like it: The other he cou'd by no means compaſs without making ſome excuſe to go to MELLIORA's Chamber, and ſhe had deſired that none might viſit her: But he overcome this Bar to his Deſign at laſt; there was a Cabinet in it, where he told ALOVISA he had put ſome Papers of great Concern, which now he wanted to look over, and deſired ſhe would make an Apology for his coming in, in, to fetch them. MELLIORA imagin'd this was only a Pretence to see her, but his Wife being with him, and he saying nothing to her, or taking any further notice than what common Civility required, was not much troubled at it. While ALOVISA was paying a Complement to the Recluse, he was dex'trous enough to slip the Key out of the Door, unperceiv'd by either of them.

As soon as he had got the Passport to his expected Joys in his Possession, he order'd a couple of Saddle Horses to be made ready, and only attended by one Servant, rid out, as if to take the Air; but when they were got about two or three Miles from his House, Commanded him to return and tell his Lady, that he should lye that Night at the *Baron* D'ESPERNAY's, the Fellow obey'd, and clapping Spurs to his Horse, was immediately lost in a Cloud of Dust.

D'ELMONT had sent this Message to prevent any of the Family sitting up expecting him, and instead of going to the *Barons*, turn'd short, and went to *Angerville*, where meeting with some Gentlemen of his Acquaintance, he pass'd the Hours 'till between Twelve and One, as pleasantly as his Impatience to be with MELLIORA would give him leave: He had not much above a Furlong to ride, and his Desires made him not spare his Horse, which he ty'd by the Bridle, hot and foaming as he was, to a huge Oak, which grew pretty near his Garden; it was incompass'd only with a Hedge, and that so low, that he got over it without any Difficulty; he look'd carefully about him, and found no Tell-tale Lights in any of the Rooms, and concluding all was as hush'd as he cou'd wish, open'd the first Door, but the encreasing Transports of his Soul, as he came up Stairs, to be so near the end of all his Wishes, are more easily imagin'd than express'd; but as violent as they were, they presently receiv'd a vast Addition, when he came into the happy Chamber, and by a most delight-full Gloom, a Friend to Lovers, (for it was neither Dark nor Light, he beheld the lovely MELLIORA in her Bed, and fast asleep, her Head was reclin'd on one of her Arms; a Pillow softer and whiter far than that it lean'd on, the other was stretch'd out, and with its extension had thrust down the Bed-cloths so far, that all the Beauties of her Neck and Breast appear'd to View. He took an inexpressible Pleasure in gazing on her as she lay, and in this silent Contemplation of her thousand Charms, his Mind was agitated with various Emotions, and the resistless Posture he beheld her in, rouz'd all that was honourable in him, he thought it Pity even to wake her, but more to wrong such Innocence; and he was sometimes prompted to return and leave her as he found her.

BUT whatever Dominion, Honour and Virtue may have over our waking Thoughts, 'tis certain that they fly from the clos'd Eyes, our Passions then exert their forceful Power, and that which is most Predominant in the Soul, agitates the Fancy, and brings even Things impossible to pass: Desire, with watchful Diligence repell'd, returns with greater Violence in unguarded Sleep, and overthrows the vain Efforts of Day. MELLIORA in spite of her self, was often happy in Idea, and possess'd a Blessing which Shame and Guilt deter'd her from in reality. Imagination at this Time was active, and brought the charming Count much nearer than indeed he was, and he, stooping to the Bed, and gently laying his Face close to hers, (possibly designing no more than to steal a Kiss from her, unperceiv'd) that Action concurring at that Instant with her Dream, made her throw her Arm (still slumbering) about his Neck, and in a soft and languishing Voice, cry out, O! D'ELMONT, cease, cease to Charm, to such a height ---- Life cannot bear these Raptures! --- And then again Embracing him yet closer, ---O! too, too lovely *Count* --- Extatick Ruiner!

WHERE

WHERE was now the Reſolution he was forming ſome Moments before? If he had now left her, ſome might have applauded an Honour ſo uncommon, but more wou'd have condemn'd his Stupidity, for I believe there are very few Men, how Stoical ſoever they pretend to be, that in ſuch a tempting Circumſtance would not have loſt all Thoughts, but thoſe, which the preſent Opportunity inſpir'd. That he did, is moſt certain, for he tore open his Waſtecoat, and joyn'd his panting Breaſt to hers, with ſuch a tumultuous Eagerneſs! Seiz'd her with ſuch a rapidity of tranſported Hope-crown'd Paſſion, as immediately wak'd her from an imaginary Felicity, to the Approaches of a ſolid one. Where have I been (ſaid ſhe, juſt opening her Eyes) where am I? --- (And then coming more perfectly to her ſelf) Heaven! What's this? -- I am D'ELMONT (cry'd the o'erjoy'd *Count*) the happy D'ELMONT! MELLIORA's, the charming MELLIORA's D'ELMONT! Oh, all ye Saints, (reſum'd the ſurpriz'd, trembling Fair) ye miniſtring Angels! Whoſe Buſineſs it is to guard the Innocent! Protect and ſhield my Virtue! O! ſay, how came you here, my Lord? Love, ſaid he, Love that does all, that Wonder-working Power has ſent me here, to charm thee, ſweet Reſiſter, into yielding. O! hold, (cry'd ſhe, finding he was proceeding to Liberties, which her Modeſty could not allow of) forbear, I do conjure you, even by that Love you plead, before my Honour I'll reſign my Life! Therefore, unleſs you wiſh to ſee me dead, a Victim to your cruel, fatal Paſſion, I beg you to deſiſt, and leave me:---I cannot---muſt not (anſwer'd he, growing ſtill more bold) what, when I have thee thus! Thus naked in my Arms, trembling, defenceleſs, yielding, panting with equal Wiſhes, thy Love confeſs'd, and every Thought, Deſire! What could'ſt thou think if I ſhould leave thee? How juſtly would'ſt thou ſcorn my eaſy Tameneſs; my Dulneſs, unworthy the Name of Lover, or even of Man! -- Come, come, no more

Reluctance,

Reluctance (continued he, gathering Kisses from her soft Snowy Breast at every Word) Damp not the Fires thou hast rais'd with seeming Coyness! I know thou art mine! All mine! And thus I--yet think (said she, interrupting him, and strugling in his Arms) think what 'tis that you wou'd do; nor, for a Moment's Joy, hazard your Peace for ever. By Heaven, cry'd he, I will this Night be Master of my Wishes, no matter what to Morrow may bring forth: As soon as he had spoke these Words, he put it out of her Power either to deny or reproach him, by stopping her Mouth with Kisses, and was just on the Point of making good what he had vow'd, when a loud knocking at the Chamber Door, put a stop to his beginning Extacy, and chang'd the sweet Confusion MELLIORA had been in, to all the Horrors, of a Shame and Guilt-distracted Apprehension: They made no Doubt but that it was ALOVISA, and that they were betray'd; the *Count's* greatest Concern was for MELLIORA, and the Knocking still continuing louder, all he cou'd do in this Exigence, was to make his Escape the Way he came: There was no time for taking leave, and he could only say, perceiving she was ready to faint with her Fears----Be comforted my Angel, and resolute in your Denials, to whatever Questions the natural Insolence of a Jealous Wife may provoke mine to ask you; and we shall meet again (if D'ELMONT survives this Disappointment without Danger, of so quick, so curst a Separation. MELLIORA was in too much Distraction to make any Answer to what he said, and he had left the Room some Moments, before she cou'd get Spirit enough to ask who was at the Door? But when she did, was as much surpriz'd to find it was MELANTHA, who desir'd to be let in, as before she was frighted at the Belief it was ALOVISA, however, she immediately slipt on her Night-Gown and Slippers, and open'd the Door.

You are a sound Sleeper indeed (Cry'd MELANTHA laughing) that all the Noise I have made cou'd not wake

wake you. I have not been all this time asleep (answer'd MELLIORA) but not knowing you were in the House, cou'd not imagine who it was that gave me this Disturbance. I heartily ask your Pardon (said MELANTHA) and I know, my Dear, you are too good Natur'd to refuse it me, especially when you know the Occasion, which is so very Whimsical, that as grave as you are, you cannot help being diverted with it --- But come (continu'd she) get on your Cloaths, for you must go along with me. Where, said MELLIORA, Nay, nay, ask no Questions (resum'd MELANTHA) but make haste, every Minute that we Idle away here, loses us the Diversion of an Age. As she spoke these Words, she fell into such an excessive Laughter, that MELLIORA thought her Mad, but being far from Sympathizing in her Gaiety; it has always (said she) been hitherto my Custom to have some Reason for what I do, tho' in never so trifling an Affair, and you must excuse me, if I do not break it now. Pish (cry'd MELANTHA) you are of the oddest Temper, ---- but I will give you your Way for once, ----- provided you'll get your self ready in the mean time. I shall certainly put on my Cloaths (said MELLIORA) lest I should take cold, for I expect you'll not permit me to sleep any more this Night. You may be sure of it (rejoyn'd MELANTHA.) But to the Purpose, ----- You must know, having an Hour or two on my hands, I came this Evening to visit ALOVYSA, and found her in the strangest Humour! ----- Good God! What unaccountable Creatures these married Women are? --- her Husband it seems had sent her Word that he wou'd lye at my Brothers, and the poor loving Soul cou'd not bear to live a Night without him. I stay'd to condole with her, (tho' on my Life, I cou'd scarce forbear Laughing in her Face) 'till it was too late to go Home. ---- About twelve a Clock she yawn'd, stretch'd, and grew most horridly out of Temper; rail'd at Mankind prodigiously, and curs'd Matrimony as heartily as one of Fourscore cou'd do, that had been twice a Widow, and was left a Maid! ---- With much ado,

ado, I made her Women thrust her into Bed, and retired to a Chamber which they shew'd me, but I had no Inclination to sleep, I remember'd my self of five or six *Billet-Doux* I had to answer,---- a Lover, that growing foolishly troublesome, I have some thoughts of discharging to Morrow --- Another that I design to Countenance, to pique a third ---- a new Suit of Cloaths, and Trimmings for the next Ball --- Half a hundred new Songs--- and --- a thousand other Affairs of the utmost Consequence to a young Lady, came into my Head in a Moment; and the Night being extreamly pleasant, I set the Candle in the Chimney, open'd the Window, and fell to considering --- But I had not been able to come to a conclusion what I should do in any one thing I was thinking of, before I was interrupted in my Cogitations, with a noise of something rushing hastily thro' the Myrtles under my Window, and presently after, saw it was a Man going hastily along toward the great Alley of the Garden.---- At first I was going to cry out and Alarm the Family; taking it for a Thief; But, Dear MELLIORA, how glad am I that I did not? --- For who do you think, when I look'd more heedfully, I perceiv'd it was? Nay, how should I know? (cry'd MELLIORA peevishly, fearing the *Count*'s Inadvertency had expos'd himself and her to this foolish Woman's Curiosity) It was *Count* D'ELMONT (resum'd MELANTHA) I'll lay my Life, that he has been on some Intreague to Night: And met with a Disappointment in it, by his quick Return.--- But prithee make hast, for I long to rally him about it. What wou'd you do Madam? (said MELLIORA) you wou'd not sure go to him? Yes, (answer'd MELANTHA: I will go down into the Garden, and so shall you.---I know you have a back Way from your Chamber --- Therefore lay aside this unbecoming Demureness, and let us go, and talk him to Death. You may do as you please, (said MELLIORA) but for my part, I am for no such Frolicks. Was ever any thing so young, so Formal as you are! (Rejoyn'd MELANTHA) but I am resolv'd to Teaze

you

you out of a humour so directly opposite to the *Beau-Monde*, and, if you will not Consent to go down with me: I will fetch him up to your Chamber---- Hold! Hold, (cry'd MELLIORA perceiving she was going) what do you mean, for Heavens sake stay, what will ALOVYSA think? --- I care not reply'd, the other; I have set my Heart on an hours Diversion with him and will not be baulk'd, if the repose of the World, much less, that of a Jealous, silly Wife, depended on it.

MELLIORA saw into the Temper of this Capricious young Lady too well not to believe she wou'd do, as she had said, and perhaps, was not over willing to venture her with the *Count* alone, at that Time of Night, and in the Humour she knew he was, therefore putting on an Air more chearful than that she was Accustom'd to wear, well (said she) I will Accompany you into the Garden, since it will so much oblige you; but if the *Count* be wise, he will, by quitting the Place, as soon as he sees us, disappoint you worse than I shou'd have done, if I had kept you here. With these Words she took her by the Hand, and they went down the Stairs, where the *Count* was but just past before them.

HE had not Power to go away, without knowing who it was, that had given him that Interruption, and had stood all this Time, on the upper Step behind the inner Door. His Vexation, and Disdain when he heard it was MELANTHA gave him as much Pain, as his Concern while he believ'd it ALOVYSA, and he cou'd not forbear muttering a thousand Curses on her Impertinence. He always despis'd, but now abhor'd her: She had behav'd her self to him in a Fashion, as made him sufficiently Sensible she was desirous of engaging him, and he resolv'd to Mortifie by the bitterest Slights, both her Pride, and Love, if 'tis proper, to call that sort of liking which Agitates the Soul of *Coquet*, by that Name.

THE

THE Ladies walk'd in the Garden for ſome time, and MELANTHA ſearch'd every Buſh, before ſhe found the *Count* who ſtood Conceal'd in the Porch, which being cover'd with *Jeſſamin*, and *Fillaree*, was Dark enough to hide him from their View, tho' they had paſs'd cloſe to him as they came out. He had certainly remain'd there 'till Morning, and diſappointed MELANTHA's ſearch in part of the Revenge he ow'd her, if his Deſires to be with MELLIORA, on any Terms, had not prevail'd, even above his Anger to the other. But he cou'd not ſee that Charmer of his Soul, and imagine there might be yet an opportunity that Night of ſtealing a Kiſs from her (now he believ'd reſiſtleſs Lips) of Touching her Hand! Her Breaſt! And repeating ſome farther Freedoms which his late Advantage over her had given him, without being fill'd with Wiſhes too Fiery and too Impatient to be reſtrain'd. He watch'd their turning, and when he ſaw that they were near an Ally which had another that led to it, he went round and met them.

MELANTHA was overjoy'd at ſight of him, and MELLIORA, tho' equally pleas'd, was Cover'd with ſuch a Confuſion, at the Remembrance of what had paſs'd, that it was happy for her that her Companions Volubility gave her no room for Speech. There is nothing more certain, than that Love, tho' it fills the mind with a thouſand charming Ideas, which thoſe untouch'd by that Paſſion, are not capable of conceiving, yet it entirely takes away the Power of Utterance, and the deeper Impreſſion it had made on the Soul, the leſs we are able to expreſs it, when willing to indulge and give a looſe to Thought; what Language can furniſh us with Words ſufficient, all are too poor, all wanting both in Sublimity, and Softneſs, and only Fancy! A lovers Fancy! can reach the Exalted ſoaring of a Lovers Meaning! But, if ſo impoſſible to be Deſcrib'd, if of ſo Vaſt, ſo Wonderful a Nature as nothing but it's ſelf can Comprehend, how

how much more impoſſible muſt it be, entirely to conceal it! What Strength of boaſted Reaſons? What Force of Reſolution? What modeſt Fears or cunning Artifice can correct the Fierceneſs of its fiery Flaſhes in the Eyes, keep down the ſtruggling Sighs, command the Pulſe, and bid trembling ceaſe? Honour and Virtue may diſtance Bodies, but there is no Power in either of thoſe Names, to ſtop the Spring, that with a rapid Whirl tranſports us from our ſelves, and darts our Souls into the Boſom of the darling Object. This may ſeem ſtrange to many, even of thoſe who call, and perhaps believe that they are Lovers, but the few who have Delicacy enough to feel what I but imperfectly attempt to ſpeak, will acknowledge it for Truth, and pity the Diſtreſs of MELLIORA.

As they were paſſing thro' a Walk of Trees on each Side, whoſe intermingling Boughs made a friendly Darkneſs, and every thing Undiſtinguiſhable, the Amorous D'ELMONT throwing his eager Arms round the Waiſt of his (no leſs tranſported) MELLIORA, and Printing burning Kiſſes on her Neck, reap'd painful Pleaſure, and created in her a racking kind of Extaſie, which might perhaps, had they been now alone, prov'd her Deſires were little different from his.

AFTER MELANTHA had vented part of the Raillery, ſhe was ſo big with, on the *Count*, which he but little regarded, being wholly taken up with other Thoughts, ſhe propos'd, going into the Wilderneſs, which was at the farther end of the Garden, and they readily agreeing to it. Come, my Lord, (ſaid ſhe) to the *Count*, you are Melancholly, I have thought of a way which will either indulge the Humour you are in, or divert it, as you ſhall chuſe: There are ſeveral little Paths in this Wilderneſs, let us take each a ſeparate one, and when we meet, which ſhall be here, where we part, agree to tell an entertaining Story, which, whoever fails in, ſhall be doom'd doom'd to the Punishment of being left here all Night: The *Count* at these Words, forgot all his Animosity, and was ready to hug her for this Proposal. MELLIORA did a little oppose it; but the others were too Powerful, and she was forc'd to submit: Thou art the dullest Creature, I'll lay my Life, (my Lord, cry'd MELANTHA, taking hold of the Count in a gay manner) that it falls to her Lot to stay in the Wilderness. Oh Madam, (reply'd the *Count*) you are too severe, we ought always to suspend our Judgment 'till after the Tryal, which I confess my self so pleas'd with, that I am Impatient for its coming on: Well then, (said she, laughing) farewel for half an Hour. Agreed (cry'd the *Count*) and walk'd away: MELANTHA saw which way he went, and took another Path, leaving MELLIORA to go forward in that, in which they were, but I believe the Reader will easily imagine that she was not long to enjoy the Priviledge of her Meditations.

AFTER the *Count* had gone some few Paces, he planted himself behind a Thicket, which, while it hid him, gave the Opportunity of observing them, and when he found the Coast clear, rush'd out, and with unhurting Gripe, seiz'd once more on the unguarded Prey. Blest turn of Fortune, (said he in a Rapture,) Happy, happy Moment! --- Lost, lost MELLIORA, (said she) most unhappy Maid! --- Oh why, my Lord, this quick Return? This is no Place to answer thee, (resum'd he, taking her in his Arms, and bearing her behind that Thicket, where he himself had stood) 'twas in vain for her to resist, if she had had the Power over her Inclinations, 'till he, sitting her softly down, and beginning to Caress her in the manner he had done when she was in Bed, she assum'd Strength enough to raise her self a little, and catching hold of his Transgressing Hands, laid her Face on them, and Bath'd them in a shower of Tears: O! D'ELMONT (said she) Cruel D'ELMONT! Will you then take Advantage of my Weakness? I confess I feel

feel for you, a Passion, far beyond all, that yet, ever bore the Name of Love, and that I can no longer withstand the too powerful Magick of your Eyes, nor deny any Thing that charming Tongue can ask; but now's the Time to prove your self the Heroe! subdue your self, as you have Conquer'd me! be satisfied with Vanquishing my Soul, fix there your Throne, but leave my Honour free! *Life of my Life* (cry'd he) *wound me no more by such untimely Sorrows: I cannot bear thy Tears, by Heaven they sink into my Soul, and quite unman me, but tell me* (continu'd he tenderly Kissing her) *coud'st thou, with all this Love, this charming* --- *something more than softness* --- *cou'dst thou I say, consent to see me Pale and Dead, stretch'd at thy Feet, consum'd with inward Burnings, rather than blest, than rais'd by Love, and thee, to all a Deity in thy Embraces? For O! Believe me when I swear, that 'tis impossible to live without thee.* No more, no more (said she letting her Head fall gently on his Breast) too easily I guess thy sufferings by my own. But yet, D'ELMONT 'tis better to die in Innocence, than to live in Guilt. *O! Why* (Resum'd he, sighing as if his Heart wou'd burst) *shou'd what we can't avoid, be call'd a Crime? Be Witness for me Heaven! How much I have struggl'd with this rising Passion, even to Madness struggl'd!* --- *but in vain, the mounting Flame blazes the more, the more I wou'd suppress it* --- *my very Soul's on Fire* --- *I cannot bear it* --- *Oh* MELLIORA! *Didst thou but know the thousandth Part, of what this Moment I endure, the strong Convulsions of my warring Thoughts, thy Heart steel'd as it is, and Frosted round with Virtue, wou'd burst it's Icy Shield, and melt in Tears of Blood, to pity me.* Unkind and Cruel! (answer'd she) do I not partake them then? ---- Do I not bear, at least, an equal share in all your Agonies? Have --- you no Charms - - or have not a Heart? --- A most susceptible and tender Heart? ---- Yes, you may feel it Throb, it beats against my Breast, like an Imprison'd Bird, and fain wou'd burst it's Cage to fly to you, the aim of all it's Wishes! -- Oh D'ELMONT!

 --- With

-- With these Words she sunk wholly into his Arms unable to speak more: Nor was he less dissolv'd in Rapture, both their Souls seem'd to take Wing together, and left their Bodies Motionless, as unworthy to bear a part in their more elevated Bliss.

BUT D'ELMONT at his returning Sense, repenting the Effects of the violent Transport, he had been in was now preparing to take from the resistless MELLIORA, the last, and only remaining Proof that she was all his own, when MELANTHA (who had contriv'd this separation only with a Design to be alone with the *Count*, and had carefully obeserv'd which way he took) was coming towards them. The rustling of her Cloaths among the Bushes, gave the disappointed Couple leave to rise from the Posture they were in, and MELLIORA to abscond behind a Tree, before she could come near enough to discern who was there.

MELANTHA, as soon as she saw the *Count*, put on an Air, of Surprize, as if it were but by Chance, that she was come into his walk, and Laughing with a visible Affectation, bless me! You here, my Lord! (said she) I vow this has the look of Assignation, but I hope you will not be so vain as to believe I came on purpose to seek you. No Madam (answer'd he coldly) I have not the least Thought of being so happy. Lord! You are strangely grave (Rejoyn'd she) but suppose I really had come with a Design to meet you, what kind of a Reception might I have expected? I know no Reason Madam (said he) that can oblige me to entertain a Supposition so unlikely. Well then (resum'd she) I'll put it past a Supposition, and tell you plainly, that I did walk this way on purpose to divert your Spleen. I am sorry (reply'd he, tir'd to Death with her Impertinence) that you are disappointed; for I am not in a Humour at present, of receiving any Diversion. Fie (said she) is this an answer for the gay, Gallant, engaging *Count* D'ELMONT, to give a Lady who makes a Declaration of admiring him ---- who thinks it not too so much to make the first Advances, and who wou'd believe her self fully recompenc'd for breaking thro' the nice Decorums of her Sex, if he receiv'd it kindly--- Madam (said he, not a little amaz'd at her Imprudence) I know of no such Person, or if I did, I must confess, I shou'd be very much puzled how to behave in an Adventure so uncommon: Pish (answer'd she, growing vext at his coldness) I know that such Adventures are not uncommon with you: I'm not to learn the Story of ALOVYSA, and if you had not been first Address'd, perhaps might have been 'till now unmarried. Well Madam (said he, more out of humour) put the Case that what you say were true, I am married; and therefore, (interrupted she) you ought to be better acquainted with the Temper of our Sex, and know, that a Woman, where she says she Loves, expects a thousand fine things in Return. But there is more than a possibility (answer'd he) of her being disappointed, and methinks Madam, a Lady of your Gaity shou'd be conversant enough with Poetry, to remember those too Lines of a famous English Poet.

All naturally fly, what does Pursue
'Tis fit Men shou'd be Coy, when Women Woe.

MELANTHA was fretted to the Heart to find him so insensible, but not being one of those who are apt to repent any thing they have done, she only pretended to fall into a violent fit of Laughter, and when she came out of it, I confess (said she) that I have lost my Aim, which was, to make you believe I was dying for Love of you, raise you to the highest Degree of Expectation, and then have the pleasure of baulking you at once, by letting you know the jest. ---- But your Lordship is too hard for me, even at my own Weapon, ridicule! I am mightily obliged to you Madam (answer'd he, more briskly than before) for your Intention, however; but 'tis probable, if I cou'd have been drawn into a Belief that you were in earnest, I might, at such a Time, and such a Place as this, have taken some Measures which wou'd have sufficiently reveng'd me on you ---- but come Madam, (continu'd he) the Morning begins to break, if you please we will find out MELLIORA, and go into the House: As he spoke these Words, they perceiv'd her coming towards them, who had only taken a little round to meet 'em, and they all three made what hast they cou'd in: *Count*, D'ELMONT asked a formal leave of MELLIORA to go thro' her Chamber, none of the Servants being yet stirring, to let him into the House any other way, which being granted, he cou'd not help sighing as he passed by the Bed, where he had been lately so cruelly disappointed, but had no opportunity to speak his Thoughts at that time to MELLIORA.

THE *Count* rung for his Gentleman to rise to undress him, and order'd him to send some body to take care of his Horse, and went to Bed, ALOVYSA was very much surpriz'd at his return from the *Baron's* at so unseasonable an Hour, but much more so, when in the Morning, MELANTHA came laughing into the Chamber, and told her, all that she knew of the Adventure of the Night before; her old fit of Jealousie now resum'd it's Dominion in her Soul, she cou'd not forbear thinking, that there was something more in it, than MELANTHA had discover'd: And presently imagin'd that her Husband stay'd not at the *Baron's*, because she was abroad; but she was more confirm'd in this Opinion, when MELANTHA calling for her Coach to go home; the *Count* told her that he wou'd accompany her thither, having urgent Business with her Brother. 'Tis almost impossible to guess the rage ALOVYSA was in, but she dissembled it 'till they were gone, then going to MELLIORA's Chamber, she vented part of it there, and began to question her about their Behaviour in the Wilderness. Tho' MELLIORA was glad to find, since she was jealous, that she was jealous of any Body rather than her self, yet she said all that she cou'd, to perswade her, that she had no Reason to be uneasie.

BUT

BUT ALOVYSA was always of too fiery a Nature to listen patiently to any thing that cou'd be offer'd, to alter the Opinion she had taken up, tho' it were with never so little an appearance of Reason, but much more now, when she thought her self, in a manner Confirm'd: Forbear (said she) Dear MELLIORA to take the part of perfidy: I know he hates me, I read it in his Eyes, and feel it on his Lips, all Day he shuns my Converse, and at night, colder than Ice, receives my warm Embraces, and when, (oh that I cou'd tear the tender folly from me Heart) with Words as soft as Love can Form, I urge him to disclose the Cause of his Disquiet, he answers but in sighs, and turns away: Perhaps? (reply'd MELLIORA) his Temper naturally is gloomy, and love it self, has scarce the Power to alter Nature. Oh no, (Interrupted ALOVYSA) far from it: Had I ne'er known him otherwise, I cou'd forgive what now I know, but he was once as kind as tender Mothers to their new born Babes, and fond as the first Wishes of desiring Youth: Oh! With what eagerness has he approach'd me, when absent but an Hour! --- Hadst thou 'ere seen him in those Days of Joy, even, thou, cold Cloyster'd Maid, must have ador'd him What Majesty, then sat upon his Brow? ----- What Matchless Glories shone around him! ---- Miriads of *Cupids*, shot resistless Darts in every Glance, --- his Voice when softned in amorous Accents, boasted more Musick, than the Poet *Orpheus*! When e're he spoke, methought the Air seem'd Charm'd, the Winds forgot to blow, all Nature listn'd, and like ALOVISA melted into Transport ---- but he is chang'd in all ---- the Heroe, and the Lover are Extinct, and all that's left, of the once gay D'ELMONT, is a dull senceless Picture: MELLIORA was too sensibly Touch'd with this Discourse, to be able presently to make any Answer to it, and she cou'd not forbear accompanying her in Tears, while ALOVYSA renew'd her Complaints in this manner; his Heart (said she) his Heart is lost for ever Ravish'd from me, that Bosom where I had Treasur'd all my Joys, my Hopes, my

Wishes, now burns and pants, with longings for a rival Curst! Curst, MELANTHA, by Heaven they are even impudent in Guilt, they Toy, they Kiss, and make Assignations before my Face, and this Tyrant Husband braves me with his falsehood, and thinks to awe me into Calmness, but, if I endure it --- No (continu'd she stamping, and walking about the Room in a disorder'd Motion) I'll be no longer the tame easie wretch I have been --- all *France* shall Eccho with my Wrongs --- The ungrateful Monster! --- Villain, whose well nigh wasted Stream of Wealth had dry'd, but for my kind of supply, shall he enslave me! --Oh MELLIORA shun the Marriage Bed, as thou woud'st a Serpents Den, more Ruinous, more Poysonous far, is Man.

'TWAS in vain that MELLIORA endeavour'd to pacifie her, she continu'd in this Humour all Day, and in the Evening receiv'd a considerable Addition to her former Disquiet: The *Count* sent a Servant of the *Barons* (having not taken any of his own with him) to acquaint her, that he shou'd not be at home that Night 'Tis well (said she ready to burst with Rage) let the *Count* know that I can change as well as he, and sha excuse his Absence tho' it lasts to all Eternity, (go con tinu'd she, seeing him surpriz'd) deliver this Messag and withal, assure him, that what I say, I mean. Sh had scarce made an end of these Words, when she flun out of the Room, unable to utter more, and lock' her self into her Chamber, leaving MELLIORA no le distracted, tho' for different Reasons, to retire to her'

SHE had not 'till now, had a moments Time fo reflection since her Adventure in the Wilderness, an the Remembrance of it, joyn'd with the Despair, an Grief of ALOVISA, which she knew her se the sole occasion of, threw her into most terrib Agonies. She was ready to die with shame, whe she consider'd how much the secret of her Soul w laid open to him, who of all the World she oug most to have conceal'd it from, and with remorse, f

th

the Miseries her fatal Beauty was like to bring on a Family for whom she had the greatest Friendship.

BUT these Thoughts soon gave way to another, equally as shocking, she was present when the Servant brought Word the *Count* wou'd lie abroad, and had all the Reason imaginable to believe that Message was only a feint, that he might have an oportunity to come unobserv'd to her Chamber, as he had done the Night before. She cou'd not presently guess by what means he had got in, and therefore was at a loss how to prevent him, 'till recollecting all the Circumstances of that tender interview, she remembred that when MELLENTHA had surpriz'd them, he made his escape by the back Stairs into the Garden, and that when they went down, the Door was lock'd: Therefore concluded it must be by a Key, that he had gain'd admittance: And began to set her Invention to Work, how to keep this dangerous Enemy to her Honour, from coming in a second Time. She had no Keys that were large enough to fill the Wards, and if she had put one in, on the inside, it wou'd have fallen out immediately on the least touch, but at last, after trying several ways, she tore her Handkerchief into small pieces, and thrust it into the hole with her Busk, so hard, that it was impossible for any Key to enter.

MELLIORA thought she had done a very Heroick Action, and sate her self down on the Bed-side in a pleas'd Contemplation of the Conquest, she believ'd her Virtue had gain'd over her Passion: But alas, How little did she know the true State of her own Heart? She no sooner heard a little noise at the Door, as presently after she did, but she thought it was the *Count*, and began to tremble not with fear, but desire.

IT was indeed *Count* D'ELMONT, who had borrow'd Horses and a Servant of the *Baron*, and got into the Garden as before, but with a much greater Assurance now of making himself entirely happy in the Gratification of his utmoſt Wiſhes. But 'tis impoſſible to repreſent the greatneſs of his vexation and ſurprize, when all his Efforts to open the Door, were in vain: He found ſomething had been done to the Lock, but cou'd not diſcover what, nor by any means remove the obſtacle which MELLIORA had put there. She, on the other hand, was in all the confuſion immaginable: Sometimes prompted by the violence of her Paſſion, ſhe wou'd run to the Door, reſolving to open it; and then, frighted with the apprehenſion of what wou'd be the Conſequence, as haſtily fly from it: If he had ſtay'd much longer, 'tis poſſible love wou'd have got the better of all other Conſiderations, but a light appearing on the other ſide of the Garden, oblig'd the thrice diſappointed Lover, to quit his Poſt. He had ſent away the Horſes by the Servant who came with him, and had no opportunity of going to the *Barons* that Night, ſo came to his own Fore-gate, and thunder'd with a force, ſuitable to the fury he was poſſeſt with; it was preſently open'd, moſt of the Family being up. ALOVISA had rav'd her ſelf into Fits, and her diſorder created full Employment for the Servants, who buſily running about the Houſe with Candles fetching things for her, occaſion'd that reflection which he had ſeen.

THE *Count* was told of his Lady's Indiſpoſition, but he thought he had ſufficient pretence not to come where ſhe was, after the Meſſage ſhe had ſent him by the *Baron*'s Servant, and order'd a Bed to be made ready for him in another Chamber.

ALOVISA ſoon heard he was come in, and it was with much ado, that her Women prevail'd on her not to riſe and go to him that moment, ſo little did ſhe remember what ſhe had ſaid She paſs'd the Night in moſt terrible Inquietudes, and early in the Morning went to his Chamber, but finding it ſhut, ſhe was oblig'd to wait, tho' with a World of impatience, 'till ſhe heard he was ſtirring, which not being till towards Noon,

Noon, she spent all that Time in considering how she shou'd accost him.

As soon as the Servant whom she had order'd to watch, brought her Word that his Lord was dressing, she went into the Room, there was no body with him but his Gentleman, and he withdrawing out of respect, imagining by both their Countenances, there might something be said, not proper for him to hear. I see (said she) my Presence is unwish'd, but I have learn'd from you to scorn Constraint, and as you openly avow your falshood, I shall my Indignation, and my just Disdain! Madam (answer'd he suddenly) if you have any thing to reproach me with, you cou'd not have chose a more unlucky Time for it, than this, nor was I ever less dispos'd to give you Satisfaction. No, barbarous cold Insulter! (resum'd she) I had not the least hope you wou'd, I find that I am grown so low in your Esteem, I am not worth pains of an Invention ---- By Heaven, this damn'd indifference is worse than the most vile Abuse! --- 'Tis plain Contempt! ---- O that I cou'd resent it as I ought ---- then Sword, or Poison shou'd revenge me --- why am I so Curst to Love you still? --- O that those Fiends (continu'd she, bursting into Tears) that have deform'd thy Soul, wou'd change thy Person too, turn every Charm to horrid Blackness, grim as thy Cruelty, and foul as thy Ingratitude, to free that Heart, thy Perjury has ruin'd. I thought Madam (said he, with an Accent maliciously Ironical) that you had thrown off, even the appearances of Love for me, by the Message you sent me Yesterday --- O thou Tormenter (interrupted she) hast thou not wrong'd me in the tenderest Point, driven me to the last Degree of Misery! To Madness! -- To Despair? And dost thou ---- can'st thou Reproach me for complaining? --- Your coldness; your unkindness stung me to the Soul, and then I said, I know not what --- but I remember well, that I wou'd have seem'd careless, and indifferent like you. You need not (reply'd he) give your self the trouble of an Apology;

logy, I have no design to make a quarrel of it: And wish, for both our Peace, you cou'd as easily moderate your Passions, as I can mine, and that you may the better do so, I leave you to reflect on what I have said, and the little Reason I have ever given you for such intemperance. He left the Chamber with these Words, which instead of quelling, more enflam'd ALOVYSA's Rage. She threw her self down into an Elbow Chair that stood there, and gave a loose to the Tempest of her Soul, Sometimes she curst, and vow'd the bitterest Revenge: Sometimes she wept, and at others, was resolv'd to fly to Death, the only Remedy for neglected Love: In the midst of these confus'd Meditations, casting her Eye on a Table by her, she saw Paper, and something written on it, which hastily taking up, found it the *Count's* Character, and read (to her inexpressible Torment) these Lines.

The Dispairing D'ELMONT to hi[s] Repenting Charmer.

WHAT Cruel Star last Night, had Influence ove[r] my Inhumane Dear? Say, to what Cause mu[st] I ascribe my Fatal Disappointment? For I wou'[d] fain believe I owe it not to Thee! ---- Such an Actio[n] after what thou hast confest, I cou'd expect from no[]thing but a Creature of MELANTHA'S *Temper -- no, 'tis too much of the vain Coquet, and indeed t[oo] much of the Jilt, for my Adorable to be guilty of -- a[nd] yet --- Oh how shall I excuse thee? when every thi[ng] was hush'd, Darkness my Friend, and all my Wish[es] rais'd, when every Nerve trembled with fierce D[e]sires, and my Pulse beat a call to Love, or Deat[h] ---- (For if I not enjoy thee, that will soon arri[ve] then, then what, but thy self, forgetting all thy Vow[s]*

t

thy tender Vows of the most Ardent Passion, cou'd have destroyed my Hopes? --- Oh where was then that Love which lately flatter'd my fond doating Soul, when sinking, dying in my Arms, my Charmer lay! And suffer'd me to reap each Prologue favour to the greatest Bliss ---- But they are past, and rigid Honour stands to Guard those joys, which ----

THERE was no more written, but there needed no more to make ALOVYSA, before half distracted, now quite so. She was now convinc'd that she had a much more dangerous Rival than MELANTHA, and her Curiosity who it might be, was not much less troublesome to her than other Passions.

SHE was going to seek her Husband with this Testimony of his Infidelity in her Hand, when he, remembring he had left it there, was coming hastily back to fetch it. The Excess of Fury which she met him with, is hardly to be imagin'd, she upbraided him in such a Fashion as might be called reviling, and had so little regard to good Manners, or even decency in what she said, that it dissipated all the confusion he was in at first, to see so plain a Proof against him in her Hands, and rouz'd him to a rage not much Inferior to her's. She endeavour'd (tho' she took a wrong Method) to bring him to a Confession, he had done amiss; and he, to lay the Tempest of her Tongue, by storming louder, but neither succeeded in their wish: And he, stung with the bitterness of her Reproaches, and tired with Clamour, at last flung from her with a solemn Vow never to eat, or Sleep with her more.

A WIFE if equally haughty and jealous, if less fond than ALOVYSA will scarce be able to comprehend the greatness of her Sufferings: And it is not to be wonder'd at, that she, so violent in all her Passions, and agitated by so many, at once, committed a thousand Extravagancies, which those who know the force but of one, by the Aid of Reason, may avoid. She tore

down

down the *Count's* Picture which hung in the Room, and ſtamp'd on it, then the Letter, her own Cloaths, and Hair, and whoever had ſeen her in that Poſture, wou'd have thought ſhe appear'd more like what the Furies are repreſented to be, than a Woman.

THE *Count* when he took leave the Night before of the *Baron* D'ESPERNAY, had promis'd to return to him in the Morning, and give him an Account of his Adventure with MELLIORA, but the vexation of his diſappointment, and quarrel with his Wife, having hindred him all this time, the *Baron* came to his Houſe, impatient to know the Succeſs of an Affair on which his own hopes depended. He was told by the Servants that their Lord was above, and running haſtily without Ceremony, the firſt Perſon he ſaw was ALOVISA, in the condition I have deſcrib'd.

THE *Baron* had paſſionately lov'd this Lady from the firſt Moment he had ſeen her, but it was with that ſort of Love, which conſiders more it's own gratification, than the Intereſt, or quiet, of the object beloved. He imagin'd by the Wildneſs of ALOVYSA's Countenance and Behaviour, that the *Count* had given her ſome extraordinary occaſion of diſtaſte, and was ſo far from being troubled at the Sorrow he beheld her in, that he rejoyc'd in it, as the advancement of his Deſigns. But he wanted not cunning to diſguiſe his Sentiments, and approaching her with a tender, and ſubmiſſive Air, entreated her to tell him the Cauſe of her diſorder. ALOVYSA had always conſider'd him as a Perſon of worth, and one who was entitled to her Eſteem by the vaſt reſpect he always paid her, and the Admiration, which in every opportunity, he expreſt for her Wit and Beauty. She was not perhaps far from gueſſing the Extent of his Deſires, by ſome Looks, and private Glances he had given her, and, notwithſtanding her Paſſion, for the *Count*, was too vain to be offended at it. On the contrary, it pleas'd her Pride, and confirm'd her in the good Opinion ſhe

had

had of her self, to think a Man of his Sense shou'd be compell'd by the force of her irresistible Attractions to adore and to despair, and therefore made no Difficulty of disburthening all the anguish of her Soul, in the Bosom of this, as she believ'd, so faithful Friend.

THE *Baron* seem'd to receive this Declaration of her Wrongs, with all imaginable concern: And accus'd the *Count* of Stupidity in so little knowing the value of a Jewel he was Master of, and gave her some hints, that he was not unsensible who the Lady was, that had been the Cause of it, which ALOVISA presently taking hold on, O speak her Name (said she) quick, let me know her, or own thy Friendship was but feign'd to undo me, and that thou hatest the wretched ALOVISA. O far (resum'd he) far be such thoughts, first let me Die, to prove my Zeal --- my Faith, sincere to you, who only next to Heaven, are worthy Adoration --- but forgive me, if I say, in this, you must not be obey'd. O why, said she? Perhaps, (answer'd he) I am a trusted Person --- A confident, and if I should reveal the secret of my Friend, I know, tho' you approv'd the Treachery, you wou'd detest the Traytor. O! Never (rejoyn'd she impatiently) 'twou'd be a Service, more than the whole Study of my Life can pay ---- am I not Rack'd, ---- Stab'd --- and Mangled in Idea, by some dark Hand shaded with Night and Ignorance? And shou'd I not be grateful for a friendly Clue to guide me from this Labyrinth of Doubt, to a full Day of Certainty, where all the feind may stand expos'd before me, and I have Scope to Execute my Vengeance? Besides, continu'd she, finding he was silent and seemingly extreamly mov'd at what she said) 'tis joyning in the Cause of Guilt to hide her from me ---- come, you must tell me --- your Honour suffers else --- both that, and pity, plead the Injur'd's Cause. Alas (said he) Honour can ne'er consent to a Discovery of what, with solemn Vows I have promis'd to Conceal; but Oh! --- There is something in my Soul, more Powerful, which says,

ſays, that ALOVYSA muſt not be deny'd. Why then (cry'd ſhe) do you delay? Why keep me on the Rack, when one ſhort Word wou'd eaſe me of my Torment? I have conſider'd (anſwer'd he after a pauſe) Madam, you ſhall be ſatisfied, depend on it you ſhall, tho' not this Moment, you ſhall have greater Proofs than Words can give you --- Occular Demonſtration ſhall ſtrike denial Dumb. What mean you? Interrupted ſhe; you ſhall behold (ſaid he) the guilty pair, link'd in each others Arms. Oh ESPERNAY (rejoyn'd ſhe) coud'ſt thou do that? --- 'Tis eaſie (anſwer'd he) as I can order Matters --- but longer Conferrence may render me ſuſpected --- I'll go ſeek the *Count*, for he muſt be my Engine to betray himſelf --- In a Day or two, at fartheſt you ſhall enjoy all the Revenge Detection can beſtow.

ALOVYSA wou'd fain have perſwaded him to have told her the Name of her Rival, in part of that full Conviction he had promis'd her, but in vain, and ſhe was oblig'd to leave the Iſſue of this Affair entirely to his Management.

THE *Baron* was extreamly pleas'd with the Progreſs he had made, and did not doubt, but for the purchaſe of this ſecret he ſhou'd obtain every thing he deſired of ALOVYSA. He found *Count* D'ELMONT full of troubled and perplexed Thoughts, and when he had heard the Hiſtory of his diſappointment: I am ſorry to hear (ſaid he) that the fooliſh Girl does not know her own mind --- but come (my Lord continued he, after a little pauſe) do not ſuffer your ſelf to ſink beneath a Caprice, which all thoſe who converſe much with that Sex muſt frequently meet with --- I have a Contrivance in my Head, that cannot fail to render all her peeviſh Virtue fruſtrate: And make her happy in her own deſpite Oh ESPERNAY! (reply'd the *Count*) thou talkeſt as Friendſhip prompts thee, I know thou wiſheſt my Succeſs, but alas! So many, and ſuch unforeſeen Accidents

cidents have happen'd hitherto to prevent me, that I begin to think the Hand of Fate has set me down for lost. For shame my Lord (Interrupted the *Baron*) be be not so poor in Spirit---- Once more I tell you that she shall be yours --- a Day or two shall make her so --- and because I know you Lovers are unbelieving, and impatient---- I will Communicate the Means. A Ball, and Entertainment shall be provided at my House, to which, all the Neighbouring People of Condition shall be invited, amongst the number, your self, your Lady, and MELLIORA; it will be late before 'tis done, and I must perswade your Family, and some others who live farthest off, to Countenance the Design) to stay all Night; all that you have to do, is to keep up your Resentment to ALOVYSA, that you may have a pretence to sleep from her: I shall take care to have MELLIORA plac'd where no Impediment may bar your Entrance. Impossible Suggestion! (cry'd D'ELMONT shaking his Head) ALOVYSA is in too much Rage of Temper to listen to such an Invitation, and without her, we must not hope for MELLIORA. How Industrious are you (resum'd the *Baron*) to create difficulties where there is none: Tho' I confess this may have, to you, a reasonable Appearance of one. But know, my Friendship builds it's hopes to serve you on a sure Foundation --- this jealous furious Wife, makes me the Confident of her imagin'd Injuries, Conjures me to use all my Interest with you for a reconcilement, and believes I am now pleading for her ---- I must for a while rail at your Ingratitude, and Condemn your want of Taste, to keep my Credit with her, and now and then sweeten her with a doubtful Hope that it may be possible at last to bring you to acknowledge, that you have been in an Error; this at once confirms her, that I am wholly on her side, and engages her to follow my Advice.

THO' nothing Palls desire so much as too easie an Assurance of Means to gratifie it, yet a little hope is absolutely

absolutely necessary to preserve it. The fiery Wishes of D'ELMONT's Soul, before chill'd by despair, and half supprest with clouding Griefs, blaz'd now, as fierce, and vigorous as ever, and he found so much probability in what the *Baron* said, that he was ready to adore him for the Contrivance.

THUS all Parties, but MELLIORA, remain'd in a sort of a pleas'd Expectation. The COUNT doubted not of being happy, nor ALOVISA of having her curiosity satisfy'd by the *Baron*'s Assistance, nor himself of the reward he design'd to demand of her for that good Service; and each long'd impatiently for the Day, or rather Night, which was to bring this great Affair to a Period. Poor MELLIORA was the only Person, who had no interval of Comfort. Restrain'd by Honour, and enflam'd by Love, her very Soul was torn: And when she found that COUNT D'ELMONT made no attempt to get into her Chamber again, as she imagin'd he wou'd, she fell into a Despair more terrible than all her former Inquietudes; she presently fancy'd that the disappointment he had met with the Night before, had driven the hopeless Passion from his Heart, and the Thoughts of being no longer beloved by him, were unsupportable. She saw him not all that Day, nor the next, the quarrel between him and ALOVISA having caus'd separate Tables, she was oblig'd in Decency, to eat at that where she was, and had the Mortification of hearing her self Curs'd every Hour, by the enrag'd Wife, in the Name of her unknown Rival, without daring to speak a Word in her own Vindication.

IN the mean time the *Baron* diligent to make good the Promises he had given the COUNT and ALOVISA, for his own Ends, got every thing ready, and came himself to D'ELMONT's House, to entreat their Company [illegible] Now Madam (said he) to ALOVISA the [illegible] come to prove your Servants Faith. This [illegible] [illegible] put an end to your uncertainty. They had no opportunity for further Speech;

MEL-

MELLIORA came that Moment into the Room, who being ask'd to go to the Ball, and seeming a little unwilling to appear at any publick Diversion, by Reason of the late Death of her Father, put the *Baron* in Mortal Apprehension for the Success of his Undertaking: But ALOVYSA joyning in his Entreaties, she was at last prevail'd upon: The COUNT went along with the *Baron* in his Chariot: And the Ladies soon follow'd in an other.

THERE was a vast deal of Company there, and the *Count* danc'd with several of the Ladies, and was extreamly gay amongst them: ALOVYSA watch'd his Behaviour, and regarded every one of them, in their Turn, with Jealousie, but was far from having the least Suspicion of her whom only she had Cause.

THO' MELLIORA's greatest Motive to go, was, because she might have the happiness of seeing her admir'd *Count*; a Blessing, she had not enjoy'd these two Days, yet she took but little Satisfaction in that View, without an opportunity of being spoke to by him, But that uneasiness was remov'd, when the serious Dances being over, and they all joyning in a grand Ballet: He every now and then, got means to say a Thousand tender Things to her, press'd her Hand whenever he turn'd her, and wou'd sometimes, when at a distance from ALOVISA, pretend to be out, on purpose to stand still, and talk to her. This kind of Behaviour banish'd part of her Sufferings for tho' she cou'd consider both his, and her own Passion in no other View, than that of a very great Misfortune to them both, yet there are so many Pleasures, even in the Pains of Love, Such tender thrillings, such Soul-ravishing Amusements, attend some happy Moments of Contemplation, that those who most Endeavour, can wish but faintly to be freed from.

WHEN

WHEN it grew pretty late, the Baron made a sign to the Count to follow him into a little Room joyning to that where they were, and when he had, now my Lord, (said he) I doubt not but this Night will make you entirely Possessor of your Wishes: I have prolonged the Entertainment, on purpose to detain those, who 'tis necessary for our Design, and have ordered a Chamber for MELLIORA, which has no Impediment to Bar your Entrance: O! Thon best of Friends, (answer'd D'ELMONT) how shall I requite thy Goodness? In making (resum'd the Baron) a right Use of the Opportunity I give you, for if you do not, you render fruitless all the Labours of my Brain, and make me wretched, while my Friend is so. Oh! fear me not (cry'd D'ELMONT in a Rapture) I will not be deny'd, each Faculty of my Soul is bent upon Enjoyment, tho' Death in all its various Horrors glar'd upon me, I'd scorn 'em all in MELLIORA's Arms --- O! the very Name transports me --- New fires my Blood, and tingles in my Veins --- Imagination points out all her Charms -- Methinks I see her lie in sweet Confusion -- Fearing -- Wishing -- Melting --- Her glowing Cheeks -- Her closing dying Eyes -- her every kindling -- Oh 'tis too vast for Thought Even Fancy flags, and cannot reach her Wonders! As he was speaking, MELANTHA, who had taken notice of his going out of the Room, and had follow'd him with a Design of talking to him, came time enough to hear the latter part of what he said but seeing her Brother with him, withdrew with as much haste as she came, and infinitely more uneasiness of Mind; she was now but too well assur'd that she had a greater difficulty than the Count's Matrimonial Engagement to get over, before she could reach his Heart, and was ready to burst with Vexation to think she was supplanted: Full of a Thousand tormenting Reflections she return'd to the Ball Room, and was so out of Humour all the Night, that she could

could hardly be commonly Civil to any Body that ſpoke to her.

AT laſt, the Hour ſo much deſired by the Count, the Baron, and ALOVISA (tho' for various Reaſons) was arriv'd: The Company broke up; thoſe who liv'd near, which were the greateſt part, went home, the others being entreated by the Baron, ſtay'd. When they were to be conducted to their Chambers, he call'd MELANTHA, and deſired ſhe would take care of the Ladies as he ſhould direct, but above all, charg'd to place ALOVISA and MELLIORA in two Chambers which he ſhewed, her.

MELANTHA was now let into the Secret ſhe ſo much deſired to know, the Name of her Rival, which ſhe had not come time enough to hear, when ſhe did the Count's Rapturous Deſcription of her. She had before found out, that her Brother was in Love with ALOVYSA, and did not doubt, but that there was a double Intrigue to be carry'd on that Night, and was the more confirm'd in that Opinion, when ſhe remembred, that the *Baron* had order'd the Lock that Day to be be taken off the Door of that Chamber where MELLIORA was to be lodg'd. It preſently came into her Head, to betray all ſhe knew to ALOVISA, but ſhe ſoon rejected that Reſolution for another, which ſhe thought would give her a more pleaſing Revenge: She conducted all the Ladies to ſuch Chambers as ſhe thought fit, and ALOVISA to that her Brother had deſired, having no deſign of diſappointing him, but MELLIORA ſhe led to one where ſhe always lay her ſelf, reſolving to ſupply her Place in the other, where the Count was to come: Yes, (ſaid ſhe to her ſelf) I will receive his Vows in MELLIORA's Room, and when I find him rais'd to the higheſt pitch of Expectation, declare who I am, and awe him into Tameneſs; 'twill be a charming Piece of Vengeance, beſides, if he be not the moſt ungrateful Man on Earth, he muſt

Adore

Adore my Generosity in not exposing him to his Wife, when I have him in my Power, after the Coldness he has us'd me with. She found something so pleasing in this Contrivance, that no Considerations whatever, could have Power to deter her from pursuing it.

WHEN the Baron found every thing was silent and ready for his Purpose, he went softly to Count D'ELMONT's Chamber, where he was impatiently expected; and taking him by the Hand, led him to that, where he had ordered MELLIORA to be Lodg'd. When they were at the Door, you see my Lord, (said he) I have kept my Promise; there lies the Idol of your Soul, go in, be bold, and all the Happiness, you wish attend you. The Count was in too great a hurry of disorder'd Thoughts to make him any other Answer than a passionate Embrace, and gently pushing open the Door which had no fastning to it, left the Baron to prosecute the remaining part of his treacherous Design.

ALOVISA had all the time of her being at the Baron's, endur'd most grievous Racks of Mind, her Husband appear'd to her that Night, more gay and lovely, if possible than ever, but that Contentment which sat upon his Face, and added to his Graces, stung her to the Soul, when she reflected how little Sympathy there was between them: Scarce a Month (said she to her self) was I bless'd with those looks of Joy, a pensive sullenness has dwelt upon his Brow e'er since, 'till now; 'tis from my Ruin that his Pleasure flows, he hates me, and rejoyces in a Pretence, tho never so poor a one, to be absent from me. She was inwardly toss'd with a Multitude of these and the like perturbations, tho the Assurance the Baron had given her of Revenge, made her conceal them tolerably well, while she was in Company, but when she was left alone in the Chamber, and perceiv'd the Baron did not come so soon as she expected. Her Rage broke

broke out in all the Violence imaginable: She gave a loose to every furious Passion, and when she saw him enter, Cruel *D' Espernay* (said she) where have you been! --- Is this the Friendship which you vow'd? To leave me here distracted with my Griefs, while my perfidious Husband, and the cursed she, that robs me of him, are perhaps, as happy, as their guilty Love can make them? Madam (answer'd he)'tis but a Moment since they are met: A Moment! (interrupted she) a Moment is too much, the smallest Particle of undivided Time, may make my Rival blest, and vastly recompence for all that my Revenge can do. Ah Madam (resum'd the Baron) how dearly do you still Love that most ungrateful Man: I had hopes that the full Knowledge of his Falshood might have made you scorn the scorner, I shall be able by to Morrow (reply'd the Cunning ALOVISA who knew his drift well enough) to give you a better account of my Sentiments than now I can: --- But why do we delay (continued she impatiently) are they not together? --- The Baron saw this was no time to press her farther, and therefore taking a Wax Candle which stood on the Table, in one Hand, and offering the other to lead her, I am ready Madam (said he) to make good my Promise, and shall esteem no other Hours of my Life happy, but those which may be serviceable to you: They had only a small part of a Gallery to go thro', and ALOVISA had no time to answer to these last Words, if she had been compos'd enough to have done it, before they were at the Door, which as soon as the Baron had brought her to, he withdrew with all possible Speed.

THO' the *Count* had been but a very little time in the Arms of his suppos'd MELLIORA, yet he had made so good use of it, and had taken so much Advantage of her complying Humour, that all his Fears were at an End, he now thought himself the most Fortunate of all Mankind; and MELANTHA was far from repenting the Breach of the Resolution she had

had made of discovering her self to him. His Behaviour to her was all Rapture, all killing extacy, and she flatter'd her self with a Belief, that when he shou'd come to know to whom he ow'd that bliss he had possess'd, he would not be ungrateful for it.

WHAT a confus'd Consternation must this Pair be in, when ALOVYSA rush'd into the Room; --- 'tis hard to say, which was the greatest, the *Count's* concern for his imagin'd MELLIORA's Honour, or MELLANTHA's for her own; but if one may form a Judgment from the Levity of the one's Temper, and generosity of the other's, one may believe that his had the Preheminence: But neither of them were so lost in Thought, as not to take what measures the Place and Time wou'd permit, to baffle the Fury of this Incens'd Wife: MELLNTHA slunk under the Cloaths and the COUNT started up in the Bed at the first Appearance of the Light, which ALOVYSA had in her Hand, and in the most angry Accent he cou'd turn his Voice to, ask'd her the Reason of her coming there: Rage, at this sight (prepar'd and arm'd for it as she was) took away all Power of utterance from her; but she flew to the Bed, and began to tear the Cloaths (which MELANTHA held fast over her Head) in so violent a manner, that the *Count* found the only way to Tame her, was to meet Force with Force; so jumping out, he seiz'd on her, and throwing her into a Chair, and holding her down in it, Madam, Madam (said he) you are Mad, and I as such shall use you, unless you promise to return quietly, and leave me. She cou'd yet bring forth no other Words, than Villain, ---- Monster! And such like Names, which her Passion and Injury suggested, which he but little regarding but for the noise she made; for shame (resum'd he) expose not thus your self and me, if you cannot command your Temper, at least confine your Clamours --- I will not stir (said she, raving and struggling to get loose) 'till I have seen the Face that has undone me, I'll tear out her bewitching Eyes --- the

curst

curst Adultress! And leave her Mistress of fewer Charms than thou canst find in me: She spoke this with so elevated a Voice, that the *Count* endeavour'd to stop her Mouth, that she might not alarm the Company that were in the House, but he cou'd not do it time enough to prevent her from schrieking out Murder. --- Help! Or the barbarous Man will kill me! At these Words the *Baron* came running in immediately, full of Surprize and Rage at something he had met with in the mean time: How came this Woman here, cry'd the *Count* to him: Ask me not my Lord said he) for I can answer nothing, but every thing this cursed Night, I think, has happened by Enchantment; he was going to say something more, but several of his Guests hearing a noise, and cry of Murder, and directed by the Lights they saw in that Room, came in, and presently after a great many of the Servants, that the Chamber was as full as it cou'd hold: The *Count* let go his Wife on the sight of the first stranger that enter'd; and indeed, there was no need of his confining her in that Place (tho' he knew not so much) for the violence of so many contrary Passions warring in her Breast at once, had thrown her into a Swoon, and she fell back when he let go his hold of her, Motionless, and in all appearance Dead. The *Count* said little, but began to put on his Cloaths, asham'd of the Posture he had been seen in; but the BARON endeavour'd to perswade the Company, that it was only a Family Quarrel of no Consequence, told them he was sorry for the disturbance it had given them, and desir'd them to return to their Rest, and when the Room was pretty clear, order'd two or three of the Maids to carry ALOVYSA to her Chamber, and apply Things proper for her Recovery; as they were bearing her out, MELLIORA who had been frighted as well as the rest, with the noise she heard, was running along the Gallery to see what had happen'd, and met them; her Trouble to find ALOVYSA in that Condition, was unfeign'd, and she assisted those that

that were employ'd about her, and accompany'd them where they carry'd her.

THE *Count* was going to the Bed-side to comfort the conceal'd Fair, that lay still under the Cloaths, when he saw MELLIORA at the Door: What Surprize was ever equal to his, at this View? ----- He stood like one transfix'd with Thunder, he knew not what to think, or rather cou'd not think at all, confounded with a seeming Impossibility. He beheld the Person, whom he thought had lain in his Arms, whom he had enjoy'd, whose Bulk and Proportion he still saw in the Bed, whom he was just going to Address to, and for whom he had been in all the Agonies of Soul imaginable, come from a distant Chamber, and unconcern'd, ask'd cooly, how ALOVISA came to be taken ill! He look'd confusedly about, sometimes on MELLIORA, sometimes towards the Bed, and sometimes on the Baron; am I awake, (said he) or is every thing I see and hear, Illusion? The Baron could not presently resolve after what manner he should answer, tho' he perfectly knew the Truth of this Adventure, and who was in the Bed; for, when he had conducted ALOVISA to that Room, in order to make the Discovery he had promised, he went to his Sister's Chamber, designing to abscond there, in case the Count should fly out on his Wife's Entrance, and seeing him there, imagine who it was that betray'd him; and finding the Door shut, knock'd and call'd to have it opened; MELLIORA, who began to think she should lye in quiet no where, ask'd who was there, and what he would have? I would speak with my Sister, (reply'd he, as much astonish'd then, to hear who it was that answer'd him, as the Count was now to see her) and MELLIORA having assur'd him that she was not with her, left him no Room to doubt, by what means the Exchange had been made: Few Men, how amorous soever themselves, care that the Female part of their Family should be so, and he was most sensibly mortify'd mortify'd with it, but reflecting that it could not be kept a Secret, at least from the Count, my Lord, (said he, pointing to the Bed) there lies the Cause of your Amazement, that wicked Woman has betray'd the Trust I repos'd in her, and deceiv'd both you and me; rise, continued he, throwing open the Curtains, thou shame of thy Sex, and everlasting Blot and Scandal of the Noble House thou art descended from; rise, I say, or I will stab thee here in this Scene of Guilt; in speaking these Words, he drew out his Sword, and appear'd in such a real Fury, that the Count, tho' more and more amaz'd with every thing he saw and heard, made no doubt but he wou'd do as he said, and ran to hold his Arm.

As no Woman that is Mistress of a great share of Wit, *will* be a Coquet, so no Woman that has not a little, *can* be one: MELANTHA, tho' frighted to Death with these unexpected Occurrences, feign'd a Courage, which she had not in reality, and thrusting her Head a little above the Cloaths, Bless me Brother (said she) I vow I do not know what you mean by all this Bustle, neither am I guilty of any Crime: I was vex'd indeed to be made a Property of, and chang'd Beds with MELLIORA for a little innocent Revenge; for I always design'd to discover my self to the Count, time enough to prevent Mischief. The Baron was not so silly as to believe what she said, tho' the Count, as much as he hated her, had too much Generosity to contradict her, and keeping still hold of the Baron, come *D'Espernay*, (said he) I believe your Sisters Stars and mine, have from our Birth been at Variance, for this is the third Disappointment she has given me; once in MELLIORA's Chamber, then in the Wilderness, and now here; but I forgive her, therefore let us retire and leave her to her Repose. The Baron was sensible that all the Rage in the World could not recall what had been done, and only giving her a furious Look, went with the Count out of the Room, without saying any thing more to her at that Time.

THE Baron with much Entreating, at last prevail'd on Count D'ELMONT to go into his Bed, where he accompan[illegible]'d him; but they were both of them too full of troubled Meditations, to Sleep: His Sister's Indiscretion vex'd the Baron to the Heart, and took away great part of the Joy, for the fresh Occasion the Count had given ALOVISA to withdraw her Affection from him. But with what Words can the various Passions that agitated the Soul of D'ELMONT be described? The Transports he had enjoy'd in an imaginary Felicity, were now turn'd to so many rea[l] Horrors; he saw himself expos'd to all the World for it would have been Vanity to the last Degree, t[o] believe this Adventure would be kept a Secret, bu[t] what gave him the most bitter Reflection, was, tha[t] MELLIORA when she should know it, as he coul[d] not doubt but she immediately wou'd be told it b[y] ALOVISA, wou'd judge of it by the Appearanc[e] and believe him, at once, the most vicious, an[d] most false of Men. As for his Wife, he though[t] not of her, with any Compassion for his Suffering[s] but with Rage and Hate, for that jealous Curiosit[y] which he suppos'd had led her to watch his Actio[n] that Night; (for he had not the least Suspicion of th[e] Baron.) MELANTHA he always despised, but no[w] detested, for the Trick she had put upon him; y[et] thought it would be not only unmanly, but barb[a]rous to let her know he did so: It was in vain f[or] him to endeavour to come to a Determination aft[er] what manner he should behave himself to any [of] them, and when the Night was past, in forming [a] thousand several Resolutions, the Morning found hi[m] as much to seek as before: He took his Leave ear[ly] of the Baron, not being willing to see any of th[e] Company after what had happened, 'till he was mo[re] Compos'd.

HE was not deceiv'd in his Conjectures concer[n]ing MELLIORA, for ALOVISA was no sooner [re]cove cover'd from her Swoon, than, ſhe, with bitter Exclamations, told her what had been the Occaſion, and put that aſtoniſh'd Fair one into ſuch a viſible Diſorder, as had ſhe not been too full of Miſery, to take Notice of it, had made her eaſily perceive that ſhe was deeply intereſted in the Story: But whatever ſhe ſaid againſt the Count, as ſhe could not forbear ſomething, calling him Ungrateful, Perjur'd, Deceitful, and Inconſtant, ALOVISA took only, as a Proof of Friendſhip to her ſelf, and the Effects of that juſt Indignation all Women ought to feel for him, that takes a Pride in Injuring any one of them.

WHEN the Count was gone, the Baron ſent to ALOVISA to enquire of her Health, and if he might have leave to viſit her in her Chamber, and being told he deſired he ſhou'd, reſolv'd now to make his Demand. MELLIORA had but juſt parted from her, n order to get herſelf ready to go Home, and ſhe vas alone when he came in. As ſoon as the firſt Ciilities were over, ſhe began afreſh to conjure him to t her know the Name of her Rival, which he artilly evading, tho' not abſolutely denying, made her lmoſt diſtracted; the Baron carefully obſerv'd her very Look and Motion, and when he found her Imatience was rais'd to the higheſt degree; Madam aid he, taking her by the Hand, and looking tenerly on her) you cannot blame a Wretch who has viſh'd all he had away to one poor Jewel, to make ne moſt he can of that, to ſupply his future Wants: have already forfeited all pretence to Honour, and ven common Hoſpitality, by betraying the Truſt hat was repos'd in me, and expoſing under my wn Roof, the Man who takes me for his deareſt riend, and what elſe I have ſuffer'd from that unaoidable Impulſe which compell'd me to do all this, our ſelf may judge, who too well know, the Pangs nd Tortures of neglected Love --- Therefore, (conued he with a deep Sigh) ſince this laſt reſerve is my Hopes dependance, do not, Oh Charming

ALOVISA, think me Mercinary, if I preſume to ſet a Price upon it, which I confeſs too high, yet nothing leſs can Purchaſe: No Price (reply'd ALOVISA, who thought a little Condeſcenſion was neceſſary to win him to her purpoſe) can be too dear to buy my Peace, nor Recompence too great for ſuch a Service: What, not your Love, ſaid the Baron, eagerly kiſſing her Hand? No (reſum'd ſhe, forcing herſelf to look kindly on him) not even that, when ſuch a Proof of yours engages it; but do not keep me longer on the Rack, give me the Name and then.--- She ſpoke theſe laſt Words with ſuch an Air of Languiſhment, that the Baron thought his Work was done, and growing bolder, from her Hand he proceeded to her Lips, and anſwer'd her only in Kiſſes, which diſtaſtful as they were to her, ſhe ſuffer'd him to take, without Reſiſtance, but that was not all he wanted, and believing this the Critical Minute, he threw his Arms about her Waiſt, and began to draw her by little and little toward the Bed; which ſhe affected to permit with a kind of an unwilling Willingneſs; ſaying, Well, if you wou'd have me able to deny you nothing you can ask, tell me the Name I ſo much wiſh to know: But the Baron was as cunning as ſhe, and ſeeing thro' her Artifice, was reſolv'd to make ſure of his Reward firſt: Yes, yes, my adorable ALOVISA (anſwer'd he, having brought her now very near the Bed) you ſhall immediately know all, thy Charms will force the Secret from my Breaſt, cloſe as it is lodg'd within my inmoſt Soul. --- Dying with Rapture I will tell thee all.--- If that a Thought of this injurious Husband, can interpoſe amidſt Extatick Joys. What will not ſome Women venture, to ſatisfy a jealous Curioſity? ALOVISA had feign'd to conſent to his Deſires, (in hopes to engage him to a Diſcovery) ſo far, and had given him ſo many Liberties, that now it was as much as ſhe cou'd do to ſave herſelf, from the utmoſt Violence, and perceiving ſhe had been outwitted, and that nothing but the really yielding up her Honour, cou'd oblige him to

reva

reveal what she desired. Villain, said she, (struggling to get loose from his Embrace) dare thy base Soul believe so vilely of me? Release me from thy detested Hold, or my Cries shall force thee to it, and proclaim thee what thou art, a Monster! The Baron was not enough deluded by her pretence of Kindness, to be much surpriz'd at this sudden turn of her Behaviour, and only cooly answer'd, Madam, I have no design of using Violence, but perceive, if I had depended on your Gratitude, I had been miserably deceiv'd. Yes (said she, looking contemptibly on him) I own thou would'st; for whatsoever I might say, or thou could'st hope, I love my Husband still, with an unbated Fondness, doat upon him! Faithless and Cruel as he is, he still is lovely! His Eyes lose nothing of their brightness, nor his Tongue its softness! His very Frowns have more Attraction in them than any others Smiles! and canst thou think! Thou, so different in all from him, that thou seemest not the same Species of Humanity, nor ought'st to stile thy self a Man since he is no more: Canst thou, I say, believe a Woman, bless'd as ALOVISA has been, can e'er blot out the dear Remembrance, and quit her Hopes of re-gain'd Paradise in his Embrace, for certain Hell in Thine? She spoke these Words with so much Scorn, that the Baron skill'd as he was in every Art to tempt, cou'd not conceal the Spite he conceiv'd at them, and letting go her Hand, (which perforce he had held) I leave you Madam (said he) to the Pleasure of enjoying your own Humour; neither that, nor your Circumstances are to be envy'd, but I'd have you to remember, that you are your own Tormentor, while you refuse the only means can bring you Ease. I will have Ease another way (said she, incens'd at the Indignity she imagin'd he treated her with) and if you still persist in refusing to discover to me the Person who has injur'd me, I shall make no difficulty of letting the Count know how much of his Secrets you have imparted, and for what Reason you conceal the other: You may do so answer'd ſwer'd he) and I doubt not but you will--- Miſchief is the darling Favourite of Woman! Blood is the Satisfaction perhaps, that you require, and if I fall by him, or he by me, your Revenge will have its aim, either on the Unloving or the Unlov'd; for me, I ſet my Life at nought, without your Love 'tis Hell; but do not think that even dying, to purchaſe Abſolution, I'd reveal one Letter of that Name, you ſo much wiſh to hear, the Secret ſhall be buried with me.---- Yes, Madam (continued he, with a malicious Air) that happy Fair unknown, whoſe Charms have made you wretched, ſhall undiſcover'd, and ungueſs'd at, Triumph in thoſe Joys you think none but your Count can give. ALOVISA had not an Opportunity to make any Anſwer to what he ſaid; MELLICRA came that Moment into the Room, and ask'd if ſhe was ready to go, and ALOVISA ſaying that ſhe was, they both departed from the Baron's Houſe, without much Ceremony on either ſide.

ALOVISA had not been long at home before a Meſſenger came to acquaint her, that her Siſter having miſs'd of her at *Paris*, was now on her Journey to *Le Beauſſe*, and wou'd be with her in a few Hours She rejoyc'd as much at this News, as it was poſſible for one ſo full of diſquiet to do, and order'd he Chariot and Six to be made ready again, and wen to meet her.

D'ELMONT heard of ANSELLINA's comin almoſt as ſoon as ALOVISA, and his Complaiſanc for Ladies, join'd with the extream deſire he had o ſeeing his Brother, whom he believ'd was with he wou'd certainly have given him Wings to have flow to them with all imaginable Speed, had not the lat Quarrel between him and his Wife, made him thinl it was improper to join Company with her on an Account whatever: He was ſitting in his Dreſſing Room Window in a melancholly and diſturb'd Me ditation, ruminating on every Circumſtance of hi la last Nights Adventure, when he perceiv'd a couple of Horsemen come galloping over the Plain, and make directly toward his House. The Dust they made, kept him from distinguishing who they were, and they were very near the Gate before he discover'd them to be the *Chevalier* BRILLIAN, and his Servant: The Surprize he was in to see him without ANSELLINA was very great, but much more so, when running down, as soon as he saw he was alighted, and opening his Arms eagerly to Embrace him; the other drawing back, No, my Lord (said he) since you are pleas'd to forget I am your Brother. I pretend no other way to merit your Embraces: Nor can think it any Happiness to hold him in my Arms, who keeps me distant from his Heart. What mean you (cry'd DELMONT, extreamly astonish'd at his Behaviour) you know so little (resum'd the *Chevalier*) of the power of Love, your self, that perhaps, you think I ought not to resent what you having done to ruin me in mine: But, however Sir, Ambition is a Passion which you are not a Stranger to, and have settled your own Fortune according to your Wish, methinks you shou'd not wonder that I take it ill, when you endeavour to prevent my doing so to: The *Count* was perfectly Confounded at these Words, and looking earnestly on him; Brother (said he) you seem to lay a heavy Accusation on me, but if you still retain so much of that former Affection which was between us, as to desire I shou'd be clear'd in your Esteem, you must be more plain in your Charge, for tho' I easily perceive that I am wrong'd, I cannot see by what means I am so. My Lord, you are not wrong'd (cry'd the *Chevalier* hastily) you know you are not: If my Tongue were silent, the despair that sits upon my Brow, my alter'd Looks, and grief-sunk Eyes, wou'd proclaim your Babrarous --- most unnatural Usage of me. Ungrateful BRILLIAN (said the COUNT, at once inflam'd with Tenderness and Anger) is this the Consolation I expected from your Presence? I know not for what Cause I am upbraided, being Innocent of any, nor what your Troubles are, but I am ſure my own are ſuch, as needed not this Weight to overwhelm me. He ſpoke this ſo feelingly, and concluded with ſo deep a ſigh as moſt ſenſibly touch'd the Heart of BRILLIAN. If I cou'd believe that you had any (reply'd he) it were enough to ſink me quite, and rid me of a Life which ANSELLINA's loſs has made me hate. What ſaid you, (interrupted the *Count*) ANSELLINA's loſs? If that be true, I pardon all the wildneſs of your unjuſt Reproaches, for well I know, deſpair has ſmall regard to Reaſon, but quickly ſpeak the Cauſe of your Misfortune: --- I was about to enquire the Reaſon that I ſaw you not together, when your unkind Behaviour drove it from my Thoughts. That Queſtion (anſwer'd the *Chevalier*) ask'd by you ſome Days ſince, wou'd have put me paſt all the Remains of Patience, but I begin to hope I am not ſo unhappy as I thought, but ſtill am bleſt in Friendſhip, tho' undone in Love ---- but I'll not keep you longer in ſuſpence, my Tale of Grief is ſhort in the Repeating, tho' everlaſting in its Conſequence. In ſaying this, he ſat down, and the *Count* doing the like, and aſſuring him of Attention, he began his Relation in this manner.

YOUR Lordſhip may remember that I gave you an Account by Letter, of ANSELLINA's Indiſpoſition, and the Fears I was in for her; but by the time I receiv'd your Anſwer, I thought my ſelf the happieſt of Mankind: She was perfectly recover'd, and every Day I receiv'd new Proofs of her Affection: We began to talk now of coming to *Paris*, and ſhe ſeem'd no leſs Impatient for that Journey than my ſelf, and one Evening, the laſt I ever had the Honour of her Converſation; ſhe told me, that in ſpite of the Phyſicians Caution, ſhe wou'd leave *Amiens* in three or four Days; You may be ſure I did not diſſwade her from that Reſolution; but, how great was my Aſtoniſhment, when going the next Morning to the *Baroneſſes*, to give the Ladies the *Bon jour*, as I conſtantly

dic

id every Morning. I perceiv'd an unusual coldness 1 the Face of every one in the Family; the *Baroness* erself spoke not to me, but to tell me that ANSEL-INA wou'd see no Company: How, Madam, said , am I not excepted from those general Orders, what an this sudden alteration in my Fortune mean? I suppose (reply'd she) that ANSELLINA has her Reaons for what she does: I said all that despair cou'd sugest, to oblige her to give me some light into this Mistery, but all was in vain, she either made me no nswers, or such as were not Satisfactory, and growg weary with being Importun'd, she abruptly went ut of the Room, and left me in a confusion not to e Express'd: I renew'd my visit the next Day, and as then deny'd admittance by the Porter: The same, e following one, and as Servants commonly form eir Behaviour, according to that of those they serve, was easy for me to observe I was far from being a elcome Guest: I writ to ANSELLINA, but had y Letter return'd unopen'd: And that Scorn so unstly thrown upon me, tho' it did not absolutely cure y Passion, yet it stirr'd up so much just Resentment me, that it abated very much of its Tenderness: bout a Fortnight I remain'd in this perplexity, and the end of it was plung'd into a greater, when I ceiv'd a little *Billet* from ANSELLINA, which as emember, contain'd these Words.

ANSELLINA to the *Chevalier* BRILLIAN.

'Sent your Letter back without Perusing, believing it might contain something of a Subject which I am solv'd to encourage no farther; I do not think it proper present to acquaint you with my Reasons for it; but

if

if I ſee you at Paris, *you ſhall know them: I ſet out for thence to Morrow, but deſire you not to pretend to Accompany me thither, if you wou'd preſerve the Eſteem of,*

ANSELLINA.

I cannot but ſay, I thought this manner of proceeding very odd, and vaſtly different from that openneſs of Nature, I always admir'd in her, but as I had been always a moſt obſequious Lover; I reſolv'd not to forfeit that Character, and give a Proof of an implicite Obedience to her Will, tho' with what Anxiety of Mind you may imagine. I ſtood at a diſtance, and ſaw her take Coach, and as ſoon as her Attendants were out of ſight, I got on Horſeback, and follow'd; I ſeveral Times lay at the ſame Inn where ſhe did, but took care not to appear before her: Never was any ſight more pleaſing to me, then that of *Paris*, becauſe I there hop'd to have my Deſtiny unravell'd; but your being out of Town, preventing her making any ſtay, I was reduc'd to another tryal of Patience; about Seven Furlongs from hence, hap'ning to Bait at the ſame *Cabaret* with her, I ſaw her Woman, who had been always perfectly obliging to me, walking alone in the Garden; I took the liberty to ſhow my ſelf to her, and ask her ſome Queſtions concerning my future Fate to which ſhe anſwer'd with all the Freedom I cou'd deſire, and obſerving the Melancholly, which was but too apparent in my Countenance: Sir, ſaid ſhe tho' I think nothing can be more blame-worthy than to betray the Secrets of our Superiors, yet I hope I ſhall ſtand excus'd for declaring ſo much of my Lady as the Condition you are in, ſeems to require; I wou'd not therefore have you believe that in this Separation, you are the only Sufferer, I can aſſure you my Lady bears her part of Sorrow too. ---- How can that be poſſible (cry'd I) when my Misfortune is brought upon me, only by the change of her Inclination? Far from it (anſwer'd ſhe) you have a Brother — he only is to blame, ſhe has receiv'd Letters from

Madam

Madam D'ELMONT which have--- as she was speaking, she was call'd hastily away, without being able to finish what she was about to say, and I was so Impatient to hear: Her naming you in such a manner, planted ten thousand Daggers in my Soul! --- What cou'd I imagine by those Words, *You have a Brother, he only is to Blame*, and her mentioning Letters from that Brother's Wife; but that it was thro' you I was made wretched? I repeated several times over to my self, what she had said, but cou'd wrest no other Meaning from it, than that you being already possess'd of the Elder Sister's Fortune, were willing to Engross the other's too, by preventing her from Marrying: Pardon me, my Lord, if I have Injur'd you, since I protest, the Thoughts of your designing my undoin g, was, if possible, more dreadful to me than the Ilit, self.

YOU will, reply'd the *Count*, be soon convinc'd how little Hand I had in those Letters, whatever they contain'd, when you have been here a few Days. He then told him of the disagreement between himself and ALOVISA, her perpetual Jealousy, her Pride, her Rage, and the little probability there was of their being ever reconcil'd, so as to live together as they ought, omitting nothing of the Story, but his Love for MELLICORA, and the Cause he had given to create this uneasiness. They both concluded, that ANSELLINA's alteration of Behaviour was entirely owing to something her Sister had written, and that she wou'd use her utmost endeavour to break off the Match wholly in Revenge to her Husband: As they were discoursing on means to prevent it, the Ladies came to the Gate; they saw them thro' the Window, and ran to receive them immediately: The *Count* handed ANSELLINA out of the Coach, with great Complaisance, while the *Chevalier* wou'd have done the same by ALOVISA, but she wou'd not permit him, which the *Count* observing, when he had paid those Complements to her Sister, which he thought civility requir'd, quir'd, Madam (said he, turning to her and frowning) is it not enough, you make me wretched by your continual Clamours, and Upbraidings, but that your ill Nature must extend to all, whom you believe I love? She answer'd him only with a disdainful Look, and haughty Toss, which spoke the Pleasure she took in having it in her Power to give him Pain, and went out of the Room with ANSELLINA.

D'ELMONT's Family was now become a most distracted one, every Body was in confusion, and it was hard for a disinterested Person, to know how to behave among them: The *Count* was ready to die with Vexation, when he reflected on the Adventure at the BARON's with MELANTHA, and how hard it wou'd be to clear his Conduct in that point with MELLIORA: She, on the other Hand, was as much tormented at his not attempting it. The *Chevalier*, was in the height of despair, when he found that ANSELLINA continued her Humour, and still avoided letting him know the occasion of it: And ALOVISA, tho' she contented herself for some Hours with relating to her Sister, all the Passages of her Husband's unkind usage of her, yet when that was over, her Curiosity return'd, and she grew so madly Zealous to find out, who her rival was, that she repented her Behaviour to the *Baron*, and sent him the next Day privately, a *Billet*, wherein she assur'd him, that she had acquainted the *Count* with nothing that had pass'd between them, and that she desir'd to speak with him. 'Tis easy to believe he needed not a second Invitation; he came immediately, and ALOVISA renew'd her Entreaties in the most pressing manner she was capable of, but in vain, he told her plainly, that if he cou'd not have her Heart, nothing but the full Possession of her Person shou'd Extort the Secret from him. 'Twould swell this Discourse beyond what I design, to recount her various States of Passions, and different Turns of Behaviour, sometimes louder than the Winds she rav'd! Commanded! Threatned! Then, still as *April* Showers,

ers, or Summer Dews ſhe wept, and only whiſper'd her Complaints, now diſſembling Kindneſs, then declaring unfeign'd Hate; 'till at laſt, finding it impoſſible to prevail by any other means, ſhe promis'd to admit him at Midnight into her Chamber: But as it was only the force of her too paſſionate Affection for her Husband, which had work'd her to this pitch of raging Jealouſie, ſo ſhe had no ſooner made the Aſſignation, and the *Baron* had left her (to ſeek the *Count* to prevent any ſuſpicion of their long Converſation) but all D'ELMONT's Charms came freſh into her Mind, and made the Thoughts of what ſhe had promis'd, Odious and Inſupportable; ſhe open'd her Mouth more than once to call back the *Baron*, and Recant all that ſhe had ſaid; but her ill Genius, or that Devil, Curioſity, which too much haunts the Minds of Women, ſtill prevented Her: What will become of me, (ſaid ſhe to her ſelf) what is it I am about to do? Shall I foregoe my Honour --- quit my Virtue, --- ſully my yet unſpotted Name with endleſs Infamy --- and yield my Soul to Sin, to Shame, and Horror, only to know what I can ne'er Redreſs? If D'ELMONT hates me now, will he not do ſo ſtill? --- What will this curs'd Diſcovery bring me but added Tortures, and freſh weight of Woe: Happy had it been for her if theſe Conſiderations cou'd have laſted, but when ſhe had been a Minute or two in this Temper, ſhe wou'd relapſe and cry, what! muſt I tamely bear it then? --- Endure the Flouts of the malicious World, and the contempt of every ſaucy Girl, who while ſhe pities, ſcorns my want of Charms -- Shall I neglected tell my Tale of Wrongs, (O, Hell is in that Thought) 'till my deſpair ſhall reach my Rival's Ears, and Crown her Adulterous Joys with double Pleaſure. --- Wre[illegible] that I am! -- Fool that I am, to heſitate, [illegible]ery is already paſt Addition, my everlaſting P[illegible] broke! Loſt even to hope, what can I mo[illegible] --- No, ſince I muſt be ruin'd, I'll have [illegible]ſfaction of dragging with me to Perdition [illegible], the Curſed ſhe that has undone me: I'll be reveng'd on her, then die

die my ſelf, and free me from Pollution. As ſhe was in this laſt Thought, ſhe perceiv'd at a good diſtance from her, the *Chevalier* BRILLIAN and ANSELLINA in Diſcourſe; the ſight of him immediately put a new contrivance into her Head, and ſhe compos'd her ſelf as ſhe cou'd, and went to meet them.

ANSELLINA having been left alone, while her Siſter was Entertaining the *Baron*, had walk'd down into the Garden to divert her ſelf, where the *Chevalier*, who was on the watch for ſuch an opportunity, had follow'd her; he cou'd not forbear, tho' in Terms full of Reſpect, taxing her with ſome little Injuſtice for her late Uſage of him, and Breach of Promiſe, in not letting him know her Reaſons for it: She, who by Nature was extreamly averſe to the diſguiſing her Sentiments, ſuffer'd him not long to preſs her for an *Eclarciſment*, and with her uſual Freedom, told him what ſhe had done, was purely in compliance with her Siſter's Requeſt; that ſhe cou'd not help having the ſame Opinion of him as ever, but that ſhe had promis'd ALOVISA to defer any Thoughts of marrying him, till his Brother ſhou'd confeſs his Error: The obliging things ſhe ſaid to him, tho' ſhe perſiſted in her Reſolution, diſſipated great part of his Chagreen, and he was beginning to excuſe D'ELMONT, and perſuade her that her Siſter's Temper was the firſt occaſion of their quarrel, when ALLOVISA interrupted them. ANSELLINA was a little out of Countenance at her Siſter's Preſence, imagining ſhe wou'd be Incens'd at finding her with the *Chevalier*; but that diſtreſſed Lady was full of other Thoughts, and deſiring him to follow her to her Chamber, as ſoon as they were ſet down, confeſs'd to him, how, fir'd with his Brother's Falſhood, ſhe endeavour'd to revenge it upon him, that ſhe had been his Enemy, but was willing to enter into any Meaſures for his Satisfaction, provided he wou'd comply with one, which ſhe ſhould propoſe, which he faithfully promiſing, after ſhe had ſworn him to Secrecy, diſcover'd to him every Circumſtance,

cumſtance, from her firſt Cauſe of Jealouſy, to the Aſſignation ſhe had made with the *Baron*; now, ſaid ſhe, it is in your Power to preſerve both your Brother's Honour, and my Life (which I ſooner will reſign than my Vertue) if you ſtand conceal'd in a little Cloſet, which I ſhall convey you to, and the Moment he has ſatisfy'd my Curioſity, by telling me her Name that has undone me, ruſh out, and be my Protector. The *Chevalier* was infinitely Surpriz'd at what he heard, for his Brother had not given him the leaſt hint of his Paſſion, but thought the requeſt ſhe made, too reaſonable to be deny'd.

WHILE they were in this Diſcourſe, MELLIORA, who had been ſitting indulging her Melancholly in that Cloſet which ALOVISA ſpoke of, and which did not immediately belong to that Chamber, but was a ſort of an Entry, or Paſſage, into another, and tir'd with Reflection, was fallen aſleep, but on the noiſe which ALOVYSA and the *Chevalier* made in coming in, wak'd, and heard to her inexpreſſible trouble, the Diſcourſe that paſs'd between them: She knew that unknown Rival was herſelf, and condemn'd the *Count* of the higheſt Imprudence, in making a confidant, as ſhe found he had, of the *Baron*; ſhe ſaw her Fate, at leaſt that of her Reputation was now upon the Criſis, that, that very Night ſhe was to be expos'd to all the Fury of an enrag'd Wife, and was ſo ſhook with apprehenſion, that ſhe was ſcarce able to go out of the Cloſet time enough to prevent their diſcovering ſhe was there; what cou'd ſhe do in this Exigence, the Thoughts of being betray'd, was worſe to her than a thouſand Deaths, and it was to be wondred at, as ſhe has ſince confeſt, that in that height of Deſparation, ſhe had not put an end to the Tortures of Reflection, by laying violent Hands on her own Life: As ſhe was going from the Cloſet haſtily to her own Appartment, the *Count* and *Baron* paſs'd her, and that ſight heightening the diſtraction ſhe was in, ſhe ſtept

to

to the *Count*, and in a faultring, ſcarce intelligible Accent, whiſper'd, for Heaven's Sake let me ſpeak with you before Night, make ſome pretence to come to my Chamber, where I'll wait for you. And as ſoon as ſhe had ſpoke theſe Words, darted from him ſo ſwift, that he had no opportunity of replying, if he had not been too much overwhelm'd with Joy at this ſeeming Change of his Fortune to have done it; he miſunderſtood part of what ſhe ſaid, and inſtead of her deſiring to ſpeak with him ***before Night***, he imagin'd, ſhe ſaid ***at Night***. He preſently communicated it to the *Baron*, who congratulated him upon it; and never was any Night more impatiently long'd for, than this was by them both. They had indeed not many Hours of Expectation, but MELLIORA thought them Ages; all her hopes were, that if ſhe cou'd have an opportunity of diſcovering to *Count* D'ELMONT what ſhe had heard between his Wife and Brother, he might find ſome means to prevent the *Baron*'s Treachery from taking Effect. But when Night grew on, and ſhe perceiv'd he came not, and ſhe conſider'd how near ſhe was to inevitable Ruin, what Words can ſufficiently expreſs her Agonies? So I ſhall only ſay, they were too violent to have long kept Company with Life; but Horrour, Fear, Remorſe, and Shame at once oppreſs'd her, and ſhe was very near ſinking beneath their Weight, when ſomebody knock'd ſoftly at the Door; ſhe made no doubt but it was the *Count*, and open'd it immediately, and he catching her in his Arms with all the eagerneſs of tranſported Love, ſhe was about to clear his Miſtake, and let him know it was not an amourous Entertainment ſhe expected from him; when a ſudden cry of Murder, and the noiſe of claſhing Swords, made him let go his hold, and draw his own, and run along the Gallery to find out the occaſion, where being in the dark, and only directed by the noiſe he heard in his Wife's Chamber, ſomething met the point, and a great ſhriek following it, he cry'd for Lights but none coming immediately; he ſtepping farther ſtumbled at the Body which had fallen, he then redoubled his outcrys,

crys, and MELLIORA, frighted as she was, brought one from her Chamber, and at the same Instant that they discover'd it was ALOVISA, who coming to alarm the Family, had by Accident run on her Husband's Sword, they saw the *Chevalier* pursuing the *Baron*, who mortally wounded, dropt down by ALOVISA's side; what a dreadful View was this? The *Count*, MELLIORA, and the Servants, who by this time were most of them rowz'd, seem'd without Sence or Motion, only the *Chevalier* had Spirit enough to speak, or think, so stupify'd was every one with what they saw. But he ordering the Servants to take up the Bodies, sent one of 'em immediately for a Surgeon, but they were both of them past his Art to cure; ALOVISA spoke no more, and the *Baron* liv'd but two Days, in which time the whole Account, as it was gather'd from the Mouths of those chiefly concern'd, was set down, and the Tragical part of it being laid before the KING, there appear'd so much of Justice in the BARON's Death, and Accident in ALOVISA's, that the *Count* and *Chevalier* found it no difficult matter to obtain their Pardon. The *Chevalier* was soon after Married to his beloved ANSELLINA; but MELLIORA look'd on herself as the most guilty Person upon Earth, as being the primary Cause of all the Misfortunes that had happen'd, and retir'd immediately to a Monastery, from whence, not all the entreaties of her Friends, nor the implorations of the Amorous D'ELMONT cou'd bring her, she was now resolv'd to punish, by a voluntary Banishment from all she ever did, or cou'd love; the Guilt of Indulging that Passion, while it was a Crime. He, not able to live without her, at least in the same Climate, committed the Care of his Estate to his Brother, and went to Travel, without an Inclination ever to return: MELANTHA who was not of a Humour to take any thing to Heart, was Married in a short Time, and had the good Fortune not to be suspected by her Husband, though she brought him a Child in Seven Months after her Wedding.

LOVE in Excess:

OR, THE

FATAL ENQUIRY.

A

NOVEL.

The THIRD and Last PART.

Success can then alone your Vows attend,
When Worth's the Motive, Constancy the End.
EPILOGUE to the *Spartan* Dame.

By *Mrs.* HAYWOOD.

LONDON:
Printed for W. CHETWOOD, J. WOODMAN, D. BROWN, and S. CHAPMAN.

Love in Excess,

OR, THE

Fatal Enquiry:

The Third and Last Part.

THO Count *Delmont* never had any tenderness for *Alovisa* and her Extravagance of Rage and Jealousie, join'd to his Passion for *Melliora*, had every Day abated it, yet the manner of her Death was too great a shock to the sweetness of his Disposition, to be easily worn off; he cou'd not remember her Uneasiness, without reflecting that it sprung only from her too violent Affection for him; and tho' there was no possibility of living happily with her, when he consider'd that she died, not only for him, but by his Hand, his Compassion for the Cause, and Horror for the unwish'd, as well as undesign'd Event, drew Lamentations from him, more sincere, perhaps, than some of those Husbands,

bands, who call themselves very loving ones, wou'd make.

To alleviate the troubles of his Mind, he had endeavour'd all he cou'd, to persuade *Melliora* to continue in his House; but that afflicted Lady was not to be prevail'd upon, she look'd on her self, as in a manner, accessary to *Alovisa*'s Death, and thought the least she ow'd to her Reputation was to see the *Count* no more, and tho' in the forming this Resolution, she felt Torments unconceivable, yet the strength of her Virtue enabled her to keep it, and she return'd to the Monastery, where she had been Educated, carrying with her nothing of that Peace of Mind with which she left it.

Not many Days pass'd between her Departure, and the *Count*'s; he took his way towards *Italy*, by the Persuasions of his Brother, who, since he found him bent to Travel, hop'd that Garden of the World might produce something to divert his Sorrows; he took but two Servants with him, and those rather for conveniency than State: *Ambition*, once his darling Passion, was now wholly extinguish'd in him by these Misfortunes, and he no longer thought of making a Figure in the World; but his *Love* nothing cou'd abate, and 'tis to be believ'd that the violence of that wou'd have driven him to the use of some fatal Remedy, if the *Chevalier Brillian*, to whom he left the Care of *Melliora*'s and her Brother's Fortune as well as his own, had not, tho' with much difficulty, obtain'd a Promise from her, of conversing with him by Letters.

This was all he had to keep hope alive, and indeed it was no inconsiderable Consolation, for she that allows a Correspondence of that Kind with a Man that has any Interest in her Heart, can never persuade herself, while she does so, to make him become indifferent to her. When we give our selves the liberty ty of even talking of the Person we have once lov'd, and find the least pleasure in that Discourse, 'tis ridiculous to imagine we are free from that Passion, without which, the mention of it would be but insipid to our Ears, and the remembrance to our Minds, tho' our Words are never so Cold, they are the Effects of a secret Fire, which burns not with less Strength for not being Dilated. The *Count* had too much Experience of all the Walks and Turns of Passion to be ignorant of this, if *Meliora* had endeavour'd to disguise her Sentiments, but she went not so far, she thought it a sufficient vindication of her Virtue, to withold the rewarding of his Love, without feigning a coldness to which she was a stranger, and he had the satisfaction to observe a tenderness in her Stile, which assur'd him, that her *Heart* was unalterably his, and very much strengthen'd his Hopes, that one Day her Person might be so too, when time had a little effac'd the Memory of those Circumstances, which had obliged her to put this constraint on her Inclinations.

HE wrote to her from every Post-Town, and waited till he receiv'd her Answer, by this means his Journey was extreamly tedious, but no Adventures of any moment, falling in his way 'till he came to *Rome*, I shall not trouble my Readers with a recital of particulars which cou'd be no way Entertaining

BUT, how strangely do they deceive themselves, who fancy that they are Lovers, yet on every little turn of Fortune, or Change of Circumstance, are agitated with any Vehemence, by Cares of a far different Nature? *Love* is too jealous, too arbitrary a Monarch to suffer any other Passion to equalize himself in that Heart where he has fix'd his Throne. When once enter'd, he becomes the whole Business of our Lives, we think ---- we Dream of nothing else, nor have a Wish not inspir'd by him: Those who have the Power to apply themselves so seriously to any other Consideration as to forget him, tho' but for a Moment,

ment, are but Lovers in Conceit, and have entertain'd Desire but as an agreeable Amusement, which when attended with any Inconvenience, they may without much difficulty shake off. Such a sort of Passion may be properly enough call'd *Liking*, but falls widely short of *Love*. *Love*, is what we can neither resist, expel, nor even alleviate, if we should never so vigorously attempt it; and tho' some have boasted, ***Thus far will I yield and no farther***, they have been convinc'd of the Vanity of forming such Resolutions by the impossibility of keeping them. *Liking* is a flashy Flame, which is to be kept alive only by ease and delight. *Love*, needs not this fewel to maintain its Fire, it survives in Absence, and disappointments, it endures, unchill'd, the wintry Blasts of cold Indifference and Neglect, and continues its Blaze, even in a storm of Hatred and Ingratitude, and Reason, Pride, or a just sensibility of conscious Worth, in vain oppose it. *Liking*, plays gaily round, feeds on the Sweets in gross, but is wholly insensible of the Thorns which guard the nicer, and more refin'd Delicacies of Desire, and can consequently give neither Pain, nor Pleasure in any superlative degree. *Love* creates intollerable Torments! Unspeakable Joys! Raises us to the highest Heaven of Happiness, or sinks us to the lowest Hell of Misery.

Count *D'elmont* experienc'd the Truth of this Assertion; for neither his just concern for the manner of *Alovisa*'s Death cou'd curb the Exuberance of his Joy, when he consider'd himself belov'd by *Melliora*, nor any Diversion of which *Rome* afforded great Variety, be able to make him support being absent from her with Moderation. There are I believe, but few modern Lovers, how Passionate and constant soever they pretend to be, who wou'd not in the *Count*'s Circumstances have found some matter of Consolation; but he seem'd wholly dead to Gaiety. In vain, all the *Roman* Nobility courted his acquaintance; in vain the Ladies made use of their utmost Artifice to engage him: He prefer'd a solitary Walk, a lonely Shade, or the

Bank

Bank of some purling Stream, where he undisturb'd might contemplate on his belov'd *Melliora*, to all the noisy Pleasures of the Court, or the endearments of the inviting Fair. In fine, he shun'd as much as possible all Conversation with the Men, or Correspondence with the Women; returning all their *Billet-Deux*, of which scarce a Day past, without his receiving some, unanswer'd.

THIS manner of Behaviour in a little time deliver'd him from the Persecutions of the Discreet; but having receiv'd one Letter which he had us'd as he had done the rest, it was immediately seconded by another; both which contain'd as follows:

LETTER I.

To the never Enough Admir'd COUNT D'ELMONT.

N your Country, where Women are allow'd the previledge of being seen and Addres'd to, it wou'd be Crime unpardonable to Modesty, to make the first dvances. But here, where rigid Rules are Bar's, as ll to Reason, as to Nature: It wou'd be as great a e, to feign an Infidelity of your Merit. I say, feign, I look on it, as an impossibility really to behold you with difference: But, if I cou'd believe that any of my x were in good earnest so dull, I must confess, I shou'd vy that happy Stupidity, which wou'd secure me from e Pains such a Passion, as you create, must Inflict; less, from the Millions whom your Charms have each'd; you have yet a corner of your Heart Unprepossess'd;

possess'd; and an Inclination willing to receive the Impression of,

Your most Passionate and Tender,
(but 'till she receives a favourable
Answer) Your unknown Adorer.

LETTER II.

To the Ungrateful D'ELMONT.

UNworthy of the Happiness design'd you! Is it thus, That you return the Condescention of a Lady? How fabulous is Report, which speaks those of your Country, warm and full of amorous Desires? -- Thou, sure, art colder than the bleak northern Islanders — dull, stupid Wretch! Insensible of every Passion which give Lustre to the Soul, and differ Man from Brute! --- Without Gratitude --- Without Love -- Without Desire --- Dead, even to Curiosity! --- How I cou'd despise Thee for this narrowness of Mind, were there not something in thy Eyes and Mein which assure me, that this negligent Behaviour is but affected; and that there are within thy Breast, some Seeds of hidden Fire, which want but the Influence of Charms, more potent perhaps than you have yet beheld, to kindle into Blaze. Make hast then to be Enliven'd, for I flatter my self 'tis in my Power to work this wonder, and long to inspire so Lovely a Form with Sentiments only worthy of it. -- The Bearer of this, is a Person who I dare Confide in - Delay not to come with him, for when once you are Taught what 'tis to Love; you'll not be Ignorant that doubtful Expectation is the worst of Racks, and from your own Experience. Pity what I feel, thus chill with Doubt, yet burning with Desire.

Yours, Impatiently.

TH

THE *Count* was pretty much surpriz'd at the odd Turn of this *Billet*; but being willing to put an End to the Ladies Trouble, as well as his own; sat down, and without giving himself much Time to think, writ these Lines in Answer to Hers.

To the Fair INCOGNITA.

MADAM,

IF you have no other design in Writing to me, than your Diversion, *methinks my Mourning Habit, to which my Countenance and Behaviour are no way Unconformable, might inform you, I am little dispos'd for Raillery. If in* Earnest *you can find any thing in me which pleases you, I must confess my self entirely unworthy of the Honour, not only by my personal Demerits, but by the Resolution I have made, of Conversing with none of your Sex while I continue in* Italy. *I shou'd be sorry however to incurr the Aspersion of an unmannerly Contemner of Favours, which tho' I do not* desire, *I pretend not to* deserve. *I therefore beg you will believe that I return this, as I did your Former, only to let you see, that since I decline making any use of your Condescentions to my Advantage; I am not ungenerous enough to do so to your Prejudice, and to all Ladies deserving the regard of a Disinterested Well-wisher; shall be an*

Humble Servant, *D'Elmont*.

THE *Count* order'd one of his Servants to deliver this Letter to the Person who brought the other; but he return'd immediately with it in his Hand, and told his Lordship that he cou'd not prevail on the Fellow to take it; that he said he had business with the *Count*,

 and

and muſt needs ſee him, and was ſo Importunate, that he ſeem'd rather to *Demand*, than *Entreat* a Grant of his Requeſt. D'ELMONT was aſtoniſh'd, as well he might, but commanded he ſhould be admitted.

NOTHING cou'd be more comical than the appearance of this Fellow, he ſeem'd to be about three-ſcore Years of Age, but Time had not been the greateſt Enemy to his Face, for the Number of Scars, was far exceeding that of Wrincles, he was tall above the common Stature, but ſo lean, that, till he ſpoke, he might have been taken for one of thoſe Wretches who have paſs'd the Hands of the Anatomiſts, nor wou'd his Walk have diſſipated that Opinion, for all his Motions, as he enter'd the Chamber, had more of the Air of Clock-work, than of Nature; his Dreſs was not leſs particular; he had on a Suit of Cloaths; which might perhaps have been good in the Days of his Great Grand-father, but the Perſon who they fitted muſt have been five times larger about the Body than him who wore them; a large broad buff Belt however remedy'd that Inconvenience, and girt them cloſe about his Waſte, in which hung a Faulchion, two Daggers, and a Sword of a more than ordinary Extent; the reſt of his Equipage was a Cloak, which buttoning round his Neck fell not ſo low as his Hips, a Hat, which in rainy weather kept his Shoulders dry much better than an *Indian* Umbrella one Glove, and a formidable pair of Whiskers. As ſoon as he ſaw the *Count*, my Lord, ſaid he, with a very impudent Air, my Orders were to bring your ſelf, not a Letter from you, nor do I uſe to be employ'd in Affairs of this Nature, but to ſerve one of the richeſt and moſt beautiful Ladies in *Rome*, who I aſſure you, it will be dangerous to diſoblige. *D'elmont* ey'd him intentively all the time he ſpoke, and cou'd ſcarce, notwithſtanding his Chagreen, forbear Laughing at the Figure he made, and the manner of his Salutation. I know not, anſwer'd he, Ironically, what Employments you have been us'd to, but certainly you appear to me, one of the most unfit Persons in the World for what you now undertake, and if the Contents of the Paper you brought me, had not inform'd me of your Abilities this Way, I should never have suspected you for one of *Cupid*'s Agents: You are merry, my Lord, reply'd the other, but I must tell you, I am a Man of Family and Honour, and shall not put up an Affront; but, continued he, shaking the few Hairs which frequent Skirmishes had left upon his Head, I shall defer my own satisfaction 'till I have procur'd the Ladies; therefore, if your Lordship will prepare to follow, I shall walk before, at a perceivable Distance, and without St. *Peter*'s Key, open the Gate of Heaven. I should be apt (said the *Count*, not able to keep his Countenance at these Words) rather to take it for the other Place; but be it as it will, I have not the least Inclination to make the Experiment, therefore, you may walk as soon as you please without expecting me to accompany you. Then you absolutely refuse to go (cry'd the Fellow, clapping his Hand on his Forhead, and staring at him, as if he meant to scare him into Compliance!) Yes (answer'd the *Count*, laughing more and more) I shall neither go, nor waste any farther time or Words with you, so wou'd advise you not to be saucy, or tarry till my Anger gets the better of my Mirth, but take the Letter and be gone, and trouble me no more. The other, at these Words laid his Hand on his Sword, and was about to make some very impudent Reply, when *D'elmont*, growing weary of his Impertinence, made a Sign to his Servants, that they shou'd turn him out, which he perceiving, took up the Letter without being bid a second time, and muttering some unintelligible Curses between his Teeth, march'd out, in the same affected Strut, with which he enter'd.

THIS Adventure, tho' surprizing enough to a Person so entirely unacquainted with the Character and Behaviour of these *Bravo*'s, as *D'elmont* was, gave him but very little matter of Reflection, and it being the time for Evening Service at St. *Peter*'s, he went, according to his Custom, to hear *Vesper*'s there.

NOTHING is more Common, than for the Nobility and Gentry of *Rome*, to divert themselves with Walking, and talking to one another in the *Collonade* after Mass. and the *Count*, tho' averse to all other publick Assemblies, wou'd sometimes spend an Hour or two there.

AS he was walking there this Evening, a Lady of a very gallant Mein pass'd swiftly by him, and flurting out her Handkerchief with a careless Air, as it were by Chance, drop'd an *Agnus Dei* set round with Diamonds at his Feet, he had too much Complaisance to neglect endeavouring to overtake the Lady, and prevent the Pain he imagin'd she wou'd be in, when she shou'd miss so rich a Jewel: But she, who knew well enough what she had done, left the Walk where the Company were, and cross'd over to the Fountain, which being more retir'd was the most proper for her Design: She stood looking on the Water, in a thoughtful Posture, when the *Count* came up to her, and bowing, with an Air peculiar to himself, and which all his Chagreen could not deprive of an irresistable Power of attraction, Presented the *Agnus Dei* to her. I think my self, Madam, said he, highly indebted to Fortune, for making me the means of your recovering a Jewel, the Loss of which wou'd certainly have given you some disquiet: Oh Heavens! cry'd she, receiving it with an affected Air of Surprize, could a Trifle like this, which I knew not that I had let fall, nor perhaps shou'd have thought on more, cou'd this, and belonging to a Woman too, meet the Regard of him, who prides in his Insensibility? Him! Who has no Eyes for Beauty, nor no Heart for Love! As she spoke these Words she contriv'd to let her Vail fall back as if by Accident, and discover'd a Face, Beautiful even to Perfection! Eyes black and sparkling, a Mouth form'd to Invite, a Skin dazlingly white, thro' which

a

a most delightful Bloom diffus'd a chearful Warmth, and glow'd in amorous Blushes on her Cheeks. The *Count* could not forbear gazing on her with Admiration, and perhaps, was, for a Moment, pretty near receeding from that Insensibility she had reproach'd him with; but the Image of MELLIORA, yet unenjoy'd, all ravishingly Kind and Tender, rose presently in his Soul, fill'd all his Faculties, and left no Passage free for rival Charms. Madam, said he after a little Pause, the *Italian* Ladies take care to skreen their too dazling Lustre behind a Cloud, and, if I durst take that Liberty, have certainly reason to Tax your Accusation of Injustice; he, on whom the Sun has never vouchsafed to shine, ought not to be condemn'd for not acknowledging its brightness; yours is the first Female Face I have beheld, since my Arrival here, and it wou'd have been as ridiculous to have feign'd my self susceptible of Charms which I had never seen, as it would be Stupidity, not to confess those I now do, worthy Adoration. Well, resum'd she smiling, if not the *Lover's*, I find, you know how to Act the *Courtier's* Part, but continued she, looking languishingly on him, all you can say, will scarce make me believe, that there requires not a much brighter Sun than mine, to Thaw a certain Frozen *Resolution*, you pretend to have made. There need no more to confirm the *Count* in the Opinion he had before conceiv'd, that this was the Lady from whom he had receiv'd the two Letters that Day, and thought he had now the fairest Opportunity in the World to put an End to her Passion, by assuring her how impossible it was for him ever to return it, and was forming an Answer to that purpose; when a pretty deal of Company coming toward them, she drew her Vail over her Face, and turning hastily from him, mingled with some Ladies, who seem'd to be of her Acquaintance.

THE *Count* knew by experience, the unutterable Perturbations of Suspence, and what agonizing Tortures rend an amorous Soul, divided betwixt Hope and Fear: Despair itself is not so Cruel as Uncertainty, and in all Ills, especially in those of Love, it is less Misery to *Know*, than *Dread* the worst. The Remembrance of what he had suffer'd thus agitated, in the Beginning of his Passion for *Melliora*, made him extreamly pity the unknown Lady, and regret her sudden Departure; because it had prevented him from setting her into so much of his Circumstances, as he believ'd were necessary to induce her to recall her Heart. But when he consider'd how much he had struggled, and how far he had been from being able to repel Desire, he began to wonder that it cou'd ever enter into his Thoughts that there was even a possibility for *Woman*, so much stronger in her Fancy, and weaker in her Judgment, to suppress the Influencce of that powerful Passion; against which, no Laws, no Rules, no Force of Reason, or Philosophy, are sufficient Guard.

THESE Reflections gave no small Addition to his Melancholy; *Amena*'s Retirement from the World; *Alloüisa*'s Jealousy and Death; *Melliora*'s Peace of Mind and Reputation, and the Despair of several, whom he was sensible, the Love of him, had rendred miserable, came fresh into his Memory, and he look'd on himself as most unhappy, in being the occasion of making others so.

THE Night which succeeded this Day of Adventures, chancing to be abroad pretty late; as he was passing thro' a Street, he heard a Clashing of Swords, and going nearer to the place where the Noise was, he perceiv'd by some Lights which glimmer'd from a distant Door, a Gentleman defending himself with much Bravery against Three, who seem'd eager for his Death. *D'elmont* was mov'd to the highest Indignation at the sight of such Baseness; and drawing his Sword, flew furiously on the Assassins, just as one of them was about to run his Sword into the Breast of the Gentleman; who, by the breaking of his own Blade, was left unarm'd. *Turn Villain*, cry'd D'elmont, *or while you are acting that Inhumaniy, receive the just Reward of it from me.* The Ruffian fac'd about immediately, and made a Pass at him, while one of his Comrades did the same on the other side; and the third was going to excute on the Gentleman, what his fellows Surprize had made him leave undone: But he now gain'd Time to pull a Pistol out of his Pocket, with which he shot him in a Moment dead, and snatching his Sword from him as he fell, ran to assist the *Count,* who 'tis likely wou'd have stood in need of it, being engag'd with two, and those the most desparate sort of *Bravo*'s, Villains that make a Trade of Death. But the Noise of the Pistol made them apprehensive there was a farther Rescue, and put 'em to flight. The Gentleman seem'd agitated with a more than ordinary Fury; and instead of staying to Thank the *Count,* or enquire how he had escap'd, ran in pursuit of those who had assaulted him, so swiftly, that it was in vain for the *Count,* not being well acquainted with the Turnings of the Streets, to attempt to follow him, if he had a Mind to it: But seeing there was a Man kill'd, and not knowing either the Persons who fought, or the occasion of their Quarrel, he rightly judg'd, that being a Stranger in the place, his Word wou'd not be very readily taken in his own Vindication; therefore thought his wisest Course wou'd be to make off, with what Speed he cou'd, to his Lodging. While he was considering, he saw something on the Ground which glitter'd extreamly; and taking it up, found that it was part of the Sword which the assaulted Gentleman had the Misfortune to have broke: The Hilt was of a fine Piece of Agate, set round on the Top with Diamonds, which made him believe the Person whom he had preserv'd, was of considerable Quality, as well as Bravery.

HE had not gone many Paces from the place where the Skirmish happened, before a Cry of Murder met his Ears, and a great Concourse of People his Eyes: He had receiv'd two or three slight Wounds, which, tho' not much more than Skin-deep, had made his Linnen bloody, and he knew wou'd be ſufficient to make him be apprehended, if he were ſeen, which it was very difficult to avoid: He was in a narrow Street, which had no Turning, and the Crowd was very near him, when looking round him with a good deal of Vexation in his Thoughts, he diſcern'd a Wall, which in one part of it ſeem'd pretty low: He preſently reſolv'd to climb it, and truſt to Fortune for what might befall him on the other ſide, rather than ſtay to be expos'd to the Inſults of the Outrageous Mob; who, ignorant of his Quality, and looking no farther than the outſide of Things, wou'd doubtleſs have conſider'd him no otherwiſe, than a Midnight *Rioter*.

WHEN he was got over the Wall, he found himſelf in a very fine Garden, adorn'd with Fountains, Statues, Groves, and every Ornament, that Art, or Nature, cou'd produce, for the Delight of the Owner At the upper End there was a Summer-houſe, into which he went, deſigning to ſtay 'till the Search was over.

BUT He had not been many Moments in his Concealment before he ſaw a Door open from the Houſe, and two Women come out; they walk'd directly up to the place where he was; he made no doubt but that they deſign'd to enter, and retir'd into the fartheſt Corner of it: As they came pretty near, he found they were earneſt in Diſcourſe, but cou'd underſtand nothing of what they ſaid, 'till ſhe, who ſeem'd to be the Chief, raiſing her Voice a little higher than ſhe had done: Talk no more, *Brione* ſaid ſhe, if e're thy Eyes are Bleſt to ſee this Charmer of my Soul, thou wil't ceaſe to wonder at my Paſſion; great as it is, 'tis wanting of his Merit.---- Oh! He is more than Raptur'd Poets feign, or Fancy can invent! Suppoſe Him ſo, *(cry'd the other,)* yet ſtill he wants that Charm which ſhou'd Endear the others to you --- Softneſs, --- Heavens! To Return your Letters! To Inſult your Meſſenger! To ſlight ſuch Favours as any Man of Soul wou'd die to obtain!

obtain! Methinks such Usage shou'd make him odious to you, --- even I shou'd scorn so spiritless a Wretch. Peace, thou Prophaner, *said the Lady in an angry Tone*, such Blasphemy deserves a Stab ---- But thou hast never heard his Voice, nor seen his Eyes, and I forgive Thee. Have you then spoke to him, *interupted the Confidant*, Yes, *answer'd the Lady*, and by that Conversation, am more undone than ever; it was to tell thee this Adventure, I came to Night into this agreeable Solitude. With these Words they came into the Summer-house, and the Lady seating her self on a Bench; Thou know'st, *resum'd she*, I went this Evening to Saint *Peter's*, there I saw the glorious Man; saw him in all his Charms; and while I bow'd my Knee, in show to Heaven, my Soul was prostrate only to him. When the Ceremony was over, perceiving he stay'd in the *Collonade*, I had no power to leave it, but stood, regardless who observ'd me, gazing on him with Transports, which only those who Love like me, can guess! --- God! With what an Air he walk'd! What new Attractions dwelt in every Motion --- And when he return'd the Salutes of any that pass'd by him, how graceful was his Bow! How lofty his Mein, and yet, how affable! ---- A sort of an inexpressible awful Grandeur, blended with tender Languishments, strikes the amaz'd Beholder at once with Fear and Joy! --- Something beyond Humanity shines round him! Such looks descending Angels wear, when sent on Heavenly Embassies to some Favourite Mortal! Such is their Form! Such Radient Beams they dart; and with such Smiles they temper their Divinity with Softness! --- Oh! With what Pain did I restrain my self from flying to him! from rushing into his Arms! From hanging on his Neck, and wildly uttering all the furious Wishes of my burning Soul! ----- I trembled ------ panted ---- rag'd with inward Agonies. Nor was all the Reason I cou'd muster up, sufficient to bear me from his Sight, without having first spoke to him. To that end I ventur'd to pass by him, and drop'd an *Agnus*

Dei at his Feet, believing that wou'd give him an Occ ſion of following me, which he did immediately, and returning it to me, diſcover'd a new Hoard of unimagin'd Charms ---- All my fond Soul confeſs'd before of his Perfections, were mean to what I now beheld! Had'ſt thou but ſeen how he approach'd me -- with what an awful Reverence --- with what a ſoft beſeeching, yet commanding Air, he kiſs'd the happy Trifle, as he gave it me, thou would'ſt have envy'd it as well as I! At laſt he ſpoke, and with an Accent ſo Divine, that if the ſweeteſt Muſick were compar'd to the more Celeſtial Harmony of his Voice, it wou'd only ſerve to prove how vaſtly *Nature* do's excell all *Art*. But, Madam, *cry'd the other*, I am impatient to know the End of this Affair; for I preſume you diſcover'd to him both what, and who you were? My Face only, reply'd the Lady, for e're I had opportunity to do more, that malicious Trifler, *Viollетta*, perhaps envious of my Happineſs, came toward us with a Crowd of Impertinents at her Heels. Curſe on the Interruption, and broke off our Converſation, juſt at that Bleſt, but Irrecoverable Moment, when I perceiv'd in my Charming Conqueror's Eyes, a growing Tenderneſs, ſufficient to encourage me to reveal my own. Yes, *Brione*, thoſe lovely Eyes, while fix'd on mine, ſhone, with a Luſtre, uncommon, even to themſelves --- A livelier Warmth o'reſpread his Cheeks ---- Pleaſure ſat ſmiling on his Lips ---- thoſe Lips, my Girl, which even when they are ſilent, ſpeak; but when unclos'd, and the ſweet Gales of balmy Breath blow on you, he kills you in a Sigh; each hurry'd Senſe is raviſh'd and your Soul glows with Wonder and Delight. Oh! To be forc'd to leave him in this Criſis, when new-deſire began to dawn; when Love its moſt lively Symptoms was apparent, and ſeem'd to promiſe all my Wiſhes covet, what Separation ever was ſo cruel? Compoſe your ſelf, dear Madam, ſaid *Brione*, if he be really in Love; as who ſo Inſenſible as not to be ſo, that once has ſeen your Charms?

Charms? That *Love* will teach him ſpeedily to find out an opportunity as favourable as that which you have lately miſs'd; or if he ſhou'd want Contrivance to procure his own Happineſs, 'tis but your writing to appoint a Meeting. He muſt --- He ſhall be mine! Cry'd the Lady in a Rapture, My Love, fierce as it was before, from Hope receives Addition to its Fury; I rave--- I burn --- I am mad with wild Deſires--- I die, *Brione*, if I not poſſeſs him. In ſpeaking theſe Words, ſhe threw her ſelf down on a Carpet which was ſpread upon the Floor; and after ſighing two or three times, continued to diſcover the Violence of her impatient Paſſion in this manner: Oh that this Night, ſaid ſhe, were paſt, --- the Bliſſful Expectation of to morrows Joys, and the diſtracting Doubts of Diſappointment, ſwell my unequal beating Heart by turns, and rack me with Viciſſitudes of Pain ----- I cannot live and bear it ---- ſoon as the Morning breaks, I'll know my Doom ---- I'll ſend to him ---- but 'tis an Age till then ---- Oh that I cou'd ſleep --- Sleep might perhaps anticipate the Bleſſing, and bring him in Idea to my Arms ---- but 'tis in vain to hope one Moment's cool Serenity in Love like mine -- my anxious Thoughts hurry my Senſes in Eternal Watchings! --- Oh *D'elmont! D'elmont!* Tranquill, Cold, and Calm *D'elmont!* Little doeſt thou gueſs the Tempeſt thou haſt rais'd within my Soul, nor know'ſt to pity theſe conſuming Fires!

THE *Count* liſt'ned to all this Diſcourſe with a World of Uneaſineſs and Impatience; and tho' at the firſt he fancy'd he remember'd the Voice, and had Reaſon enough from the beginning, eſpecially when the *Agnus Dei* was mention'd, to believe it cou'd be no other than himſelf, whom the Lady had ſo paſſionately deſcrib'd; yet he had not Confidence to appear till ſhe had nam'd him; but then, no conſideration was of force to make him neglect this opportunity of undeceiving her; his good Senſe, as well as good Nature, kept him from that Vanity, too many of his Sex imitate

tate the weaker in, of being pleas'd that it was in his Power to create Pains, which it was not in his Power, so devoted as he was, to Ease.

HE stept from his Retirement as softly as he cou'd, because he was loath to alarm them with any Noise, 'till they shou'd discover who it was that made it, which they might easily do, in his advancing toward them never so little, that part of the Bower being much lighter than that where he had stood; but with his over-caution in sliding his Feet along, to prevent being heard, one of them tangled in the Corner of the Carpet, which happened not to lie very smooth, and not being sensible presently what it was that Embarrass'd him: He fell with part of his Body cross the Lady, and his Head in *Brione*'s Lap, who was sitting on the Ground by her. The Manner of his Fall was lucky enough, for it hinder'd either of them from rising, and running to alarm the Family, as certainly in such a fright they wou'd have done, if his Weight had not detain'd them; they both gave a great Shriek, but the House being at a good distance, they cou'd not easily be heard; and he immediately recovering himself, beg'd Pardon for the Terror he had occasion'd them; and addressing to the Lady, who at first was dying with her Fears, and now with Consternation: *D'elmont*, Madam, said he, cou'd not have had the Assurance to appear before you, after hearing those undeserv'd Praises your Excess of Goodness has been pleas'd to bestow upon him, but that his Soul wou'd have reproach'd him of the highest Ingratitude, in permitting you to continue longer in an Error, which may involve you in the greatest of Misfortunes, at least I am ---- As he was speaking, three or four Servants with Lights came running from the House; and the Lady, tho' in more Confusion than can be well exprest, had yet Presence of Mind enough to bid the *Count* retire to the place where he had stood before, while she and *Brione* went out of the Summer-house to learn the Cause of this

In-

Interruption: Madam, cry'd one of the Servants, as ſoon as he ſaw her, the Officers of Juſtice are within; who being rais'd by an Alarm of Murther, come to beg your Ladyſhips Permiſſion to ſearch your Garden, being, as they ſay, inform'd that the Offender made his Eſcape over this Wall. 'Tis very improbable, reply'd the Lady, for I have been here a conſiderable Time, and have neither heard the leaſt Noiſe, nor ſeen any Body: However they may ſearch, and ſatisfy themſelves ---- go you, and tell them ſo. Then turning to the *Count*, when ſhe had diſmiſs'd her Servants; My Lord, ſaid ſhe Trembling, I know not what ſtrange Adventure brought you here to Night, or whether you are the Perſon for whom the Search is made; but am ſenſible, if you are found here, it will be equally injurious to your Safety, and my Reputation; I have a Back-door, thro' which you may paſs in Security: But, if you have Honour, (continu'd ſhe) Sighing, Gratitude, or good Nature, you will let me ſee you to morrow Night. Madam, (reply'd he,) aſſure your ſelf that there are not many things I more earneſtly deſire than an opportunity to convince you, how ſenſibly I am touch'd with your Favours, and how much I regret my want of Power to --- you, (interrupted ſhe,) can want nothing but the *Will* to make me the happieſt of my Sex --- but this is no Time for you to *Give*, or me to *Receive* any Proofs of that Return which I expect ---- Once more I conjure you to be here to morrow Night at Twelve, where the Faithful *Brione* ſhall attend to admit you. Farewell --- be punctual and ſincere -- 'Tis all I ask --- when I am not, (anſwer'd he,) may all my Hopes forſake me. By this time they were come to the Door, which *Brione*, opening ſoftly, let him out, and ſhut it again immediately.

THE *Count* took care to Remark the place that he might know it again, reſolving nothing more than to make good his Promiſe at the appointed Hour, but

cou'd

cou'd not help being extreamly troubled, when he consider'd how unwelcome his Sincerity wou'd be, and the Confusion he must give the Lady, when instead of those Raptures the Violence of her mistaken Passion made her hope, she shou'd meet with only cold Civility, and the killing History of the Pre-engagement of his Heart. In these and the like melancholly Reflections he spent the Night; and when Morning came, receiv'd the severest Augmentation of them, which Fate cou'd load him with.

IT was scarce full Day when a Servant came into his Chamber to acquaint him, that a young Gentleman, a Stranger, desir'd to be admitted, and seem'd so impatient till he was, That, said the Fellow, not knowing of what Consequence his Business may be, I thought it better to Risque your Lordship's Displeasure for this early Disturbance, than by dismissing him, fill you with an unsatisfy'd Curiosity. The *Count* was far from being Angry, and commanded that the Gentleman should be brought up, which Order being immediately obey'd, and the Servant withdrawn out of Respect: Putting his Head out of the Bed, he was surpriz'd with the Appearance of one of the most beautiful *Chevaliers* he had ever beheld, and in whose Face, he imagin'd he trac'd some Features not Unknown to him. Pardon, me Sir, said he, throwing the Curtains more back than they were before, that I receive the Honour you do me, in this manner --- but being ignorant of your Name, Quality, the Reason of your desire to see me, or any thing but your Impatience to do so, in gratifying that, I fear, I have injur'd the Respect. which I believe, is due, and which, I am sure, my Heart is inclinable to pay to you. Visits, like mine, reply'd the Stranger, require but little Ceremony, and I shall easily remit that Respect you talk of, while I am unknown to you, provided you will give me one Mark of it, that I shall ask of you, when you do. There are very few, reply'd *D'elmont,*

D'elmont, that I cou'd refuſe to one, whoſe Aſpect Promiſes to deſerve ſo many. Firſt then, cry'd the other pretty warmly, I demand a Siſter of you, and not only her, but a Reparation of her Honour, which can be done no otherwiſe than by your Blood. It is impoſſible to repreſent the *Count*'s aſtoniſhment at theſe Words, but conſcious of his Innocence in any ſuch Affair: I ſhou'd be ſorry *Seignior*, ſaid he cooly, that Precipitation ſhould hurry you to do any Action you wou'd afterwards Repent; you muſt certainly be miſtaken in the Perſon to whom you are talking -- Yet, if I were raſh like you, what fatal Conſequences might enſue; but there is ſomething in your Countenance which engages me to wiſh a more friendly Interview than what you ſpeak of: Therefore wou'd perſuade you to conſider calmly, and you will ſoon find, and acknowledge your Miſtake; and, to further that Reflection, I aſſure you, that I am ſo far from Converſing with any Lady, in the Manner you ſeem to hint, that I ſcarcely know the Name, or Face of any one. --- Nay, more, I give you my Word, to which I joyn my Honour, that, as I never *have*, I never *will* make the leaſt Pretenſions of that kind to any Woman during the Time of my Reſidence here. This poor Evaſion, reply'd the Stranger with a Countenance all inflam'd, ill ſuits a Man of Honour. --- This is no *Roman*, no, *Italian Bono-Roba*, who I mean ---- but *French* like you ---- like both of us. ---- And if your Ingratitude had not made it neceſſary for your Peace, to erace all Memory of *Monſieur Frankville*, you wou'd before now, by the near reſemblance I bear to him, have known me for his Son, and that 'tis *Melliora*'s --- the fond --- the loſt --- the ruin'd *Melliora*'s Cauſe which calls for Vengeance from her Brother's Arm! Never was any Soul agitated with more violent Emotions, than that of Count *D'elmont* at theſe Words. Doubt, Grief, Reſentment, and Amazement, made ſuch a Confuſion in his Thoughts, that he was unable for ſome Moments to anſwer this cruel Accuſation; and when he did, the Brother of

Melliora

Melliora ſaid he with a deep Sigh, wou'd certainly have been, next to her ſelf, the moſt welcome Perſon upon Earth to me; and my Joy to have Embrac'd him as the deareſt of my Friends, at leaſt have equall'd the Surprize I am in, to find him without Cauſe, my Enemy.--- But, Sir, if ſuch a Favour may be granted to an unwilling Foe, I wou'd deſire to know, Why you joyn *Ruin* to your Siſters Name? Oh! Give me Patience Heaven, cry'd young *Frankville* more enrag'd; is this a Queſtion fit for you to ask, or me to Anſwer? Is not her Honour Tainted --- Fame betray'd. --- Her ſelf a Vagabond, and her Houſe abus'd, and all by you; the unfaithful Guardian of her injur'd Innocence? --- And can you ask the Cauſe? --- No, rather riſe this Moment, and if you are a Man, who dare maintain the ill you have done, defend it with your Sword not with vain Words and Womaniſh Excuſes: All the other Paſſions which had warr'd within *D'elmont's* Breaſt, now gave way to Indignation: Raſh young Man, ſaid he, jumping haſtily out of the Bed, and beginning to put his Cloaths on: Your Father wou'd no[t] thus have us'd me; nor, did he Live, cou'd blame me for vindicating as I ought my wounded Honour --- That I do Love your Siſter, is as True, as that you hav[e] wrong'd me --- Baſely wrong'd me. But that he[r] Vir[tu]e ſuffers by that Love, is falſe! And I muſt writ[e] the Man that ſpeaks it, *Lyar*, tho' in her Brother' Heart. Many other violent Expreſſions to the ſam[e] Effect, paſs'd between them, while the *Count* wa[s] dreſſing himſelf, for he wou'd ſuffer no Servan[t] to come in, to be Witneſs of his Diſorder. But th[e] ſteady Reſolution with which he had atteſted his In-nocence, and that inexpreſſible ſweetneſs of Deport-ment, equally Charming to both Sexes, and whic[h] not even *Anger* cou'd render leſs graceful, extreaml[y] cool'd the Heat *Frankville* had been in a little befor[e] and he in ſecret, began to recede very much fron[m] the ill Opinion he had conceiv'd, tho' the greatneſs o[f] his Spirit kept him from acknowledging he had bee[n] in an Error; 'till chancing to caſt his Eyes on a Table which ſtood in the Chamber, he ſaw the hilt of the broken Sword which *D'elmont* had brought home the Night before, lying on it; he took it up, and having firſt look'd on it with ſome Confuſion in his Countenance. My Lord, ſaid he, turning to the *Count*, I conjure you, before we proceed further, to acquaint me truely, how this came into your Poſſeſſion, Tho' *D'elmont* had as great a Courage, when any laudable Occaſion appear'd to call it forth, as any Man that ever liv'd, yet his natural Diſpoſition had ſuch an uncommon Sweetneſs in it, as no Provocation cou'd ſowre; it was always a much greater Pleaſure to him to *Forgive* than *Puniſh* Injuries; and if at any time he was *Angry*, he was never *Rude*, or *Unjuſt*. The little ſtarts of Paſſion, *Frankville*'s raſh Behaviour had occaſion'd, all diſſolv'd in his more accuſtomary Softneſs, when he perceiv'd the other growing Calm. And anſwering to his Queſtion, with the moſt obliging Accent in the World: It was my good Fortune, (ſaid he) to be inſtrumental laſt Night, in the Reſcue of a Gentleman who appear'd to have much Bravery, and being Attack'd by odds, behav'd himſelf in ſuch a Manner, as wou'd have made him ſtand but little in need of my Aſſiſtance, if his Sword had been equal to the Arm which held it; but the breaking of that, gave me the Glory of not being unſerviceable to him. After the Skirmiſh was over, I took it up, hoping it might be the means ſometime or other of my diſcovering who the Perſon was, who wore it; not out of Vanity of receiving Thanks for the little I have done, but that I ſhou'd be glad of the Friendſhip of a Perſon, who ſeems ſo worthy my Eſteem. Oh far! (cry'd *Frankville*, with a Tone and Geſture quite alter'd,) infinitely far from it -- It was my ſelf whom you preſerv'd; that very Man whoſe Life you but laſt Night ſo generouſly redeem'd, with the hazard of your own, comes now prepar'd to make the firſt uſe of it againſt you --- Is it poſſible that you can be ſo heavenly good to Pardon my wild Paſſions Heat? Let

this

this be witness, with what Joy I do, answer'd the *Count*, tenderly Embracing him, which the other eagerly returning; they continu'd lock'd in each others Arms for a considerable Time, neither of them being able to say more, than --- And was it *Frankville* I Preserv'd! --- And was it to *D'elmont* I owe my Life!

AFTER this mutual Demonstration of a perfect Reconcilement was over: See here, my Lord, said *Frankville*, giving a Paper to the *Count*, the occasion of my Rashness, and let my just concern for a Sisters Honour, be at least some little Mittigation of my Temerity, in accosting your Lordship in so rude a Manner. *D'elmont* made no Answer, but looking hastily over the Paper found it contain'd these Words.

To Monsieur FRANKVILLE.

WHILE your Sisters Dishonour was known but to few, and the injurious Destroyer of it, out of the reach of your Revenge; I thought it would ill become the Friendship I have always profess'd to your Family, to disquiet you with the Knowledge of a Misfortune, which it was no way in your Power to Redress.

BUT Count D'elmont, *having by the Solicitation of his Friends, and the remembrance of some slight Services, obtain'd a Pardon from the KING, for the Murder of his Wife; has since taken but little care to conceal the Reasons which induc'd him to that barbarous Action; and all* Paris *is now sensible that he made that unhappy Lady's Life a Sacrifice to the more attractive Beautie*

Beauties of Melliora, *in bloody Recompence for the Sacrifice she had before made him of her Virtue.*

IN short, the Noble Family of the Frankvilles *is for ever dishonour'd by this Unfaithful* Guardian; *and all who wish you well, rejoice to hear that his ill Genius has led him to a place which, if he knew you were at, certainly Prudence wou'd make him of all others most avoid; for none believes you will so far degenerate from the Spirit of your Ancestors, as to permit him to go unpunish'd.*

IN finding the Count, *you may probably find your Sister too; for tho', after the Death of* Alovisa, *shame made her retire to a Monastry, she has since privately left it without acquainting the* Abbess, *or any of the Sisterhood, with her Departure; nor is it known to any one, where, or for what Cause she absconds; but most People imagine, as indeed it is highly reasonable, that the Violence of her guilty Passion for* D'elmont *has engag'd her to follow him.*

I am not unsensible how much I shock your Temper by this Relation, but have too much real concern for your Honour, to endure you shou'd, thro' Ignorance of your Wrongs, remain Passive in such a Cause, and perhaps hug the Treacherous Friend in your most strict Embrace? Nor can I forbear, tho' I love not Blood, urging you to take that just Revenge, which next to Heaven you have the greatest Claim to.

I am, Sir, with all due Respect,

Yours, *Sanseverin.*

THE *Count* swell'd with Indignation at every Paragraph of this malicious Letter; but when he came to that, which mention'd *Melliora's* having withdrawn her self from the Monastry, he seem'd to be wholly abandon'd by his Reason; all Endeavours to represent his Agonies

Agonies wou'd be vain, and none but those who have felt the same, can have any Notion of what he suffer'd. He read the fatal Scroll again and again, and every time grew wilder than before; he stamp'd, bit his Lips, look'd furiously about him, then, starting from the place where he had stood, measur'd the Room in strange, disorder'd, and unequal Paces; all his Motions, all his Looks, all his Air were nothing but Distraction: He spoke not for some time, one Word, either prevented by the rising Passions in his Soul, or because it was not in the Power of Language to express the greatness of his Meaning; and when, at last, he open'd his Mouth, it was but to utter half Sentences, and broken Complainings: Is it possible, he cry'd, ---- gone, --- left the Monastry unknown --- and then again ---- false ---- false Woman? ---- Wretched --- wretched Man! There's no such Thing on Earth as Faith --- is this the Effect of all her tender Passion? -- So soon forgot --- what can be her Reason? --- This Action suits not with her Words, or Letters. In this manner he rav'd with a Thousand such like Breathings of a tormented Spirit, toss'd and confounded between various Sentiments.

Monsieur *Frankville* stood for a good while silently observing him; and if before, he were not perfectly assur'd of his Innocence, the Agonies he now saw him in, which were too natural to be suspected for Counterfeit, entirely convinc'd him he was so. When the first gust of Passion was blown over, and he perceiv'd any likelyhood of being heard, he said a Thousand tender and obliging Things to perswade him to Moderation, but to very little Effect, till finding, that that which gave him the most stinging Reflection was, the Belief that *Melliora* had forsook the Monastry, either because she thought of him no more, and was willing to divert her enfranchis'd Inclination with the Gaieties of the Town or that some happier Man had supplanted him in her Esteem. Judge not, my Lord, (said

(said he) so rashly of my Sister's Fidelity, nor know so little of your own unmatch'd Perfections, as to suspect that she, who is Blest with your Affection, can consider any other Object as worthy her Regard: For my part, since your Lordship *knows*, and I firmly *believe*, that this Letter contains a great many Untruths, I see no Reason why we should not imagine it all of a piece: I declare I think it much more improbable that she should leave the Monastry, unless sollicited thereto by you, than that she had the Power to deny you any thing your Passion might request. The *Count's* Disorder visibly abated at this Remonstrance; and stepping hastily to his Cabinet, he took out the last Letter he receiv'd from *Melliora*, and found it was dated but two Days before that from Monsieur *Sanseverin*; he knew she had not Art, nor was accustom'd to endeavour to disguise her Sentiments; and she had written so many tender things in that, as when he gave himself leave to consider, he could not, without believing her to be either the most Dissembling, or most fickle of her Sex, continue in the Opinion which had made him, a few Moments before, so uneasy, that she was no longer, what she always subscrib'd her self, *Entirely His*.

THE Tempest of Rage and Grief being hush'd to a little more Tranquillity, Count *D'elmont*, to remove all Scruples which might be *yet* remaining in the Breast of Monsieur *Frankville*, entertain'd him with the whole History of his Adventures, from the Time of his Gallantry with *Amena*, to the Misfortunes which had induc'd him to Travel, disguising nothing of the Truth, but some part of the Discourses which had pass'd between him and *Melliora* that Night when he surpriz'd her in her Bed, and in the Wilderness: For tho' he freely confess'd the Violence of his own unbounded Passion, had hurry'd him beyond all Considerations but those of gratifying it; yet he was too tender of *Melliora*'s Honour, to relate any thing of her, which

which her Modesty might not acknowledge, without the Expence of a Blush.

Frankville list'ned with abundance of Attention to the Relation he made him, and could find very little in his Conduct to accuse: He was himself too much susceptible of the Power of Love, not to have Compassion for those that suffer'd by it, and had too great a share of good Sense not to know that, that Passion is not to be Circumscrib'd; and being not only, not *Subservient*, but absolutely *Controller* of the *Will*, it it would be meer Madness, as well as ill Nature, to say a Person was Blame-worthy for what was unavoidable.

WHEN Love once becomes in our Power, it ceases to be worthy of that Name; no Man really possest with it, *can* be Master of his Actions; and whatever Effects it may Enforce, are no more to be Condemn'd, than Poverty, Sickness, Deformity, or any other Misfortune incident to Humane Nature. Methinks there is nothing more absur'd than the Notions of some People, who in other Things are wise enough too; but wanting Elegance of Thought, Delicacy, or Tenderness of Soul, to receive the Impression of that harmonious Passion, look on those to be mad, who have any Sentiments elevated above their own, and either Censure, or Laugh, at what they are not refin'd enough to comprehend. These *Insipids*, who know nothing of the Matter, tell us very gravely, that we *ought* to Love with Moderation and Discretion, --- and take Care that it is for our Interest,-- that we should never place our Affections, but where Duty leads, or at least, where neither Religion, Reputation, or Law, may be a Hindrance to our Wishes --- Wretches! We know all this, as well as they; we know too, that we both do, and leave undone many other Things, which we ought not; but Perfection is not to be expected on this side the Grave: And since 'tis impossible for Humanity to avoid Frail-

ties

ties of some kind or other, those are certainly least blamable, which spring only from a too great Affluence of the nobler Spirits. *Covetousness*, *Envy*, *Pride*, *Revenge*, are the Effects of an Earthly, Base, and Sordid Nature, *Ambition*, and *Love*, of an Exalted one; and if they are Failings, they are such as plead their own Excuse, and can never want Forgiveness from a generous Heart, provided no indirect Courses are taken to procure the Ends of the *former*, nor Inconstancy, or Ingratitude, stain the Beauty of the *latter*.

NOTWITHSTANDING all that Monsieur *Frankville* could say, the *Count*, tho' not in the Rage of Temper he had been in, was yet very melancholly; which the other perceiving, Alas, my Lord, said he Sighing, if you were sensible of the Misfortunes of others, you would think your own more easy to be born: You Love, and are Belov'd; no Obstacle remains between you and your Desires; but the Formality of Custom, which a little time will Remove, and at your return to *Paris* you will doubtless be happy, if 'tis in my Sister's Power to make you so: You have a sure Prospect of Felicity to *come*, but mine is *past*, never, I fear, to be retriev'd. What mean you? Cry'd the *Count* pretty much surpriz'd at his Words, and the Change which he observ'd in his Countenance; I am in Love! Reply'd He, Belov'd! Nay, have Enjoy'd---- Ay, there's the Source of my Despair ---- I know the Heaven I have lost, and that's my Hell. ---- The Interest *D'elmont* had in his Concerns, as being Son to the Man whom he had loved with a kind of filial Affection, and Brother to the Woman whom he ador'd above the World, made him extreamly desirous to know what the Occasion of his Disquiet was, and having exprest himself to that purpose; I shall make no Difficulty, reply'd *Frankville*, to reveal the Secret of my Love, to him who is a Lover, and knows so well, how to pity, and forgive, the Errors which that Passion will sometimes lead us into. The *Count* was too impatient to hear the Relation he was about to give him, to make any other Anſwer to theſe Words than with a half Smile; which the other perceiving, without any farther Prelude, began to ſatisfy his Curioſity in this manner.

The Hiſtory of Monſieur FRANKVILLE.

YOU know, my Lord, ſaid he, that I was bred at *Rheims* with my Uncle, the Biſhop of that Place, and continu'd with him,' till after, prompted by Glory, and hope of that Renown you have ſince ſo gallantly acquir'd; you left the Pleaſures of the *Court* for the Fatigues aud Dangers of the Field: When I came home, I never ceas'd ſolliciting my Father to permit me to Travel, 'till weary'd with my continual Importunies, and perhaps, not much diſpleas'd with my Thirſt of Improvement, he at laſt gave leave. I left *Paris* a little before the Concluſion of the Peace, and by that means remain'd wholly a Stranger to your Lordſhip's Perſon, tho' perfectly acquainted with thoſe admirable Accompliſhments which Fame is every where ſo full of.

I HAVE been in the Courts of *England, Spain,* and *Portugal,* but nothing very material hapning to me in any of thoſe Places, it would be rather Impertinent than Diverting, to defer, for Trifles, the main Buſineſs of my Life, that of my Love, which had not a Being 'till I came into this City.

I HAD been here but a little Time before I had a great many Acquaintance, among the Number of them was Seignior *Jaques Honorius Cittolini*: He, of all th reſt, I was moſt intimate with; and tho' to the Generality of People he behav'd himſelf with an Air o Imperiouſneſs, he was to me, all free, and eaſy; h ſeem'd as if he took a Pleaſure in Obliging me; carry'd me every where with him; introduc'd me to the beſ Company: When I was abſent he ſpoke of me, as o a Perſon who he had the higheſt Eſteem for; and when I was preſent, if there were any in Company whoſe rank oblig'd him to place them above me in the *Room*; he took care to teſtify that I was not below them in his *Reſpect*; in fine, he was never more happy than when he was giving me ſome Proof how much he was my Friend; and I was not a little ſatisfy'd that a Man of almoſt twice my Years ſhould believe me qualify'd for his Companion in ſuch a manner as he made me.

WHEN the melancholly Account of my Fathers Death came to my Ears, he omitted nothing to perſuade me to ſell my Eſtate in *France*, and ſettle in *Rome*; he told me he had a Daughter, whoſe Heart had been the aim of the chiefeſt Nobility; but that he wou'd buy my Company at that Price and to keep me here, wou'd give me her. This Propoſition was not altogether ſo pleaſing to me, as perhaps, he imagin'd it wou'd be: I had heard much Talk of this Lady's Beauty, but I had never ſeen her; and at that Time, Love was little in my Thoughts, eſpecially that ſort which was to end in Marriage. However, I wou'd not abſolutely refuſe his Offer, but evaded it, which I had the better pretence for, becauſe *Violleta*, (ſo was his Daughter call'd) was gone to *Vitterbo* to Viſit a ſick Relation, and I cou'd not have the opportunity of ſeeing her. In the mean time, he made me acquainted with his deepeſt Secrets; among many other Things he told me, that tho' their Family was one of the greateſt in *Rome*, yet by the too great Liberality of his Father, himſelf and one Siſter was left with very little to Support the Grandeur of their Birth; but that his Siſter who was acknowledg'd a Woman of an uncommon Beauty, had the good Fortune to appear ſo, to Seignior *Marcarius Fialaſco*: he was the poſſeſſor of immenſe Riches, but very Old; but the young Lady found Charms enough in his Wealth to ballance all other Deficiencies. She Married, and Buried him in a Month's Time, and he dy'd ſo full of fondneſs to his lovely Bride, that he left her Miſtreſs of all he had in the

World; giving only to a Daughter he had by a former Wife, the Fortune which her Mother had brought him, and that too, and herself to be dispos'd of, in Marriage, as this Triumphant Widow should think fit; and she, like a kind Sister, thought none worthy of that Alliance, but her Brother; and in a few Days he said, he did not doubt but that I shou'd see him a Bridegroom. I ask'd him if he was happy enogh to have made an Interest in the young Lady's Heart; and he very frankly answer'd, That he was not of a Humour to give himself much uneasiness about it, since it was wholly in his Sister's Power to make him Master of her Person, and she resolv'd to do that, or Confine her in a Monastry for ever. I cou'd not help feeling a Compassionate concern for this Lady, tho' she was a Stranger to me, for I cou'd not believe, so Beautifu and accomplish'd a Woman, as he had often describ'c her to be, cou'd find any thing in her design'd Hus band which cou'd make this Match agreeable. No thing can be more different from Graceful, than th Person of *Cittolini*; he is of a black swarthy Complexior hook'd-Nos'd, wall Ey'd, short of Stature; and the he is very Lean, the worst shap'd Man I ever saw then for his Temper, as friendly as he behav'd to m I discern'd a great deal of Treachery, and Baseness i it to others; a perpetual peevishness and Pride appear in his Deportment to all those who had any depe dance on him: And I had been told by some wl knew him perfectly well, that his cruel Usage of h first Lady had been the means of her Death; but th was none of my Business, and tho' I pity'd the Lac yet my gratitude to him engag'd me to wish him Su cess in all his Undertakings. 'Till one Day, unlucl ly both for him and me, as it has since prov'd; desir'd me to Accompany him to the House of C *mara*, for so is his Sister call'd, being, willing I su pose, that I shou'd be a Witness of the extraordin State she liv'd in; and indeed, in all the Courts I h been at, I never saw any thing more Magnificent th her Apartments; the vast quantity of Plate; the Ri ness of the Furniture, and the number of Servants attending on Her, might have made her be taken rather for a Princess, than a private Woman. There was a very noble Collation, and she sit at Table with us her self, a particular Favour from an *Italian* Lady. She is by many Years younger than her Brother, and extreamly Handsome; but has, I know not what, of fierceness in her Eyes, which renders her, at least to me, a Beauty, without a Charm. After the Entertainment, *Cittolini* took me into the Gardens, which were answerable to what I had seen within, full of Curiosities; at one end there was a little Building of Marble, to which he led me, and entering into it, see here, *Monsieur*, said he, the Place where my Sister spends the greatest part of her Hours, and tell me if 'tis in this kind of Diversion that the *French* Ladies take Delight. I presently saw it was full of Books, and guess'd those Words were design'd as a Satyr on our Ladies, whose disposition to Gallantry seldom affords much time for Reading; but to make as good a Defence for their Honour as I was able. *Seignior*, reply'd I, it must be confest, that there are very few Ladies of any Nation, who think the *Acquisition* of Knowledge, worth the Pains it must cost them in the *Search*, but that ours is not without some Examples, that all are not of that Mind; our famous *D'anois*, and *D'acier* may evince. Well, Well, interrupted he laughing; the propensity which that Sex bears to Learning is so trifling, that I shall not pretend to hold any Argument on its Praise; nor did I bring you here so much to engage you to Admire my Sisters manner of Amusement, as to give you an Opportunity of diverting your self, while I go to pay a Compliment to my Mistress; who, tho' I have a very great Confidence in you, I dare not trust with the sight of so accomplish'd a *Chevalier*. With these Words he left me, and I, designing to do as he had desir'd; turn'd to the Shelves to take down what Book I cou'd find most suitable to my Humour; but good God! As I was tumbling them over, I saw thro' a Window which look'd into a Garden behind the Study; tho' both belonging to one Perſon: A Woman, or rather Angel, coming down a Walk directly oppoſite to where I was, never did I ſee in one Perſon ſuch various Perfections blended, never did any Woman wear ſo much of her Soul in her Eyes, as did this Charmer: I ſaw that moment in her Looks, all I have ſince experienc'd of her Genius, and her Humour; Wit, Judgment, good Nature and Generoſity are in her Countenance, conſpicuous as in her Actions; but to go about to make a Deſcription, were to wrong her; She has Graces ſo peculiar, that none without knowing her, can be able to conceive; and tho' nothing can be finer than her Shape, or more regular than her Features; yet thoſe, our Fancy or a *Painters* Art may Copy: There is ſomething ſo inexpreſſibly ſtriking in her Air; ſuch a delightful Mixture of awful and attractive in every little Motion, that no Imagination can come up to. But if Language is too poor to paint her Charms, how ſhall I make you ſenſible of the Effects of them on me! The Surprize --- the Love --- the Adoration which this fatal View involv'd me in, but by that which, you ſay, your ſelf felt at the firſt Sight of *Melliora*. I was, methought all Spirit, --- I beheld her with Raptures, ſuch as we imagine Souls enjoy when freed from Earth, they meet each other in the Realms of Glory; 'twas Heaven to gaze upon her: But Oh! The Bliſs was ſhort, the Envious Trees obſcur'd her Luſtre from me. --- The Moment I loſt Sight of her, I found my *Paſſion* by my *Pain*, the *Joy* was vaniſh'd, but the *Sting* remain'd --- I was ſo bury'd in Thought, that I never ſo much as ſtirr'd a Step to endeavour to diſcover which way ſhe went; tho' if I had conſider'd the Situation of the Place, it would have been eaſy for me to have known, there was a Communication between the two Gardens, and if I had gone but a few Paces out of the Study, muſt have met her; but Love had for the preſent depriv'd me of my Sences; and it but juſt enter'd into my Head that there was a Poſſibility of renewing my Happineſs, when I perceiv'd *Cittolini*

tolini returning. When he came pretty near; Dear *Frankville,* said he, pardon my Neglect of you; but I have been at *Camilla*'s Apartment, and am told she is in the lower Garden; I will but speak to her, snatch a Kiss and be with you again: He went hastily by me without staying for any Answer, and it was well he did so, for the Confusion I was in, had made me little able to reply. His Words left me no room to hope it was any other than *Camilla* I had seen, and the Treachery I was guilty of to my Friend, in but wishing to invade his Right, gave me a Remorse which I had never known before: But these Reflections lasted not long; Love generally exerts himself on these Occasions, and is never at a loss for means to remove all the Scruples that may be rais'd to oppose him. Why, said I to my self, should I be thus Tormented? She is not yet married, and 'tis almost impossible she can with Satisfaction, ever yield to be so, to him. Could I but have opportunity to Talk to her, to let her know my Passion, --- to endeavour to deliver her from the Captivity she is in, perhaps she would not condemn my Temerity: I found a great deal of Pleasure in this Thought, but I was not suffer'd to enjoy it long; *Honour* suggested to me, that *Cittolini* lov'd me, had Oblig'd me, and that to supplant him would be Base and Treacherous: But would it not be more so, cry'd the Dictates of my *Love,* to permit the Divine *Camilla* to fall a Sacrifice to one so every way undeserving of her; one who 'tis likely she abhors; one who despises her Heart, so he may but possess her Fortune to support his Pride, and her Person to gratify a Passion far unworthy of the Name of *Love*; One! who 'tis probable, when Master of the one and satiated with the other, may treat her with the utmost Inhumanity. Thus, for a time, were my Thoughts at Strife; but Love at length got the Victory, and I had so well compos'd my self before *Cittolini*'s Return that he saw nothing of the Disorder I had been in; but it was not so with him, his Countenance, at the best displeasing enough, was now the perfect

Representative of Ill Nature, Malice, and Discontent. *Camilla* had assur'd him, that nothing could be more her Aversion, and that she was resolv'd, tho' a Monastick Life was what she had no Inclination to, yet she would fly to that Shelter, to avoid his Bed. You may imagine, my Lord, I was Transported with an Excess of Joy, when he told me this; but Love taught me to dissemble it, 'till I had taken leave of him, which I made an Excuse to do, as soon as possible.

NOW all that troubled me was to find an Opportunity to declare my Passion; and, I confess, I was so dull in Contrivance, that tho' it took up all my Thoughts, none of them were to any purpose: Three or four Days I spent in fruitless Projections, the last of which I met with a new Embarrassment; *Cittolini's* Daughter was return'd, he renew'd his Desires of making me his Son, and invited me the next Evening to his House, where I was to be entertain'd with the sight of her; I could not well avoid giving him my Promise to be there, but resolv'd in my Mind to behave my self in such a manner as should make her disapprove of me. While I was thus busied in Contriving how to avoid *Violletta*, and engage *Camilla*, a Woman wrapt up very closely in her Vail came to my Lodgings, and brought me a Note, in which I found these Words.

To Monsieur FRANKVILLE.

MY *Father is resolv'd to make me Yours; and if he has your Consent, mine will not be demanded; he has Commanded me to receive you to morrow, but I have a particular Reason to desire to see you sooner; I am to pass this Night with* Camilla *at my Aunt* Ciamara's;

mara's; *there is a little Wicket that opens from the Garden, directly opposite to the Convent of St.* Francis, *if you will favour me so far as to come there at Ten a Clock to Night, and give Seven gentle Knocks at the Gate: You shall know the Cause of my Entreating this private Interview, which is of more Moment than the Life of*

Violetta.

NEVER had I been more pleasingly surpriz'd, than at the Reading these Lines; I could not imagine the Lady could have any other Reason for seeing me in private, than to confess that her Heart was pre-engag'd, and disswade me from taking the Advantage of her Father's Authority, a secret Hope too, sprung within my Soul, that my Adorable *Camilla* might be with her; and after I had dismiss'd the Woman, with an Assurance that I would attend her Lady, I spent my Time in vast Idea's of approaching Happiness 'till the appointed Hour arriv'd.

BUT how great was my Disappointment, when being admitted, I cou'd distinguish, tho' the Place was very dark, that I was receiv'd but by one, and accosted by her, in a manner very different from what I expected: I know not, *Monsieur*, said she, how you interpret this Freedom I have taken; but whatever we pretend, our Sex, of all Indignities, can the least support those done to our Beauty; I am not vain enough of mine to assure my self of making a Conquest of your Heart; and if the World should know you have *seen*, and *refus'd* me, my slighted Charms would be the Theme of *Mirth* to those whose *Envy* now they are: I therefore beg, that if I am dislik'd, none but my self may know it; when you have seen my Face, which you shall do immediately, give me your Opinion freely; and if it is not to my Advantage, make some pretence to my Father to avoid coming to our House. I protest to you, my Lord that I was so much surpriz'd at this odd kind of proceeding, that I knew not presently how to Reply, which she imagining by my Silence: Come, come, *Monsieur*, said she, I am not yet on even Terms with you, having often seen *your* Face, and you wholly a Stranger to *mine*: But when our Knowledge of each other is Mutal, I hope you will be as free in your Declaration as I have been in my Request. These Words I thought were as proper for my purpose as I cou'd wish, and drawing back a little, as she was about to lead me: Madam, said I, since you have that Advantage, methinks it were but just, you shou'd reveal what sort of Sentiments the sight of me has inspir'd, for I have too much Reason from the Knowledge of my Demerit, to fear, you have no other design in exposing your Charms, than to Triumph in the Captivating a Heart you have already doom'd to Misery; I will tell you nothing, answer'd she, of *my* Sentiments 'till I have a perfect knowledge of *yours*. As she spoke this, she gave me her Hand to conduct me out of that Place of Darkness; as we went, I had all the Concern at the apprehension of being too much approv'd of by this young Lady, as I shou'd have had for the contrary, if I had imagin'd who it was I had been talking with, for as soon as we came out of the Grotto, I saw by the light of the Moon, which shone that Night with an uncommon Lustre, the Face which in those Gardens had before so Charm'd me, and which had never since been absent from my Thoughts. What Joy, what a mixture of Extacy and Wonder, then fill'd my raptur'd Soul at this second view, I cou'd not presently trust my Eyes, or think my Happiness was real: I gaz'd, and gaz'd again, in silent Transport, for the big Bliss, surpass'd the reach of Words. What *Monsieur*, said she, observing my Confusion, are you yet Dumb, is there any thing so dreadful in the form of *Violetta*, to deprive you of your Speech? No Madam, reply'd I, 'tis not *Violetta* has that Power, but she, who unknowing that she did so, caught at first sight the Victory o're my Soul; she! for whom I have vented so many

Sighs! ſhe for whom I languiſh'd and almoſt dy'd for; while *Violetta* was at *Vitterbo:* She! The Divine *Camilla* only cou'd inſpire a Paſſion ſuch as mine! -- Oh Heavens! cry'd ſhe, and that inſtant I perceiv'd her lovely Face all crimſon'd o're with Bluſhes; is it then poſſible that you know me, have ſeen me before, and that I have been able to make any Impreſſion on you? I then told her of the Viſit I had made to *Ciamara* with *Cittolini*, and how by his leaving me in the Marble-Study, I had been bleſt with the ſight of her; and from his Friend became his Rival: I let her know the Conflicts my Honour and my Obligations to *Cittolini* had engag'd me in; the thouſand various Inventions Love had ſuggeſted to me, to obtain that Happineſs I now enjoy'd, the opportunity of declaring my ſelf her Slave; and in ſhort, conceal'd not the leaſt Thought, tending to my Paſſion, from Her. She, in requital, acquainted me, that ſhe had often ſeen me from her Window, go into the Convent of St. *Francis*, walking in the *Collonade* at St. *Peter*'s, and in ſeveral other Places, and, prompted by an extravagance of good Nature, and Generoſity, confeſs'd, that her Heart felt ſomething at thoſe Views, very prejudicial to her Repoſe: That *Cittolini*, always diſagreeable, was now grown Odious; that the Diſcourſe ſhe had heard of my intended Marriage with his Daughter, had given her an alarm impoſſible to be expreſs'd, and that, unable longer to ſupport the Pangs of undiſcover'd Paſſion, ſhe had writ to me in that Ladies Name, who ſhe knew I had never ſeen, reſolving, if I lik'd her as *Violetta*, to own her ſelf *Camilla*, if not, to go the next Day to a Monaſtry, and devote to Heaven thoſe Charms which wanted force to make a Conqueſt where alone ſhe wiſh'd they ſhou'd

I muſt leave it to your Lordſhip's imagination to conceive the wild tumultuous hurry of diſorder'd Joy which fill'd my raviſh'd Soul at this Condeſcention; for I am now as unable to deſcribe it, as I was then to thank the Dear, the tender Author of it; but what

Words

Words had not Power to do, *Looks* and *Actions* testified: I threw my self at her Feet, Embrac'd her Knees, and kiss'd the Hand she rais'd me with, with such a Fervor, as no false Love cou'd feign; while she, all softness, all divinely Kind, yielded to the pressure of my glowing Lips, and suffer'd me to take all the freedom which Honour and Modesty wou'd permit. This interview was too felicitous to be easily broken off, it was almost broad Day when we parted, and nothing but her Promise, that I shou'd be admitted the next Night, cou'd have enabled me to take leave of her.

I went away highly satisfy'd, as I had good Reason, with my Condition, and after recollecting all the tender Passages of our Conversation; I began to consider after what manner I shou'd proceed with *Cittolini:* To Visit and Address his Daughter, I thought, wou'd be Treacherous and Deceitful to the last degree; and how to come off, after the Promise I made of seeing her that Evening, I cou'd not tell; at last, since Necessity oblig'd me to one I resolv'd of, the two Evils to chuse the least, and rather to seem *Rude*, then *Base*, which I must have been, had I by counterfeiting a Desire to engage *Violetta*, left room for a possibility of creating one in her. I therefore, writ, to *Cittolini* an Excuse for not waiting on Him and his Daughter, as I had promis'd, telling him that I, on more serious Reflection found it wholly inconsistent, either with my Circumstances, or Inclinations, to think of passing all my Life in *Rome*; that I thank'd him for the Honour he intended me, but that it was my Misfortune, not to be capable of accepting it. Thus, with all the Artifice I was Master of, I endeavour'd to sweeten the bitter Pill of Refusal, but in vain; for he was so much Disgusted at it, that he visited me no more: I cannot say, I had Gratitude enough to be much concern'd at being compell'd to use him in this Fashion; for, since I had beheld, and Ador'd *Camilla*, I cou'd consider him no longer as a Friend, but as the most dangerous Enemy to my Hopes and me. All this time I ſpent the beſt part of the Nights with *Camilla*; and in one of them, after giving, and receiving a thouſand Vows of everlaſting Faith, I ſnatch'd a lucking Moment, and obtain'd from the Dear, melting Charmer, all that my Fondeſt, and moſt eager Wiſhes cou'd aſpire to. Yes, my Lord, the ſoft, the trembling Fair, diſſolv'd in Love; yielded without Reſerve, and met my Tranſports with an equal Ardor; and I truly proteſt to your Lordſhip, that what in others, *palls* Deſire, added freſh *Force* to mine; the more I knew; the more I was Inflam'd, and in the higheſt Raptures of Enjoyment, the Bliſs was daſh'd with Fears, which prov'd alas, but too Prophetick, that ſome curſt Chance might drive me from my Heaven: Therefore, to ſecure it mine for ever, I preſs'd the lovely Partner of my Joys, to give me leave to bring a Prieſt with me the next Night; who by giving a Sanction to our Love, might put it paſt the Power of Malice to Diſunite us: Here, I experienc'd the greatneſs of her Soul, and her almoſt unexampled Generoſity; for in ſpite of all her Love, her Tenderneſs, and the unbounded Condeſcentions ſhe had made me, it was with all the difficulty in the World, that I perſuaded her to think of Marrying me without a Fortune; which by her Father's *Will*, was wholly in the Diſpoſal of *Ciamara*, who it wou'd have been Madneſs to Hope, wou'd ever beſtow it upon me. However, my Arguments at laſt prevail'd; I was to bring a Fryar of the Order of St. *Francis*, who was my intimate Friend, the next Night to join our Hands; which done, ſhe told me, ſhe wou'd adviſe to leave *Rome* with what ſpeed we cou'd, for ſhe doubted not but *Cittolini* wou'd make uſe of any means, tho' never ſo baſe or Bloody, to Revenge his Diſappointment. This Propoſal infinitely pleas'd me, and after I had taken leave of her, I ſpent the remainder of the Night, in contriving the means of our Eſcape: Early in the Morning I ſecur'd Poſt-Horſes, and then went to the Convent of St. *Francis*; a Purſe of

Lewis,

Lewis D'ors ſoon engag'd the Fryar to my Intereſt, and I had every thing ready in wonderful Order, conſidering the ſhortneſs of the Time, for our Deſign: When returning Home towards Evening, as well to take a little reſt after the Fatigue I had had, as to give ſome other neceſſary Directions, concerning the Affair to my Servants, when one of them gave me a Letter, which had been juſt left for me.

Monſieur Frankville cou'd not come to this Part of his Story, without ſome Sighs, but ſuppreſſing them as well as he was able, he took ſome Papers out of his Pocket, and ſingling out one, read to the *Count* as follows.

To Monſieur FRANKVILLE.

W*ITH what Words can I repreſent the greatneſs of my Misfortune, or Exclaim againſt the Perfidy of my Woman? I was oblig'd to make her the Confidant of my Paſſion, becauſe without her Aſſiſtance, I cou'd not have enjoy'd the Happineſs of your Converſation, and 'tis by her that I am now Betray'd ---- undone, --- loſt to all hopes of ever ſeeing you more --- What have I not endur'd this Day, from the upbraidings of* Ciamara *and* Cittolini, *but that I ſhou'd deſpiſe, nay, my own Ruin too, if you were ſafe ---- But Oh! their Malice aims to wound me moſt, through you ---- Bravo's are hir'd, the Price of your Blood is paid, and they have ſworn to take your Life --- Guard it I conjure you, if you wou'd preſerve that of* Camilla's. *Attempt not to come near this Houſe, nor walk alone, when Night may be an Umbrage to their Deſigns. --- I hear my cruel Enemies returning to renew their Perſecutions, and I have Time to inform you no more. than that 'tis*

to

to the Generous Violetta *you are indebted for this Caution: She, in pity of my Agonies, and to prevent her Father from executing the Crime he intends; conveys this to you, slight it not, if you wou'd have me believe you Love,*

Camilla.

WHAT a turn was here (continu'd he, sadly) in my Fortune? How on a sudden was my Scene of Happiness chang'd to the blackest Despair? --- But not to tire your Lordship, and spin out my Narration, which is already too long with unavailing Complainings. I every Day expected a Challenge from *Cittolini*, believing he wou'd, at least, take that Method at first, but it seems he was for chusing the *surest*, not the *fairest* way: And I have since prov'd, that my Dear *Camilla* had too much Reason for the Caution she gave me. Ten Days I lingred out without being able to invent any means, either to see her, or write to Her; at the end of which, I receiv'd another Letter from Her, which, if I were to tell you the Substance of, wou'd be to wrong her; since no Words but her own are fit to Express her Meaning, and 'tis for that Reason only, I shall Read it.

To Monsieur FRANKVILLE.

OF all the Woes which wait on humane Life, sure there is none Equal to that a Lover feels in Absence; 'tis a kind of Hell, an earnest of those Pains, we are told, shall be the Portion of the Damn'd ---- Ten whole Nights, and Days, according to the vulgar Reckoning, but in mine, as many Ages, have roll'd their tedious Hours away since last I saw you, in all which time, my Eyes have never known one Moments cessation from

from my Tears, nor my sad Heart from Anguish; restless I wander thro' this hated House --- Kiss the clos'd Wicket --- stop, and look at every Place which I remember your dear steps have blest, then, with wild Ravings, think of past Joys, and curse my present Woes --- yet you perhaps are Calm, no sympathizing Pang invades your Soul, and tells you what mine suffers, else, you wou'd, you must have found some Means to ease your self and me -- 'tis true, I bid you not attempt it -- but Oh! If you had lov'd like me, you cou'd not have obey'd ---- Desire has no regard to Prudence, it despises Danger, and over-looks even Impossibilities ---- but whether am I going? --- I say, I know not what --- Oh, mark not what Distraction utters! Shun these detested Walls! --- 'tis Reason now commands! fly from this House, where injur'd Love's enslav'd, and Death and Treachery reign --- I charge thee come not near, nor prove thy Faith so hazardous a way --- forgive the little Fears, which ever dwell with Love --- I know thou art all sincerity! --- all God-like Truth, and can'st not change --- yet, if thou shouldst, --- tormenting Thought! ---- Why then, there's not a Heaven-abandon'd Wretch, so lost --- so Curst as I --- What shall I do to shake off Apprehension? in spite of all thy Vows --- thy ardent Vows, when I but think of any Maid, by Love, and fond Belief undone, a deadly cold runs thro' my Veins, congeals my Blood, and chills my very Soul! --- Gazing on the Moon last Night, her Lustre brought fresh to my Memory those transporting Moments, when by that Light I saw you first a Lover, and, I think Inspired me, who am not usually fond of Versifying, to make her this Complaint.

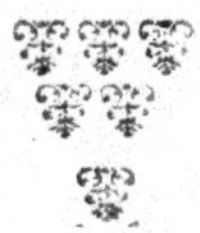

The

The Unfortunate CAMILLA's Complaint to the *Moon*, for the Absence of her Dear HENRICUS FRANKVILLE.

Mild Queen of Shades! Thou sweetly shining Light!
Once, more than Phœbus, *welcome to my Sight:*
'Twas by thy Beams I first HENRICUS *saw*
Adorn'd with softness, and disarm'd of awe!
Never did'st thou appear more fair! more bright!
Than on that Dear, that Cause-remembred Night!
When the dull Tyes of Friendship he disclaim'd,
And to Inspire a tend'rer Passion aim'd:
Alas! he cou'd not long, in vain, implore
For that, which tho' unknown, was his before;
Nor had I Art the Secret to Disguise,
My Soul spoke all her Meaning thro' my Eyes,
And every Glance bright'ned with glad Surprize!
Lost to all Thought, but His Transporting Charms,
I sunk, unguarded! Melting in his Arms!
Blest at that lavish rate, my State, that Hour
I'd not have Chang'd for all in fortune's Pow'r,
Nay, had descending Angel's from on High
Spread their bright Wings to waft me to the Sky,
Thus clasp'd'! Cœlestial Charms had fail'd to move
And Heav'n been slighted, for HENRICUS *Love.*
How did I then thy happy Influence Bless?
How watch each joyful Night, thy Lights encrease?
But Oh! How alter'd since --- Despairing now,
I View thy Lustre with contracted Brow:
Pensive, and sullen from the Rays wou'd hide,
And scarce the glimmering Star's my Griefs abide,
In Death-like darkness wou'd my Fate deplore,
And wish Thee to go down, to Rise no more!

PITY

PITY the Extravagance of a Passion which only Charms like thine cou'd Create, nor too severely chide this soft Impertinence, which I cou'd not refrain sending you, when I can neither see you, nor hear from you: to write, gives some little respite to my Pains, because I am sure of being in your Thoughts, while you are Reading my Letters. The Tender Heared Violetta, *preferring the Tyes of Friendship to those of Duty, gives me this happy opportunity, but my Ill-fortune deprives me too of her, she goes to Morrow to her Fathers* Villa, *and Heaven knows when I shall find means to send to you again.*

Farewel, Thou Loveliest, Dearest, and Divine Charmer ---Think of me with a Concern full of Tenderness, but that is not enough; and you must pardon me, when I confess, that I cannot forbear wishing you might feel some of those Pains, impatient longing brings.--- All others be far away, as far, as Joy is, when you are Absent from

Your Unfortunate

Camilla.

P.S. *Since I writ this, a Fancy came into my Head, that if you cou'd find a Friend Trusty enough to confide in, and one unknown to our Family, he might gain admittance to me in* Cittolini's *Name, as sent by him, while he is at the* Villa. *I flatter my self you will take as much pleasure in endeavouring to let me hear from you, as I do in the hope of it. Once more* Adieu.

YOUR Lordship may judge, by what I have told you of the Sincerity of my Passion, how glad I should have been to have comply'd with her Request, but it was utterly impossible to find any body fit for such a Business: I pass'd three or four Days more, in Disquietudes too great to be exprest; I saunter'd up and down

down the Street where she liv'd, in hopes to see her at some of the Windows, but Fortune never was so favourable to me, thus I spent my Days, and left the sight of those dear Walls at Nights, but in obedience to the Charge she had given me of preserving my Life.

THUS, my Lord, has the business of my Love engrossed my Hours, ever since your Lordships arrival, and tho' I heard that you were here, and extreamly wish'd to kiss your Hands, yet I cou'd never get one Moment compos'd enough to wait on you in, 'till what my Desires cou'd not do, the rashness of my Indignation effected: Last Night, being at my Bankers where all my Bills and Letters are directed, I found this, from Monsieur *Sanseverin*, the Rage which the Contents of it put me in, kept me from remembring that Circumspection, which *Camilla* had enjoyn'd, and I thought of nothing but revenging the injury I imagin'd you had done me: As I was coming Home, I was attack'd as you saw, when you so generously preserv'd me, the just Indignation I conceiv'd at this base procedure of *Cittolini*'s transported me so far, as to make me forget what I owed to my Deliverer, to run in pursuit of those who assaulted me, but soon lost sight of them, and returning, as Gratitude and Honour call'd me, to seek, and thank you for your timely Assistance, I found a Throng of People about the Body of the Villain I had killed, some of them were for Examining me, but finding no Wounds about me, nor any marks of the Engagement I had been in, I was left at my Liberty.

THUS, my Lord, have I given you, in as brie a . manner as the Changes of my Fortune wou'd permit, the Account of my present melancholly Circumstances, in which, if you find many things blameable, you must acknowledge there are more which require Compassion.

I see no Reason, answer'd the Count, either for the one or the other, you have done nothing but what any Man who is a Lover, wou'd gladly have it in his Power to do, and as for your Condition, it certainly is more to be envy'd than pity'd: The Lady loves, is Constant, and doubtless will some way or other, find means for her Escape, ---- Impossible! Cry'd *Frankville*, interrupting him, she is too strictly watch'd to suffer such a Hope. If you will prepare a Letter, resum'd *D'elmont*, my self will undertake to be the Bearer of it; I am entirely a Stranger to the People you have been speaking of, or if I should chance to be known to them, cannot be suspected to come from you, since our Intimacy, so lately born, cannot yet be talk'd of, to the prejudice of our Design; and how do you know, continu'd he smiling, but, if I have the good Fortune to be introduc'd to this Lady, that I shall not be able to assist her Invention to form some Scheme, for both your future Happiness. This offer was too agreeable to be refus'd, *Frankville* accepted it with all the Demonstrations of Gratitude and Joy imaginable, and setting himself down to the *Count's* Scrutore, was not long Writing the following *Billet* which he gave him to read before he seal'd it.

To the most Lovely and Adorable CAMILLA.

" IF to consume with inward Burnings, to have
" no Breath but Sighs, to wish for Death, or
" Madness to relieve me from the racks of Thought,
" be Misery consummate, such is mine! And yet my
" too unjust CAMILLA thinks I feel no Pain, and
" chides my cold Tranquility; cou'd I be so, I were
indeed

" indeed a Wretch deſerving of my nate, but far un-
" worthy of your Pity or Regard. No, no, thou
" Loveliest, Softest, most angelic Creature, that
" Heaven, in laviſh Bounty, ever ſent to charm the
" adoring World; he that cou'd know one Moments
" ſtupid Calm in ſuch an *Abſence*, ought never to be
" bleſt with thoſe unbounded Joys thy *Preſence* brings:
" What wou'd I not give, what wou'd I not hazard
" but once more to behold thee, to gaze upon thy
" Eyes, thoſe Suns of kindling Tranſports! to touch
" thy enlivening Hand! to feed upon the raviſhing
" ſweetneſs of thy Lips! Oh the Imagination's Ex-
" tacy! Life were too poor to ſet on ſuch a Caſt, and
" you ſhou'd long e're this, have prov'd the little Va-
" lue I have for it, in competition with my Love
" if your Commands had not reſtrain'd me. *Citto-*
" *lini*'s Malice, however, had laſt Night been gratify'd,
" if the Noble Count *D'elmont* had not been inſpir'd
" for my Preſervation, it is to him I am indebted,
" not only for my Life, but a much greater Favour,
" that of conveying to you the Aſſurance, how much
" my Life, my Soul, and all the Faculties of it are
" eternally Yours. Thank him, my *Camilla*, for
" your *Frankville*, for Words like thine are only fit to
" Praiſe, as it deſerves, ſuch an exalted Generoſity;
" 'tis with an infinite deal of Satisfaction I reflect
" how much thy Charms will juſtify my Conduct
" when he ſees thee, all that exceſs of Paſſion, which
" my fond Soul's too full of to conceal, that height
" of Adoration, which offer'd to any other Woman
" wou'd be Sacriledge, the wonders of thy Beauty
" and thy Wit, claim as their due, and prove *Camilla*,
" like *Heaven*, can never be too much Reverenc'd!
" Be too much Lov'd! ---- But, Oh! How poor is
" Language to expreſs what 'tis I think, thus Rap-
" tur'd with thy Idea, thou beſt, thou Brighteſt ----
" thou moſt Perfect ---- thou ſomething more than
" Excellence it ſelf -- thou far ſurpaſſing all that Words
" can ſpeak, or Heart, unknowing thee, conceive:

" yet

" yet I cou'd dwell for ever on the Theme, and ſwell " whole Volumes with enervate, tho' well-meaning " Praiſes, if my Impatience, to have what I have " already writ, be with you, did not prevent my ſay- " ing any more than, that but in you I live, nor cou'd " ſupport this Death-like abſence, but for ſome little " intervals of Hope, which ſometimes flatter me, that " Fortune will grow weary of perſecuting me, and " one Day re-unite my Body to my Soul and make " both inſeparably Yours,

Frankville.

THESE new made Friends having a fellow-feeling of each others Sufferings, as proceeding from one Source, paſs'd the time in little elſe but amorous Diſcourſes, till it was a proper Hour for the Count to perform his Promiſe, and taking a full Direction from *Frankville* how to find the Houſe, he left him at his Lodgings to wait his return from *Ciamara*'s, forming, all the way he went, a thouſand Projects to communicate to *Camilla* for her Eſcape, he was ſtill extreamly uneaſy in his Mind concerning *Melliora*, and long'd to be in *Paris* to know the Truth of that Affair, but thought he cou'd not in Honour leave her Brother in this Embaraſſment, and reſolv'd to make uſe of all his Wit and Addreſs to perſwade *Camilla* to hazard every thing for Love, and was not a little pleas'd with the Imagination, that he ſhould lay ſo conſiderable an obligation on *Melliora*, as this Service to her Brother wou'd be. Full of theſe Reflections he found himſelf in the *Portico* of that magnificent Houſe he was to enter, and ſeeing a Crowd of Servants about the Door, deſir'd to be brought to the preſence of *Donna Camilla Fialaſo*, one of them, immediately conducted him into a ſtately Room, and leaving him there, told him, the Lady ſhou'd be made acquainted with his Requeſt; preſently after came in a Woman, who, tho' very Young, ſeem'd to be in the nature of a *Duenna*, the *Count* ſtood with his Back toward her as

ſhe

ſhe enter'd, but hearing ſomebody behind him, and turning haſtily about, he obſerv'd ſhe ſtartled at ſight of him, and appear'd ſo confus'd that he knew not what to make of her Behaviour, and when he ask'd if he might ſpeak with *Camilla*, and ſaid he had a Meſſage to deliver from *Cittolini*, ſhe made no other Anſwer than ſeveral times, with an amaz'd Accent, Ecchoing the names of *Camilla* and *Cittolini*, as if not able to comprehend his Meaning; he was oblig'd to repeat his Words over and over before ſhe cou'd recollect herſelf enough to tell him, that ſhe wou'd let him know her Lady's pleaſure inſtantly. She left him in a good deal of Conſternation, at the Surprize he perceiv'd the Sight of him had put her into, he form'd a thouſand uncertain Gueſſes what the occaſion ſhou'd be, but the Miſtery was too deep for all his Penetration to fathom, and he waited with abundance of Impatience for her return, or the appearance of her Lady, either, of which, he hop'd, might give a Solution to this ſeeming Riddle.

HE attended a conſiderable time, and was beginning to grow exceſſive uneaſy, at this Delay, when a magnificent *Anti-porta* being drawn up, he ſaw thro' a Glaſs Door, which open'd into a Gallery, the *Duenna* approaching: She had now entirely compos'd her Countenance, and with an obliging Smile told him, ſhe wou'd conduct him to her Lady. She led him thro' ſeveral Rooms, all richly furniſh'd and adorn'd, but far inferior to the laſt he came into, and in which he was again left alone, after being aſſur'd that he ſhould not long be ſo.

Count D'elmont cou'd not forbear giving Truce to his more ſerious Reflections, to admire the Beauties of the Place he was in; where e'er he turn'd his Eyes, he ſaw nothing but was ſplendidly Luxurious, and all the Ornaments contriv'd in ſuch a manner, as might fitly be a Pattern, to Paint the Palace of the Queen

Queen of Love by: The Ceiling was vastly high and beautify'd with most curious Paintings, the Walls were cover'd with Tapestry, in which, most artificially were woven, in various colour'd Silk, intermix'd with Gold and Silver, a great number of Amorous Stories; in one Place he beheld a Naked *Venus* sporting with *Adonis*, in another, the Love transform'd *Jupiter*, just resuming his Shape, and rushing to the Arms of *Leda*; there, the seeming Chast *Diana* Embracing her entranc'd *Endimion*; here, the God of soft Desires himself, wounded with an Arrow of his own, and snatching Kisses from the no less enamour'd *Psiche*: betwixt every one of these Pieces hung a large Looking-Glass, which reach'd to the top of the Room, and out of each sprung several crystal Branches, containing great Wax-Tapers, so that the number of Lights vy'd with the Sun, and made another, and more glorious Day, than that which lately was withdrawn. At the upper End of this magnificent Chamber, there was a Canopy of Crimson Velvet, richly emboss'd, and trim'd with Silver, the Corners of which were supported by two golden *Cupids*, with stretch'd out Wings, as if prepar'd to fly; two of their Hands grasp'd the extremity of the *Valen*, and the other, those nearest to each other, joyn'd to hold a wreath of Flowers, over a Couch, which stood under the Canopy. But tho' the Count was very much taken at first with what he saw, yet he was too sincere a Lover to be long delighted with any thing in the absence of his Mistress: How Heavenly (said he to himself Sighing) wou'd be this Place, if I expected *Melliora* here! But Oh! how preferable were a Cottage blest with her, to all this Pomp and Grandeur with any other; this Consideration threw him into a deep Musing, which made him forget either where he was, or the Business which brought him there, till rous'd from it by the dazling Owner of this sumptuous Apartment. Nothing could be more glorious than her Appearance; she was by Nature, a Woman of a most excellent Shape, to which, her desire of Pleasing, had made her add all

by

the aids of Art; she was drest in a Gold and Silver Stuff Petticoat, and a Wastcoat of plain blew Sattin, set round the Neck and Sleeves, and down the Seams with Diamonds, and fastned on the Breast, with Jewels of a prodigeous largeness and lustre; a Girdle of the same encompass'd her Waste; her Hair, of which she had great quantity, was black as Jet, and with a studied Negligence, fell part of it on her Neck in careless Ringlets, and the other was turn'd up, and fasten'd here and there with Bodkins, which had pendant Diamonds hanging to 'em, and as she mov'd, glittered with a quivering Blaze, like Stars darting their fires from out a sable Sky; she had a Vail on, but so thin, that it did not, in the least, obscure the shine of her Garments, or her Jewels, only she had contriv'd to double that part of it which hung over her Face, in so many folds, that it serv'd to conceal her as well as a *Vizard* Mask.

THE Count made no doubt but this was the Lady for whom he waited, and throwing off that melancholy Air he had been in, assum'd one all gay and easy, and bowing low, as he advanc'd to meet her; Madam, said he, if you are that incomparable *Camilla*, whose Goodness nothing but her Beauty can equalize, you will forgive the intrusion of a Stranger, who confesses himself no other way worthy of the Honour of your Conversation, but by his Desires to serve him who is much more so: A Friend of *Cittolini's*, answer'd she, can never want admittance here, and if you had no other Plea, the Name you come in, is a sufficient Warrant for your kind Reception: I hope, resum'd he in a low Voice, and looking round to see if there were no Attendants in hearing, I bring a Letter, from *Frankville*, Madam, the adoring *Frankville*, I have these Credentials to Justify my Visit; in speaking this, he deliver'd the Letter to her, which she retiring a few Paces from him to read, gave him an opportunity of admiring the Majesty of her Walk,

 and

and the agreeable loftineſs of her Mein, much more than he had time to do before.

SHE dwelt not long on the Contents of the Letter, but throwing it careleſly down on a Table which ſtood near her, turn'd to the Count, and with an Accent which expreſs'd not much Satisfaction; and was it to you, my Lord! ſaid ſhe, that Monſieur *Frankville* ow'd his Preſervation? I was ſo happy, reply'd he, to have ſome little hand in it, but ſince I have known how dear he is to you, think my ſelf doubly bleſt by Fortune for the means of acting any thing conducive to your Peace: If you imagine that this is ſo, reſum'd ſhe haſtily, you are extreamly miſtaken, as you will always be, when you believe, where Count *D'elmont* appears, any other Man ſeems worthy the regard of a diſcerning Woman; but, continu'd ſhe, perceiving he look'd ſurpriz'd, to ſpare your ſuſpence, and my ſelf the trouble of repeating what you know already, behold who ſhe is, you have been talking to, and tell me now, if *Frankville* has any Intereſt in a Heart to which this Face belongs? With theſe Words ſhe threw off her Vail, and inſtead of leſſening his Amazement, very much encreas'd it, in diſcovering the Features of the Lady, with whom he had diſcourſed the Night before in the Garden, He knew not what to think, or how to reconcile to Reaſon, that *Camilla*, who ſo lately lov'd, and had granted the higheſt Favours to *Frankville*, ſhou'd on a ſudden be willing, uncourted, to beſtow them on another, nor cou'd he comprehend how the ſame Perſon ſhou'd at once live in two ſeveral Places, for he conceiv'd the Houſe he was in, was far diſtant from the Garden which he had been in the Night before

THEY both remain'd for ſome Moments in a profound Silence, the Lady expecting when the Count ſhou'd ſpeak, and he endeavouring to recollect himſelf enough to do ſo, 'till ſhe, at laſt, poſſibly gueſſing at his Thoughts, reſum'd her Diſcourſe in this manner;

My

My Lord, said she, wonder not at the Power of Love, a Form like yours might soften the most rugged Heart, much more one, by Nature so tender as is mine. ---- Think but what you are, continu'd she sighing, and making him sit down by her on the Couch, and you will easily excuse whatever my Passion may enforce me to commit. I must confess Madam, answer'd he very gravely, I never in my Life wanted presence of mind so much as at this juncture, to see before me here, the Person, who, I believ'd, liv'd far from hence, who, by Appointment, I was to wait on this Night at a different Place. ---- To find in the Mistress of my Friend, the very Lady, who seems unworthily to have bestow'd her Heart on me, are Circumstances so Incoherent, as I can neither account for, or make evident to *Reason*, tho' they are too truly so to *Sense*: It will be easy, reply'd she, to reconcile both these seeming Contradictions, when you shall know that the Gardens blonging to this House, are of a very large Extent, and not only that, but the turning of the Streets are so order'd, as make the Distance between the fore, and back Door appear much greater than really it is: And for the other, as I have already told you, you ought to be better acquainted with your self, than to be surpriz'd at Consequences, which must infallibly attend such Charms: In saying this, she turn'd her Head a little on one side, and put her Handkerchief before her Face, affecting to seem confus'd at what she spoke; but the Count redned in good Earnest, and with a Countenance which express'd Sentiments, far different from those she endeavour'd to Inspire: Madam, said he, tho' the good Opinion you have of me is owing entirely to the *Error* of your *Fancy*, which too often, especially in your Sex, blinds the *Judgment*, yet, 'tis certain, that there are not many Men, whom such Praises, coming from a Mouth like yours, wou'd not make Happy and Vain; but if I was ever of a Humour to be so, it is now wholly mortify'd in me, and 'tis but with the utmost regret, that I must receive the Favours you confer on me to the prejudice of my

Friend: And is that, interrupted ſhe haſtily, is that the *only* Cauſe? Does nothing but your Friendſhip to *Frankville* prevent my Wiſhes? That, of itſelf, anſwer'd he, were a ſufficient Bar to ſunder us for ever, but there's another, if not a greater, a more tender one, which, to reſtore you to the Path, which Honour, Gratitude, and Reaſon call you to, I muſt inform you of, yes, I muſt tell you, Madam, all lovely as you are, that were there no ſuch Man as *Frankville*, in the World, ---- were you as free as Air, I have a defence within, which all your Charms can never pierce, nor ſoftneſs melt --- I am already bound, not with the weak Ties of Vows or formal Obligations, which confine no farther than the Body, but Inclination! ---- the fondeſt Inclination! That ever ſwell'd a *Heart* with Rapturous Hopes: The Lady had much ado to contain herſelf till he had done ſpeaking; ſhe was by Nature extreamly Haughty, Inſolent of her Beauty, and impatient of any thing ſhe thought look'd like a ſlight of it, and this open Defyance of *her* Power, and acknowledging *anothers*, had ſhe been leſs in Love wou'd have been inſupportable to her: Ungrateful and uncourtly Man, ſaid ſhe, looking on him with Eyes that ſparkled at once with Indignation and Deſire, you might have ſpar'd yourſelf the trouble of Repeating, and me the Confuſion of hearing, in what manner you ſtand Engag'd, it had been enough to have told me you never cou'd be mine, without appearing tranſported at the Ruin which you make; if my too happy Rival poſſeſſes Charms, I cannot boaſt, methinks your *good Manners* might have taught you, not to inſult my Wants, and your *good Nature*, to have mingled *Pity* with your *Juſtice*; with theſe Words ſhe fell a Weeping, but whether they were Tears of Love or Anger, is hard to determine, 'tis certain that both thoſe Paſſions rag'd this Moment in her Soul with equal Violence, and if ſhe had had it in her Power, wou'd doubtleſs have been glad to have hated him, but he was, at all times, too lovely to ſuffer a poſſibility of that, and much more ſo at this, for in

ſpite

ſpite of the Shock, that Infidelity he believ'd her guilty of to *Frankville*, gave him; he was by Nature ſo Compaſſionate, he *felt* the Woes he *ſaw*, or *heard* of, even of thoſe who were moſt indifferent to him, and cou'd not now behold a Face, in which all the Horrors of Deſpair were in the moſt lively manner repreſented, without diſplaying a Tenderneſs in his, which in any other Man, might have been taken for Love; the dazling Radience of his Eyes, gave place to a more dangerous, more bewitching ſoftneſs, and when he ſigh'd, in Pity of her Anguiſh, a Soul Inchanting Languiſhment diffus'd itſelf thro' all his Air, and added to his Graces; ſhe preſently perceiv'd it, and forming new Hopes, as well from that, as from his Silence, took hold of his Hand, and preſſing it eagerly to her Boſom, Oh my Lord! reſum'd ſhe, you cannot be ungrateful if you wou'd. ---- I ſee you cannot ---- Madam, interrupted he, ſhaking off as much as poſſible that ſhow of Tenderneſs, which he found had given her Incouragement; I wiſh not to convince you how nearly I am touch'd, with what you ſuffer, leaſt it ſhou'd *encreaſe* an Eſteem, which, ſince prejudicial to your Repoſe, and the Intereſt of my Friend; I rather ought to endeavour to *leſſen*. ---- But, as this is not the Entertainment I expected from *Camilla*, I beg to know an Anſwer of the Buſineſs I came upon, and what you decree for the unfortunate *Frankville*: If the Lady was agitated with an extremity of Vexation at the *Count*'s Declaration of his Paſſion for another, what was ſhe now, at this Diſappointment of the Hopes ſhe was ſo lately flatter'd with! inſtead of making any direct reply to what he ſaid ſhe rag'd, ſtamp'd, tore her Hair, curs'd *Frankville*, all Mankind, the World, and in that height of F[illegible] ſpar'd Heaven itſelf: but the violence of [illegible] Reſentment being a little vented, [illegible] turn, again ſhe wept, again ſhe preſt his Hand, [illegible] knelt and hung upon his Feet, as he wou'd have broke from her, and begg'd him with Words as eloquent as Wit cou'd Form, and deſperate dying Love Suggeſt to pity and relieve her Misery: But he had now learn'd to dissemble his Concern, lest it shou'd a second time beguile her, and after raising her, with as careless and unmov'd an Air, as he was capable of putting on: My Presence, Madam, said he, but augments your Disorder, and 'tis only by seeing you no more, that I am qualify'd to conduce to the recovery of your Peace: With these Words he turn'd hastily from her, and was going out of the Room, when she, quick as Thought, sprung from the Place where she had stood, and being got between him and the Door, and throwing her self into his Arms, before he had time to prevent her; you must not, shall not go, she cry'd, till you have left me dead: Pardon me, Madam, answer'd he fretfully, and struggling to get loose from her Embrace, to stay after the Discovery you have made of your Sentiments, were to be guilty of an Injustice almost equal to your's, therefore I beg you'd give me liberty to pass. ---- Hear me but speak, resum'd she, grasping him yet harder; return but for a Moment, ---- lovely Barbarian, ---- Hell has no torments like your Cruelty. Here, the different Passions working in her Soul, with such uncommon Vehemence, hurry'd her Spirits beyond what Nature cou'd Support; her Voice faulter'd in the Accent, her trembling Hands by slow degrees relinquish'd what so eagerly they had held, every Sense forgot its Use, and she sunk, in all appearance, lifeless on the Floor: The Count was, if possible, more glad to be releas'd, than griev'd at the occasion, and contented himself with calling her Women to her Assistance, without staying to see when she wou'd recover.

He went out of that House with Thoughts much more discompos'd than those with which he had enter'd it, and when he came Home, where *Frankville* impatiently waited his Return, he was at the greatest loss in the World, how to discover his Misfortune to him; the other observing the trouble of his Mind, which was very visible in his Countenance;

nance; my Lord, said he, in a melancholly Tone, I need not ask you what Success, the gloom which appears on your Brow, tells me, my ill Fortune has deny'd you the means of speaking to *Camilla?* Accuse not Fortune, answer'd *D'elmont*, but the influence of malicious Stars which seldom, if ever, suits our Dispositions to our Circumstances; I have seen *Camilla*, have talk'd to her, and 'tis from that Discourse that I cannot forbear reflection on the Miseries of Humanity, which, while it mocks us with a show of *Reason*, gives us no Power to curb our *Will*, and guide the erring Appetites to Peace. Monsieur *Frankville* at these Words first felt a jealous Pang, and, as 'tis natural to believe every Body admires what we do, he presently imagin'd Count *D'elmont* had forgot *Melliora* in the presence of *Camilla*, and that it was from the Consciousness of his own Weakness and Inconstancy, that he spoke so feelingly: I wonder not my Lord, said he coldly, that the Beauties of *Camilla* shou'd inspire you with Sentiments, which, perhaps, for many Reasons, you wou'd desire to be free from, and I ought, in Prudence, to have consider'd, that tho' you are the most excellent of your Kind, you are still a *Man*, and not have the Passions incident to *Man*, and not have expos'd you to those Dangers the sight of *Camilla* must necessarily involve you in: I wish to Heaven answer'd the Count, easily guessing what his Thoughts were, no greater threaten'd you, and that you cou'd think on *Camilla* with the same indifference as I can, or she of me with more; then, in as brief a manner as he cou'd, he gave him the Substance of what had happen'd. *Frankville*, whose only Fault was rashness, grew almost wild at the Recital of so unexpected a Misfortune, he knew not for a good while what to believe, loath he was to suspect the Count, but loather to suspect *Camilla*, yet flew into extremities of Rage against both, by turns: The Count pitied, and forgave all that the violence of his Passion made him utter, but offer'd not to argue with him, 'till he found him capable of admitting his Reasons, and then, that open Sincerity, that honest noble Assurance which always accompany'd his Sweetness, and made it difficult to doubt the Truth of any thing he said, won the disorder'd Lover to an entire Conviction; he now concludes his Mistress false, repents the tenderness he has had for her, and tho' she still appears as lovely to his *Fancy* as ever, she grows odious to his *Judgment*, and resolves to use his utmost Efforts to banish her Idea from his Heart.

IN this Humour he took leave of the Count, it growing late, and his last Nights Adventure taught him the danger of Nocturnal Walks, but how he spent his time till Morning, those can only guess, who have loved like him, and like him, met so cruel a Disappointment.

THE Count pass'd not the Night in much less Inquietude than *Frankville*, he griev'd the powerful Influence of his own Attractions, and had there not been a *Melliora* in the World, he wou'd have wish'd himself Deform'd, rather than have been the Cause of so much Misery, as his Loveliness produc'd.

THE next Morning the Count design'd to visit *Frankville*, to strengthen him in his Resolution of abandoning all Thoughts of the unconstant *Camilla*, but before he cou'd get drest, the other came into his Chamber: My Lord, said he, assoon as they were alone, my perfidious Mistress, failing to make a Conquest of your Heart, is still willing to preserve that she had attain'd over mine, but all her Charms and her Delusions are but vain, and to prove to your Lordship that they are so, I have brought the Letter I receiv'd from her, scarce an Hour past, and the true Copy of my Answer to it.

To

To Monsieur FRANKVILLE

THO' *nothing proves the value of our Presence, so much as the Pangs our absence occasions. and in my last I rashly wish'd you might be sensible of mine, yet on examining my Heart, I presently recall'd the hasty Prayer, and found I lov'd with that extravagance of Tenderness, that I had rather you return'd it too little than too much, and methinks cou'd better bear to represent you to my Fancy, careless and calm as common Lovers are, than think, I saw you, Burning,-- Bleeding,--- Dying, like me, with hopeless Wishes, and unavailing Expectations; but Ah! I fear such Apprehensions are but too un-necessary ---- You think not of me, and, if in those happy days, when no cross Accident interven'd to part me from your Sight, my Fondness pleas'd, you now find nothing in* Camilla *worth a troubled Thought, nor breath one tender sigh in memory of out Transports past.---- If I wrong your Love, impute it to Distraction, for Oh! 'tis sure, I am not in my Senses, nor know to form one regular Desire: I act, and speak, and think, a thousand Incoherent things, and tho' I cannot forbear Writing to you, I write in such a manner, so wild, so different from what I wou'd, that I repent me of the Folly I am guilty of, even while I am committing it; but to make as good a Defence as I am able for these, perhaps, unwelcome Lines, I must inform you that they come not so much to let you know my Sentiments, as to engage a Discovery of yours:* Ciamara *has discharg'd one of her Servants from her Attendance, who no longer courting her Favour or regarding her Frowns, I have prevail'd upon, not only to bring this to you, but to convey an Answer back to me, by the help of a String which I am to let down to him from my Window, therefore, if you are but as Kind, as he has promis'd to be*

Faithful, we may often enjoy the Bleſſing of this diſtant Converſation; Heaven only knows when we ſhall be permitted to enjoy a nearer. Cittolini *is this Evening return'd from his* Villa, *and nothing but a Miracle can ſave me from the neceſſity of making my Choice of him, or a Monaſtery, either of which is worſe than Death, ſince it muſt leave me the Power to wiſh, but take away the means, of being what I ſo oft have ſwore to be*

Eternally Yours, and,

Yours alone,

Camilla.

THE Count could not forbear lifting up his Eyes and Hands in token of Amazement, at the unexampled Falſhood this Woman appeared guilty of, but perceiving Monſieur *Frankville* was about to read the following Anſwer, wou'd not Interrupt him, by asking any Queſtions 'till he had done.

To *Donna* CAMILLA.

IF Vows are any conſtraint to an Inclination ſo addicted to Liberty as Yours, I ſhall make no difficulty to releaſe you of all you ever made to me! Yes Madam, you are free to diſpoſe both of your Heart and Perſon wheresoever you think fit, nor do I deſire you ſhou'd give your ſelf the pains of farther Diſſimulation. I pay too entire an Obedience to your Will, to continue in a Paſſion which is no longer pleaſing: Nor will, by an ill tim'd and unmannerly Conſtancy, diſturb the ſerenity of your future Enjoyments with any happier Man than

Frankville.

YOU

YOU see, my Lord, said he with a sigh, that I have put it out of her Power to Triumph over my Weakness, for I confess my Heart still wears her Chains, but e'er my Eyes or Tongue betray to her the shameful Bondage, these Hands shou'd tear them out; therefore I made no mention of her Behaviour to you, nor of my sending any Letter by you, not only because I knew not if your Lordship wou'd think it proper, but lest she shou'd imagine my Resentment proceeded from Jealousy, and that I lov'd her still. ---- No, she shall ne'er have Cause to guess the truth of what I suffer ---- Her *real perfidy* shall be repaid with *seeming Inconstancy* and Scorn --- Oh! How 'twill sting her Pride, ---- By Heaven, I feel a gloomy kind of Pleasure in the Thought, and will indulge it, even to the highest insults of Revenge.

I rather wish, reply'd the Count, you cou'd in *earnest* be indifferent, than only *feign* to be so, her unexampled Levity Deceit, renders her as unworthy of your Anger as your Love, and there is too much Danger while you preserve the *one*, that you will not be able to throw off the *other*. ---- Oh! I pretend not to it, cry'd *Frankville*, interupting him, she has too deep a root within my Soul ever to be remov'd --- I boast no more than a concealment of my Passion, and when I dress the horrors of a bleeding, breaking Heart, in all the calm of cold Tranquility; methinks, you shou'd applaud the *Noble* Conquest: Time, said the *Count*, after a little Pause, and a just Reflection how little she deserves your Thoughts, will teach you to obtain a a *Nobler*; that of numbering your Love, among things that *were*, but *are* no more, and make you, with me, acknowledge that 'tis as great an argument of *Folly* and *meaness of Spirit* to continue the same Esteem when the Object ceases to deserve, which we profess'd before the discovery of that unworthiness, as it wou'd be of *Villany* and *Inconstancy of Mind*, to change, without

without an Efficient Cauſe: A great deal of Diſcourſe paſs'd between them to the ſame Effect, and it was but in vain that Count *D'elmont* endeavour'd to perſwade him to a real forgetfulneſs of the Charmer, tho' he reſolv'd to ſeem as if he did ſo.

WHILE they were diſputing, one of *D'elmont's* Servants gave him a Letter, which, he told him, the Perſon who brought it, deſir'd he wou'd anſwer immediately; he no ſooner broke it open, and caſt his Eye over it, than he cry'd out in a kind of Tranſport, Oh, *Frankville*, what has Fate been doing! You are Happy. ---- *Camilla* is Innocent, and perhaps the moſt deſerving of her Sex; I only am Guilty, who, by a fatal Miſtake have wrong'd her Virtue, and Tormented you; but Read, continu'd he, giving him the Letter, Read, and Satisfy your ſelf.

MONSIEUR *Frankville* was too much aſtoniſh'd at theſe Words to be able to make any reply, but immediately found the Interpretation of them in theſe Lines.

To the dear cruel Deſtroyer of my Quiet, the never too much Admir'd *Count* D'ELMONT.

"'TIS no longer the Miſtreſs of your Friend, a perjur'd and unjuſt *Camilla*, who languiſhes and "dies by your Contempt, but one, whom all the "Darts of Love had ſtrove in vain to reach, 'till from "your Charms they gain'd a God-like Influence, and "un-erring Force! One, who tho' a Widow, brings "you the Offering of a Virgin Heart.

" As I was ſitting in my Cloſet, watching the " progreſs of the lazy Hours, which flew not half ſo " ſwift as my Deſires to bring on the appointed time " in which you promis'd to be with me in the Gar- " den; my Woman came running in, to acquaint me, " that you were in the Houſe, and waited to ſpeak " with *Camilla*: Surprize, and Jealouſy at once Aſ- " ſaulted me, and I ſunk beneath the Apprehenſion " that you might, by ſome Accident, have ſeen her, " and alſo loved her, to eaſe my ſelf of thoſe torment- " ing Doubts I reſolv'd to appear before you, in her " ſtead, and kept my Vail over my Face, 'till I found " that hers was unknown to you: ----- You are not " Ignorant what follow'd, the Deceit paſs'd upon " you for Truth, but I was ſufficiently puniſh'd for " it, by the ſeverity of your Uſage: I was juſt going " to diſcover who I was, when the violence of my " Love, my Grief, and my Deſpair threw me into " that Swoon, in which, to compleat your Cruelty, " you left me; 'twou'd be endleſs to endeavour to re- " preſent the Agonies of my Soul, when I recovered, and " heard you were gone, but all who truly Love, as " they *fear much*, ſo they *hope much*, my Tortures " at length abated, at leaſt, permitted me to take ſome " intervals of Comfort, and I began to flatter my ſelf " that the Paſſion you ſeem'd tranſported with, for " a nameleſs Miſtreſs, was but a *feint* to bring me " back to him you thought I was oblig'd to Love, " and that there was a poſſibility, that my Perſon " and Fortune might not appear deſpicable to you, " when you ſhou'd know, I have no Ties but thoſe " of Inclination, which can be only yours while I am

Ciamara.

" *P.S.* If you find nothing in me worthy of your " Love, my Sufferings are ſuch, as juſtly may de- " ſerve your Pity; either relieve or put an end to them " I conjure you --- Free me from the ling'ring Death " of "of Doubt, at once decree my Fate, for, like a God, "you rule my very Will, nor dare I, without your "Leave, throw off this wretched Being; Oh then, "permit me once more to behold you, to try at least, "to warm you into Kindness with my Sighs, to melt "you with my Tears, --- to sooth you into softness "by a thousand yet undiscover'd Fondnesses --- and, "if all fail to die before your Eyes.

THOSE who have experienc'd the force of Love, need not to be inform'd what Joy, what Transport swell'd the Heart of Monsieur *Frankville*, at this unexpected *Eclairciffment* of his dear *Camilla*'s Innocence; when every thing concurs to make our Woes seem real, when Hopes are dead, and even Desire is hush'd by the loud Clamours of Despair and Rage, then, --- then, to be recall'd to Life, to Light, to Heaven and Love again, is such a torrent of o're powering Happiness, -- such a surcharge of Extacy, as Sense can hardly bear.

WHAT now wou'd *Frankville* not have given that it had been in his Power to have recall'd the last Letter he sent to *Camilla*? his Soul severely reproach'd him for so easily believing she cou'd be False; tho' his Experience of the sweetness of her Disposition, made him not doubt of a Pardon from her, when she shou'd come to know what had been the Reason of his Jealousy; his impatience to see her, immediately put it into his Head, that as *Ciamara* had been the occasion of the mis-understanding between them, *Ciamara* might likewise be made the property to set all right again; to this end, he entreated the Count to write her an answer of Compliance, and a promise to come to her the next Day, in which Visit, he wou'd, in a Disguise attend him, and being once got into the House, he thought it wou'd be no difficulty to steal to *Camilla*'s Apartment.

BUT he found it not so easy a Task as he imagin'd, to persuade Count *D'elmont* to come into this Design, his

his generous Heart, averse to all Deceit, thought it base and unmanly to abuse with Dissimulation the real tenderness this Lady had for him, and tho' press'd by the Brother of *Melliora*, and conjur'd to it, even by the Love he profess'd for her, it was with all the reluctance in the World, that he, at last, consented, and his Servant came several times into the Room to remind him that the Person who brought the Letter, waited impatiently for an Answer, before he cou'd bring himself into a Humour to write in the manner Monsieur *Frankville* desir'd; and tho', scarce any Man ever had so sparkling a Fancy, such a readiness of Thought, or aptitude of Expression, when the dictates of his Soul, were the Employment of his Tongue or Pen, yet he now found himself at a loss for Words, and he wasted more time in these few Lines, than a Thousand times as many on any other Subject wou'd have cost him.

To the Beautiful and Obliging CIAMARA.

Madam,

"IF I did not Sin against Truth when I assur'd you "that I had a Mistress to whom I was engag'd by In-"clination, I certainly did, when I appear'd guilty "of a harshness which was never in my Nature; the "Justice you do me in believing the Interest of my "Friend was the greatest Motive for my seeming Un-"kindness I have not the Power sufficiently to ac-"knowledge, but, cou'd you look into my Soul, you "wou'd there find the Effects of your Inspiration, "something so tender, and so grateful, as only favours, "such as you confer, cou'd merit or create.

" I deſign to make my ſelf happy in waiting on " you to Morrow Night about Eleven, if you will " order me admittance at that Back-gate, which was " the Place of our firſt Appointment, 'till then, I am " the lovely *Ciamara*'s

Moſt Devoted Servant

D'elmont.

" *P.S.*There are ſomeReaſons why I think it not ſafe " to come alone,therefore beg you'll permit me to bring " a Servant with me, on whoſe ſecrecy I dare rely.

WHEN the Count had ſent away this little Billet, Monſieur *Frankville* grew very gay on the hopes of his Deſign ſucceeding; and laughing, my Lord ſaid he, I queſtion whether *Melliora* wou'd forgive me, for engaging you in this Affair; *Ciamara* is extreamly handſome, has Wit, and where ſhe attempts to Charm, has doubtleſs, a thouſand Artifices to obtain her wiſh; the Count was not in a temper to reliſh his Raillery, he had a great deal of Compaſſion for *Ciamara*, and thought himſelf inexcuſable for deceiving her, and all that *Frankville* cou'd do to diſſipate the Gloom that reflection ſpread about him, was but vain,

THEY ſpent the greateſt part of this Day together, as they had done the former; and when the time came that *Frankville* thought it proper to take Leave, it was with a much more chearful Heart, than he had the Night before; but his Happineſs was not yet ſecure, and in a few Hours he found a conſiderable alteration in his Condition.

AS ſoon as it was dark enough for *Camilla* to let down her String to the Fellow whom ſhe had order'd to wait for it, he receiv'd another Letter faſten'd to it, and finding it was Directed as the other, for Monſieur *Frankville*, he immediately brought it to him.

It was with a mixture of Fear and Joy, that the impatient Lover broke it open, but both these Passions gave Place to an adequate Despair, when having un-seal'd it, he read these Lines.

To Monsieur FRANKVILLE.

" I HAVE been already so much deceiv'd, that I " ought not to boast of any skill in the Art of " Divination, yet, I fancy, 'tis in my Power to form " a juster Guess than I have done, what the Sentiments " of your Heart will be when you first open this ---- " Methinks, I see you put on a scornful Smile, resol- " ving to be still unmov'd, either at Upbraidings or " Complaints, for to do one of these, I am satisfied, " you imagine is the reason of my troubling you with " a Letter: But Sir, I am not altogether silly enough " to believe the tenderest Supplications the most hum- " ble of my Sex cou'd make, has efficacy to restore " Desire, once Dead, to Life; or if it cou'd, I am " not so mean Spirited as to accept a return thus " caus'd; nor wou'd it be less impertinent to Re- " proach; to tell you that you are Perjur'd --- Base --- " Ungrateful, is what you know already, unless your " Memory is so Complaisant as not to remind you " of either Vows or Obligations: But, to assure you, " that I reflect on this sudden Change of your Hu- " mour without being fir'd with Rage, or stupify'd " with Grief, is perhaps, what you least expect. ---- " Yet, strange as it may seem, it is most certain, that " she, whom you have found the Softest, Fondest, " Tenderest of her Kind, is in a moment grown the " most Indifferent, for in spight of your Inconstancy, " I never shall deny that I have Lov'd you, --- Lov'd " you, even to Dotage, my Passion took birth long be- " fore I knew you had a thought of feigning one for me,

" me, which frees me from that Imputation Women " too frequently deserve, of *loving* for no other Reason " than because they are *beloved*, for if you ne'er had " *seem'd* to love, I shou'd have continu'd to do so in " *Reality*. I found a thousand Charms in your Person " and Conversation, and believ'd your Soul no less " transcending all others in excellent Qualities, than I " still confess your Form to be in Beauty; I drest you " up in vain Imagination, adorn'd with all the Orna-" ments of Truth, Honour, good Nature, Generosi-" ty, and every Grace that raise mortal Perfection to " the highest pitch, and almost reach Divinity, --- but " you have taken care to prove your self, meer *Man*, " to like, dislike, and wish you know not what, nor " why! If I never had any Merits, how came you " to think me worthy the pains you have taken to " engage me? And if I had, how am I so suddenly " depriv'd of them? --- No, I am still the same, and " the only reason I appear not so to you, is, that you " behold me now, no more, with Lover's Eyes; the " few Charms, I am Mistress of, look'd lovely at a " distance, but lose their Lustre, when approach'd too " near; your Fancy threw a glittering Burnish o're me, " which free Possession has worn off, and now, the *Wo-* " *man* only stands expos'd to View, and I confess I justly " suffer for the guilty Folly of believing that in your Sex " Ardors cou'd survive Enjoyment, or if they cou'd, " that such a Miracle was reserv'd for me; but thank " Heaven my Punishment is past, the Pangs, the Tor-" tures of my bleeding Heart, in tearing your Idea " thence, already are no more! The fiery Tryal is " over, and I am now arriv'd at the Elizium of per-" fect Peace, entirely unmolested by any warring Pas-" sion; the Fears, the Hopes, the Jealousies, and all " the endless Train of Cares which waited on my " hours of Love and fond Delusion, serve but to endear " re-gain'd Tranquility; and I can cooly *Scorn*, not " *hate* your Falshood; and tho' it is a Maxim very " much in use among the Women of my Country,

" that,

" that, *not to Revenge, were to deserve Ill-usage*, yet " I am so far from having a wish that way, that I " shall always esteem your *Virtues*, and while I par-" don, pity your *Infirmities*; shall praise your flow-" ing Wit, without an Indignant remembrance how " oft it has been employ'd for my undoing; shall " acknowledge the brightness of your Eyes, and not " in secret Curse the borrow'd softness of their Glan-" ces, shall think on all your past Endearments, your " Sighs, your Vows, your melting Kisses, and the " warm Fury of your fierce Embraces, but as a plea-" sing Dream, while Reason slept, and wish not to " renew at such a Price.

" I desire no Answer to this, nor to be thought of " more, go on in the same Course you have begun, " Change 'till you are tir'd with roving, still let " your Eyes Inchant, your Tongue Delude, and Oaths " Betray, and all who look, who listen, and believe, " be ruin'd and forsaken like

Camilla.

THE calm and resolute Resentment which appear'd in the Stile of this Letter, gave *Frankville* very just Grounds to fear, it would be no small Difficulty to obtain a Pardon for what he had so rashly Written; but when he reflected on the seeming Reasons, which mov'd him to it, and that he should have an Opportunity to let her know them, he was not altogether Inconsolable, he pass'd the Night however in a World of Anxiety, and as soon as Morning came, hurried away, to communicate to the *Count* this fresh Occasion of his Trouble.

IT was now *D'elmont*'s turn to Rally, and he laugh'd as much at those Fears, which he imagin'd Causeless, as the other had done, at the Assignation he had perswaded him to make with *Ciamara*, but tho' as most of his Sex are, he was pretty much of the

the *Count*'s Opinion, yet, the Re-instating himself in *Camilla*'s Esteem, was a Matter of too great Importance to him, to suffer him to take one Moment's ease 'till he was perfectly Assur'd of it.

AT last, the wish'd for Hour arriv'd, and he, disguis'd so, as it was impossible for him to be known, attended the *Count* to that dear Wicket, which had so often given him Entrance to *Camilla*; they waited not long for Admittance, *Brione* was ready there to Receive them; the Sight of her, inflam'd the Heart of Monsieur *Frankville* with all the Indignation imaginable, for he knew her to be the Woman, who, by her Treachery to *Camilla*, had gain'd the Confidence of *Ciamara*, and involv'd him in all the Miseries he had endur'd! but he contain'd himself, 'till she taking the *Count* by the Hand, in order to lead him to her Lady, bad him wait her Return, which she told him should be immediately, in an outer Room which she pointed him to.

IN the mean Time she conducted the *Count* to the Door of that magnificent Chamber, where he had been receiv'd by the suppos'd *Camilla*, and where he now beheld the real *Ciamara*, drest, if possible, richer than she was the Night before, but loose as wanton Fancy cou'd invent; she was lying on the Couch when he enter'd, and affecting to seem as if she was not presently Sensible of his being there, rose not to receive him 'till he was very near her; they both kept silence for some Moments, she, waiting till he should speak, and he, possibly, prevented by the uncertainty after what manner he should Form his Address, so as to keep an equal Medium between the two Extreams, of being Cruel, or too Kind, till at last the Violence of her impatient Expectation burst out in these Words, - - - - Oh that this Silence were the Effect of Love! - - - - and then perceiving he made no Answer; tell me, continu'd she, am I forgiven for thus intruding on your *Pity* for a Grant, which

which *Inclination* would not have allow'd me? Ceaſe Madam, reply'd he, to encreaſe the Confuſion which a juſt Senſe of your Favours, and my own Ingratitude has caſt me in: How can you look with Eyes ſo tender and ſo kind, on him who brings you nothing in Return? Rather deſpiſe me, hate me, drive me from your Sight, believe me as I am, unworthy of your Love, nor ſquander on a Bankrupt Wretch the noble Treaſure: Oh Inhuman! interrupted ſhe, has then that Miſtreſs of whoſe Charms you boaſted, engroſs'd all your ſtock of Tenderneſs? and have you nothing, nothing to repay me for all this waſte of Fondneſs, ---- this laviſh Prodigality of Paſſion, which forces me beyond my Sexes Pride, or my own natural Modeſty, to ſue, to Court, to kneel and weep for Pity: Pity, reſum'd the *Count* wou'd be a poor Reward for Love like yours, and yet alas! continu'd he Sighing, 'tis all I have to give; I have already told you, I am ty'd by Vows, by Honour, Inclination, to another, who tho' far abſent hence, I ſtill preſerve the dear Remembrance of! My Fate will ſoon recall me back to her, and *Paris*; yours fixes you at *Rome*, and ſince we are doom'd to be for ever ſeparated, it wou'd be baſe to Cheat you with a vain Pretence, and lull you with Hopes pleaſing Dreams a while, when you muſt quickly wake to added Tortures, and redoubled Woe: Heavens, cry'd ſhe, with an Air full of Reſentment, are then my Charms ſo mean, my Darts ſo weak, that near, they cannot intercept thoſe, ſhot at ſuch a Diſtance? And are you that dull, cold Platoniſt, which can prefer the viſionary Pleaſures of an *abſent* Miſtreſs, to the warm Tranſports of the Subſtantial *preſent*: The *Count* was pretty much ſurpriz'd at theſe Words, coming from the Mouth of a Woman of Honour, and began now to perceive what her Aim was, but willing to be more confirm'd, Madam, ſaid he, I dare not hope your Virtue wou'd permit. - - - - Is this a Time (Interrupted ſhe, looking on him with Eyes which ſparkled with wild Deſires, and left no want of further Expla-

Explanation of her meaning) Is this an Hour to preach of Virtue? ---- Married, ---- betroth'd, engag'd by Love or Law, what hinders but this Moment you may be mine, this Moment, well improv'd, might give us Joys to baffle a whole Age of Woe; make us, at once, forget our Troubles past, and by its sweet remembrance, scorn those to come; in speaking these Words, she sunk supinely on *D'elmont's* Breast; but tho' he was not so ill-natur'd, and unmannerly as to repel her, this sort of Treatment made him lose all the Esteem, and great part of the Pity he had con-conceiv'd for her.

THE Woes of Love are only worthy Commiseration, according to their Causes; and tho' all those kinds of Desire, which the difference of Sex creates, bear in general, the name of Love, yet they are as vastly wide, as Heaven and Hell; that Passion which aims chiefly at Enjoyment, in Enjoyment ends, the fleeting Pleasure is no more remembred, but all the stings of Guilt and Shame remain; but that, where the interiour Beauties are consulted, and *Souls* are Devotees, is truly Noble, Love, *there* is a Divinity indeed, because he is immortal and unchangeable, and if our earthy part partake the Bliss, and craving Nature is in all obey'd; Possession thus desired, and thus obtain'd, is far from satiating, *Reason* is not here debas'd to *Sense*, but *Sense* elevates itself to *Reason*, the different Powers unite, and become pure alike.

IT was plain that the Passion with which *Ciamara* was animated, sprung not from this last Source; she had seen the Charming Count, was taken with his Beauty, and wish'd no farther than to possess his lovely *Person*, his *Mind* was the least of her Thoughts, for had she the least Ambition to reign there, she wou'd not have so meanly sought to obtain the one, after he had assured her, the other, far more noble part of him was dispos'd of. The Grief he had been in, that it was not in his Power to return her Passion, while

he

he believ'd it meritorious, was now chang'd to the utmoſt Contempt, and her Quality, and the State ſhe liv'd in, did not hinder him from regarding of her, in as indifferent a manner, as he wou'd have done a a common *Courtezan*.

LOST to all Senſe of Honour, Pride or Shame, and wild to gratify her furious Wiſhes, ſhe ſpoke, without reſerve, all they ſuggeſted to her, and lying on his Breaſt, beheld, without concern, her Robes fly open, and all the Beauties of her own expos'd, and naked to his View: Mad at his Inſenſiblity, at laſt ſhe grew more bold, ſhe kiſs'd his Eyes, --- his Lips, a thouſand times, then preſs'd him in her Arms with ſtrenuous Embraces, ---- and ſnatching his Hand and putting it to her Heart, which fiercely bounded at his Touch, bid him be witneſs of his mighty Influence there.

THO' it was impoſſible for any Soul to be capable of a greater, or more conſtant Paſſion than his felt for *Melliora*, tho' no Man that ever liv'd, was leſs addicted to looſe Deſires, ---- in fine, tho' he really was, as *Frankville* had told him, the moſt excellent of his Kind, yet, he was ſtill a *Man!* And, 'tis not to be thought ſtrange, if to the force of ſuch united Temptations, Nature and Modeſty a little yielded; warm'd with her fires, and perhaps, more mov'd by Curioſity, her Behaviour having extinguiſh'd all his reſpect, he gave his Hands and Eyes a full Enjoyment of all thoſe Charms, which had they been anſwer'd by a Mind worthy of them, might juſtly have inſpir'd the higheſt Raptures, while ſhe, unſhock'd, and unreſiſting, ſuffer'd all he did, and urg'd him with all the Arts ſhe was Miſtreſs of, to more, and it is not altogether improbable, that he might not entirely have forgot himſelf, if a ſudden Interruption had not reſtor'd his Reaſon to the conſideration of the Buſineſs which had brought him here.

MONSIEUR *Frankville* had all this time been employ'd in a far different manner of Entertainment; *Brione* came to him, according to her promise, assoon as she had introduc'd the *Count* to *Ciamara*, and having been commanded by that Lady to Discourse with the suppos'd Servant, and get what she cou'd out of him, of the *Count*'s Affairs, she sat down and began to talk to him with a great deal of Freedom; but he who was too impatient to lose much time, told her he had a Secret to discover, if the place they were in was private enough to prevent his being over-heard, and she assuring him that it was, he immediately discover'd who he was, and clap'd a Pistol to her Breast, swearing that Moment shou'd be the last of her Life, if she made the least Noise, or attempted to intercept his passage to *Camilla*: The terror she was in, made her fall on her Knees, and conjuring him to spare her Life, beg'd a thousand Pardons for her Infidelity, which she told him was not occasion'd by any particular Malice to him; but not being willing to leave *Rome* herself, the fear of being expos'd to the revenge of *Ciamara* and *Cittolini*, when they shou'd find out that she had been the Instrument of *Camilla*'s Escape, prevail'd upon her timerous Soul to that Discovery, which was the only means to prevent what she so much dreaded: *Frankville* contented himself with venting his Resentment in two or three hearty Curses, and taking her roughly by the Arm, bid her go with him to *Camilla*'s Apartment, and discover before her what she knew of *Ciamara*'s Entertaining Count *D'elmont* in her Name, which she trembling promis'd to obey, and they both went up a pair of back Stairs which led a private way to *Camilla*'s Chamber; when they enter'd, she was sitting in her night Dress on the Bed-side, and the unexpected sight of *Brione*, who, till now, had never ventured to appear before her, since her Infidelity, and a Man with her whom she thought a Stranger, fill'd her with such a surprize, that it depriv'd her of her

Speech,

Speech, and gave *Frankville* time to throw off his Disguise, and catch her in his Arms, with all the Transports of unfeign'd Affection, before she cou'd enough recover her self to make any resistance, but when she did, it was with all the Violence imaginable, and indeavouring to tear herself away; Villain, said she, comest thou again to triumph o're my Weakness,---- again to Cheat me into fond Belief? There needed no more to make this obsequious Lover relinquish his Hold, and falling at her Feet, was beginning to speak something in his Vindication; when she, quite lost in Rage, prevented him, by renewing her Reproaches in this manner; have you not given me up my Vows? Resum'd she, have you not abandon'd me to ruin,--- to Death -- to Infamy,---- to all the stings of self-accusing Conscience and Remorse? And come you now, by your detested Presence, to alarm Remembrance, and new point my Tortures? ----- That Woman's Treachery, continu'd she, looking on *Brione*, I freely Pardon, since by that little Absence it occasion'd, I have discovered the wavering disposition of your Soul, and learn'd to scorn what is below my Anger. Here me but speak, cry'd *Frankville*, or if you doubt my Truth, as I confess you have almighty Cause, let her inform you, what seeming Reasons, what Provocations urg'd my hasty Rage to write that fatal, ---- that acursed Letter. I will hear nothing, reply'd *Camilla*, neither from you nor her, ---- I see the base Design, and scorn to joyn in the Deceit, -- You had no Cause, ---- not even the least Pretence for your Inconstancy but one, which, tho' you all are guilty of, you all Disown, and that is, being lov'd too well.---- I Lavish'd all the fondness of my Soul, and you, unable to reward, despiz'd it: -- But think not that the rage, you now behold me in, proceeds from my Despair -- No, your Inconstancy is the Fault of Nature, a Vice which all your Sex are prone to, and 'tis we, the fond Believers only, are to blame, *that* I forgave, my Letter told you that I did ---- but thus to come ---- thus Insolent in Imagination, to dare to hope I were that mean Soul'd

L Wretch

Wretch, whose easy Tameness, and whose doating Love, with Joy would welcome your return, clasp you again in my deluded Arms, and swear you were as dear as ever, is such an affront to my Understanding, as merits the whole Fury of Revenge! as she spoke these Words, she turn'd disdainfully from him with a Resolution to leave the Room, but she could not make such hast to go away, as the despairing, the distracted *Frankville* did to prevent her, and catching hold of her Garments, stay Madam, said he, wildly, either permit me to clear my self of this barbarous Accusation, or, if you are resolv'd, Unhearing, to Condemn me, behold me, satiate all your Rage can wish, for by Heaven, continued he, holding the Pistol to his own Breast, as he had done a little before to *Brione's*, by all the Joys I have Possest, by all the Hell I now endure, this Moment I'll be receiv'd your *Lover*, or expire your *Martyr*. These Words pronounc'd so passionately, and the Action that accompany'd them, made a visible alteration in *Camilla's* Countenance, but it lasted not long, and Resuming her fierceness; your Death, cry'd she, this way would give me little Satisfaction, the World would judge more Noble of my Resentment, if by my Hand you fell---- Yet, continu'd she, snatching the Pistol from him, and throwing it out of the Window, which happen'd to be open, I will not --- cannot be the Executioner. -- No, Live! And let thy Punishment be, in *Reality*, to endure what thou well *Dissemblest*, the Pangs, the racking Pangs, of hopeless, endless Love! -- May'st thou *indeed*, Love *Me*, as thou a thousand Times hast falsely sworn, --- for ever *Love*, and I, for ever *Hate!* In this last Sentence, she flew like Lightning to her Closet, and shut her self in, leaving the amaz'd Lover still on his Knees, stupify'd with Grief and Wonder, all this while *Brione* had been casting about in her Mind, how to make the best use of this Adventure with *Ciamara*, and encourag'd by *Camilla's* Behaviour and taking advantage of *Frankville's* Confusion, made but one Step to the Chamber Door, and running out into the Gallery, and down

Stairs.

Stairs, cry'd Murder, ---- Help, a Rape ---- Help, or *Donna Camilla* will be carry'd away. --- She had no occasion to call often, for the Pistol which *Camilla* threw out of the Window chanc'd to go off in the fall, and the report it made, had alarm'd some of the Servants who were in an out-House adjoyning to the Garden, and imagining there were Thieves, were gathering to search: some arm'd with Staves, some with Iron Bars, or any thing they could get in the Hurry they were in, as they were running confusedly about, they met Monsieur *Frankvile* pursuing *Brione*, with a design to stop her Mouth, either by Threatnings or Bribes, but she was too nimble for him, and knowing the ways of the House much better than he did, went directly to the Room where *Ciamara* was Carressing the Count in the manner already mention'd: Oh Madam, said she, you are impos'd on, the Count has deceiv'd your Expectations, and brought Monsieur *Frankville* in Disguise to rob you of *Camilla*. These Words made them both, tho' with very different Sentiments, start from the posture they were in, and *Ciamara* changing her Air of Tenderness for one all Fury, Monster! Cry'd she to *D'elmont*, have you then betray'd me? This is no time, reply'd he, hearing a great Bustle, and *Frankville*'s Voice pretty loud without, for me to answer you, my Honour calls me to my Friend's assistance; and drawing his Sword, run as the Noise directed him to the Place where *Frankville* was defending himself against a little Army of *Ciamara*'s Servants, she was not much behind him, and enrag'd to the highest degree, cry'd out, kill, kill them both! But that was not a Task for a much greater Number of such as them to Accomplish, and tho' their Weapons might easily have beat down, or broke the Gentlemens Sword; yet their Fears kept them from coming too near, and *Ciamara* had the Vexation to see them both Retreat with Safety, and her self disappointed, as well in her Revenge, as in her Love.

NOTHING cou'd be more surpriz'd, than Count *D'elmont* was, when he got Home, and heard from *Frankville* all that had pass'd between him and *Camilla*, nor was his Trouble less, that he had it not in his Power to give him any Advice in any Exigence so uncommon: He did all he cou'd to comfort and divert his Sorrows, but in vain, the Wounds of bleeding Love admit no Ease, but from the Hand which gave them; and he, who was naturally rash and fiery, now grew to that height of Desparation and violence of Temper, that the Count fear'd some fatal Catastrophe, and wou'd not suffer him to stir from him that Night, nor the next Day, till he had oblig'd him to make a Vow, and bind it with the most solemn Imprecations, not to offer any thing against his Life.

BUT, tho' plung'd into the lowest depth of Misery, and lost, to all Humane probability, in an inextricable Labyrinth of Woe, *Fortune* will find, at last some way, to raise, and disentangle those, whom she is pleas'd to make her Favourites, and that Monsieur *Frankville* was one, an unexpected Adventure made him know.

THE third Day from that, in which he had seen *Camilla*, as he was sitting in his Chamber, in a melancholly Conversation with the Count, who was then come to Visit him, his Servant brought him a Letter, which he said had been just left, by a Woman of an extraordinary Appearance, and who the Moment she had given it into his Hand, got from the Door with so much speed, that she seem'd rather to vanish than to walk.

WHILE the Servant was speaking, *Frankville* look'd on the Count with a kind of a pleas'd Expectation in his Eyes, but then casting them on the Direction of the Letter, Alas! Said he, how vain was my Imagination, this is not *Camilla*'s, but a Hand, to which I am utterly a Stranger; these Words were clos'd with a sigh, and he open'd it with Negligence which wou'd have been unpardonable, cou'd he have guess'd at the

the Contents, but assoon as he saw the Name of *Violetta* at the bottom, a flash of Hope re-kindled in his Soul, and trembling with Impatience he Read.

To Monsieur FRANKVLLE.

I *Think it cannot be call'd Treachery, if we betray the Secrets of a Friend, only when Concealment were an Injury, but however I may be able to answer this breach of Trust, I am about to make to my self, 'tis your Behaviour alone, which can absolve me to* Camilla, *and by your Fidelity she must judge of* mine.

THO' Daughter to the Man she hates, she finds nothing in me Unworthy of her Love and Confidence, and as I have been privy, ever since your mutual Misfortunes, to the whole History of your Amour, so I am now no Stranger to the Sentiments, your last Conversation has inspir'd her with -- She loves you still, Monsieur *-- with an extremity of Passion loves you, ---- But, tho' she ceases to believe you unworthy of it, her Indignation for your unjust Suspicion of her will not be easily remov'd -- She is resolv'd to act the* Heroine, *tho' to purchase that Character it shou'd cost her Life: She is determin'd for a Cloyster, and has declared her Intention, and a few Days will take away all Possibility of ever being yours; but I, who know the conflicts she endures, wish it may be in your Power to prevent the Execution of a Design, which cannot, but be fatal to her: My Father and* Ciamara, *I wish I cou'd not call her Aunt, were last Night in private Conference, but I over heard enough of their Discourse, to know there has been some ungenerous Contrivance carry'd on to make you, and* Camilla *appear guilty to each other, and 'tis from that Knowledge I derive my Hopes, that you have Honour enough to make a right Use of this*

Discovery, if you have any thing to say, to further the Intercessions I am imploy'd in, to serve you; Prepare a Letter, which I will either prevail on her to read, *or oblige her, in spite of the Resolution she has made, to* Hear: *But take care, that in the least, you hint not that you have receiv'd one from me, for I shall perswade her that the Industry of your Love has found means of conveying it to me, without my Knowledge: Bring it with you this Evening to St.* Peter's, *and assoon as Divine Service is over, follow her who shall drop her Handkerchief as she passes you, for by that Mark you shall distinguish her whom you yet know, but by the Name of*

Violetta.

P.S. *One thing, and indeed not the least, which induc'd me to write, I had almost forgot, which is, that your Friend the Accomplish'd Count* D'elmont, *is as much endangered by the Resentment of* Ciamara, *as your self by that of my Father, bid him beware how he receives any Letter, or Present from a Hand unknown, lest he should Experience, what he has doubtless heard of, our* Italian *Art of Poysoning by the smell.*

WHEN Monsieur *Frankville* had given this Letter to the Count to read, which he immediately did, they both of them broke into the highest Encomiums on this young Lady's Generosity, who contrary to the custom of her Sex, which seldom forgives an affront of that kind, made it her study to serve the Man who had refus'd her, and make her Rival blest.

THESE Testimonies of a grateful Acknowlegement being over, *Frankville* told the Count, he believ'd the most, and indeed the only effectual Means to extinguish *Camilla's* Resentment wou'd be entirely to remove the Cause, which cou'd be done no other way, than by giving her a full Account of *Ciamara's* behaviour, while she pass'd for her: *D'elmont* readily consented,

conſented, and thought it not at all inconſiſtent with his Honour to Expoſe that of a Woman who had ſhewn ſo little Value for it herſelf: And when he ſaw that *Frankville* had finiſh'd his Letter, which was very long, for Lovers cannot eaſily come to a Concluſion, he offer'd to write a Note to her, encloſ'd in the other, which ſhou'd ſerve as an Evidence of the Truth of what he had alledged in his Vindication: *Frankville* gladly embrac'd the kind Propoſal, and the other immediately made it good in theſe Words.

To *Donna* CAMILLA.

Madam,

I*F the Severity of your Juſtice requires a* Victim, *I only am Guilty, who being Impoſ'd upon my ſelf,* endeavour'd, *for I cannot ſay I cou'd* Accompliſh *it, to involve the Unfortunate* Frankville *in the ſame fatal Error, and at laſt, prevail'd on him to* Write, *what he cou'd not be brought, by all my Arguments to* Think.

LET the Cauſe which led me to take this Freedom, excuſe the Preſumption of it, which, from one ſo much a Stranger, wou'd be elſe unpardonable: But when we are conſcious of a Crime, the firſt reparation we can make to Innocence, is, to acknowledge we have offended; and, if the Confeſſion of my Faults, may purchaſe an Abſolution for my Friend, I ſhall account it the nobleſt Work of Supererogation.

BE assur'd, that as inexorable as you are, your utmost Rigour wou'd find its Satisfaction, if you cou'd be sensible of what I suffer in a sad Repentance for my Sin of injuring so Heavenly a Virtue, and perhaps, in time be mov'd by it, to Pity and Forgive

The Unhappily deceiv'd

D'elmont.

THE time in which they had done Writing, immediately brought on that of *Violetta*'s Appointment, and the Count wou'd needs accompany Monsieur *Frankville* in this Assignation, saying, he had an acknowledgment to pay to that Lady, which he thought himself oblig'd, in good Manners and Gratitude, to take this Opportunity to do; and the other being of the same Opinion, they went together to St. *Peter*'s.

WHEN Prayers were done, which, 'tis probable, *One* of these Gentlemen, if not *Both*, might think too tedious, they stood up, and looking round, impatiently expected when the promis'd Signal shou'd be given; but among the great Number of Ladies, which pass'd by them, there were very few, who did not stop a little to gaze on these two Accomplish'd *Chevaliers*, and they were several times Tantaliz'd with an *imaginary* Violetta, before the *real* one appear'd. But when the Crowd were almost dispers'd, and they began to fear some Accident had prevented her coming, the long expected Token was let fall, and she who threw it, trip'd hastily away to the farther end of the *Collonade*, which hapned to be entirely void of Company: The Count and his Companion, were not long behind her, and Monsieur *Frankville* being the Person chiefly concern'd, address'd himself to her in this manner: With what Words, Madam, said he, can a Man so infinitely Oblig'd, and so desirous to be Grateful, as *Frankville*, sufficiently make known

known his admiration of a Generosity like yours? Such an unbounded Goodness, shames all Discription! Makes Language vile, since it affords no Phrase to suit your Worth, or speak the mighty Sense my Soul has of it. I have no other Aim, reply'd she, in what I have done, than Justice; and 'tis only in the proof of your sincerity to *Camilla*, that I am to be thank'd. *Frankville* was about to answer with some assurances of his Faith, when the Count stepping forward, prevented him: My Friend, Madam, said he bowing, is most happy in having it in his Power to obey a Command, which is the utmost of his Wishes; but how must I acquit my self of any part of that Return which is due to you, for that generous Care you have been pleas'd to express for the preservation of my Life? There needs no more, interrupted she, with a perceivable alteration in her Voice, than to have *seen* Count *D'elmont*, to be interested in his Concerns -- she paus'd a little after speaking these Words, and then, as if she thought she had said too much, turn'd hastily to *Frankville*, the Letter, *Monsieur*, continu'd she, the Letter, --- 'tis not impossible but we may be observ'd, --- I tremble with the apprehension of a Discovery: *Frankville* immediately deliver'd it to her, but saw so much Disorder in her Gesture, that it very much surpriz'd him: She trembled indeed, but whether occasioned by any danger she perceiv'd of being taken notice of, or some other secret Agitation she felt within, was then unknown to any but herself, but whatever it was, it transported her so far, as to make her quit the Place, without being able to take any other Leave than a hasty *Curtisie*, and bidding *Frankville* meet her the next Morning at *Mattins*.

HERE was a new Cause of Disquiet to *D'elmont*; the Experience he had of the too fatal influence of his dangerous Attractions, gave him sufficient Reason to fear this young Lady was not insensible of them, and that his Presence was the sole Cause of her Disorder; however, he said nothing of it to *Frankville* 'till the other

other mentioning it to him, and repeating her Words, they both joyn'd in the Opinion, that Love had been too busy in her Heart, and that it was the feeling the Effects of it in herself, had inclined her to so much Compassion for the Miseries she saw it inflicted upon others. The Count very well knew that when Desires of this Kind are springing in the Soul, every Sight of the beloved Object, encreases their growth, and therefore, tho' her generous manner of Proceeding had created in him a very great Esteem, and he wou'd have been pleas'd with her Conversation, yet he ceas'd to wish a farther Acquaintance with her, lest it should render her more Unhappy, and forbore going the next Day to Church with *Frankville*, as else he wou'd have done.

VIOLETTA fail'd not to come as she had promis'd, but instead of dropping her Handkerchief, as she had done the Evening before, she knelt as close to him as she cou'd, and pulling him gently by the Sleeve, oblig'd him to regard her, who else, not knowing her, wou'd not have suspected she was so near, and slip'd a Note into his Hand, bidding him softly, not take any farther notice of her: He obey'd, but 'tis reasonable to believe, was too impatient to know what the Contents were, to listen with much Attention and Devotion to the remainder of the Ceremony; as soon he was releas'd, he got into a Corner of the *Cathedral*, where, unobserv'd he might satisfy a Curiosity, which none who Love, will condemn him for, any more than they will for the thrilling Extacy which fill'd his Soul at the Reading these Lines.

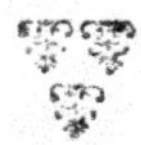

To

To Monsieur FRANKVILLE.

FOR fear I should not have an Opportunity of speaking to you, in safety, I take this Method to inform you, that I have been so Successful in my Negotiation, as to make Camilla *repent the Severity of her Sentence, and wish for nothing more than to recall it: you are now entirely justified in her Opinion, by the Artifice which was made use of to Deceive you, and she is, I believe, no less enrag'd at* Ciamara, *for depriving her of that Letter you sent by the* Count, *than she was at you for that unkind one, which came to her Hands. She is now under less restraint, since* Brione's *Report of her Behaviour to you, and the everlasting Resentment she vow'd, and I have prevail'd on her to accompany me in a Visit I am to make, to morrow in the Evening, to* Donna Clara Metteline, *a Nun, in the Monastery of* St. Augustine. *and if you will meet us there, I believe it not impossible but she may be brought to a Confession of all I have discover'd to you of her Thoughts.*

THE Count's *Letter was of no small Service to you, for tho' without that Evidence she wou'd have been convinc'd of your Constancy, yet she wou'd hardly have acknowledged she was so! and if he will take the Pains to come with you to morrow I believe his Company will be acceptable, if you think it proper, you may let him know as much from*

Violetta.

P S. *I beg a thousand Pardons both of you and the* Count, *for the abruptness of my Departure last Night; something happen'd to give me a Confusion from which I cou'd not at that time recover, but hope for the future to be more Mistress of my self.*

MONSIEUR

MONSIEUR *Frankville* hasted to the *Count's* Lodgings, to commuuicate his good Fortune, but found him in a Humour very unfit for Congratulations; the Post had just brought him a Letter from his Brother, the Chevalier *Brillian*, the Contents whereof were these.

To Count D'LMONT.

MY LORD,

'TIS with an inexpressible Grief that I obey the Command you left me, for giving you from Time to Time an exact Account of Melliora's *Affairs, since what I have now to acquaint you with, will make you stand in Need of all your Moderation to support it. But, not to keep your Expectation on the Rack, loth as I am, I must inform you, that* Melliora *is, by some unknown Ravisher stolen from the Monastery ---- The manner of it, (as I have since learn'd from those who were with her) was thus: As she was walking in the Fields, behind the Cloyster Gardens, accompanied by some young Lady's, Pensioners there as well as her self, four Men well mounted, but Disguis'd and Muffled, rode up to them, three of them jump'd off their Horses, and while one seiz'd on the defenceless Prey; and bore her to his Arms, who was not alighted, the other two caught hold of her Companions, and prevented the Out-cries they would have made, 'till she was carry'd out of sight, then Mounting again their Horses, immediately lost the amaz'd Virgins all Hopes of recovering her.*

I Conjure my dearest Brother to believe there has been nothing omitted for the Discovery of this Villany, but

but in spite of all the Pains and Care we have taken in the search; None of us have yet been happy enough to hear the least Account of her: That my next may bring you more welcome News, is the first wish of

My Lord,
Your Lordship's most
Zealously Affectionate
Brother, and Humble Servant
Brillian.

P.S. *THERE are some People here, Malicious enough to Report, that the Design of carrying away* Mellora, *was contriv'd by you, and that it is in* Rome *she only can be found. It wou'd be of great Advantage to my Peace, if I cou'd be of the Number of those who believe it, but I am too well acquainted with your Principles to harbour such a Thought. Once more, my dear Lord, for this Time,* Adieu.

AFTER the Count had given this Letter to *Frankville* to read, he told him, he was resolv'd to leave *Rome* the next Day, that no body had so great an Interest in her Recovery as himself, that he would Trust the Search of her to no other, and swore with the most dreadful Imprecations he could make, never to rest, but wander, *Knight-Errand* like, over the whole World 'till he had found her.

THO' Monsieur *Frankville* was extreamly concern'd at what had happen'd to his Sister, yet he endeavour'd to disswade the Count from leaving *Rome*, till he knew the result of his own Affair with *Camilla*; but all his Arguments were for a long time ineffectual, 'till, at last, showing him *Violetta*'s Letter, he prevail'd on him to defer his Journey till they had first seen *Camilla*, on Condition, that if she persisted in her Rigour, he shou'd give over any further fruitless Solicitations, and accompany him to *Paris:* This *Frankville* promis'd to perform, and they pass'd the time in very uneasy and impatient Cogitations, 'till the next Day about Five in the Evening they prepar'd for the Appointment.

Count

Count *D'elmont* and his longing Companion, were the first at the Rendezvous, but in a very little while they perceiv'd two Women coming towards them: The Idea of *Camilla* was always too much in *Frankville*'s Thoughts, not to make him know her, by that charming Air (which he so much ador'd her for) tho' she was Veil'd never so closely, and the Moment he had sight of them, Oh Heaven (cry'd he to *D'elmont*) yonder she comes, that, ---- that my Lord, is the divine *Camilla*, as they came pretty near, she that indeed prov'd to be *Camilla*, was turning on one Side, in order to go to the Grate where she expected the *Nun*. Hold! Hold *Donna Camilla*, cry'd *Violetta*, I cannot suffer you shou'd pass by your Friends with an Air so unconcern'd, if Monsieur *Frankville* has done any thing to merit your Displeasure, my Lord the Count certainly deserves your Notice, in the Pains he has taken to undeceive you. One so much a Stranger as Count *D'elmont* is, answer'd she, may very well excuse my Thanks for an explanation, which had he been acquainted with me he would have spar'd. Cruel *Camilla!* Said *Frankville*, is then the knowledge of my Innocence unwelcome? --- Am I become so hateful, or are you so chang'd, that you wish me guilty, for a justification of your Rigour? If it be so, I have no Remedy but Death, which tho' you depriv'd me of, the last time I saw you, I now can find a Thousand means to compass; he pronounc'd these Words in so Tender, yet so resolv'd an Accent, that *Camilla* cou'd not conceal part of the Impression they made on her, and putting her Handkerchief to her Eyes, which in spite of all she had done to prevent it, overflow'd with Tears; talk not of Death, said she, I am not Cruel to that degree, Live *Frankville*, Live! ---- but Live without *Camilla!* Oh, 'tis impossible! Resum'd he, the latter part of your Command entirely destroys the first. --- Life without your Love, would be a Hell, which I confess my Soul's a Coward, but to think of.

THE Count and *Violetta* were Silent all this Time, and perceiving they were in a fair way of Reconciliation

liation, thought the beſt they cou'd do to forward it, was to leave 'em to themſelves, and walking a few Paces from them; You ſuffer my Lord, ſaid ſhe, for your Generoſity in accompanying your Friend, ſince it condemns you to the Converſation of a Perſon, who has neither *Wit*, nor *Gaiety* ſufficient to make her ſelf Diverting. Thoſe, reply'd he, who wou'd make the Excellent *Violletta* a Subject of Diverſion, ought never to be bleſt with the Company of any, but ſuch Women who merit not a ſerious Regard: But you indeed, were your Soul capable of deſcending to the Follies of your Sex, wou'd be extreamly at a Loſs in Converſation ſo little Qualify'd as mine, to pleaſe the Vanities of the Fair; and you ſtand in need of all thoſe more than *Manly* Virtues you poſſeſs, to pardon a *Chagreen*, which even your Preſence cannot Diſſipate: If it cou'd, interrupted ſhe, I aſſure your Lordſhip, I ſhou'd much more *rejoice* in the happy Effects of it on you, than *Pride* my ſelf in the Power of ſuch an Influence -- And yet continu'd ſhe with a Sigh, I am a very Woman, and if free from the uſual Affectations and Vanities of my Sex, I am not ſo from Faults, perhaps, leſs worthy of forgiveneſs: The Count cou'd not preſently reſolve what reply to make to theſe Words; he was unwilling ſhe ſhould believe he wanted Complaiſance, and afraid of ſaying any thing that might give room for a Declaration of what he had no Power of anſwering to her wiſh; but after the conſideration of a Moment or two, Madam, ſaid he, tho' I dare not Queſtion your Sincerity in any other Point, yet you muſt give me leave to disbelieve you in this, not only, becauſe, in my Opinion, there is nothing ſo contemptibly ridiculous as that ſelf ſufficiency, and vain deſire of pleaſing, commonly known by the Name of *Coquetry*, but alſo, becauſe ſhe who eſcapes the Contagion of this Error, will not without much difficulty be led into any other: Alas my Lord, cry'd *Violetta*, how vaſtly wide of Truth is this Aſſertion? That very foible, which is moſt pernicious to our Sex, is chiefly by *Coquetry* prevented: I need not tell you that 'tis Love I mean, and as blamable as you think the *one*, I believe the *other* wou'd find less favour from a Person of your Lordship's Judgment: How Madam, interrupted the Count, pretty warmly, have I the Character of a Stolick? --- Or do you, imagine that my Soul, is compos'd that course Stuff, not to be capable of receiving, or approving a Passion, which, all the Brave, and generous think it their glory to Profess, and which can only give refin'd delight, to Minds enobled. ---- But I perceive, continu'd he growing more cool, I am not happy enough in your Esteem, to be thought worthy the Influence of that God. Still you mistake my Meaning, said *Violetta*, I doubt not of your Sensibility, were there a possibility of finding a Woman worthy of Inspiring you with soft Desires: and if that shou'd ever happen, Love wou'd be so far from being a weakness, that it wou'd serve rather as an Embellishment to your other Graces; it's only when we stoop to Objects below our Consideration, or vainly wing our wishes to those above our Hopes, that makes us appear ridiculous or contemptible; but either of these is a Folly which, ---- which the incomparable *Violetta*, interrupted *D'elmont*, never can be guilty of: You have a very good Opinion of my Wit resum'd she, in a melancholly Tone, but I shou'd be much happier than I am, if I were sure I cou'd secure my self from doing any thing to forfeit it: I believe, reply'd the Count there are not many things you have less Reason to apprehend than such a Change; and I am confident were I to stay in *Rome* as many *Ages*, as I am determin'd to do but *Hours*, I shou'd, at last, leave it, with the same Esteem and Admiration of your singular Vertues, as I now shall do. *Violetta* cou'd not prevent the Disorder these Words put her into, from discovering it self in the Accent of her Voice, when, How! My Lord, said she, are we then to lose you? --- Lose you in so short a Time? As the Count was about to answer, *Frankvillle* and *Camilla* joyn'd them, and looking on *Frankville*, if any Credit, said he, may be given to the Language of the Eyes, I am certain

yours

yours ſpeak Succeſs, and I may congratulate a Happineſs you lately cou'd not be perſuaded to hope; had I a thouſand Eyes, cry'd the tranſported Lover, a thouſand Tongues, they all wou'd be but inſignificant to expreſs the Joy! ---- he unbounded Extacy, my Soul is full of, ---- but take the mighty Meaning in one Word, ---- *Camilla*'s mine --- for ever mine! --- the Storm is paſt, and all the ſunny Heaven of Love returns to bleſs my future Days with ceaſeleſs Raptures: Now, my Lord, I am ready to attend you in your Journey, this Bright! This beauteous Guardian Angel, will partake our Flight! And we have nothing now to do, but to prepare with ſecrecy and ſpeed fit means for our Eſcape. As ſoon as *Frankville* had left off ſpeaking, Count *D'elmont* addreſſing himſelf to *Camilla*, made her abundance of Retributions, for the happineſs ſhe gave his Friend, which ſhe receiving with a becoming Chearfulneſs, and unaffected Gaiety, I am afraid ſaid ſhe, your Lordſhip will think a Woman's Reſolution is, henceforth, little worth regarding; but, continu'd ſhe, taking *Violetta* by the Hand, I ſee well, that this unfaithful Creature, has betray'd me, and to puniſh her Infidelity, will, by leaving her, put it out of her Power to deceive my Confidence again: *Viollett*a either did not hear, or was not in a condition to return her *Raillery*, nor the Praiſes which the Count and Monſieur *Frankville* concurr'd in of her Generoſity, but ſtood motionleſs and loſt in Thought, till *Camilla* ſeeing it grow towards Night, told the Gentlemen, ſhe thought it beſt to part, not only to avoid any Suſpicion at Home of their being out ſo long, but alſo that the others might order every thing proper for their Departure, which it was agreed on between *Frankville* and her, ſhould be the next Night, to prevent the Succeſs of thoſe miſchievous Deſigns ſhe knew *Ciamara* and *Cittolini* were forming, againſt both the Count and Monſieur *Frankville*.

MATTERS being thus adjuſted to the entire Satisfaction of the Lovers, and not in a much leſs proportion

tion to the Count, they all thought it best to avoid making any more Appointments till they met to part no more; which was to be at the Wicket at dead of Night. When the Count took leave of *Violletta*, this being the last time he cou'd expect to see her; she was hardly able to return his Civilities, and much less to answer those which *Frankville* made her, after the Count had turn'd from her to give him way; both of them guess'd the Cause of her Confusion, and *D'elmont* felt a concern in observing it, which nothing but that for *Melliora* cou'd surpass.

THE next Day found full Employment for them all; but the Count, as well as *Frankville*, was too impatient to be gone, to neglect any thing requisite for their Departure, there was not the least particular wanting, long before the time they were to wait at the Wicket for *Camilla*'s coming forth: The Count's Lodging being the nearest, they stay'd there, watching for the long'd for Hour; but a little before it arriv'd, a Youth, who seem'd to be about 13 or 14 Years of Age, desir'd to be admitted to the Count's presence, which being granted, pulling a Letter out of his Pocket, and blushing as he approach'd him: I come my Lord, said he, from *Donna Violetta*, the Contents of this will inform you on what Business; but lest the Treachery of others, shou'd render me suspected, permit me to break it open, and prove it carries no Infection: The Count look'd earnestly on him while he spoke, and was strangely taken with the uncommon Beauty and Modesty which he observ'd in him: You need not give your self the trouble of that Experiment, answer'd he, *Donna Violetta*'s Name, and your own engaging Aspect, are sufficient Credentials, if I were liable to doubt; in saying this, he took the Letter, and full of Fears that some Accident had happen'd to *Camilla*, which might retard their Journey, hastily read over these Lines.

To

To the Worthy Count D'ELMONT.

My LORD,

IF any Part of that Esteem you Profess'd to have for me, be real, you will not deny the Request I make you to accept this Youth, who is my Relation, in Quality of a Page: He is inclin'd to Travel, and of all Places, France *is that which he is most desirous of going to: If a diligent Care, a faithful Secresy, and an Unceasing watchfulness to please, can render him acceptable to your Service, I doubt not but he will, by those, Recomend himself, hereafter: In the mean Time beg you will receive him on my Word: And if that will be any Inducement to prejudice you in his Favour, I assure you, that tho' he is one degree nearer in Blood to my Father, he is by many in Humour and Principles to*

Violetta.

P.S. *May Health Safety and Prosperity attend you in your Journey, and all the Happiness you wish for, crown the End.*

THE Young *Fidelio,* for so he was call'd, cou'd not wish to be receiv'd with greater Demonstrations of Kindness than those the Count gave him: And perceiving that *Violetta* had trusted him with the whole Affair of their leaving *Rome* in private, doubted not of his Conduct, and consulted with him, who they found knew the Place perfectly well, after what manner they should Watch, with the least danger of being discover'd, for *Camilla*'s opening the Wicket: *Frankville* was for going alone, lest if any of the Servants shou'd happen to be about, one Person would be less

less liable to suspicion, than if a Company were seen; the Count thought it most proper to go all together, remembring *Frankville* of the danger he had lately scap'd, and might again be brought into; but *Fidelio* told them, he wou'd advise that they two should remain conceal'd in the *Portico*, of the Convent of St. *Francis*, while himself wou'd watch alone at the Wicket for *Camilla*, and lead her to them, and then afterwards they might go altogether to that Place where the Horses and Servants shou'd attend them; the Page's Counsel was approv'd by both of them, and the time being arriv'd, what they had contriv'd was immediately put in Execution.

EVERY thing happen'd according to their Desire, *Camilla* got safely to the Arms of her impatient Lover, and they all taking Horse, rode with such Speed, as some of them wou'd have been little able to bear, if any thing less than Life and Love had been at Stake.

THEIR eager wishes, and the goodness of their Horses brought them, before Day-break many Miles from *Rome*; but tho' they avoided all high Roads, and travell'd cross the Country to prevent being met, or overtook by any that might know them, yet their desire of seeing themselves in a Place of Security was so great that they refus'd to stop to take any Refreshment 'till the next Day was almost spent; but when they were come into the House where they were to lye that Night, not all the fatigue they had endur'd, kept the Lovers from giving and receiving all the Testimonies imaginable of mutual Affection.

THE sight of their Felicity added new Wings to Count *D'elmont's* impatience to recover *Melliora*, but when he consider'd the little probability of that hope, he grew inconsolable, and his new Page *Fidelio*, who lay on a *Pallet* in the same Room with him, put all his Wit, of which he had no small Stock, upon the stretch,

ſtretch to divert his Sorrows, he talk'd to him, ſung to him, told him a hundred pretty Stories, and, in fine, made good the Charact[illegible] *[illegible]etta* had given him ſo well, that the Count [illegible] him as a Bleſſing ſent from Heaven to leſſen his Misfortunes, and make his Woes ſit eaſy.

THEY continu'd Travelling with the ſame Expedition as when they firſt ſet out, for three or four Days, but then, believing themſelves ſecure from any Purſuit, began to ſlacken their Pace, and make the Journey more delightful to *Camilla* and *Fidelio*, who not being accuſtomed to ride in that manner, wou'd never have been able to ſupport it, if the ſtrength of their *Minds*, had not by far, exceeded that of their *Bodies*.

THEY had gone ſo much about, in ſeeking the By-roads, that they made it three times as long before they arriv'd at *Avigno*, a ſmall Village on the Borders of *Italy*, as any, that had come the direct way wou'd have done; but the Caution they had obſerv'd, was not altogether needleſs, as they preſently found.

A Gentleman who had been a particular Acquaintance of Monſieur *Frankville's*, overtook them at this Place, and after expreſſing ſome Amazement to find 'em no farther on their Journey, told Monſieur *Frankville* he believ'd he cou'd inform him of ſome things which had happen'd ſince his Departure, and cou'd not yet have reach'd his Knowledge, which the other deſiring him to do, the Gentleman began in this manner.

IT was no ſooner Day, ſaid he, than it was nois'd over all the City, that Donna *Camilla*, Count *D'elmont*, and your ſelf, had privately left *Rome*; every Body ſpoke of it, according to their Humour, but the Friends of *Ciamara* and *Cittolini* were outragious, a Complaint was immediately made to the *Conſiſtory*, and all imaginable Deligence us'd, to overtake, or ſtop

you,

you, but you were so happy as to Escape, and the Pursuers return'd without doing any thing of what they went about: Tho' *Cittolini*'s disappointment to all appearance, was the greatest, yet *Ciamara* bore it with the least Patience, and having vainly rag'd, offer'd all the Treasure she was Mistress of, and perhaps spent the best part of it in fruitless means to bring you back, at last she swallow'd Poison, and in the raving agonies of Death, confess'd, that it was not the loss of *Camilla*, but Count *D'elmont* which was the Cause of her Despair: Her Death gave a fresh occasion of Grief to *Cittolini*, but the Day in which she was interr'd, brought him yet a nearer; he had sent to his *Villa* for his Daughter *Violetta* to assist at the Funeral, and the Messenger return'd with the surprizing Account of her not having been there as she pretended she was, nothing was ever equal to the Rage, the Grief, and the Amazement of this distracted Father, when after the strictest Enquiry, and Search that cou'd be made, she was no where to be found or heard of, it threw him into a Fever, of which he linger'd but a small Time, and dy'd the same Day on which I left *Rome*.

THE Gentleman who made this recital, was entirely a Stranger to any of the Company but Monsieur *Frankville*, and they were retired into a private Room during the time of their Conversation, which lasted not long; *Frankville*, was impatient to communicate to *Camilla* and *D'elmont* what he had heard, and as soon as Civility wou'd permit, took leave of the Gentleman.

THE Count had too much Compassion in his Nature not to be extreamly troubled when he was told this mellancholly Catastrophe; but *Camilla* said little; the ill usage of *Ciamara*, and the impudent, and interested Pretensions of *Cittolini* to her, kept her from being so much *concern'd* at their Misfortunes, as she wou'd have been at any other Persons, and the generosity of her Temper, or some other Reason which the

the Reader will not be ignorant of, hereafter, from expressing any *Satisfaction* in the Punishmeut they had met: But when the Count, who most of all lamented *Violetta*, express'd his Astonishment and Affliction, at her Elopement, she joyn'd with him in the Praises of that young Lady, with an eagerness which testify'd, she had no part in the Hatred she bore her Father.

WHILE they were discoursing, *Camilla* observ'd, that *Fidelio* who was all this while in the Room, grew very pale, and at last saw him drop on the Ground, quite Senseless, she run to him, as did his Lord, and Monsieur *Frankville*, and after, by throwing Water in his Face, they brought him to himself again, he appear'd in such an Agony that they fear'd his Fit wou'd return, and order'd him to be laid on a Bed, and carefully attended.

AFTER they had taken a short Repast, they began to think of setting forward on their Journey, designing to reach *Piedmont* that Night: The Count went himself to the Chamber where his Page was laid, and finding he was very ill, told him he thought it best for him to remain in that Place, that he wou'd order Physicians to attend him, and that when he was fully recover'd, he might follow them to *Paris* with Safety. *Fidelio* was ready to faint a second time at the hearing these Words, and with the most earnest Conjurations, accompany'd with Tears, begg'd that he might not be left behind: I can but die, said he, if I go with you, but I am sure, that nothing if I stay can *save* me: The Count seeing him so pressing, sent for a *Litter*, but there was none to be got, and inspite of what *Camilla* or *Frankville* cou'd say to diswade him, having his Lord's Leave, he ventured to attend him as he had done the former part of the Journey.

THEY Travell'd at an easy rate, because of *Fidelio*'s Indisposition, and it being later than they imagin'd, Night came upon 'em before they were aware of it, Usher'd

Usher'd in, by one of the most dreadful Storms that ever was; the Rain, the Hail; the Thunder, and the Lightning, was so Violent that it oblig'd 'em to mend their Pace to get into some Place of shelter, for there was no House near: But to make their Misfortune the greater, they miss'd the Road, and rode considerably out of their way, before they perceiv'd that they were wrong; the darkness of the Night, which had no Illumination than, now and then, a horrid flash of Lightning, the wildness of the Desart, which they had stray'd into, and the little Hopes they had of being able to get out of it, at least till Day, were sufficient to have struck Terror in the boldest Heart: *Camilla* stood in need of all her Love, to Protect her from the Fears which were beginning to Assault her; but poor *Fidelio* felt an inward Horror, which, by this dreadful Scene encreas'd, made him appear wholly desparate: Wretch that I am, cry'd he, 'tis for me the Tempest rises! I justly have incurr'd the wrath of Heaven, --- and you who are Innocent, by my accurs'd Presence are drawn to share a Punishment only due to Crimes like Mine! In this manner he exclaim'd wringing his Hands in bitter Anguish, and rather *Exposing* his lovely Face to all the Fury of the Storm, than any way endeavouring to *Defend* it: His Lord, and the two generous Lovers, tho' Harass'd almost to Death themselves, said all they cou'd to comfort him; the Count and Monsieur *Frankville* consider'd his Words, rather as the Effects of his Indisposition, and the fatigue he endur'd, than remorse for any Crime he cou'd have been guilty of, and the pity they had for one so young and innocent, made the cruelty of the Weather more insupportable to them.

AT last, after long wandring, and the Tempest still encreasing, one of the Servants, who was before, was happy enough to explore a Path, and cry'd out to his Lord with a great deal of Joy, of the Discovery he had made; they were all of Opinion that it must lead to some House, because the

Ground was beat down, as if with the Feet of Passengers, and entirely free from Stubble, Stones and stumps of Trees, as the other part of the Desart they come thro' was Encumber'd with.

THEY had not rode very far before they discern'd Lights, the Reader may imagine the Joy this Sight produc'd, and that they were not slow in making their approach, Encourag'd by such a wish'd for Signal of Success: When they came pretty near, they saw by the Number of Lights, which were dispers'd in several Rooms distant from each other, that it was a very large and magnificent House, and made no doubt, but that it was the Country-Seat of some Person of great Quality: The wet Condition they were in, made them almost asham'd of appearing, and they agreed not to Discover who they were, if they found they were unknown.

THEY had no sooner knock'd, than the Gate was immediately open'd by a Porter, who asking their Business, the Count told him they were Gentlemen, who had been so Unfortunate to mistake the Road to *Piedmont*, and desir'd the Owners leave for Refuge in his House, for that Night; that is a Curtesy, said the Porter, which my Lord never refuses; and in Confidence of his Assent, I may venture to desire you to alight, and bid you welcome: They all accepted the Invitation, and were conducted into a stately Hall, where they waited not long before the Marquess *De Saguillier*, having been inform'd they appear'd like People of Condition, came himself to confirm the Character his Servant had given of his Hospitality. He was a Man perfectly well Bred, and in spite of the Disadvantages their Fatigue had subjected them to, he saw something in the Countenance of these Travellers, which commanded his Respect, and engag'd him to receive them with a more than ordinary Civility.

ALMOST the first thing the Count desir'd, was, that his Page might be taken care of; he was presently carry'd to Bed, and *Camilla* (to whom the Marquess made a thousand Apologies, that being a Batchellor, he cou'd not Accommodate her, as he cou'd the Gentlemen) was show'd to a Chamber, where some of the Maid Servants attended to put her on dry Cloaths.

THEY were splendidly Entertain'd that Night, and when Morning came, and they were preparing to take Leave, the Marquess, who was strangely Charm'd with their Conversation, Entreated them to stay two or three Days with him, to recover themselves of the Fatigue they had suffer'd: The Count's impatience to be at *Paris*, to enquire after his Dear *Melliora*, wou'd never have permitted him to consent, if he had not been oblig'd to it, by being told, that *Fidelio* was grown much worse, and not in a Condition to Travel; *Frankville* and *Camilla* had said nothing, because they wou'd not Oppose the *Count*'s Inclination, but were extreamly glad of an Opportunity to rest a little longer, tho sorry for the Occasion.

THE Marquess omitted nothing that might make their Stay agreeable; but tho' he had a longing Inclination to know the Names, and Quality of his Guests, he forbore to ask, since he found they were not free to discover themselves: The Conversation between these accomplish'd Persons was extreamly Entertaining, and *Camilla*, tho' an *Italian*, spoke *French* well enough to make no inconsiderable part of it; the Themes of their Discourse were various, but at last happning to mention Love, the Marquess spoke of that Passion so feelingly, and express'd himself so vigorously when he attempted to excuse any of those Errors, it leads its Votaries into, that it was easy to Discover, he felt the Influence he endeavour'd to represent.

NIGHT

NIGHT came on again, *Fidelio's* Diſtemper encreas'd to that degree, that they all began to deſpair of his Recovery, at leaſt they cou'd not hope it for a long Time, if at all, and Count *D'elmont* fretted beyond meaſure at this unavoidable delay of the progreſs of his Journey to that Place, where he thought there was only a poſſibility of hearing of *Melliora*: As he was in Bed, forming a thouſand various Idea's, tho' all tending to one Object, he heard the Chamber Door unlock, and opening his Curtains perceiv'd ſomebody come in; a Candle was burning in the next Room, and gave Light enough at the opening the Door, to ſhow it was a Woman, but what Sort of one he cou'd not Diſcern, nor did he give himſelf the trouble of asking who was there, believing it might be one of the Servants come in to fetch ſomething ſhe wanted, 'till coming pretty near the Bed, ſhe cry'd twice in a low Voice, are you a Sleep, no, anſwer'd he, a little ſurpriz'd at this Diſturbance, what wou'd you have? I come ſaid ſhe, to talk to you, and I hope you are more a *Chevalier*, than to prefer a little Sleep, to the Converſation of a Lady, tho' ſhe Viſits you at Midnight: Theſe words made *D'elmont* believe he had met with a ſecond *Ciamara*, and leſt he ſhou'd find the ſame Trouble with this as he had done with the former, he reſolv'd to put a ſtop to it at once, and with an Accent as peeviſh as he cou'd turn his Voice to, the Converſation of Ladies reply'd he, is a Happineſs I neither Deſerve, nor much Deſire at any Time, eſpecially at this; therefore whoever you are, to oblige me, you muſt leave me to the freedom of my Thoughts, which at preſent afford me matter of Entertainment more ſuitable to my Humour than any thing I can find here! Oh Heavens! Said the Lady, is this the Courtly, the Accompliſh'd Count *D'elmont*? So fam'd for Complaiſance and Sweetneſs? Can it be he, who thus rudely Repels a Lady, when ſhe comes to make him a Preſent of her Heart? The Count was very much amaz'd to find he was known in a Place where he thought himself wholly a Stranger, I perceive, answer'd, he, with more Ill-humour if possible, than before, you are very well acquainted with my Name, which I shall never deny (tho' for some Reasons I conceal'd it) but not at all with my Character, or you wou'd know, I can esteem the Love of a Woman, only when 'tis *Granted*, and think it little worth acceptance, *Proffer'd*. Oh unkind! Said she, but perhaps the sight of me, may inspire you with Sentiments less Cruel: With these Words she went hastily out of the Room to fetch the Candle she had left within; and the Count was so much surpriz'd and vex'd at the Immodesty and Imprudence he believ'd her Guilty of, that he thought he cou'd not put a greater affront upon her, than her Behaviour deserv'd, and turn'd himself with his Face the other way, designing to deny her the satisfaction even of a look; she return'd immediately, and having set down the Candle pretty near the Bed, came close to it her self, and seeing how he was laid; this is unkind indeed, said she, 'tis but one look I ask, and if you think me unworthy of another, I will for ever shun your Eyes: The Voice in which these Words were deliver'd, for those she spoke before were in a feign'd Accent, made the Heart-ravish'd *D'elmont* turn to her indeed, with much more hast, than he had done to avoid her; those Dear, those well-remember'd sounds infus'd an Extacy, which none but *Melliora*'s cou'd create; he hear'd --- he saw, --- 'twas she, that very she, whose Loss he had so much deplor'd, and began almost to despair of ever being able to Retrieve! Forgetting all Decorum, he flew out of the Bed, catch'd her in his Arms, and almost stifl'd her with Kisses; which she returning with pretty near an equal eagerness, you will not chide me from you now she cry'd? Those who have Experienc'd any part of that Transport, *D'elmont* now was in, will know it was impossible for him to give her any other Answer, than repeating his Caresses; Words were too poor to Express what 'twas he felt, nor had he time to spare for Speech, employ'd in a far dearer, softer

softer Oratory, than all the force of Language cou'd come up to!

BUT, when at last, to gaze upon her with more freedom, he releas'd her from that strict Embrace he had held her in, and she blushing, with down cast Eyes, began to reflect on the Effects of her unbounded passion. a sudden pang seiz'd on his Soul, and trembling, and convuls'd between extremity of *Joy*, and extremity of *Anguish*, I find thee *Melliora*, cry'd he, but Oh, my Angel! Where is it thou art found? --- in the House of the young Amorous *Marquese D' Sanguillier!* Cease, cease, interrupted she, your causeless Fears, ---- where ever I am found, I am, ---- I can be only yours.---- And if you will return to Bed, I will Inform you, not only what Accident brought me hither, but also every particular of my Behaviour since I came.

THESE Words first put the Count in mind of the Indecency his Transport had made him Guilty of, in being seen in that manner, and was going hastily to throw on his Night Gown, when *Melliora* perceiving his Intent, and fearing he wou'd take cold, told him she wou'd not stay a Moment, unless he granted her Request of returning to his Bed, which he, after having made her sit down on the Side of it, at last consented to: And contenting himself with taking one of her Hands, and pressing it between his, close Prisoner in his Bosom, gave her Liberty to begin in this Manner, the Discovery she had Promis'd.

AFTER the sad Accident of *Alovysa*'s Death. said she, at my return to the Monastry I found a new *Pensioner* there; it was the young *Madamoselle Charlotta D'Mezray*, who being lately left an Orphan, was entrusted to the Care of our *Abbess*, being her near Relation, 'till her time of Mourning was expir'd, and she shou'd be married to this Marquess *D'Sanguillier*, at whose House we are; they were Contracted by their Parents in their Infancy, and nothing but the sudden Death of her Mother, had put a ſtop to to the Conſummation of what, *then*, they both wiſh'd with equal Ardour: But alas! Heaven which decreed the little Beauty I am Miſtreſs of, ſhou'd be pernicious to my own repoſe, ordain'd it ſo, that this unfaithful Lover, ſeeing me one Day at the *Grate* with *Charlotta*, ſhou'd fancy he found ſomething in *Me* more worthy of creating a Paſſion, than he had in her, and began to wiſh himſelf releas'd from his Engagement with her, that he might have Liberty to enter into another, which he imagin'd wou'd be more pleaſing: Neither ſhe, nor I had the leaſt ſuſpicion of his Sentiments, and we having commenc'd a very great Friendſhip, ſhe wou'd for the moſt part, deſire me to partake in the Viſits he made her: He ſtill continu'd to make the ſame proteſtations of Affection to her as ever; but if on any occaſion, ſhe but turn'd her Head, or caſt her Eyes another way, he wou'd give me ſuch looks, as, tho' I then but little regarded, I have ſince underſtood the meaning of, but too well; in this manner he proceeded for ſome Weeks, 'till at laſt he came one Day extreamly out of Humour, and told *Charlotta* the occaſion of it was, that he had heard ſhe gave Encouragement to ſome other Lover; ſhe, amaz'd, as well ſhe might, Avow'd her Innocence, and endeavour'd to Undeceive him, but he, who reſolv'd not to be convinc'd, at leaſt not to ſeem as if he was, pretended to be more enrag'd at what he call'd weak Excuſes; ſaid, he was ſatisfy'd ſhe was more Guilty, even than he wou'd ſpeak, ---- that he knew not if it were conſiſtent with his Honour, ever to ſee her more.---And in ſhort, behav'd himſelf in ſo unaccountable a manner, that there was no room to Doubt that he was either the moſt *Impos'd* on, or moſt *Baſe* of Men: It wou'd be endleſs for me to endeavour to repreſent poor *Charlotta*'s affliction. So I ſhall only ſay, it was anſwerable to the Tenderneſs ſhe had for him, which, cou'd by nothing be exceeded, but by that, continu'd ſhe Sighing, and looking Languiſhingly on him, which contrary to all the Reſolutions I had made, brings *me*

to

to seek the Arms of my Enchanting *D'elmont*, to rouze Remembrance of his former Passion! To strengthen my Idea in his Heart! And Influence him a new with Love and Softness! This kind Digression made the Count give Truce to his *Curiosity*, that he might Indulge the Raptures of his *Love*, and raising himself in Bed, and pressing her slender fine proportioned Body close to his, wou'd permit her no otherwise, than in this Posture to continue her Discourse.

SEVERAL Days resum'd *Melliora*, were past, and we heard nothing of the Marquess, all which, as he has since told me, were spent in fruitless Projections to steal me from the Monastry; but at last, by the means of a *Lay Sister*, he found means to convey a Letter to me; the Contents of it, as near as I can remember, were these.

To the Divine MELLIORA.

'TIS *not the falshood of* Charlotta, *but the Charms of* Melliora *have produc'd this Change in my Behaviour, do not therefore, at the reading this, affect a surprize at Effects, which I am sure cannot be uncommon to such Excellence! Nor accuse an Inconstancy, which I rather esteem a Virtue than a Vice: To Change from you indeed wou'd be the biggest Sin, as well as Stupidity: but to Change for you, is what all must, and ought to do, who boast a Capacity of distinguishing. I love you, Oh Divinest* Melliora, *I burn, I languish for you in unceasing Torments, and you wou'd find it impossible for you to condemn the boldness*

 of

of this Declaration, if you cou'd be sensible of the Racks which force me to it, and which must shortly End me, if not happy enough to be receiv'd

Your Lover,

D'SANGULLIER.

'TIS impossible for me to express the Grief, and Vexation this Letter gave me, but I forbore showing it to *Charlotta*, knowing how much it would encrease her Anguish, and resolv'd when next I saw him, as I made no doubt but I should quickly do, to use him in such a fashion, as in spite of his Vanity, shou'd make him know I was not to be won in such a manner; for I confess, my dear *D'elmont*, that his Timerity gave no less a shock to my *Pride*, than his Infidelity to her I really lov'd, did to my *Friendship*. The next Day I was told, a Gentleman enquir'd for me, I presently imagin'd it was he, and went to the Grate, with a Heart full of Indignation; I was not deceiv'd in my Conjecture, it was indeed the Marquess, who appear'd on the other side, but with so much Humility in his Eyes, and awful fear, for what he saw in Mine, as half disarm'd my Anger for what concern'd my self, and had his Passion not proceeded from his Inconstancy, I might have been drawn to *pity* what was not in my Power to Reward; but his base Usage of a Woman so deserving as *Charlotta*, made me Express my self in Terms full of Disdain and Detestation, and without allowing him to Reply, or make any Excuses, pluck'd the Letter he had sent me out of my Pocket, with a design to return it him, just at that Moment when a *Nun* came hastily to call me from the Grate: Some body had overheard the beginning of what I said, and had told the *Abbess*, who, tho' she was not displeas'd at what she heard of my Behaviour to him, yet she thought it improper for me to hold any Discourse with a Man, who declar'd himself

himself my Lover: I did not, however, let her know who the Person was, fearing it might come to *Charlotta*'s Ears, and encrease an Affliction, which was already too violent: I was vext to miss the Opportunity of giving back his Letter, but kept it still about me, not in the least Questioning, but that boldness which had encourag'd him to make a discovery of his Desires, wou'd again lead him to the Prosecution of them in the same manner, but I was deceiv'd, his Passion prompted him to take other, as he believ'd, more effectual Measures: One Day, at least a Fortnight after I had seen the *Marquess*, as I was walking in the Garden with *Charlotta*, and another young *Pensioner*, a Fellow who was imploy'd in taking away Rubbish, told us there were some Statues carry'd by the Gate, which open'd into the Fields, which were the greatest Master-pieces of Art that had ever been seen: They are going, said he, to be plac'd in the *Seiur Valiers* Garden. if you step but out, you may get a Sight of them: We, who little suspected any Deceit, run without Consideration, to satisfie our Curiosity, but instead of the Statues we expected to see, four Living Men disguis'd, muffl'd, and well Mounted, came Galloping up to us, and, as it were surrounded us, before we had Time to get back to the Gate we came out at: Three of them alighting, seiz'd me and my Companions, and I, who was the destin'd Prey, was in a Moment thrown into the Arms of him who was on Horseback, and who no sooner receiv'd me, than as if we had been mounted on a *Pegasus*, we seem'd rather to *fly* than *Ride*; in vain I struggl'd, shriek'd, and cry'd to Heaven for help, my Prayers were lost in Air, as quickly was my Speech, surprize, and rage, and dread, o'rewhelm'd my sinking Spirits, and unable to sustain the Rapidity of such violent Emotions, I fell into a Swoon, from which I recover'd not, till I was at the Door of some House, but where I yet am ignorant; the first thing I saw, when I open'd my Eyes, was one of those Men who had been Assistant in my carrying away, and was now about to lift me from the Horſe: I had not yet the power to Speak, but when I had, I vented all the Paſſions of my Soul in terms full of Diſtraction and Deſpair: By what means the People of the Houſe were gain'd to my Raviſhers Intereſt, I know not, but they took little Notice of the Complaints I made, or my Implorations for Succour: I had now, not the leaſt ſhadow of a Hope, that any thing but Death cou'd ſave me from Diſhonour, and having vainly Rag'd, I at laſt ſate down meditating by what means I ſhou'd Compaſs that only Relief from the worſe Ruin which ſeem'd to threaten me: While my Thoughts were thus employ'd, he who appear'd the chief of that inſolent Company, making a Sign that the reſt ſhou'd withdraw, fell on his Knees before me, and plucking off his Vizard, diſcover'd to me the Face of the Marqueſs *D' Saguillier.* Heavens! How did this Sight inflame me? Mild as I am, by Nature, I that Moment was all Fury! ---- Till now I had not the leaſt Apprehenſion who he was, and believ'd 'twas rather my *Fortune* than my *Perſon*, which had prompted ſome daring Wretch to take this Method to obtain it; but now, my Woes appear'd, if poſſible, with greater Horror, and his Quality and Engagement with *Charlotta* made the Act ſeem yet more Baſe. I blame you not, ſaid he, Oh Divineſt *Melliora!* The Preſumption I am guilty of, is of ſo high a Nature, as juſtly may deſerve your utmoſt Rigour! ----- I know, and confeſs my Crime; Nay, hate my ſelf for thus offending you.-- But Oh! 'Tis unavoidable.---be then, like Heaven, who when Injured moſt, takes moſt delight to pardon: Crimes unrepented, anſwer'd I, can have no plea for Mercy, ſtill to perſiſt, and ſtill to ask forgiveneſs, is *Mocking* of the Power we ſeem to *Implore*, and but encreaſes Sin.---- Releaſe me from this Captivity, which you have betray'd me into, Reſtore me to the Monaſtry ---- And for the *future*, ceaſe to ſhock my Ears with Tales of violated Faith, deteſted Paſſion! Then, I perhaps, *may* pardon what is *paſt.* His reply to all this was very little to the Purpoſe, only I perceiv'd he was ſo far from complying

complying with my Requeſt, or repenting what he had done, that he reſolv'd to proceed yet further, and one of his Aſſociates coming in, to tell him that his Chariot, which it ſeems he had order'd to meet him there, was ready, he offer'd to take me by the Hand to lead me to it, which I refuſing, with an Air which teſtify'd the Indignation of my Soul, Madam, ſaid he, you are not here leſs in my Power, than you will be in a Place, where I can Accommodate you in a manner more ſuitable to your Quality, and the Adoration I have for you: If I were capable of a baſe Deſign on you, what hinders but I now might perpetrate it? But be aſſur'd, your Beauties are not of that kind, which inſpire Sentiments diſhonourable; nor ſhall you ever find any other Treatment from me, than what might become the humbleſt of your Slaves; my Love, fierce as it is, ſhall know it's Limits, and never dare to Breath an Accent leſs Chaſt than your own Virgin Dreams, and Innocent as your Deſires.

THO' the boldneſs he had been guilty of, and ſtill perſiſted in, made me give but little Credit to the latter part of his Speech, yet the Beginning of it awak'd my Conſideration to a reflection, that I cou'd not indeed be any where in a greater danger of the Violence I fear'd, than where I was; but on the contrary, it might ſo happen, that in leaving that Place, I might poſſibly meet ſome Perſons who might know me, or at leaſt be carry'd ſomewhere, whence I might with more likelihood, make my Eſcape: In this laſt Hope, I went into the Chariot, and indeed, to do him juſtice, neither in our Journey, nor ſince I came into his Houſe, has he ever violated the Promiſe he made me; nothing can be with more Humility than his Addreſſes to me, never Viſiting me without firſt having obtain'd my leave! But to return to the particulars of my Story, I had not been here many Days, before a Servant-Maid of the Houſe, being in my Chamber doing ſomething about me, ask'd me if it were poſſible I cou'd forget her; the Queſtion

ſurpriz'd

ſurpriz'd me, but I was much more ſo, when looking earneſtly in her Face, which I had never done before, I perfectly diſtinguiſh'd the Features of *Charlotta*: Oh Heavens! cry'd I, *Charlotta!* The very ſame, ſaid ſhe, but I dare not ſtay now to unfold the Miſtery, leſt any of the Family take Notice; at Night when I undreſs you, you ſhall know the Hiſtory of my Transformation.

NEVER any Day ſeem'd ſo long to me as that, and I feign'd my ſelf indiſpos'd, and rung my Bell for ſome body to come up, ſeveral Hours before the time I us'd to go to Bed, *Charlotta* gueſſing my impatience, took care to be in the way, and as ſoon as ſhe was with me, not ſtaying for my Requeſting it of her, begun the Information ſhe had promis'd, in this manner.

YOU ſee, ſaid ſhe, forcing her ſelf to put on a half ſmile, your unhappy Rival follows to interrupt the Triumph of your Conqueſt; but I proteſt to you, that if I thought you eſteem'd my perjur'd Lover's Heart an offering worthy your Acceptance, I never wou'd have diſturb'd your happineſs, and 'tis as much the Hopes of being able to be Inſtrumental in ſerving you in your Releaſment, as the prevention of that Bleſſing the injurious *D'Sanguillier* aims at, which has brought me here: Of all the Perſons that bewail'd your being carry'd away, I was the only one who had any Gueſs at the Raviſher, nor had I been ſo wiſe, but that the very Day on which it happen'd, you drop'd a Letter, which I took up, and knowing it the *Marqueſs's* Hand, made no ſcruple of Reading it. I had no opportunity to upbraid you for the concealment of his falſhood, but the manner of your being ſeiz'd, convinc'd me you were Innocent of favouring his Paſſion, and his Vizard ſlipping a little on one Side, as he took you in his Arms, diſcover'd enough of that Face, I have ſo much ador'd, for me to know who it was, that had took this Method to gain you: I will not

not continu'd ſhe, weeping, trouble you with any Recital of what I endur'd from the Knowledge of my Misfortune, but you may judge it by my Love, however, I bore up againſt the Oppreſſive weight, and reſolv'd to ſtruggle with my Fate, even to the Laſt; I made an Excuſe for leaving the Monaſtry the next Day, without giving any ſuſpicion of the Cauſe, or letting any body into the Secret of the Marqueſs, and Diſguis'd as you ſee, found means to be receiv'd by the Houſe-keeper, as a Servant, I came here in three Days after you, and have had the opportunity of being confirm'd by your Behaviour, of what I before believ'd, that you were far from being an Aſſiſtant in his Deſign.

HERE the ſorrowful *Charlotta* finiſh'd her little Account, and I teſtify'd the Joy I felt in ſeeing her, by a thouſand Embraces, and all the Proteſtations of Eternal Friendſhip to her, that I could make: All the times we had any opportunity of Talking to each other, were ſpent in forming Schemes for my Eſcape, but none of them appear'd feaſible; however the very Contrivance was a kind of Pleaſure to me, for tho' I began to baniſh all my Fears of the Marqueſs's offering any violence to my Virtue, yet I found his Paſſion wou'd not permit him to ſuffer my Departure, and I was almoſt Diſtracted when I had no Hopes of being in a Capacity of hearing from you, or writing to you: In this faſhion, my deareſt *D'elmont* have I liv'd, ſometimes flattering my ſelf with vain Projects, ſometimes deſponding of being ever free: But laſt Night, *Charlotta* coming up, according to her Cuſtom, told me in a kind of Rapture, that you, and my Brother were in the Houſe, ſhe, it ſeems knew you at *Paris* while her Mother was yet Living, and to make her entirely eaſy as to the Marqueſs, I had now made her the Confidant of my Sentiments concerning you: I need not tell you the Extacy this News gave me, you are too well acquainted with my Heart, not to be able to conceive it more juſtly than Language

Language can Expreſs; but I cannot forbear Informing you of one thing, of which you are ignorant, tho' had Prudence any ſhare in this Love-directed Soul, I ſhou'd conceal it: My impatience to behold you, was almoſt equal to my Joy to think you were ſo near, and tranſported with my eager wiſhes, by *Charlotta*'s Aſſiſtance, I laſt Night found the way into your Chamber: I ſaw you, Oh *D'elmont!* My longing Eyes enjoy'd the ſatisfaction they ſo much deſir'd, but yours were cloſs'd, the Fatigue of your Journey had laid you faſt a Sleep, ſo faſt, that even Fancy was unactive, and no kind Dream, alarm'd you with one Thought of *Melliora!*

SHE cou'd not pronounce theſe laſt Words very Intelligibly, the greedy Count devour'd 'em as ſhe ſpoke, and tho' Kiſſes had made many a Parentheſis in her Diſcourſe, yet he reſtrain'd himſelf as much as poſſible, for the Pleaſure of hearing her; but perceiving ſhe was come to a Period, he gave a looſe to all the furious Tranſports of his ungovern'd Paſſion: A while their Lips were Cemented! Rivetted together with Kiſſes, ſuch Kiſſes! As Collecting every Sence in one, exhale the very Soul, and mingle Spirits! Breathleſs with bliſs, then wou'd they pauſe and gaze, then joyn again, with Ardour ſtill encreaſing, and Looks, and Sighs, and ſtraining Graſps were all the Eloquence that either cou'd make uſe of: Fain wou'd he now have obtain'd the aim of all his Wiſhes, ſtrongly he preſs'd, and faintly ſhe repuls'd: Diſſolv'd in Love, and melting in his Arms, at laſt ſhe found no Words to form Denials, while he, all fire, improv'd the lucky Moment, a thouſand Liberties he took. --- A thouſand Joys he reap'd, and had infallibly been poſſeſt of all, if *Charlotta*, who ſeeing it broad Day, had not wonder'd at *Melliora*'s ſtay, and come and knock'd at the Chamber Door, which not being faſten'd, gave way to her Entrance, but ſhe made not ſuch haſt, but that they had time enough to Diſengage themſelves from that cloſe Embrace they had held each other

other in: Heavens! *Melliora*, cry'd the careful Interrupter, what mean you by this ſtay, which may be ſo prejudicial to our Deſigns; the Marqueſs is already ſtirring, and if he ſhou'd come into this Room, or ſend to yours, what might be the Conſequence: I come, I come, ſaid *Melliora*, alarm'd at what ſhe heard, and riſing from the Bed-ſide: Oh, you will not, ſaid the Count in a Whiſper, and tenderly preſſing her Hand, you muſt not leave me thus! A few Hours hence, anſwer'd ſhe aloud, I hope to have the Power to own my ſelf all yours, nor can the Scheme we have laid fail of the Effects we wiſh, if no Diſcovery happens to Poſtpone it: She was going with *Charlotta* out of the Chamber, with theſe Words, but remembring her ſelf, ſhe turn'd haſtily back, let not my Brother, Reſum'd ſhe, know my Weakneſs, and when you ſee me next, feign a ſurprize equal to his own.

IT is not to be ſuppos'd that after ſhe was gone, *D'elmont*, tho' kept awake all Night, cou'd ſuffer any Sleep to enter his Eyes; exceſs of Joy, of all the Paſſions, hurries the Spirits moſt, and keeps 'em longeſt buſied: *Anger* or *Grief*, rage violently at firſt, but quickly flag, and ſink at laſt into a Lethargy, but *Pleaſure* warms, exhillerates the Soul, and every rapturous Thought infuſes new Deſires, new Life, and added Vigour,

THE Marqueſs *D' Saguillier* was no leſs happy in imagination than the Count, and it was the force of that Paſſion which had rouz'd him ſo early that Morning, and made him wait impatiently for his Gueſts coming out of their Chambers, for he wou'd not diſturb them: As ſoon as they were all come into the Drawing-Room, I know not Meſſiures, ſaid he, with a Voice and Eyes wholly chang'd from thoſe he wore the Day before, whether you have ever Experienc'd the force of Love to that Degree that I have, but I dare believe you have Generoſity enough to rejoyce in the good Fortune I am going to be

poſſeſs'd

poſſeſs'd of; and when I ſhall inform you how I have long languiſh'd in a Paſſion, perhaps, the moſt extravagant that ever was, you will confeſs the Juſtice of that God, who ſoon or late, ſeldom ſuffers his faithful Votaries to miſs their Reward: The Count cou'd not force himſelf to a Reply to theſe Words, but *Frankville* and *Camilla*, who were entirely Ignorant of the Cauſe of them, heartily Congratulated him. I am Confident, reſum'd the Marqueſs, that Deſpair has no Exiſtance but in weak and timerous Minds, all Women may be won by Force or Stratagem, and tho' I had, almoſt, invincible Difficulties to ſtruggle with, Patience, Conſtancy, and a bold and artful Management has at length ſurmounted them: Hopeleſs by Diſtant Courtſhip to obtain the *Heart* of my Adorable, I found means to make my ſelf Maſter of her *Perſon*, and by making no other uſe of the Power I had over her, than humbly Sighing at her Feet, convinc'd her my Deſigns were far from being Diſhonourable; and laſt Night, looking on me, with more kindneſs than ſhe had ever done before: My Lord, ſaid ſhe, your Uſage of me has been too Noble, not to vanquiſh what ever Sentiments I may have been poſſeſt with to your Prejudice, therefore ſince you have Company in the Houſe, who may be Witneſs of what I do, I think I cannot chuſe a fitter time, than this, to beſtow my ſelf, before them, on him who moſt Deſerves me: I will not now, continu'd he, delay the Confirmation of my Happineſs ſo long, as to go about to deſcribe the Extacy I felt, for this ſo wiſh'd, and ſo unhop'd a Condeſcenſion, but when, hereafter, you ſhall be told the whole Hiſtory of my Paſſion, you will be better able to conceive it; the Marqueſs had ſcarce done ſpeaking, when his Chaplain came into the Room, ſaying, he believ'd it was the Hour his Lordſhip order'd him to attend; it is! it is, cry'd the tranſported Marqueſs. Now my worthy Gueſts you ſhall behold the lovely Author of my Joys; with theſe Words he left them, but immediately return'd, leading the intended Bride: Monſieur

Frankville,

ville, tho' he had not ſeen his Siſter in ſome Years, knew her at the firſt Glimpſe, and the Surprize of meeting her ---- Meeting her in ſo unexpected a manner was ſo great, that his Thoughts were quite confounded with it, and he cou'd no otherwiſe Expreſs it, than by throwing his Eyes wildly, ſometimes on her, ſometimes on the Count, and ſometimes on the Marqueſs; the Count tho appris'd of this, felt a Conſternation for the Conſequence little inferior to his, and both being kept ſilent by their different Agitations, and the Marqueſs, by the ſudden Change, which he perceiv'd in their Countenances, *Melliora* had liberty to explain her ſelf in this manner. I have kept my Word, my Lord, ſaid ſhe to the Marqueſs, this Day ſhall give me to him who beſt deſerves me; but who that is, my Brother and Count *D'elmont* muſt determine, ſince Heaven has reſtor'd them to me, all Power of diſpoſing of my ſelf muſt ceaſe; 'tis they muſt, henceforth, rule the will of *Melliora*, and only their conſent can make me yours; all Endeavours wou'd be vain to repreſent the Marqueſs's confuſion at this ſudden Turn, and 'tis hard to ſay whether his Aſtoniſhment, or Vexation was greateſt; her Brother he wou'd little have regarded, not doubting but his Quality, and the Riches he was poſſeſt of, wou'd eaſily have gain'd his Compliance; but Count *D'elmont*, tho' he knew him not (having, for ſome diſguſt he receiv'd at Court, been many Years abſent from *Paris*,) yet he had heard much talk of him; and the Paſſion he had for *Melliora*, by the Adventure of *Alovyſa*'s Death, had made too great a Noiſe in the World not to have reach'd his Ears; he ſtood Speechleſs for ſome time, but when he had a little recover'd himſelf, have you then Deceiv'd me, Madam, Said he? No, anſwer'd ſhe, I am ſtill ready to perform my promiſe, whenever theſe Gentlemen ſhall command me.---- The one my Brother, the other my Guardian, obtain but their Conſent, and ---- Mine, he can never have, Interrupted *Frankville* haſtily, and laying his Hand on his Sword. Nor mine,

mine, cry'd the Count, while I have Breath to form Denials, or my Arm strength to Guard my Beauteous Charge; hold Brother, ---- Hold, my Lord, said *Mellicora*, fearing their Fury wou'd produce some fatal Effects, the *Marquess* has been so truly Noble, that you rather ought to Thank, than resent his Treatment of me, and tho' *I* see Rage in *your* Eyes, and all the Stings of disappointment glowing fierce in *his*, yet I have Hopes, a general Content may Crown the End. ---- Appear! Continu'd she, raising her Voice, appear! Thou lovely faithful Maid! Come forth and Charm thy roving Lovers Heart again to Constancy, to Peace, and thee! She had no sooner spoke, then *Charlotta* entred, drest like a Bride indeed, in a Suit of Cloaths, which she had brought with her, in case any happy Opportunity shou'd arise for her to discover herself: If the *Marquess* was before confounded, how much more so was he now? That injur'd Ladies Presence, just at this juncture, and the Surprize by what means she came there, made him utterly unable to resolve on any thing, which she observing, and taking advantage of his Confusion, run to him, and catching hold of his Hand; wonder not my Lord, said she, to see *Charlotta* here, nothing is impossible to Love like mine, tho' slighted and abandon'd by you, still I pursue your Steps with Truth, with Tenderness, and Constancy untir'd! --- Then, perceiving he still was silent, come, my Lord, continu'd she, you must at last take Pity on my Sufferings, my Rival, Charming as she is, wants a just sensibility of your Deserts, and is by that, less worthy even than I; Oh, then remember, if not to me, what 'tis you owe your self your own exhalted Merits, and you will soon determine in my Favour, and confess that she, who knows you best, ought most to have you; she spoke these Words in so moving an Accent, and they were accompany'd with so many Tears, that the most rocky Heart must have relented, and that the Marquess was sensibly touch'd with 'em, his Countenance Testify'd, when sighing, and turning his Head a little away, not with disdain, but Remorse,

morſe, for the Infidelity he had been guilty of: Oh, ceaſe, ſaid he, this Flood of Softneſs, it gives me Pains I never felt before, for 'tis impoſſible you can forgive --- Oh Heaven! cry'd the tranſported *Charlotta*, all you have done, or ever can do of Unkindneſs, is by one tender Word made full amends for; ſee at your Feet, (continued ſhe, falling on her Knees) thus in this humble Poſture, which beſt becomes my proſtrate Soul, I beg you to accept the Pardon which I bring, to baniſh from your Mind all Thoughts that you have injured me, and leave it free from all the generous Joys, the making others happy, muſt create: This Action of *Charlotta*'s, join'd to the Reflection, how ſtrangely every Thing happen'd to prevent his Deſigns on the other, won him entirely, and raiſing her with a tender Embrace, put it out of her Power to regret his ever being Falſe, ſince his Return gave her a Taſte of Joys, which are not, but in Reconciliation to be found.

THE Count, Monſieur *Frankville*, and the two Ladies who had waited all this while in an impatient Expectation for the end of this Affair, now paid their ſeveral Congratulations, all highly applauding the Conſtancy of *Charlotta*, and the timely Repentance of the Marqueſs: Theſe Ceremonies being over, the Marqueſs deſir'd *Charlotta* to acquaint him by what means ſhe had gain'd Admittance to his Houſe unknown to him; which Curioſity ſhe immediately ſatisfying, engag'd a new, the Praiſes of the whole Company, and more endear'd herſelf to her belov'd Marqueſs's Affections.

TRANQUILITY now reign'd in thoſe Hearts, which lately heav'd with various and diſturb'd Emotions, and Joy ſate ſmiling upon every Cheek, entirely happy in their ſeveral Wiſhes: They could now talk of paſt Woes with Pleaſure, and began to enter into a very delightful Converſation, when *Frankville* on a ſudden miſſing *Camilla*, and asking for her, one

of

of the Servants told him ſhe was gone to the Sick Page's Chamber, this News gave him ſome little alarm, and the rather, becauſe he had obſerv'd ſhe expreſſed a more than ordinary Tenderneſs and Care for this Page, all the Time of their Journey: he ran immediately to the Room where he heard ſhe was, and found her lying on the Bed, with her Arms round *Fidelio*'s Neck, and her Face cloſe to his; this ſhocking Sight had certainly driven the Raſhneſs of his Temper to commit ſome Deed of Horror, if the Amazement he was in had not prevented it; he drew his Sword half out, but then, as if ſome Spell had charm'd his Arm, remain'd in that Poſture, fix'd and motionleſs as Marble: *Camilla* half blinded with the Tears which fell from her Eyes, ſaw not the Confuſion he was in, nor conſidered the ſeeming Reaſon he had to be ſo, but raiſing her Head a little to ſee who it was that came into the Chamber, Oh *Frankville!* ſaid ſhe, ſee here the Ruins of Love, behold the Tyranny of that fatal *Paſſion* in this expiring Fair! But haſte, contin'd ſhe, finding him ready to faint, let Count *D'elmont* know, the faithful, generous *Violetta!* Dies --- ſhe dies for him, and asks no other Recompence, than a laſt Farewell -- *Violetta!* interrupted *Frankville,* what means *Camilla*? This, this is *Violetta,* reſum'd ſhe, who like a Page diſguis'd, has followed the too lovely Count, and loſt herſelf: The Rage which at his firſt Entrance had poſſeſt the Heart of *Frankville,* now gave Way to Grief, and coming near the Bed, he began to teſtify it, by all the Marks which an unfeign'd Concern cou'd give, but this unfortunate Languiſher, finding her Strength decay, prevented him from making any long Speeches, by renewing that Requeſt which *Camilla* had already made known, of ſeeing her dear Lord before ſhe dy'd, which *Frankville* making haſte to fulfil, ſhe call'd to him as loud as her Weakneſs would permit to come back, and as ſoon as he was, *Camilla,* ſaid ſhe, has inform'd me of my Lord's good Fortune in meeting with the Charmer of his Soul, I would not deprive him of a

Moments

Moments Happiness. I therefore beg she'd give a dying Rival, leave to wish her Joy, and as neither my Death, nor the Cause of it can be a Secret to any of the Company here, I desire they all may be Witnesses, with what Pleasure I welcome it; *Frankville*, Fiery as he was, had a vast deal of Compassion in his Nature, and could not see so beautiful a young Lady, and one whom he had so many Obligations to, on the Account of his Affair with *Camilla*, in this despairing and dying Condition, without being seiz'd with an Anguish inexpressible; but all the Pangs he felt were nothing when compar'd to those he gave *D'elmont* in the Delivery of her Message; he ran into the Room like a Man distracted, and in the Hurry of his Grief forgot even the Complaisance he ow'd to *Melliora*, but she was too generous to disapprove his Concern, immediately followed with her Brother, the Marquess and *Charlotta*: What is it that I hear Madam, cry'd the Count, throwing himself on the Bed by her? Can it be possible that the admir'd *Violetta* cou'd forsake her Father, --- Country, --- Friends, --- forego her Sexes Pride, --- the Pomp of Beauty, --- gay Dresses, and all the Equipage of State and Grandeur; to follow in a mean Disguise, a Man unworthy her Thoughts? Oh! no more, said she, weeping, you are but too, too worthy Adoration; nor do I yet believe my Love a Crime, tho' the Consequence is so: I might in *Rome*, with Honour and Innocence have died, but by my shameful Flight, I was the Murderer of my Father --- that --- that's a Guilt, which all these Floods of Penitence can never wash away --- Yet, bear me Witness Heaven, how little I suspected the sad Event, when first, unable to support your Absence, I contriv'd this Way, unknown, to keep for ever in your Sight; I lov'd, 'tis true, but if one unchaste Wish, or an impure Desire e'er stain'd my Soul, then may the purging Fire to which I am going, miss its Effect, my Spots remain, and not one Saint vouchsafe to own me: Here the Force of her Passion, agitating her Spirits with too much

Violence

Violence for the Weakness of her Body, she sunk fainting in the Bed: And tho' the Count and *Camilla* felt the most deeply her Afflictions, the one because they proceeded from her Love to him, and the other as having long been her Friend, and Partner of her Secrets, yet those in the Company who were most Strangers to her, participated in her Sufferings, and commiserated the Woes they could not heal; and as soon as she recovered from her Swoon, the generous *Melliora* (not in the least possest with any of those little Jealousies, which Women of narrow Souls harbour on such Occasions) came nearer to the Bed, and taking her kindly by the Hand, Live and be comforted, said she, a Love so innocent shall never give me any Disquiet. --- Live and Enjoy the Friendship of my Lord, and if you please to favour me with yours, I shall esteem it as it deserves, a Blessing. No Madam, answered the now almost Expiring *Violetta*, Life, after this shameful Declaration, wou'd be the worst of Punishments, but, not to be Ungrateful to so generous an Offer, for a few Moments I accept it, and like Children, placing their darling Play things on their Pillow, and then contented to go to Sleep, so I would keep your Lord, would view him still while I awake to Life, then drop insensibly into a Slumber of eternal Peace. This mournful Tenderness peirc'd *D'elmont*, to the very Soul, and putting his Arm gently under her Head, which, he perceiv'd she was too weak to raise when she endeavoured it, and laying his Face on one of her Hands, cou'd not forbear washing it in Tears, she felt the cordial Drops, and, as if they gave her a new Vigour, exerting her Voice to the utmost of her Strength; this is too kind, said she, I now can feel none of those Agonies which render Death the King of Terrors, and thus, thus happy in your Sight,------ your Touch------ your tender Pity, I can but be Translated from one Heaven to another, and yet, forgive me Heaven, if it be a Sin, I cou'd wish, methinks, to know no other Paradise than you, to be be permitted to hover round you, to Form your Dreams, to ſit upon your Lips all Day, to mingle with your Breath, and glide in unfelt Air into your Boſom: She wou'd have proceeded, but her Voice faultered in the Accent, and all ſhe ſpoke diſtinguiſhable was, Oh *D'elmont*! receive in this one Sigh, my lateſt Breath----- it was indeed her laſt, ſhe died that Moment, died in his Arms, whom more than Life ſhe priz'd, and ſure there are none who have liv'd in the Anxieties of Love, who wou'd not envy ſuch a Death!

THERE was not in this noble Company, one whoſe Eyes were dry, but Count *D'elmont* was for ſome Time inconſolable, even by *Melliora*; he forbore the celebrating of his ſo eagerly deſired Nuptials, as did the Marqueſs and Monſieur *Frankville* theirs, in Complaiſance to him, 'till after *Violetta* was interr'd, which the Count took Care ſhould be in a Manner becoming her Quality, her Merit, and the Eſteem he profeſs'd to have born her: But when this melancholly Scene was paſt, a Day of Joy ſucceeded, and one happy Hour confirm'd the Wiſhes of the three longing Bridegrooms; the Weddings were all kept in a ſplendid Manner at the Marqueſs's, and it was not with out a great deal of Reluctance, that he and *Charlotta* ſuffered the Count, Monſieur *Frankville*, and their Ladies to take leave of them. When they came to *Paris*, they were joyfully received by the Chevalier *Brillian* and *Anſellina*, and thoſe, who in the Count's Abſence had taken a Liberty of cenſuring and condemning his Actions, aw'd by his Preſence, and in Time, won by his Virtues, now ſwell his Praiſes with an equal Vehemence: Both he and *Frankville* are ſtill living, bleſt with a numerous and hopeful Iſſue, and continue with their fair Wives, great and lovely Examples of conjugal Affection.

F I N I S.

BOOKS Printed for, and Sold by D. BROWNE, without *Temple-Bar*.

1. A Collection of Poems on various Subjects. By Sir *Richard Blackmore*, Kt. M. D. Fellow of the Royal Colledge of Physicians.

2. The Art of *English* Poetry. Containing, 1st, Rules for making Verses. 2d, A Collection of the most natural, agreeable, and sublime Thoughts, *viz*. Allusions, Similies, Descriptions and Characters of Poems and Things that are to be found in the best *English* Poets. 3d, A Dictionary of Rhymes. By *Edward Bysshe*, Gent. The 6th Edition Corrected and Enlarged, in 2 Vol. 12o.

3. A Collection of Poems, *viz*. The Temple of Death, by the Marquis of *Normandy*, an Epistle to the Earl of *Dorset*: By *Charles Mountague*, Lord *Halifax*; the Duel of the Stags by Sir *Robert Howard*. With several Original Poems never before Printed; By the Earl of *Roscommon*, the Earl of *Rochester*, the Earl of *Orrery*, the Lord *Lansdowne*, Sir *Charles Lesley*, Sir *George Etheredge*, Mr. *Stepney*, Mr. *Dryden*, &c.

4. The

BOOKS Printed for D. Browne.

4. The Dramatick and Poetical Works of *Nicholas Rowe*, Esq; late Poet Laureat; Containing all his Plays and Poems, in three neat Pocket Volumes, with Cutts.

5. The Works of Mr. *John Oldham*, together with his Remains, in 2 Vol. in 12o. To this Edition are added, Memoirs of his Life and explanatory Notes upon some obscure Passages of his Writings, adorn'd with Cutts, Price 6 *s*.

6. The Poetical Works of *Samiel Daniel*, Author of the *English* History. To which is prefix'd Memoirs of his Life and Writing, in 2 Vol. 12o.

7. Poems by the Earl of *Roscommon*, to which is added an Essay on Poetry by the Earl of *Mulgrave*, now Duke of *Buckingham*, together with Poems. By Mr. *Rich. Duke*.

8. Letters of Gallantry. By M. de *Fontenelle*; translated into *English*. By Mr. *Ozell*.

9. The Lover and Reader. By Sir *Richard Steele*. The Second Edition.

BOOKS Printed for *W. Chetwood*.

1. THE Voyages, Travels, and dangerous Adventures of Capt. *Richard Falconer*. Containing the Laws, Customs and Manners of the *Indians*, in several Parts of *America*, his Shipwrecks, his being left on Shore on the Island of *Dominica*, where to save his Life, he was obliged to Marry an *Indian* Wife; his narrow Escape from thence after his Wife was Kill'd; Intermix'd with the Voyages of *Thomas Randal*, a West *Indian* Pilot, his being cast away in the *Baltick*, &c.

N being

being the only Man ſav'd upon an uninhabited Iſland, &c. With a curious Frontiſpiece Bound 5 *s.*

2. The Seige of *Damaſcus*: A Tragedy. By the late Mr. *Hughes.*

3. Spartan Dame, a Tragedy, by Mr. *Southern.* Price 1 *s.* 6 *d.*

4. Ximena, or the Heroick Daughter, Written by Mr. *Cibber*, Dedicated to Sir *Richard Steele.* 1 *s.* 6 *d.*

5. Bond-man, or Love and Liberty, a Tragedy, 1 *s.* 6 *d.*

6. Earl of *Warwick*, or the Britiſh Exile, a Tragedy. 1 *s.* 6 *d.*

7. Love in a Veil, a Comedy, by Mr. Savage. 1 *s.* 6 *d.*

8. Traytor, a Tragedy. 1 *s.* 6 *d.*

9. Two Harlequins in *French* and *Engliſh*, a Comedy. 1 *s.* 6 *d.*

10. Fair of St. Germains, a Comedy. 1 *s.*

11. Antiochus and Stratonice, a Novel, by Mr. *Theobald.* Bound 2 *s.*

12. *Crawford*'s Novels Compleat, Bound 2 *s.* 6 *d.*

13. Orpheus and Eurydice, by Mr. *Weaver.* 1 *s.*

14. The Chevalier de St. *George*, a Heroick-comical Poem. 1 *s.*

15. Cynegetica, or the Force and Pleaſure of Hunting, by Mr. *Morgan.* 1 *s.*

16. Richard the Third, a Tragedy, by Mr. *Cibber.* 1 *s.*

17. Diſtreſs'd Mother by Mr. *Ambroſe Philips.* 1 *s.*

18. Sir Walter Raleigh by Mr. *Sewel.* 1 *s.* 6 *d.*

19. Jane

BOOKS Printed for *W. Chetwood.*

19. Jane Shore, a Tragedy, by Mr. *Rowe.* 1 *s.* 6 *d.*

20. Jane Gray by the same Author. 1 *s.*

21. The Spaniard, or don Zara del Fogo, a Novel. 1 *s.* 6 *d.*

22. Amorous Widow, or the wanton Wife. 1 *s.*

23. The most entertaining History of *Hyppolito* and *Aminta*, being a Collection of delightful Novels. Price Bound 2 *s.* 6 *d.*

24. The Pastoral Amours of Daphnis and Chloe, with Cutts curiously engrav'd. 1 *s.* 6 *d.*

25. *Steel's* Christian Heroe. 1 *s.*

26. Amours and Letters of Abelard and Heloise. 1 *s.* 6 *d.*

27. *Etheridge's* Plays Compleat or Single.

28. *Rowe's* Works Compleat, in 3 Vol. with Cutts. Bound 10 *s.*

29. Letters of Love and Gallantry, in 2 Vol. with Cutts. 5 *s.*

BOOKS Printed for *S. Chapman.*

1. Fables and Dialogues of the Dead; Written in *French* by the late Archbishop of *Cambray*, Author of *Telemachus*, and done into *English* from the *Paris* Edition of 1718. Then Corrected and Revised, with the Authors own Original Manuscript.

------De Te
Fabula Narratur.-----

2. *Roma Illustrata*, or a Description of the most beautiful pieces of Painting, Sculpture and Architecture, Antique and Modern, at and near *Rome.*

3. The fair *Circassian*, a Dramatick Performance; Done from the Original by a Gentleman Commoner of *Oxford*,---*Sine me, liber,*

ber, ibis in urbem. Ovid. The Second Edition corrected: To which are added, the following Poems by the ſame Author.

The *Midſummer* Wiſh. [*Sylvia* to *Sylvia*] Heathen Prieſtcraft. The naked Truth. On *Florida*, ſeen while ſhe was Bathing.

4. The paſtoral Amours of *Daphnis* and *Chloe*; Tranſlated from the *Greek* of *Longus*, with nine curious Cutts.

5. *Plautus*, three Comedies; Tranſlated by Mr. *Echard*.

6. The Spartan Dame by Mr. *Southern*, the Fifth Edition; to which is added above 400 Lines left out in the Repreſentation. The 1ſt Edition.

7. *Sophonisba*; or *Hannibal's* Overthrow. A Tragedy; by Mr. *N. Lee*.

8. The Country Wit, or Sir Mannerly Shallow, a Comedy; by Mr. *Crown*.

9. Don *Carlos*, a Tragedy. *Venice* preſerv'd, a Tragedy; the Orphan, or the unhappy Marriage, a Tragedy. By Mr. *Otway*.

10. The Ninth, Tenth, Eleventh and Twelfth Parts of the *Arabian* Nights Entertainment, in 2 Vol. in 12o. never before Tranſlated into *Engliſh*.

11. Sir *Walter Rawleigh*, a Tragedy: By Mr. *Sewell*.

12. *Les Deux* Harlequins, a Comedy in *French* and *Engliſh*, being one of the moſt admir'd of the *French* Plays, and Recommended by the moſt Eminent Maſters of *London*, for the uſe of thoſe who deſire to attain to the perfection of the *French* Language.

With all Sorts of Plays, Novels, &c.

FINIS.

Lightning Source UK Ltd.
Milton Keynes UK
UKHW011818190620
365269UK00004B/999